House of Lords

Also by Philip Rosenberg

The Seventh Hero:
Thomas Carlyle and the Theory of Radical Activism

Contract on Cherry Street

Point Blank

Tygers of Wrath

House
of Lords

Philip Rosenberg

HarperCollins*Publishers*

FIRST EDITION

Designed by Nancy B. Field

Printed on acid-free paper

Library of Congress Cataloging-in-Publication Data

Rosenberg, Philip
House of Lords / Philip Rosenberg. — 1st ed.
    p. cm.
ISBN 0-06-019415-4
1. Capitalists and financiers—Fiction. 2. Money laundering—Fiction. 3. New York (N.Y.)—Fiction. 4. Organized crime—Fiction. 5. Wall Street—Fiction. 6. Mafia—Fiction. I. Title.

PS3568.07877 H68 2002
813'.54—dc21   2001046502

02 03 04 05 06 ❖/RRD 10 9 8 7 6 5 4 3 2 1

To the memory of my father
Who was always there for us
And always will be.

OSCAR ROSENBERG
October 10, 1910–March 9, 1995

The greatest gambling enterprise in the United States has not been significantly touched by organized crime. That is the stock market . . . The reason is that the market works too well.

—THOMAS SCHELLING

Part One

1

Jeffrey Blaine gave himself a moment to take it all in. His eyes ran quickly from the bar on his right to the tables that glowed with gold and russet wildflowers all the way to the bandstand at the far end of the room. People were still coming in, the men brushing snow from their shoulders, the women carefully lifting the plastic covers they had put over their hair, the girls gloriously shaking their heads, letting the melting droplets spray anyone lucky enough to be around.

In a minute he would check outside, to make sure the streets were being kept clear. Now he just wanted to take stock.

Judge Borklund and his wife found Jessica and kissed her, offering their congratulations. She glowed in their admiration. Her closest friends, Renée and Amy and Grace, hovered by her bare, smooth shoulder, smiling restlessly, the bored glow of perfect and beautiful girls when a party hasn't yet come alive. In a minute the greetings will be over and the guest of honor won't have to hear again how radiant she is and how splendid the room looks and how utterly unbelievable it is that anyone could actually have her birthday party at a restaurant like Stasny's (as though there were a restaurant like Stasny's), and *Does she know how lucky she is?* and *Nonsense, dear, she deserves every bit of it,* and *How did your father ever manage to get this place?*

The band would be playing in a few minutes. Their instruments were already on the bandstand, which had been erected for the occasion at the side of the room nearest the kitchen. The musicians weren't in sight, though. They came out, set up, and then withdrew back to the kitchen.

Jeffrey watched his daughter as she luxuriated in the certainty of being, for this moment at least, the center of the known universe. Outside, he knew, the photographers who were kept penned behind police barricades on the other side of the street, who were limited to long-lens shots of Jeffrey Blaine's guests, or Jessica Blaine's guests, as they arrived, would have killed for a picture of the radiant Jessica being kissed by the Jacob Krentses, shaking the hands of the Willard Botins, bending her long Botticelli neck to listen to a whispered confidence from Itzhak Perlman.

A waiter slid up beside Jeffrey with a tray of the braised stuffed mushrooms that were one of Stasny's more celebrated hors d'oeuvres. Jeffrey waved the man off and walked briskly toward the back of the room. He was captured on the way by Ed Wuorinen but hesitated just long enough for a handshake from Ed and a kiss from Ed's wife Thelma. "I'll be right back," he said, apologizing for running off. As he turned to go, his hand was caught by Wilton Maser, who said, "I won't take your time, you must have a million things to do. Your daughter's beautiful, everything's beautiful," and Jeffrey said, "Wilton, since when do you know anything about what's beautiful?" They both laughed.

Jeffrey threaded his way through the busy kitchen toward the office. He had told the band he would want to talk to them before they started, and so they were waiting for him, the four of them, sprawled across the available space in Erill Stasny's private office as though they imagined themselves to be common fixtures one would find in any well-run kitchen. Their names were Johnny Balls, Ted Diddle, Bo Job, and Jake August. They called themselves Falling Rock Zone, and the one named Johnny Balls, who identified himself as the lead singer, had a tattoo of a penis that ran the length of his upper arm. It seemed to Jeffrey that they were nowhere near as young as they wanted to appear. He guessed that Jake August, who said he was the bassist, was at least thirty if not up into his thirties, and the others weren't much younger. A jumble of facial hardware and a lot of streaky black makeup that made them look like demented raccoons were all apparently designed to put them into a much younger bracket.

"You know there's no amplification," Jeffrey reminded them.

"Right, right," Johnny Balls agreed.

"I wanted to ask you about your lyrics."

"Like what about them?"

"Well"—Jeffrey stumbled, not quite sure how to pose the question—"what about obscenity?"

"Some."

"Some?"

"You got words you don't want us to say? How about *cunt*? We won't say *cunt*. Okay, guys, no *cunt*."

The others all agreed, each of them repeating "No cunt" like a mantra.

"That isn't exactly what I meant," Jeffrey said.

Johnny Balls raised an eyebrow, waiting. Two rings and a stud raised with it.

"I was more concerned with violence," Jeffrey said.

"For or against?"

Now it was Jeffrey's turn not to answer.

"Sorry, man, just jakin'," the singer said. "You mean like kill pigs and knife the bitch, that kind of shit. That's rap. We don't do rap."

"What do you do?"

"You won't like it," Johnny Balls said, with the first sign of candor he had displayed so far. "But the kids will. That's the point, right?"

"Part of the point."

"Right. You don't want to be getting a lot of shit from a lot of people."

"Now you've got it."

"But it's got to be real, right? 'Cause we can do wedding shit if you want. 'Hava Nagilah.' 'September Song.' Which sucks. You don't want that."

"Right," Jeffrey agreed. "It's got to be real."

• • •

Phyllis was talking to Everett Layne, the only surviving direct descendant of either Jacob Layne or Ezra Vaughan Bentley, the long dead founders of Layne Bentley, the investment firm in which her husband was now a partner. Jeffrey came up behind her and slipped his arm around her waist. Everett Layne greeted him with a thin-lipped smile and said something gracious about the party.

In his early eighties now, the gaunt old patriarch came into the office only once a week. He had never before been known to attend the social functions of the firm's partners, yet here he was, still wearing his overcoat, a plaid wool muffler around his neck. His servant Gregory, a man of almost his own age, stood mutely at his shoulder. Obviously Mr. Layne wouldn't be staying, but for Jeffrey it was a triumph of sorts that he had at least deigned to put in an appearance. Everett Layne was ratifying Jeffrey's unique position at the firm.

Phyllis glanced at her husband with a radiant smile the moment she felt the touch of his hand. She was wearing pale gold silk, a magnificent dress that followed the still-perfect lines of her body the way a man's hands would, caressing her thighs and hips. She was, Jeffrey realized, still quite beautiful, in fact the most beautiful woman he knew. She leaned her body to his, subtly, not suggestively, just enough to put anyone looking on notice that Jeffrey and Phyllis Blaine had the perfect marriage. Jeffrey returned her smile. There were moments like this, not many of them, but enough to unnerve him, when she put on that perfect smile and made her perfect body touch his, that made him realize how easy it might have been to be still in love with her.

"Mr. Layne was just telling me that he finds the music surprisingly pleasant," she said.

"Indeed," the old man said. "But why must they look like that?"

Jeffrey laughed. Phyllis laughed. They looked at each other as they laughed, sharing the pleasure of being together for the wittiest thing they had ever heard in their lives.

Not far away, Jim Thornton peered over the top of his whiskey glass and gestured with a slight waggle of his head toward where the old man was standing with the Blaines. Holden Martins and Todd Wynebrook looked in the direction indicated. All three of them were partners at Layne Bentley. Everett Layne hadn't attended Wynebrook's wedding, or Thornton's either, for that matter, and that was almost ten years ago, when he was a much younger man still putting in a full week at the office. They looked at each other, trying to decide how they should feel about his appearance at Blaine's daughter's birthday party.

"Way to go, Jeffrey," Wynebrook said at last, raising his glass.

Thornton, who had been on the verge of giving voice to his envy, thought better of it. It wouldn't have sat right. No one begrudged Jeffrey Blaine his success. There was something about the man that simply made you feel happy for him.

Or at least that's what you were supposed to feel.

Clint Bolling came out of the men's room and looked around, like a man getting off a train. He sighed. This party had all the earmarks of a waste of time, but at least he felt a lot better. There was a slight buzz between his ears that just might be enough to turn a goddamned birthday party for a teenage girl he had never met into a decent enough way to spend an evening two thousand miles from home.

He had been here since eight o'clock even though he knew it was stupid showing up exactly at eight just because Blaine told him eight. It was just that he hated hotel rooms. For some reason he felt obliged to put in an appearance because Blaine invited him. If he had to guess, he would guess that Blaine had that effect on most people. They wanted to do what he wanted them to do. The guy was just so fuck-ing *sincere* it made your skin crawl. The fact of the matter was that Blaine wanted to be his banker. By rights Jeffrey Blaine should be kissing his ass, not dragging him off to kiddie parties.

What the hell, Bolling thought. If he wasn't here, where would he be? Probably picking up a cocktail waitress, for Christ's sake. He was better off here, where he could avoid temptation. Or at least, if there was going to be temptation, it would be with a better class of people.

He spent his first hour at the party trying to find a reason why he shouldn't simply find Blaine, shake his hand, thank him for the invite, and leave. Now he was feeling better about everything.

At least a dozen teenage girls rushed passed him, heading somewhere in a hurry. He looked around for a movie star or a rock star or something.

The girls all looked delicious, teenage girls at that age when a female can look innocent and blatant at the same time, their hair sleek and dramatic, brilliantly blond or midnight black, cropped short like show dogs, flared back from their faces as though they had been caught in a sharp, surprising wind, their eyes and lips bathed in colors like exotic insects. Maybe he'd ask one of them to dance.

The headlong rush of all these girls in evening dresses, Clint Bolling discovered, was aimed at a rather remarkable looking young woman in her middle twenties who wasn't dressed for this kind of party at all. She was wearing a sheepskin coat and a peasant skirt that reached down to the floor, the kind of thing Bolling's wife wore all the time back in Oklahoma. She also had on burgundy-red calf-high boots, and she had that magical kind of presence that announced that she was *someone*, certainly someone Clint Bolling wouldn't have minded getting to know.

"I think it's Mia Hamm," he heard a woman say. The name meant nothing to Bolling. He turned to see who had spoken, and his eyes and the tilt of his head asked the next question. "The soccer player," she explained.

The *soccer* player, Bolling thought. Why in god's holy name would a bunch of teenagers be excited about a soccer player? Bolling had only a vague memory of a female soccer team that had done something illustrious a year or so ago, maybe more. Typical, he thought. A man like Blaine would pick up the phone and call a soccer player he didn't even know simply because his little girl probably played the game. Or maybe he called her agent. Did soccer players have agents? Probably. Everybody had agents. She probably charged for showing up.

Still, it was an opportunity not to be missed. He liked athletic women, even though they made him feel his age. Under that sheepskin coat there was undoubtedly a great body, firm and relentless.

He squared off his shoulders and moved forward to introduce himself. He was conscious of cutting an impressive figure in his lizard boots and string tie. He had been born and raised in Oklahoma and he still lived there, so he enjoyed a sort of natural right to the rough-and-ready cowboy air he affected. Still, it was an affectation. Like an actor playing himself in a film, he often found himself weighing his words and actions not so much in terms of what should be said or done under the circumstances, but more in terms of what Clint Bolling would say or do. For as long as he could remember, this double consciousness had been part of his being. At eighteen he carried it with him when he enrolled at Yale, eight years before Jeffrey Blaine's freshman year. Beyond the fact of their Yale educations, however, the two men had little in common. Bolling came east with a firm and almost fanatical resolve to let nothing he learned there change him, a pledge that was, if anything, solidified when he found himself surrounded by hundreds of guys like Jeffrey Blaine, blond and good-looking small-town bearers of civic pride who showed up precisely to collect on the college's implicit promise to change everything.

Four years after he came east to be a Yale freshman, Clint Bolling was able to return to Oklahoma essentially a wilier version of the youth who left. He was for this reason understandably reluctant to credit his Ivy League education with any significant role in sharpening the skills that enabled him to amass an incredible fortune over the next two and a half decades. He didn't own oil but his company was sitting on about a hundred patents for interesting things to do with oil. No one, including Bolling, actually knew what all of them were, but that didn't matter. Some of them had to do with medicine, while others involved food actually synthesized out of petrochemicals. There was a lot of interest, which translated into an explosive rise in the value of Clint Bolling's company, PetroBoll.

The story of how Bolling came to control these patents told a great deal about the man. He raided the petrochemistry departments of three large universities in Texas and Oklahoma by offering immense cash donations that the fortunate institutions eagerly transformed into libraries, laboratories, and endowed professorships. None of the scientists involved ever knowingly went to work for Clint Bolling or PetroBoll. They all remained in the employ of their universities, even though a series of Bolling trusts paid their salaries. But the fine print in the deeds of trust that created the funds turned out to give the trusts, which in turn turned out to be PetroBoll under a series of other names, the patents on the work products generated by the recipients of the trusts' generosity. No one but Bolling had understood that this would be the case at the time the gifts were made and accepted. Naturally, the universities bellowed like bulls when they realized what was happening. The courts, though, upheld Bolling, although they went out of their way in each separate ruling to cluck their judicial tongues about the sharp practices on the one hand and the slovenly lawyering on the other that forced them to such unpleasant but unavoidable conclusions.

Bolling himself remained the same crude but ingratiating man he had always been, boisterously friendly in a way that served double duty as both welcome and warning, *Hi buddy*, and *Don't fuck with me* at the same time. Where the ladies were concerned, he was conscious of holding an immense advantage over these New York types. Just by not being one of them.

He had come to New York because he was looking for things to do with his money and Blaine's name kept coming up whenever he asked about investment bankers. Before getting on a plane, he had his research people do a bit of digging. They started with the Yale yearbook and followed it back as far as they conveniently could. They weren't interested in what the banker had accomplished after he left Yale because it went without saying that he had accomplishments. Clint Bolling believed that you knew what a man was only when you knew where he came from. What they found was more or less what Bolling expected they would find. Jeffrey Blaine was a Bright Young Kid from a failing industrial town in central Massachusetts—which could just as easily have been New Hampshire or Mississippi, Georgia or Vermont. The story would be the same anywhere. Inevitably this Bright Young Kid would be the only son in a family that traced itself back through twelve generations, not one of which had ever amounted to anything. Families like that regarded their insignificance as a direct result of their virtue, and so their hearts were filled with a grubby pride that was in no way diminished by the fact that the world around them refused to validate it. On the contrary, these people looked at failure as a badge of distinction, leaning on their rectitude the way simpler folk leaned on religion. Sooner or later one of the males in the line would marry a woman who was fed up with inadequacy, who put no faith in rectitude, who possessed enough ambition to raise her only son to believe that he was entitled to more. Off he would go to Yale or Princeton, Harvard or Dartmouth, certain only of two things: that he would never come back, and that he would become in reality everything that his family had always imagined itself to be.

The Jeffrey Blaines of the world, Bolling believed, were young men with missions, ambitious but grounded. What this meant, as far as Bolling was concerned, was that they were fighters but you could trust them. They had a duty to fulfill and a calling to answer, and so they programmed themselves to make vast multiples of the money their mothers thought their fathers should have made, but they had principles at the same time. He contrasted them in his mind with people like himself, people without either grounding or principles. He knew better than to trust people like himself. He had found, over the years, that there were men he liked and men he trusted, and they were hardly ever the same men. What his research told him about Blaine put the banker in the second category, which is why Clint Bolling was in New York. Ready now to take advantage of what the situation offered.

He moved toward the girls clustered around the soccer player. One of them was certain to be Blaine's daughter. The almost-blonde in the blue dress, he guessed as he headed toward them, taking stock, suddenly thankful for having no children, especially no daughters. Their bodies sheathed in golds and blues and blacks offered tantalizing views of young legs, young thighs, young breasts.

"One of you must be Jessica," he drawled.

"I am," Jessica said.

Just as he thought. The prettiest one in the lot. Did each girl get a turn at being the prettiest at her own party? he wondered. It was a lovely world these children lived in.

The Blaine girl's restless eyes never met his as he offered and she took his hand. He told her his name and wished her a happy birthday. "There's Daddy," she said, pulling her hand from his. "Nice meeting you."

He watched her run across the restaurant, as though she were in sneakers and jeans. There was something magic about rich girls, he thought, and then he put her out of his mind.

"You're Mia Hamm, aren't you?" he said, turning to the soccer player.

She seemed pleased to be recognized.

Considering the weather, it was probably a good thing Chet Fiore wasn't going anywhere. It made tailing him that much easier. With the engine idling smoothly, the heater didn't even have to be set very high to keep the two men comfortable in the car. Warm, in fact, warmer than they needed to be. Wally Schliester wouldn't have minded opening a window, but that wasn't an option because Gogarty was behind the wheel, and when Gogarty was behind the wheel Gogarty controlled what he liked to call the environmental variables.

Gogarty was always behind the wheel. It was one of the perks that came with his seniority, and Schliester, who had no seniority at all, was in no position to question it.

This was their third night of tailing Chet Fiore and so far they hadn't seen anything worth staying awake for. Blind, random tailing of a subject is widely regarded as just about the worst way to conduct an investigation, and with good reason. For the most part it's a waste of manpower. They had been investigating Chet Fiore for a little under two months and had absolutely nothing to show for it. They resorted to random tailing simply to have something to put in their reports.

Schliester fought to keep his eyes open in the stupefying warmth of the car. They were parked just down the street from a restaurant called Seppi's on Elizabeth Street in lower Manhattan. There was no Giuseppe. The place was run by a man named Artie, but Chet Fiore owned it, named it after his grandfather, and used it more or less as his office. He didn't involve himself in the management of the establishment. He declared a small income from the restaurant on his income tax so that you couldn't get him in trouble that way.

The only difference between this night and the two before it was that tonight a blizzard was raging around them, which added an interesting wrinkle. If they cleared the windows, their presence in the car would be obvious from a block and a half away. If they let the snow accumulate, as it was accumulating on all the other cars parked on the street, they wouldn't be able to see a fucking thing.

Schliester raised this issue as a conversational gambit. Once in a while it helped to have something to talk about. Gogarty countered by suggesting they go with the flow. He claimed to be able to make out the front of the restaurant just fine through the snow.

Schliester shrugged and gave up the struggle to keep his eyes open. They weren't doing him any good anyway.

Chloe Adams Todd hugged Phyllis Blaine as though they were sisters. She kissed her as though they hadn't seen each other in years.

"I was in a total panic," Chloe whined in her high-pitched voice. She was thirty-eight years old and talked as though she were a teenager. "I mean, if he doesn't take me, who exactly is going to do my hair? He's the only man who has so much as *touched* my head since I was sixteen years old."

Phyllis managed a laugh. "Well, it worked out fine. You look stunning. Really," she said, trying to make her getaway.

There were people she *had* to talk to. And the waiters needed another reminder about the wine now that most of Jessica's friends had arrived. As she walked across the dining room, her eyes swept over thousands upon thousands of flowers, a Rose Parade of blooming colors dominated by the stalky daffodils, yellow with orange centers, the rainbows of tulips, all of them deferring, as though on orders from Phyllis Blaine herself, to the discreetly muted tints of the clustered wildflower blossoms that surrounded the flowers and set the tone for the evening. What, Phyllis had wondered out loud when she first conceived the theme of the floral arrangements, would announce the birthday of a young woman with more perfect candor than the blossoms of wildflowers?

But Chloe Todd wasn't about to let her get away. She moved around so that she was in front of Phyllis. "I couldn't believe it when I called," she went on. "The girl said he didn't have anything. I mean, didn't have *anything*? Please. I said to myself, this can't be Adrian, it's got to be a new girl. She doesn't know who I am. But it was Adrian. Can you believe that?"

Phyllis was threading her way between the tables, Chloe keeping pace with her. Phyllis stopped to adjust a floral arrangement.

"I said, 'Let me talk to him,' and she said, 'Really, Mrs. Todd.' As though I was the one being troublesome. So I said, 'Yes. Really. And *now*, if you know what's good for you.' I actually heard her gasp. Well, not a gasp, but that sound people like that make. And then he comes on the line. 'You know I love you, Chloe,' he says, 'you know I'd do anything I can,' and I say, 'I cannot go to the Blaines' party with my hair like a rat's nest,' and he says, 'Well, that's the problem, because all the girls are being done, there isn't—you know I wouldn't lie to you—a minute, not a minute the whole day.' You know how he talks."

Phyllis said to a waiter, "Eduardo, you promise me you'll keep your eye on the wine bottles."

She absolutely was not going to let the children get their hands on the wine. At Jessica's seventeenth a distressing number of the kids managed to get themselves drunk. It wasn't going to happen again.

"Yes, Mrs. Blaine," Eduardo agreed enthusiastically. The entire staff had been given enough pep talks to last a football team a whole season.

Phyllis moved on. She sampled one of the shrimp-and-avocado hors d'oeuvres and her eye caught Erill Stasny's. She nodded her approval. He answered with a curt nod. His own approval was really all that mattered to him.

All the while Chloe Adams Todd continued her eternal chatter. "He actually offered me an appointment on Thursday. *Thursday.* What good was Thursday going to do me? What was I supposed to do? Sit with my head in the refrigerator?"

"Well, it worked out," Phyllis said.

It worked out because Phyllis called Kenneth herself. "Please do something for this woman," she told him, "before she drives me out of my mind."

Phyllis stopped in front of Monsignor Fennessy, an insufferably pompous archbishop who was on the boards of some of the same charities as Phyllis. "Monsignor," she said, "you know Chloe Todd, don't you?"

She slipped away while the monsignor pumped Chloe's hand. Perhaps the saga of Chloe Todd's hair would be of interest to a Prince of the Church.

According to the official version of the story, Erill Stasny was a Czech from Paris, where he worked for five years as sous-chef at Archistrate under Alain Senderans. Stasny was certainly Czech, and he knew Paris intimately. But Archistrate? Senderans? Three prominent food critics came out and doubted it in print. None of the people who frequented the best of the Parisian restaurants could recall ever having seen him there. Or anywhere else, for that matter. He simply showed up in New York one day in 1994 and announced his presence.

Six months after his arrival, Stasny's was open for business on two floors of a brownstone in the East Forties between Third and Lexington, an auspicious location for a restaurant intended for instant primacy. It didn't matter in the least that Erill Stasny probably wasn't who he claimed to be. The upper end of the restaurant business has always operated with a higher quotient of lies per word spoken than any other industry in the world. Charm and genius are all that matter, and even charm doesn't matter greatly. With enough talent, one is assumed to be charming. Stasny was rude to virtually everyone, without exception, but as word spread, even before the first glowing reviews came in, his surliness came to be seen as an important, even an essential, part of his appeal. So, too, did the air of mystery that surrounded everything about the man and his establishment.

The biggest mystery was how to get a table. The secretaries of some of New York's most influential people, including elected officials, commissioners, financiers, and the owners of major-league baseball, football, basketball, and hockey teams, called for reservations only to be told that no tables were available for six, seven, eight weeks. Others called Stasny's in the afternoon and were dining there that night. No one ever managed to figure out if there was a list or how to get on it. The pecking order seemed whimsical, or at least it seemed whimsical to those to whom it didn't seem outrageous.

Jeffrey Blaine was the first person who ever approached Stasny about buying out the entire dining room for an evening. Le Cirque had been the scene of lavish parties, Lutèce even in the days of its greatest glory surrendered itself to private affairs. But Stasny's? Never. Because it hadn't been done, it was generally assumed that it couldn't be done.

The whole thing started out as Jessica's idea. Her seventeenth birthday party had been held at the Yale Club, with sushi and roast beef, stuffed mushrooms and cotton candy, with carnival-style booths set up in the three downstairs reading rooms where the kids could pitch rings around little plastic frogs or throw softballs into milk jugs and darts at balloons. Smashing Pumpkins played in the large room upstairs, filling the building with sounds the Yale Club had never heard before. *People* devoted three pages of pictures to the party, which was also featured on Page Six of the *Post*, where photos of teenagers with champagne glasses in their hands were accompanied by a satirical text by Noel Garver proclaiming that the Eighties were alive and well on the East Side of Manhattan.

The party was more than a success. It was a triumph. The kids loved it and talked about it for months. Parties of two and three years earlier, the sixteenth and seventeenth birthday parties of Jessica's friends' older brothers and sisters that had seemed so wonderful at the time, were suddenly second rate as Jessica Blaine's party set a new standard. In the months that followed, no one managed to outdo Jessica's party despite unimaginable expenditures. Money, after all, couldn't buy originality. Copies were only copies.

Nevertheless, Jeffrey could have done with less publicity. The Eighties were *not* alive and well, not in the least. Hedonism wasn't part of his makeup and never had been. He prided himself on being a sensible and socially responsible man. Yes, he had money, and of course he was willing to spend some of it on his only child. What parent wouldn't? But he wasn't in any sense of the word an extravagant man. Although he never said anything to Phyllis or Jessica about the press comments on the party, they hurt him in a way he couldn't fully explain. Besides, an elderly bartender who had been at the Club since the Korean War lost his job as a result of the scandal. And so, as one season rounded into the next and Jessica's eighteenth birthday loomed on the distant horizon, Jeffrey worried about how they could celebrate it without either disappointing her or opening him up to more criticism.

And then one night over dinner at Stasny's, Jessica looked up from her dessert and said, "Why don't we have my party here?"

She was only joking, she said later, but Jeffrey glanced at Phyllis, whose eyes went to his at the same time, and the decision was made.

For more reasons than Jessica could have possibly understood, it was a wonderful idea. Stasny's reputation was based almost as much on his discretion as on his food. A senator, a tenor, or a police commissioner could take his mistress to Stasny's without worrying that the paparazzi would be on the sidewalk when he came out.

The very next morning, hours before the restaurant opened for business, Jeffrey Blaine was at the door. A waiter who pulled a suit coat over his T-shirt to answer the door seated him in the empty dining room. Coffee was brought. Erill Stasny himself followed a few minutes later, smiling and smelling of an herbal cologne. When Jeffrey told him what was on his mind, Stasny was cool to the idea. He wanted no part of carnivals or Smashing Pumpkins. There wasn't, he said haughtily, enough money in the world to make him turn his restaurant into a circus.

He left Jeffrey at the table and walked back to his kitchen.

Jeffrey followed him there. "All right," he said. "What do you suggest?"

When Jeffrey Blaine wanted someone to do something, he always asked questions. He never gave orders. When the people answered his questions they were telling themselves what it was they were supposed to do. Stasny, though, didn't take the bait. He looked at Jeffrey the way he might have looked at a roach in the risotto. Customers did not walk into Erill Stasny's kitchen. Ever. Under any circumstances. Not when it was functioning in the evening, not when it lay in morning torpor, manned only by two sullen young men uncrating vegetables.

"I cannot permit this," Stasny said.

That seemed to be the end of the matter. On his way to the office, Jeffrey called Phyllis to tell her that Stasny's was out.

But it wasn't out. Later that afternoon, Stasny himself telephoned Jeffrey at the office. He didn't say what had changed his mind, but now he seemed willing to explore the idea. "I have question for you, Monsieur Blaine," he said in his strange, unidentifiable accent. "This young woman"—he pronounced it *ooman*—"is to be eighteen years old. Why must she celebrate like a heathen child?"

Negotiations began that afternoon and lasted through the fall and into winter. It took three months just to get Stasny to relent on the question of music, and then only on the condition that there be no amplifiers and no microphones. "Unplugged," Jessica said, nodding her approval, surprising her father with her enthusiastic acceptance of the terms.

"No, no," Stasny said. "No plug, no noise, no machines."

"Yes, right, exactly," Jessica said, enunciating clearly to boost her words over the language barrier. "*Un*plugged. No plugs. No machines."

With barely a month to go until the party, there remained only a few details of the menu to be worked out. The dinner wouldn't be catered in the usual sense. Jessica's guests would order from the menu. But, since the menu changed every day, depending on the whims of Stasny and the market, Jessica wanted to assure herself that at least a few of her favorite dishes would be available. The lobster crepes. The Morello mushrooms in a beef broth. The sautéed veal with dill and lemon. And above all, the poached cherries and raspberries in a mousse of white chocolate with a light orange glaze. Jeffrey and Phyllis insisted that Jessica be there for all these negotiations. She was, after all, going to be eighteen. It was time she learned to accept responsibility.

Phyllis made the reservations and made Jessica cancel her plans for a weekend on Long Island with her friends so that she could be there. Stasny himself seated them when they came in, gesturing to a waiter with a crook of his finger as he bent close to Jeffrey's ear. "Your drinks will be presently, Monsieur Blaine," he said.

Their waiter, dark-haired, dark-eyed, dark-suited, materialized immediately with the drinks they hadn't ordered yet, a Bushmill's on the rocks for Jeffrey, a chilled Chardonnay for Phyllis, a diet Coke for Jessica. They were given no menus. Stasny said, "Stasny makes the selection," adding a flourish of the eyebrows that turned it into a question.

"Yes, please," Jeffrey said.

Stasny bowed and withdrew. Jessica said, "Is he weird or what?"

"He's very nice," her mother corrected. "He is being extremely cooperative."

"I'm sure Daddy's paying him a fortune," Jessica said.

"Then you could show some appreciation."

"To Mr. Stasny?"

"And to your father."

Jeffrey looked away, annoyed. It seemed to him that Phyllis was picking on the girl more and more lately, most of the time for no discernible reason. Jessica didn't fall all over herself saying thank you, but she was certainly appreciative of the things she enjoyed in her life. Most of the girls in her set had no idea, really, of how privileged they were, but Jessica wasn't like that in the least. She knew she was lucky and she even said so from time to time. "She expresses appreciation," he said coldly, not looking at his wife.

Phyllis reached for her wine glass and looked around the room over the rim of it. She didn't like being corrected, especially where Jessica was concerned. It had always been her belief that Jeffrey stood up for the girl too much and that this was why she was so spoiled. Sometimes, it seemed to her, it was as though the two of them had two different daughters.

Stasny joined them when the salads were served. Jessica let her mother do the talking, and the menu was finalized by the time the soup arrived.

Jessica, Amy, Grace, and Renée swept this way and that across the dining room with the force of a tide and the capriciousness of ripples on a pond, pushed and pulled by the need to talk to this boy, to that girl, to share a joke or whisper a story. Jeffrey's eyes followed his daughter's movements. He heard her tell someone, an older woman, one of Phyllis's guests, that it was all so *beautiful, really, just beautiful,* and the warmth of her smile reached across the space to where Jeffrey stood watching, wanting only, first and last, to make his little girl happy.

Well, she was happy. Radiantly happy. He couldn't have asked for more.

And yet, as he watched her, a distinct and troubling shiver ran the length of his back. There is a sense one has, when one has everything, that everything is surely enough. For a moment Jeffrey Blaine felt this, but the feeling never lasted. As always, other things got in the way. These were the times he could have cursed himself for his nervous inability to enjoy what he had.

Shaking off this unexpected and inexplicable feeling of discomfort, he told himself that it was time he checked outside. As he reached the front door, Jessica ran up to him and threw her arms around his neck. "Oh, Daddy," she gushed, hanging on him, "everything is so utterly perfect."

He put his arms around her, tightening the hug. He felt her warmth the way he used to feel it when she was a baby and he had to carry her around the apartment until she fell asleep. They didn't hug much anymore, because of her age, and he missed it. This felt good. Still, he found himself inexplicably unable to manage more than a forced and fleeting smile or to shake off that sense of sudden apprehension that seemed all the more gripping because there was no reason in the world to feel it. This was a recent thing, it seemed. It had been going on for less than a year. He nodded to Phyllis as he left, holding up a finger to indicate that he'd be back in a minute.

On the other side of the inner door, he paused for a slow, deep breath. He had no idea what was wrong. In fact, he doubted that anything was wrong. It was just that . . .

No, he almost said aloud, it wasn't *just* anything. Everything was exactly as it should be. Almost all the guests had arrived, none of them kept away by the storm. Jessica's guests, his guests, Phyllis's. And Phyllis, of course, had overlooked nothing. In a closet in the office off the kitchen at this very moment there hung half a dozen dresses in different sizes—dresses by Badgley Mischka and Donna Karan, Carolina Herrera and Vera Wang, dresses with sequins and without, dresses in black and pink and turquoise, thousands of dollars' worth of dresses—waiting on hangers just in case anything got spilled. Everything was under control. Everything had been foreseen and seen to. Jeffrey knew all this and knew that he had no business feeling anxious. Or restless. Or anything less than perfectly satisfied.

The problem, he told himself as he pushed open the street door, was simply that he was not the sort of man who could ever permit himself to settle into contentment. It was his nature to be restless. Nothing wrong with that. A man's reach, etc., etc., whatever that saying was. If he was restless, he told himself, as he always did at moments like this, it was only because, even with all his success, even with the emblems and reminders of it all around him, there was still so much to be done with his life. He didn't pursue this line of thought further because he knew that he wouldn't have been able to say what exactly remained to be done, other than endlessly more of what he was doing already.

Sometimes, not often, but more often than he cared to acknowledge, the prospect made him numb.

Outside, the snow swirled around him as though the whole world were a shaken globe. Four sanitation workers in foulweather gear swept the snow with broad, straight-bladed pushbrooms. Beyond the small rectangle where they were working, to their left, to their right, across the street, and in the street, the snow was accumulating steadily, already more than three inches deep. But the broom battalion didn't allow a single flake to settle in front of Stasny's. A pair of garbage trucks with plows mounted on their front ends came around the corner from Lexington, one following on the other's flank, their plow blades angled in opposite directions. As Jeffrey took a deep breath and walked out to the curb, enjoying the feel of the snow on his face and on his hair, a waiter, obviously acting on urgent orders from inside, rushed out from the restaurant clutching an umbrella, which he deployed over Jeffrey's head with a push of a button and an explosion of springs. Startled, Jeffrey whirled to the young man. He hadn't asked for an umbrella and his first impulse was to send it back. But that was impossible. The waiter would only be sent out again.

"Thank you," Jeffrey said, resigned to having this person hovering over him as though he required looking after. He crossed the street to pay a courtesy call on the reporters and photographers herded behind police barricades set up well away from the restaurant entrance.

"Look," he said, letting his eyes move from face to face as though these people were his friends, "we want to keep things orderly. The police tell me they don't want any congestion in front, especially with this storm. I'll see what I can do later to get you some pictures."

No one quite believed him but that was okay because it wasn't meant to be believed. The reporters knew they were on the other side of the street because Jeffrey Blaine wanted them there. But that was Blaine's style. He got what he wanted but he made nice.

"Right," one of the photographers had the bad grace to mutter loud enough to be heard.

Jeffrey came right back at him. "Lighten up," he said. "It's only a birthday party."

The reporters all laughed.

"Ah, yes," Noel Garver purred. "But not just any party. The party of parties. Isn't that the idea?"

Noel Garver was an outlandishly gay and desperately alcoholic former actor, former novelist, and former journalist whose multiple careers had all come to a complete stop until a few years ago when he miraculously massaged his knack for cadging invitations into a position as society columnist for the *Post*. When he was too drunk to write, which was much of the time, his columns were ghosted from press releases by the twenty-two-year-old Princeton graduate who constituted Garver's entire staff. But when he could manage it, he cranked out hilariously scathing commentaries on social events to which he nevertheless continued to be invited. His secret, insofar as he had one, was that he reserved his satire for the husbands who paid for the bashes, but was unfailingly kind, even generous, in his flattery of the hostesses. He never got too drunk at a party to remember who was wearing what or even who disappeared for how long with whose husband. It was Noel Garver who wrote the critique of Jessica's seventeenth birthday party in which her father was compared to Ivan Boesky.

Which of course Jeffrey knew. And ignored. "Just a party, Noel," he answered graciously.

Not even his eyes betrayed the animosity he felt for this man.

• • •

For just a minute Jessica wanted to be by herself. She stood at the side of the room, letting her eyes drift at random while she thought pleasantly satisfying thoughts about Eddie Vincenzo. He had the most beautiful black eyes she had ever seen.

She was in love with Eddie Vincenzo and her parents didn't even know he existed. But they were going to find out tonight. The thought sent a delicious shiver down her back.

2

In her mind, if not out loud, Sharon Lamm was swearing like a
sailor. She wasn't a gossip columnist like the drunk standing
next to her. She was a goddamned fucking journalist. She was a
respected journalist. She hadn't won any Pulitzer Prizes or anything
like that, but she had been told on good authority that she had
been considered for one. So what in heaven's name was she doing
covering the birthday party of the little bitch daughter of the big
bitch wife of some arrogant prick with the cash and the connections to buy out Stasny's for a night? *The little cunt showed up in a
blue silk dress that showed off her rather impressive and expensive set of
tits.* How was that for a lead? Oh, you don't like it? Then you tell
me how the hell you cover a birthday party. Do you pretend it's
news? How exactly do you do that?

For a moment she toyed with the notion of taking a taxi back to
the office and plunging a letter opener all the way in between the
shoulder blades of Herb Adkin, the moronic city editor with bad
skin who dreamed up this pathetic excuse for an assignment. She
didn't even work for him. She was on the Wall Street desk, where a
pusillanimous editor whose name she couldn't even *think* without
wanting to scream consented to lending her out to that imbecile
Adkin, who actually believed that assigning a financial reporter to
cover a birthday party would give the piece an interesting *slant*.

Sharon Lamm had found, over the years, that editors who

talked about *slants* missed their calling. They should have been in television.

The drunk standing next to her was Noel Garver, who thought he was I. F. Stone and that East Forty-seventh Street was the Tonkin Gulf. He actually didn't mind standing out in the snow because he swore, promised, *guaranteed*—that was the word he actually used, *guaranteed*—that before the party was over he would get inside, and that if Sharon was a good girl he'd let her come in with him.

It was tempting to tell him he was an asshole, and an alcoholic asshole at that, and that she had no more interest in being inside than she had in being outside. Unfortunately, she couldn't say any of this, because she *was* here, and the only thing worse than being here at all was being here against one's will. She would willingly succumb to hypothermia here in the snow before she let Mr. Noel Garver of the *New York Post*, or anyone else for that matter, know that she had been sent off on a story like a twenty-year-old kid just off the copy desk.

"Well, lookee here, what have we?" Garver crooned, screwing the silver cap back onto the flat silver flask he kept in his breast pocket. It bore the initials NFG in an elaborately filigreed script.

"No Fucking Good?" Sharon asked the first time he offered her a drink.

He grinned that grin that showed off a row of tiny teeth, like chicken teeth, she thought, perfectly aware that chickens don't have teeth but amused by the notion anyway. "That's probably what my parents had in mind," he said, "but no, my middle name is Frederick."

Sharon looked where Garver was looking. She saw four young men walking down the street. There was a swagger to the way they walked. These weren't just *any* young men, although it wasn't quite clear what made them special. Maybe it was the way they walked, commanding the sidewalk as though anyone else who happened along in the opposite direction—there was no one else, but that didn't matter—would have to make way. Gangs walked like this, but gang kids lacked the intense purposefulness that seemed to flow from these young men with a palpable wave of energy. They were wearing suits, and they seemed comfortable in suits. Not preppy suits. Slick and shining, like their hair, wet with the snow. The one in front, Sharon noticed before laughing at herself for the observation, was a strikingly handsome young man, black-haired, with the deepest of deep black eyes and an intense set to his jaw.

Under the spell of those gorgeous eyes, she found herself wondering where they might be going and wishing for a moment that she could go with them. It sure as hell beat staking out a rich girl's birthday party. They looked like they knew how to have a good time.

Like a well-drilled phalanx, the four young men swung around in formation and moved up the stoop to the door of Stasny's establishment.

It seemed to be a mistake. It had to be a mistake.

She glanced to Garver. Who shrugged and grinned, showing his row of chicken teeth.

For three years Elaine Lester had been dating a man named Gil Gehringer. She met him at the gym. He was thirty-eight years old, a professor of literature at Columbia University who was working on a novel. She was impressed with the parts he let her read. He had a good mind and a keenly satiric sense of humor. As a couple, they were solicitous of each other's feelings and respectful of each other's careers. They enjoyed an active and exciting sex life together. It was a problem, but not much of a problem, that neither one of them was in love with the other.

The men in her office were shocked when an engagement announcement appeared in the Sunday *Times*. Gilbert Gehringer came from a wealthy family from Katonah and the announcement was his mother's idea. No one in the office could imagine their Dragon Lady seriously involved with a man, or even not seriously, although it had been suggested more than once that something along those lines was just what she needed. They assumed that her social life consisted of reading case files at home. She was, in fact, a beautiful woman, tall and slender, small-breasted but with great hips. They all grudgingly acknowledged her fine and at moments even splendid qualities, but what good was having an ass like that when she was so damned *serious* all the time?

When she got to the office the Monday morning after the announcement, the first thing she saw on her desk was a copy of the *Times* opened to the social page. A moment later half a dozen young lawyers appeared in the doorway to her cubicle. She took their teasing well. "And all this time you thought all I needed was a good fuck," she said.

They all laughed and Elaine enjoyed laughing with them. If Elaine Lester had laughed at all in the past three years, it wasn't at the office.

That was only Monday, four days ago. Now, on Friday night, with a gorgeous February snowstorm careening around her, Elaine put on her coat and went out onto the balcony of Gil's Claremont Avenue apartment. It was a back apartment and the balcony faced the river. She could barely make out Grant's Tomb to her left in the swirling snow. Beyond the highway, the snow vanished into the black waters of the Hudson River, blacker than she had ever seen it, catching no light from either shore. Gil came out to join her, and they stood in silence for a moment, enjoying the storm together. Then she said, "I'm not so sure this is such a good idea, Gil."

Gil didn't even have to ask her what she meant. "No," he said, "I'm not sure either."

They were both relieved that it was over. After watching the snow a few more minutes, they went inside and made love, and then after a little while Elaine got out of bed and went home to her own apartment in Chelsea.

She figured she would wait until Monday, while he was teaching a class, to go back to his apartment for her things.

Eddie Vincenzo had his invitation in his hand even before the maître d' came up to him, double time, a sense of urgency in his eyes and in his stride. He was preparing for a confrontation. He held out his hand for the invitation but only glanced at it when Eddie presented it. He seemed to be more interested in Eddie's polyester suit, his slicked-back hair, and his three friends cut from the same cloth.

"Hey, I'm sorry, this is the best I could do," Eddie smiled ingratiatingly. "I'm a friend of Jessica's."

The maître d' returned Eddie's smile in a very perfunctory way. He was British. His name was Franklin, and he didn't like being a hard-ass. "You are not headmaster of school," Stasny had explained long before the first guest arrived. "You are host. If there must be headmaster of school, I am headmaster of school."

"Could you wait right here a moment?" Franklin suggested.

"Hey, no problem," Eddie said, grinning. "You're doing your job."

When Franklin turned to walk away, Eddie said, "One thing." There was an edge in his voice, as though the one thing wouldn't be anything Franklin wanted to hear.

It was a tone Franklin hadn't heard quite so clearly since his own boyhood in East London. It was one of those meaningless phrases the tough kids with the scars above their eyebrows said when you tried to walk away from them. You turned and you caught a right hook on the cheekbone. Not that Franklin expected a right hook here in America, at Stasny's, at a birthday party. Still, there was no mistaking the challenge in the young man's voice, sly and assured. Franklin turned back to him, expecting that no good would come of it.

"Yes?" he said.

"I wouldn't check with her folks if I were you," the young man answered. "I'd check with Jessica."

"My instructions are to check all, um—"

"Questionable cases," Eddie suggested.

Franklin smiled in spite of himself. This wasn't something one saw very much of among young people these days. Franklin himself had a son almost this boy's age who never would have been capable of realizing he was a questionable case. One couldn't help being impressed with the young man's worldliness.

"I'll check with Mr. Blaine or Mrs. Blaine, yes," he said with cold professionalism, giving no hint of his admiration.

"And they'll tell you we don't exist," Eddie said, with a gesture that took in his three friends. "There must be some mistake, that's what they're going to say."

"Then it's a good thing I check with them, isn't it?"

"Except I'm going to say, 'No, it's no mistake, check with your daughter.' You see what I'm saying?"

Franklin saw. Of course he saw. Franklin was no fool. In American families like the Blaines, the children were nothing less than a permanent obsession. The sheer magnitude of their dependence gave them appalling power, the way a house one sinks one's fortune into shapes one's spirit more than the spirit shapes the house. Which was simply a more abstract way of saying that teenage girls who are given seventy-five-thousand-dollar birthday parties can pretty much do as they please. Affairs with dangerous boys were never out of the question because nothing was out of the question.

Already the Blaine girl was walking toward him, looking past Franklin to Eddie and his three friends, all blond hair and pale skin and pale pink lips and the palest of blue silk. She kissed this young man on the lips and said, "I thought you were never going to get here."

Franklin stepped aside and let the boys pass just as the band started to play with an explosion of drums.

Phyllis and Jeffrey saw none of this. As a matter of tact, they were keeping themselves almost exclusively on the side of the dining room reserved de facto for the adult guests. They were planning to take a tour of the "young people's" side of the room just before dinner, which was scheduled to be served shortly before ten. At that time they would socialize with their daughter's friends for a few minutes, welcoming them with all the grace at their disposal, encouraging them to have a good time, accepting their gratitude. It was only a little after nine when Eddie Vincenzo and his friends walked through the door, which meant that for more than half an hour Phyllis and Jeffrey had no idea that anything untoward was under way.

Phyllis gasped when she saw them. She was talking with Carly Westergaard, who was on Jessica's soccer team and had won what amounted to an athletic scholarship to Wesleyan. She was a short, boyish girl, powerfully built, who knew how to capitalize on the popularity she won on the playing field. Her family was Dutch, like the Roosevelts, with whom Carly's grandparents and great-grandparents had shared weekends upstate. Phyllis was just congratulating the girl on the scholarship, which of course would be turned back to the college, when she noticed three Italian boys moving around the edge of the dance floor. They couldn't have looked more Italian if they had been selling cannoli from pushcarts. It looked to Phyllis, from where she was standing, as though they had drinks in their hands.

"Excuse me," she said, interrupting herself in the middle of a sentence. "I'll talk to you later."

She hurried off in search of her husband. She found him in what looked like an earnest conversation with Longley Millsap, a Collegiate boy who would be going to Harvard in the fall. "Jeffrey," she interrupted in an urgent tone that left no room for apology.

That was all she said, but when she turned to locate the three interlopers, Jeffrey's eyes followed hers.

"Please," she said. "Find out who they are."

Drinks were now in the hands of Amy Laidlaw, Grace Tunney, and Renée Goldschmidt, Jessica's closest friends, and the boys had them surrounded like sheepdogs around sheep.

Jeffrey made his way across the floor toward them, weaving among the guests like a holiday shopper hurrying up Fifth Avenue. When he got to them, the drinks were back in the hands of the young men. Jeffrey nodded to the girls but addressed himself to the nearest boy, who happened also to be the smallest, a stocky kid at least twenty years old, probably a few years older. "I'm Mr. Blaine," he said. "I don't believe I know who you are."

"Friends of Eddie's," the kid answered.

"Eddie?"

From behind him, his daughter said, "Daddy, I'd like you to meet Eddie Vincenzo."

There was a certain portentousness to *I'd like you to meet* that signified far more than Jeffrey, or any father for that matter, could possibly deal with in the middle of a party. The boy was good-looking in a way that made matters even worse, an arrogant sort of way available only to those who know themselves to be sexually irresistible. It was the kind of charm Jeffrey would have liked to believe his daughter could have resisted easily. Apparently not. He couldn't help wondering how well he knew his own child.

She had her arm around the young man's waist.

"It's a wonderful party, Mr. Blaine. I'm glad to meet you," this Eddie character said, offering his hand.

Jeffrey shook his hand but spoke to his daughter. "Am I forgetting something? I don't remember his name on the invitation list."

"He was on *my* list," Jessica said. "Don't you remember Mommy said I could . . ."

Jeffrey remembered and waved off the rest of her explanation. She had asked for permission to send out some invitations on her own. Neither Jeffrey nor Phyllis understood why she would want to do that. All her friends, and their dates, were on the list anyway.

Clearly that wasn't the case, Jeffrey realized with a very unpleasant sense of disorientation, even perhaps betrayal. In a family that prided itself on having no secrets, here was a secret. His daughter had friends neither he nor her mother knew about. He wanted to say something sharp, something that would make her realize that her parents' trust was not something to be trifled with.

"And these other young men were on your list as well?" His tone left no room for possible misunderstanding.

The three young men all sipped on their drinks as though the conversation didn't in the least concern them. Jeffrey took some satisfaction, but not much, from the fact that the boy with Jessica, the one she introduced as Eddie, didn't have a drink.

"That's right," Jessica answered in the cold and precise tone she used whenever she was faced with parental disapproval. "They're friends of Eddie's. George is Amy's date."

Jeffrey didn't know which one was George. It didn't matter. This was neither the time nor the place to deal with the larger issues involved. "I'm not going to ask them for identification," he said. "I assume if they have drinks in their hands that they're over twenty-one."

"Yeah, we are," one of the boys said, although he certainly hadn't been spoken to.

"Fine," Jeffrey said. "Just don't let me see any of you sharing those drinks with Jessica's friends. We wouldn't want the party to end on a note like that."

This was the strongest threat at his disposal. None of the young people said anything. Silence was the response Jeffrey wanted, and so he waited a moment to assure himself that he got it. Then he told them all to enjoy themselves and walked away. He could hear the urgently melodramatic whispers with which Renée and Amy and Grace questioned Jessica the moment his back was turned. *What was* that *about? What did you* say? *My dad would have had a total fit.*

He smiled to himself as he made his way back to Phyllis, pleased with the way he'd handled the situation, getting his point across without having to resort to a *total fit.* "They're friends of Jessica's," he told her

"What do you mean, friends of Jessica's? They're drinking."

"They're twenty-one," he said. "At least."

"At least?"

"They look older."

"For god's sake, Jeffrey, she's eighteen years old."

"They're friends of Jessica's," he repeated. "I don't think we can inquire into that tonight."

A few minutes before ten, Erill Stasny came out of the kitchen to inspect the room and the attentive rank of waiters lined along the wall by the kitchen door, a general reviewing the troops before battle. Jessica and Eddie Vincenzo happened to be near the kitchen door at the time. She thanked Mr. Stasny for a wonderful party.

"You are enjoying, Ms. Blaine?" he asked.

"Very much."

"And you, Edward?"

"Yeah," Eddie said. "Great. Really."

"Ah, this is the important thing," Stasny purred. "Everybody must enjoy. You sit down now. We eat in two moments. Perfection. You see."

He floated off, snapping his fingers to the waiters, who dutifully filed into the kitchen.

For just a second a question flashed through Jessica's mind. How did Mr. Stasny know Eddie's name? If she had been more collected, she would have asked herself if she had introduced them. She was certain she hadn't. Maybe the puckish restaurateur had studied the guest list. Maybe that was what you had to do if you ran an exclusive restaurant. If she had thought these questions through, she probably would have said more than simply, "Have you ever been here, Eddie?" and he would have had to say more than just "C'mon."

Because it was silly. This was Eddie Vincenzo, whom she met at a convenience store on York Avenue one morning when she stopped in with Amy Laidlaw for Amy to get a pack of cigarettes, and he was at the counter buying a lottery ticket, his truck double-parked at the curb. This was Eddie Vincenzo, who never in a million years would have seen the inside of a restaurant like Stasny's if it weren't for the fact that Amy turned out not to have the price of a pack of cigarettes, and while Jessica looked in all her pockets Eddie Vincenzo put a five on the counter and said, "My treat."

They both thought he was beautiful, and when they walked out to the street together, he said, "You girls go to school around here?"

They showed him where, and when they reached the school gate, it was Jessica he asked if she were free that afternoon.

Amy settled in the end for being introduced to Georgie Vallo. She called him George because she couldn't understand a grown man being called Georgie.

3

he band had been told that they didn't have to play through dinner. Johnny Balls and Jake August, the lead singer and the bassist, took advantage of the opportunity and went outside to check out the snowstorm, but the other two remained at their posts, the guitarist settling into a series of gentle obligato riffs mixed in with some intricate jazzlike fingering, while the drummer dug into his kit for a set of brushes he hadn't used in years. The two musicians looked as mellow and relaxed as they sounded. They seemed to be enjoying themselves.

No one, especially the kids, expected anything like this from Falling Rock Zone. Chris Mamoulian, a Trinity senior whose father started out as an A&R man at Columbia Records and now ran his own label, led his date to the bandstand and struck up a conversation with the drummer as though he meant to sign him for his father's company.

The music set a pleasantly relaxed tone for the dinner, which turned out to be everything Stasny promised. The braised duck, the oyster-stuffed shrimp, and the roast lamb were especially popular, recommended by the waiters and earning sighs of satisfaction and enthusiastic congratulations when Stasny himself came out of the kitchen after the main course had been served. The soups had been exquisite as well, the salad—only one salad was ever served on any given night at Stasny's—so crisp and tart it sent shivers down people's backs.

The only ones not enjoying themselves were Jeffrey and Phyllis Blaine, who kept finding excuses to get up from their table and wander at least far enough to look over at where Jessica was sitting with her three best friends and their four dark-haired beaux. Nothing seemed to be going on, at least as far as alcohol was concerned. But that wasn't the question, was it? Phyllis knew already that no good would come of this. She believed in the magic of blood and breeding with an intensity found only among those who were born with neither. Twenty-odd years ago she came east after graduating from Macalester and found Jeffrey Blaine within a matter of months. Success was already written all over him. He wasn't at Layne Bentley yet, and hadn't really staked out any territory of his own, but it was clear that the world would be his before very long. He was the first boy she had ever fallen in love with, and she knew before they had been dating six months that he would give her the kind of life she knew she wanted. She expected they would have three children but settled happily for one, upon whom she lavished every possible attention, whose proper upbringing became the center and focus of her life. She saw in Jessica the perfect culmination of her own journey. She had made no detours and she expected none from her daughter.

Jeffrey didn't see it quite the same way, perhaps because he regretted to some extent the straightness of the path his own life had followed. In retrospect, he wouldn't have minded a few false starts, a few wrong turns before he finally found himself on the right road, and that made him willing to tolerate in Jessica the kinds of errors he himself had never made.

Besides, he wasn't quite as convinced as he knew he should have been that the young man sitting next to his daughter, her head bent to him with all the intensity of adolescent intimacy, was ipso facto as objectionable as he appeared to be. Obviously, there was an element of betrayal in the secrecy of her relationship with this boy, as well as in the sheer presumption of presenting him to her parents as a conspicuously accomplished fact. Jeffrey himself, to the best of his knowledge, had never betrayed anyone, certainly not his parents and certainly not their painfully arrived at expectations. All the more reason, he thought, to see how this thing played itself out.

Amy Laidlaw stared at her dessert as though it were alive and moving around on the plate. Her head floated back and forth with the effort of keeping it in one place. George put his arm around her and she sagged onto his shoulder. Grace and Renée were almost as drunk.

Jessica looked over at Eddie and smiled. She put her hand on his and said, "I think she is totally totaled."

Eddie shrugged. He hadn't had anything to drink because Jessica asked him not to. Besides, he never drank much anyway and never got drunk even when he did.

The others had flasks from which they topped off the girls' Cokes under the table.

Georgie stood up and said "C'mon." He put a hand under Amy's arm and helped her to her feet.

"Where are you going?" Jessica laughed. "You're not going to try and make her dance, are you?"

The band was back and had started playing again as the dessert service ended.

Amy swayed on her feet. "I don't think I can dance, Georgie," she said, and then giggled. "I just called you Georgie, didn't I?"

"Yeah, you did," he said. "C'mon."

He led her across the room.

"Where are they going?" Jessica asked again. This time she asked Eddie.

"It's all right," Eddie said.

"He's not taking her home, is he?"

She sounded horrified at the idea that the party would end so early for her closest friend.

"They'll be back," Eddie said. He asked her to dance.

The band specialized in a kind of screaming punk music, but tonight, free of their amplifiers and microphones, they turned all their best songs, "Birthday Loser," "Grimkeeper," "Rodeo Drive Explosion," into pulsing rhythmic numbers where the melodies, normally hidden in the overwhelming bass line, emerged in unexpected places. Johnny Balls, it turned out, knew how to do things with the lyric, twisting his usual shout into a kind of brittle irony. Which wouldn't have been a surprise to his fans if they knew that ten years ago Johnny Balls was Johnny Gill, with a Top 40 hit covering Dinah Washington's "What a Difference a Day Makes."

Eddie held her close and they danced slow to a fast song. It was, she was thinking, the most wonderful birthday party ever. Even her parents, she reflected mellowly, were behaving decently. They could have made a scene about Eddie and his friends, but they didn't. Not that they wouldn't later, but that was okay.

When Jessica and Eddie got back to their table, Grace and Renée and their dates were gone as well.

There were four private dining rooms at Stasny's. They were upstairs. Each had been a bedroom before the conversion of the town house into a restaurant. Each contained only a single table for two and an Early American breakfront that held a king's ransom in gold-inlaid china, eighteenth-century crystal, silver service, and linens. There was also a sitting area with a love seat and two brocaded chairs. The two largest rooms had fireplaces, but even the smallest of the four was ample enough to allow for the substitution of a larger table, although this was rarely done.

Even some of the most celebrated of Stasny's best customers didn't know of the existence of these rooms. The Clintons had been in one of the private dining rooms. So had Lauren Bacall, because Stasny admired her films. Rupert Murdoch. And Princess Diana the last time she was in New York before she died. But Governor Pataki, on the rare occasions when he was in town, was seated in the main dining room along with everybody else. The mayor ate in the main dining room. So did Arnold and Maria. So did Peter Jennings and Joe Torre, Bill Gates and Wayne Gretzky. Society-column pundits never troubled themselves trying to divine the laws of social hierarchy that dictated who got a private room and who didn't for the simple reason that they didn't even know there were such rooms. Erill Stasny knew how to keep a secret.

On most nights the rooms remained empty, even when some of New York's most illustrious political, financial, and entertainment figures called for reservations and were told that nothing was available. Never for a moment would Stasny consider putting someone upstairs simply because he didn't have room for them downstairs.

"Where are we going?" Amy asked, trying not to sound stupid. She made an effort to remember that they had just come up a flight of carpeted stairs, and now they were standing in front of a door that seemed to swim before her eyes.

Georgie said, "Nowhere. We're there."

"No, really," she giggled.

"Yeah," he said. "Really. C'mon."

He opened the door with one hand and put the other at the small of her back. A light pressure pushed her forward. He could feel the bones of her spine. She was just about the thinnest girl he had ever seen, all straight up and down. Except that she had surprisingly full breasts. If those were actually her breasts. He didn't think it likely that a girl her age would have had a boob job, although nothing these rich people did would have surprised him.

Whatever. He was about to find out.

Amy's eyes drifted around the room, as though she were expecting George to question her about what she saw.

"There's no one here," she said, a pouting note of doubt in her voice. She thought perhaps they had come to the wrong place.

"Us," he said. "We're going to have our own party."

He took her arm and turned her around, pulling her body tight to him, kissing her hard.

Her lips were slack, her mouth so unresponsive he thought for a moment that she had passed out in his arms. He grabbed her ass and pulled her into him, hips grinding against hips. Now she made a purring sound and then he felt her tongue move across his teeth. This girl wasn't asleep. Not at all. No way.

Her hips were moving now, back and forth against him, as her tongue prowled around in his mouth. Christ, she was doing all the work. Which was great as far as he was concerned. He liked girls who didn't just wait around for things to happen.

She pulled her face away from him and tipped her head to the side, as though it were easier for her to see him this way. She reminded him, for some reason, of old people when they try to read small print. Georgie had an aunt who held her head that way when she read the paper.

"I like you, George," she said.

He put a finger to her lips and let her kiss it. Then he drew a line down her chin to her neck and down her neck to her chest. Her dress was high, showing no cleavage at all. Which was why he didn't think he'd find much except paper and stuffing inside. He reached under her collar if that's what it was called, anyway the top of her dress, and drove his hand down. There was no give in the fabric and none in her chest, so that the pressure of that band of ribbonlike stuff at the top of the dress plus his own body leaning against her plus the awkward position with his wrist twisted around backward was like a tourniquet and he thought for sure he was going to lose circulation in his hand if he didn't get the dress unzipped in a hurry.

He could feel the top of one of her tits with his fingertips and he was surprised at the softness. She wasn't flat-chested, that was for sure. His other hand prowled her back looking for a zipper. He found it and started rocking it back and forth to work it down. Already he could feel the pressure on his knuckles easing, although his wrist was still being strangled by the stringy band at the top of the dress, which hadn't opened at all.

Amy was making a kind of moaning sound and her head rocked back and forth, her lips so tight against his it hurt. And then he realized she wasn't moaning, she was trying to talk. He also realized that he didn't want to hear whatever it was she had to say. But her lips came free and she said, "Oh, George, there's . . . shit," just as the hook at the top of the dress ripped out of the fabric and everything came loose.

"There's a damn hook, George," she said, sounding surprisingly sober all of a sudden.

"Why the hell didn't you tell me?"

"I was trying."

"What do you mean *trying*?"

"You wouldn't let go of me, for Christ's sake."

"I wasn't holding you," he said.

"You weren't?"

She thought a second, and then she said, "Oh," and giggled.

Georgie said, "How many hands do you think I got?" and she said, "I don't know, George. How many?"

There was definitely something flirtatious in the way she said it, drunkenly teasing, challenging.

She stepped back from him, and her dress, ripped and unzipped, fell to her waist. He was looking at just about the biggest and whitest and firmest and roundest tits he had ever seen. They filled a strapless bra that was cut as low as the dress was high.

"You're amazing," he said.

"You like?" she said, grinning, thrusting her breasts forward as she reached behind her back to unhook the bra.

Amy Laidlaw was proud of her breasts. Her mother had large breasts, too. That was where she got them. But her mother was short and thick-bodied whereas Amy was as lean as a model.

Georgie hadn't felt this excited just looking at a girl's chest since he was thirteen years old. He touched both breasts, one with each hand, and her nipples sprang to life.

"Hey, take it easy," she said.

He was kneading her flesh with his fingers.

And then she said, "Shit. Oh, hey. What?" and all of a sudden she wasn't there anymore. She was lying on the floor at his feet, and she had landed there with a thud that was more alarming than provocative. Even Georgie, who thought of himself as the kind of no-nonsense guy who would have fucked her then and there even if she died or passed out or had a foaming-at-the-mouth seizure right in front of him, even Georgie had to kneel down next to her and ask her if she was all right.

He couldn't hear her answer, so he lowered his ear closer to her lips and asked her again. This time he thought he heard what she said. He thought she said, "Oh, wow."

"Drunk?" he asked.

"No shit."

Drunk was fine. Drunk was good in fact.

He didn't bother with her tits now. He kissed her hard and grabbed her leg with his left hand. He moved his hand up to the crotch of her pantyhose, taking the lay of the land. His hand went to her waist and he thrust it down, under the tight, slick fabric, until he found what he wanted. The thick fur of her pussy was a tangle under his fingers. And then he felt the wetness and his finger was inside her and she made a strange sharp sound of surprise.

Her head twisted back and forth, trying to get away from his kiss, and she grabbed his wrist with both hands. But she was drunk and she wasn't strong in any case.

She bit at his lip, and when he pulled back she said, "Don't, George."

"Yeah right," he said.

The girl was fucking wet. Where did this *don't* shit come from?

But it sure came from somewhere, because she fought him hard, flailing with her legs, even though she accomplished nothing with her wiggling around except for driving his hand deeper into her. She managed to wrench her hips around until she was on her side, and this freed her for a second until his fingers bit hard into the bone of her hip and he pushed her back down, flat onto the floor. She spat at him, but the glob of saliva fell on her own chin and she started to cry.

"What the fuck is with you?" he growled. "All of a sudden you're a virgin or something?"

"Oh shut up, George, shut up shut up," she cried.

The fact of the matter was that Amy Laidlaw was a virgin. She had taken off her blouse, her shirt, her bathing-suit top on just about every date she'd been on since the eighth grade. She did it gladly, even triumphantly, and she loved the effect her chest had on boys. She wasn't a tease either. She always took care of their needs. She gave them hand jobs or let them rub their cocks between her breasts until they came on her chest. But she was, as far as she knew, the only girl in her class whose mother never took her to the doctor and provided her with a prescription for pills, never even had a talk with her about condoms and safe sex. Amy believed in sex, but she didn't believe it was something two people shared. She thought it was something girls gave to boys, except that in her case she didn't have to because she was giving enough.

The boys all knew that. If they didn't like it, they could find someone else. They had no future with Amy Laidlaw.

So far they had all liked it.

Girls like Renée got on Richie Demarest's nerves. Not that he knew any girls like Renée. But he sure as hell knew what they were like. Rich bitches who didn't have the least idea that there were people in the world who had to make car payments, people who had only one house, people who bought dresses when they went on sale. Nothing girls like Renée said ever sounded real. They sounded like they were on a stage or something, saying things people made up for them to say. *Absolutely* this and *positively* that and *totally* something else. If she didn't like something, she said she was *aghast*.

Well, Richie Demarest thought, we'll see about that.

He closed the door. When he looked at Renée she was looking around the room.

"What a delightful little room," she said. "How did you know this was here?"

She leaned against the wall just inside the door to steady herself.

Richie was in no mood for answering questions.

Renée was on the pudgy side, and she wasn't really *that* pretty, although she looked nice enough with her hair done up in such a complicated way and a dress she would never wear again as long as she lived because she had worn it already. But it looked fine, no question about that. Sleek. That's how Richie would have described it if he had to. It made her look a little thinner than she really was.

He stepped right up to her and kissed her. She kissed back like she was trying to suck his tongue right out of his mouth.

Okay, he thought, if that was the way she wanted to play, he could play that way.

Her hands went around behind him, kneading his shoulders and the thick muscles of his back, holding him, but he took a firm grasp of her wrist, pulled her hand free, and pushed it down until it was at his crotch. This time he wasn't surprised when it turned out she knew what to do. Christ, did she ever. It took her less than two seconds flat to get his zipper down.

Her hand was inside his pants, stroking his cock, one finger stretched out to tickle under his balls.

He put a hand on her shoulder and she knelt in front of him. He knew it wasn't supposed to be this easy but he didn't really give a damn.

In the next room, Grace Tunney was suddenly frightened enough to ask herself what she had gotten herself into. She hardly knew this boy. He was a friend of Jessica's friend Eddie, but she had broken up with Todd Galen, who had been her boyfriend for three years, so she was kind of glad when Jessica asked her if it was okay for Eddie's friend Billy Franco to come as her date.

Now Billy Franco was walking toward her with the door closed in back of him and she didn't know whether she should laugh or scream or what. And then he was on top of her and she was on the floor and she could have screamed but she didn't want to ruin Jessica's party.

Franklin remained at his post near the front door until just after eleven o'clock. He later denied that Noel Garver bribed him to leave the door unattended, insisting that he left the door simply to get something to drink. In another version of his story, he said that he went to the bar not for a drink but to relieve Albert, who had been on duty there since before the party began. He wasn't asked and didn't say who told him to do this. No one questioned him further because the excuses didn't particularly matter. If he was lying, he was lying. What mattered was that no one was at the door to prevent Noel Garver's entrance, with Sharon Lamm on his arm.

The two journalists stayed close together, hugging the side of the room, knowing there was bound to be a scene the moment either of the Blaines spotted them. Which was, in a sense, the whole idea. A scene would serve Garver's purposes perfectly. A lead paragraph about being thrown out of the finest birthday party of the new millennium was already taking shape in his mind. Still, he wanted to see as much as possible before that happened.

Sharon Lamm didn't share her colleague's sentiments. In fact, she didn't consider Noel Garver a colleague at all. She would be mortified if she were to be thrown out, and the prospect made her almost sorry she had let herself be talked into coming in. If she hadn't been thoroughly frozen, certain she was suffering from frostbite already and would be suffering from pneumonia by morning, she would have taken a pass. In fact, she tried to. "Just leave me alone," was what she said.

"It's warmer inside, my dear," Garver purred in his most effete and simpering tone. Here was a grown man, in fact a man well along in years, who apparently modeled himself on Clifton Webb. He didn't deserve an answer and didn't get one.

"If you'd rather stay out here, that's fine," Garver said. "I'm offering you the journalistic chance of a lifetime."

And so they ended up trudging across the street together. Garver nodded to the police captain on duty, who nodded back but made no effort to stop them. A few seconds later they were inside Stasny's watching a bunch of spoiled teenagers and spoiled adults dancing to unidentifiable but unabashedly raucous music.

Sharon looked around the room, taking in the whole scene. Those who weren't dancing were chatting each other up in tight little groups scattered around the floor. No more than a dozen people remained at their tables. Wall Street was her beat, and she realized she was looking at more financial wizards per square foot than she had ever seen collected together in one place. One well-placed bomb, she thought, would send the American economy crashing all the way back to the nineteen-fifties.

"Is this really what you do for a living?" she asked Garver in a whisper. She knew the answer perfectly well, and knew, without needing to be reminded, that Noel Garver made slightly over three and a half times the living she did.

Garver reminded her anyway, making the point with a simple but supercilious arch of his eyebrows. Which looked like they had been drawn on with a pencil.

"Fine. You're a credit to the profession, Noel. What exactly are we looking for?" she asked.

The eyebrows did a little dance. "What they're wearing. Who's drunk. Who's here."

"Who's not here?" she suggested, her eyes scanning the room again.

For the first time since they had been together, he looked at her as one might look at another sentient being. "Is it possible you're telling me something?" he purred.

"Grace Tunney," she said. "Don't you remember, she came in with Jessica Blaine and Amy Laidlaw, that whole crowd?"

"You actually *know* these children?" Garver asked, oozing sarcasm.

Grant Tunney, Grace's father, had been indicted six months ago for insider trading. It was Sharon who broke the story, but in the subsequent months she became quite friendly with the family in the course of researching a series of articles on the excesses of the Nassau County District Attorney's Office in its handling of the case. Just last week she revealed that the SEC and the U.S. Attorney's Office for the Southern District had examined the same evidence as the Nassau prosecutor and declined to prosecute. It made the Nassau case look cheap and flimsy and put a lot of pressure on them to drop it. Sharon interviewed Tunney in the palatial seventeen-room house in Plainview where he lived with his mistress ever since he moved out of the York Avenue apartment where Grace still lived with her mother. It was a Saturday and Grace was there for her regular weekend visit. Sharon liked the girl, who struck her as shy and confused.

"My, this is interesting," Garver scoffed. "Perhaps you weren't aware of it, but even rich girls have to pee."

But it was more than that. Sharon Lamm noticed that none of the girls Jessica came in with—the Tunney girl, the Laidlaw girl, the Goldschmidt girl—was in evidence. A few minutes passed. Then a few more. The girls were gone far too long for a girlish meeting in the loo. She decided, for what it was worth, not to mention this to Garver.

She didn't have a chance to say anything in any case because at that very moment Phyllis Blaine said, "This is a private party, Noel. Really, Sharon, this isn't very becoming. You should know better."

It was also the moment when Amy Laidlaw's scream seemed to come through the ceiling and fill the room. It was a long, piercing scream that roared in over the unamplified sound of the band, who stopped playing at once and looked around in alarm. Every conversation in the room stopped at the same time.

It wasn't clear at first where the sound came from. After a few seconds of horrible silence, the room began to buzz with hushed conversation as people speculated on whether the sound came from outside or the basement or the kitchen. Maybe someone in the kitchen cut herself or burned herself. It was definitely a woman's scream.

Phyllis looked around in panic, trying to locate her daughter. Jeffrey ran across the room toward Stasny, who himself was hurrying toward the kitchen. The rapid movement of the two men dialed up the level of confusion in the room almost to the point of panic. No one was quite sure what was going on, except that somewhere someone had screamed. Everywhere men were moving about at random, asking one another questions and getting no answers. For some reason the women stood still, as though they were waiting for their men to bring them news. Phyllis called out Jessica's name, almost a shriek, which added to the confusion and convinced half a dozen women that it had been Jessica who screamed. In a moment, though, they saw the girl, with Eddie Vincenzo at her shoulder, running toward her mother, which some took to mean she was all right and some took to mean she wasn't. A wave of people drifted toward them.

Jeffrey caught Stasny's arm just before the restaurateur disappeared into his kitchen. "What's going on?" he demanded.

"If I knew, monsieur, I would tell you," Stasny snapped back, pulling himself free, pushing the door back.

"Someone screamed," Jeffrey said. He wasn't saying it to impart information. He wanted an appropriate response and wasn't getting one.

Stasny looked back at him with something distinctly forlorn, perhaps even desperate, in his eyes. "I know nothing, monsieur. I can do nothing," he said with a sense of urgency that seemed to imply that nothing would be accomplished by detaining him.

A second scream, briefer than the first, came from somewhere above the dining room. Jeffrey glanced around wildly but couldn't locate it. When his eyes went back to Stasny, the dandified little man was already in motion along the wall toward an inconspicuous-looking door at the side of the room.

But it was Noel Garver who got to the door first, which put him in a position to lead the charge up the stairs. Jeffrey, who dashed past Stasny, shouldered his way through other men hurrying in the same direction and grabbed at Garver's shoulder. It didn't even matter that this man had no business being here. In fact, Jeffrey barely even registered who it was he was shoving aside. He simply wanted to get upstairs and get there fast.

Garver, though, flung out an arm and lurched into Jeffrey's path. He knew an exclusive when he heard one, and he wasn't about to let Jeffrey Blaine or anyone else stop him. For a moment the two of them became tangled up with each other, blocking the way of all those behind. But only for a moment. Jeffrey slammed Garver aside and ran to the first door he came to at the top of the stairs. He threw it open.

Renée Goldschmidt was scrambling into her dress. The stocky young man with whom Jeffrey had exchanged words earlier in the evening was fully clothed but obviously disarranged. He held his hands up in front of him as though he were trying to keep Blaine from charging into the room and he said, "That wasn't her, man, we're fine."

Renée said, "I am, I'm fine. Really."

She was holding up the top of her dress with her hands.

An avalanche of jumbled thoughts cascaded through Jeffrey's mind. He didn't know where his daughter was, and all he could do now was hope that it hadn't been her screaming. How the hell had he let those boys out of his sight for a moment?

He turned and bolted from the room, pushing past Noel Garver, who was on his way in. Richie Demarest stepped toward Garver and said, "Get out of here."

"Who are you?" Garver asked. "What's going on?"

Richie Demarest slammed Garver back against the wall so hard that for a moment the supercilious old gossip columnist thought he had lost consciousness. He thought he had fallen, even though he was still on his feet. Richie Demarest grabbed a fistful of Garver's shirt in each hand and shoved the man through the door, then slammed it in his face.

Meanwhile, Jeffrey had charged up to the next door and tried to open it. It was locked. He pounded with his fist. "Open this door and open it now," he called.

He could hear movement inside the room.

"Open it," he repeated. "Now."

A crowd had gathered behind him, at least half a dozen men, and maybe a few women.

He heard the bolt turn and he opened the door himself. Georgie Vallo looked him right in the eye and said, "She's okay. It's nothing."

Amy Laidlaw was on the floor and she wasn't moving. Her pantyhose were on the floor by her head and the heavy brocaded skirt of her Ungaro dress was bunched around her waist.

• • •

Wally Schliester hadn't really been asleep. He was resting with his eyes closed, dreaming in a sort of half-assed way, perfectly aware of where he was, perfectly aware that the images dancing around in his brain weren't quite real. He could see himself back home in St. Louis, sitting in a car outside town on the banks of the river, with sleet lashing the car and the levee and the water but the windows wide open anyway so they could smoke without asphyxiating each other. They smoked cigarettes and cheap cigars because they liked the way the cigars looked. There were three of them and they had three six-packs they kept on the floor so that they could shove them under the seat in case the cops wandered by. It had happened a couple of times, but it wasn't the same cops the second time, so the boys were simply sent home with a warning. If it had been the same cops, they could have lost their licenses.

Honest, Officer, we're not doing anything, Schliester remembered himself saying. *We're just sitting here like a bunch of Heinekens.*

He didn't actually say that to the cop. He said it when they were rehearsing what they would say if the cops showed up again. They laughed till they thought they were going to be sick, which, considering the cigar smoke, the cigarette smoke, and half a dozen brewskies apiece, was certainly within the realm of possibility. It wasn't such a great line, they agreed later, although it was a pretty good joke. It was the way he said it, with just the right mix of earnestness and drunken slur. You had to be there. For months after that, they could crack each other up just with the word *Heinekens.*

Those were good days. Like something out of a Bruce Springsteen song. He laughed in his drowsy recollection, just as Gogarty's elbow prodded him awake, and wondered for a second if either of the guys would laugh if he called them up right now, in the middle of the night, ten years later, and said it again. They weren't in touch with each other anymore.

"Ready to rumble, *boychik*?" Gogarty asked.

Schliester was only twenty-eight years old, young for assignment to an organized crime task force. Gogarty hadn't called him anything but *boychik* since the day he joined the unit on loan from the St. Louis PD.

Gogarty opened his door and a shock wave of brittlely cold air slammed into Schliester, bringing him completely awake. He wasn't in St. Louis, he was on a street in Little Italy near the bottom of Manhattan Island, New York, New York. Gogarty was sweeping bushels of snow off the windshield with his forearm, so the quality of the light in the car kept improving every second. The heater had kept the windshield nice and warm, so the layer touching the glass wasn't frozen. Otherwise, Gogarty would have been scraping for hours. Instead, he was back inside in less than a minute, pulling the door closed behind him.

"He's moving," he said. "Don't you want to see where he goes?"

"He's probably going home if he has any sense," Schliester suggested.

Gogarty slammed the car into gear and Schliester leaned over to see out of the part of the windshield that was clear. His head was practically on Gogarty's shoulder. In fact it *was* on Gogarty's shoulder. "What the fuck's the matter with you?" Gogarty growled.

Schliester sat up a little straighter. He felt the car slip and skate sideways. He heard the wheels spin and then the back end came around another couple dozen degrees, apparently giving up on the effort to climb through the slush pile between the curb lane and the traffic lane. They were sideways and they were stuck.

"He's in that fucking Mercedes," Gogarty said in the same growl, and then, apparently addressing his own car, he said, "C'mon c'mon c'mon."

Schliester couldn't see any Mercedes. He weighed the advisability of telling Gogarty to ease back on the pedal so the back wheels wouldn't spin but he knew better than to tell his partner anything. Maybe in a couple months. "Is he moving or sliding?" he asked instead.

"Fucking funny," Gogarty shot back. "We're going to lose him."

Normally when tires are spinning they keep spinning unless

someone does something else. Gogarty wasn't doing anything else. He kept stomping on the accelerator, swearing, and stopping, stomp, swear, stop, stomp-swear-stop. But someone must have been listening to his curses, because all of a sudden the tires caught something under the slush and the car jumped forward with a weird kind of leap that sent it like a thrown dart straight at a snow-covered car parked at the opposite curb.

"Good Christ," Gogarty said, and spun the wheel like a kid in a bumper car.

That wasn't what kept them from hitting, because the direction the wheels were facing had nothing to do with the direction the car was going. The only reason they didn't hit was because they stopped a few inches short.

Gogarty slammed it into reverse, backed out till he was straight, and then set out after the Mercedes, which had just made a right turn about a block and a half ahead.

Gogarty made the right.

The rest was easy.

In his Mercedes, Chet Fiore led them up First Avenue into the middle Forties, where he turned left.

"What the fuck is a slug like Chet Fiore doing in a neighborhood like this?" Schliester wondered out loud.

Chet Fiore was anything but a slug. He was thirty-five years old, so good-looking even men acknowledged the fact. No more than a quarter inch under six feet tall, with smooth, even features and dark eyes that could have made him a movie star. But why be a movie star when you had a chance to be the most important crime boss in New York City?

Right now he was Gaetano Falcone's right hand. If not his right nut. Imagine what kind of future a guy like that had.

"He's getting out of the fucking car is what he's doing," Gogarty said.

Fiore got out of the backseat of the Mercedes. His driver kept the engine idling. A whole bunch of people with cameras was clustered on the other side of the street behind a barricade, with a police captain standing in front of them. Given the neighborhood, with the United Nations only a few blocks away, Schliester assumed that one of these buildings had to be an embassy, but he didn't see any flags. Gogarty assumed the same thing.

They watched Fiore hurry across a cleared chunk of sidewalk, under an awning, and into a building that wasn't identified in any way.

"What have we here?" Schliester asked.

It was a rhetorical question, but Gogarty hated rhetorical questions even more than real questions, unless he was the one asking them. Of course they didn't know what the fuck they had here. If they knew that, they wouldn't have to be here, would they?

Schliester got out of the car and walked over to the captain. He showed his ID. "What's going on?" he asked.

A minute later he was back in the car.

Gogarty looked over at him, which was as close as he would come to asking what his partner found out.

"It's a fucking birthday party," Schliester said. "Do you fucking believe that?"

Jeffrey assumed the man was a cop because of the way he took charge instantly, with an assurance that was nothing short of breathtaking. He pushed through the men ringed outside the door like a running back breaking through the line and into the clear. He looked down at Amy Laidlaw, still lying on the floor, still crying, then up at Jeffrey.

"You're Blaine?" he asked.

"That's right."

"And this is your party?"

"My daughter's birthday party," Jeffrey said, and then realized that might have sounded like an evasion, so he quickly added, "Yes, that's right."

Chet Fiore's eyes met his for a moment, a brief moment in which it seemed as though he had asked and received answers to a whole series of questions he hadn't bothered to say aloud. Jeffrey felt the way he imagined women feel when men undress them with their eyes.

Then Fiore crouched down over the girl, kneeling on the floor by her head. She was lying on her side, curled up. He bent so low his lips were practically at her ear, and he said something Jeffrey couldn't hear. The girl rolled onto her back and opened her eyes. Fiore brushed the tears out of them with a fingertip. The gentleness of the gesture surprised Jeffrey, and he would have smiled if smiling had been a possibility at a time like this.

Amy didn't say anything, and Fiore got to his feet, reassuring the girl with a gesture that it was all right for her to stay where she was. "Is this the boy?" he asked, indicating Georgie Vallo.

Jeffrey simply said, "Yes."

Fiore nodded. By this time it was clear to him that Blaine mistook him for a cop and he didn't see any need, for the time being at least, to disabuse him of the notion. It made things simpler. "Don't let anyone in here," he said. "Have someone call her folks."

Jeffrey turned to go make the call. He felt like a husband being sent for boiling water by the midwife.

"Not you," Fiore barked. "Have someone else do it. You stay with her." To Georgie Vallo he said, "Come with me."

Roger Bogard, a junior man at Layne Bentley, was one of the men at the door. He said he'd make the call.

Amy said, "Call my mom," in a small voice that made her sound like a very young child. They were the first words she had spoken, and it came as a relief to hear her speak.

Jeffrey didn't like being trapped with Amy, who didn't seem to require any attention. The situation was ugly already, but if it wasn't handled correctly events would follow their own law of entropy, turning quickly and irredeemably uglier. It was obvious to Jeffrey that the first thing he had to do was talk to the officer. He wanted a line drawn between the things that had to be done and the things that could be avoided. As he looked around to see if there was anyone in the room he could get to stay with Amy, he saw Phyllis squeezing sideways through the door, wiggling past the men who seemed to be stuck in the doorway like leaves in a drain.

Phyllis didn't ask any questions and Jeffrey didn't feel the need to tell her anything. She took up a position by Amy's head and said a few reassuring words to the girl while Jeffrey hurried out into the hallway. He checked the other rooms on the floor, but they were closed and empty, except for a busboy sweeping up some broken crockery in the room where Jeffrey found Renée Goldschmidt. The busboy looked up when the door opened and then back to the tip of his broom, as though the mess at his feet were the only mess that mattered.

Jeffrey stepped back out to the corridor and pulled the door closed after him. The incongruous sound of music came up from downstairs and he wondered who had asked the band to start playing again. Maybe it was a good idea, turning the party back into a party. He hurried to the stairs and started down, then stopped halfway when he saw the detective coming up.

"Let's take her downstairs," the man said. "There's an office. She'll be better off there."

Jeffrey followed him back to the room. The man's suit was Italian, expensive, following the lines from his broad middleweight shoulders to his narrow, welterweight hips. His shoes didn't look like anything a cop would wear, either, and for the first time Jeffrey wondered who this man might be.

Before Fiore stepped into the room, he dispersed the men still milling in the corridor, sending them all back down to the party. He waited until they were gone before opening the door.

Amy was sitting up, on a chair. She was dressed, and it even seemed that her hair had been fixed up, restored to order. Phyllis's doing. She put a great deal of stock in these things. She was sitting next to the girl. It didn't seem they had been speaking.

"We're all going to go downstairs," Fiore suggested. "There's an office. No one will come in."

Amy shook her head with surprising vehemence, like someone who has been struck mute and struggles to make up for the indignity of silence with an intensity of gesture.

"No, no," Fiore said. "You don't want to stay here."

He held out a hand and she took it. They went down a different set of stairs that led them directly to the kitchen, and then into Stasny's office, where Fiore sat next to Amy on a small couch. The shelves were lined with supplies and ledgers, and the desk was piled with invoices and receipts. Phyllis and Jeffrey stood just inside the door.

"Do you want to tell me what happened?" Fiore asked softly.

Amy shook her head.

"What's the boy's name?" he asked, to give her a question that she could answer without talking about anything.

"George," she said. "Georgie."

Okay, that was a start. He asked her if this was her first date with Georgie and she shook her head. "Amy, have you ever had sex with him before?" he asked.

She started to cry and Phyllis stepped forward protectively. But Fiore held up a hand to stop her there, halfway into the room. Amy sobbed silently for what seemed like a long time, and then words started to come in a blubbering incoherent jumble. They never had sex before. They fooled around, but they never went all the way. She shook her head to reinforce the point. And then she said, "I kind of promised him," and fell silent again.

Fiore said nothing for a long time, waiting with fathomless patience. Finally he said simply, "You promised him?"

"I told him it would be different. I told him Jessica's party would be different."

Phyllis winced almost as though she had been slapped. What right did this girl have making promises about Jessica's party?

"That it would be different?" Fiore asked.

Amy nodded again, her body shaking with sobs. She looked across the room and said, "I'm sorry, Mrs. Blaine," as though she knew what Jessica's mother was thinking.

There was a soft knock on the door and Jeffrey turned to open it. Stasny leaned in and said, "Her father is here."

He pronounced it *vatter.*

"He'll kill me," Amy wailed, clasping both of Fiore's hands in hers. "I said Mom, I said call my mom."

"I'll talk to him," Fiore said, getting to his feet.

For an awkward moment she seemed not to realize that she was required to release him. Jeffrey said, "Tell him to wait right there," and then Fiore was stepping past him through the door. Did he already know what he was going to say to the father? Jeffrey wondered. Just from the way this man held himself, Jeffrey knew the answer. There are some people who are always at least one conversation ahead, with the words unrolling as though they had been said already. Jeffrey followed him out of the office.

Heavyset, with a scowling Easter Island head that even on his thick body seemed to be far too big, Winston Laidlaw wore a scowl that had nothing to do with the events of the moment. It was his perpetual look. Laidlaw was a senior partner in one of the city's most exclusive accounting firms, a major Republican campaign contributor and fund-raiser, and the owner of an impressive string of horses, including one, Governor's Friend, that was talked about as Triple Crown material. The people who did business with him rarely had anything positive to say about the experience. He was regarded as a force to be reckoned with, but no one ever looked forward to reckoning with it.

He saw the dark-haired man approaching him but zeroed in on Jeffrey instead. "What's going on here, Blaine?" he demanded in a tone that conveyed accusation without anger.

"She's in the office," Jeffrey said. "I was just with her."

Laidlaw's eyes moved from Jeffrey to Fiore and then back again, where they held for a moment, as though he were calculating already what would be the simplest way to make all these extraneous people go away. Then he stepped past Jeffrey and Fiore, bulling toward the office door.

"She seems to have been raped," Fiore said, stopping the man in his tracks.

Laidlaw turned on him. "Who are you?" he demanded.

"Chet Fiore."

"And who seems to have raped her?" He put a sneering emphasis on the word *seems*.

"His name is George."

"George what?"

"You don't need to know that," Fiore said.

The small dark eyes in Laidlaw's immense face burned like

embers under ashes. The identity of the boy who raped his daughter was something he did need to know, and he had no experience at all of having his will thwarted. "Where is he?" he demanded.

"I sent him home."

Laidlaw took a step forward, but Fiore held his ground, waiting with that masterful patience he had exhibited with the daughter. There was a well-circulated and fairly well-corroborated story about a subordinate Laidlaw had thrown through a plate-glass window. There were stories about him knocking over occupied chairs and flinging tables at people who crossed him. You could practically see the waves of rage coming off him like heat off a pavement.

Fiore must have seen it, too, but everything about him said he was a match and more for this man's wrath. It wasn't simply a matter of confidence, although confidence had a lot to do with it. He had seen this film already, his eyes seemed to say. He knew how it ended. "She went upstairs with him," he said. "That part was consensual. She's going to college in the fall. Do you want a trial?"

Now it was Laidlaw's turn to keep his own counsel.

"You don't," Fiore said. "Take her home."

Laidlaw said nothing because there was nothing that could possibly be said. He stormed to the office door and pushed through.

Jeffrey followed him in.

Amy said, "Daddy please," the moment Laidlaw entered the office, and then she said, "I asked him to call Mom."

Laidlaw said, "Your mother's out somewhere. Let's go."

Amy started crying again. "I'm staying with Mom," she protested.

Laidlaw said, "We'll talk about that in the car."

When Laidlaw took the girl out, Jeffrey realized that Fiore hadn't come back into the office when he did. He was alone with Phyllis. It seemed, in the cluttered emptiness of the office, that the episode was over. Although it hardly seemed possible it could be.

"Who the hell is that guy?" he asked.

He knew she would know whom he meant.

"I believe he's a gangster," Phyllis said.

Part Two

4

Chet Fiore's Mercedes wasn't on the street when he came out of Stasny's. What he saw instead was a nondescript Plymouth idling across the street a few doors down.

Fiore smiled to himself. Jimmy must have spotted the tail. He was clever, Jimmy. He spotted the tail and he drove off, giving them the choice between following an empty car or waiting here. They chose to wait. No problem. He and Jimmy had pulled this trick before.

Hunching his shoulders against the slanting sleet, Fiore headed west toward Lexington and then across to Madison, where he turned north, putting the wind at his back. The sleet that had been biting at his face now nipped at his neck, edging down under his collar. He felt reasonably certain the cops in the Plymouth were right behind him but he didn't bother to look. One of them probably got out to follow on foot, with his partner inching along the curb behind him. It didn't matter what they did because he had to assume they were there whether he saw them or not.

Fiore liked the idea of making the cops work for their paychecks. He imagined they were surprised when they saw his car drive away without him, even more surprised to see the subject of their surveillance leave on foot. If they hadn't been good enough to tail him here without being seen, how they imagined they'd manage it now on nearly deserted ice-covered streets was a mystery that couldn't be explained except in terms of their dogged stupidity.

Here's how stupid. He knew they were there and they knew he knew it. Yet they would follow him anyway. Apparently they worked on the assumption that other people were as lead-headed as they were. And why not? The only way anyone gets to go to jail in this country is by being dumber than the cops, and the prisons are full. Which proves something.

Despite the ice slithering down his neck onto his shoulders, Fiore was enjoying himself as his mind formed a picture of the detective who got stuck outside following on foot on a night like this. He could almost hear the man cursing into the microphone under his coat while his partner lagged back in the warmth of the car, enjoying his good fortune. Seniority, Fiore figured. The older man got to stay in the car. Someday the younger one would be older and he'd have a new partner and it would be his turn to stay inside. It all worked out in the end.

Unless of course the prick caught pneumonia and died before that. Which would be fine, too.

Fiore walked north on Madison Avenue for three blocks, and then turned right, heading back to Lexington. He had just made up his mind that the men following him were federal agents rather than cops. Cops would have packed it in and gone to bed by this point.

He had been walking for almost twenty minutes now, making slow time on the slippery sidewalks, stopping at all the corners to wait for the lights to change. Chet Fiore was a law-abiding citizen. Besides, the cold didn't bother him. Weather never bothered him. It was a matter of principle. There were Eskimos living at the North Fucking Pole and it didn't seem to bother them any, so what sense did it make to moan about a pathetic little New York snowstorm?

When he got back to Lexington Avenue Fiore entered the subway station, where he bought a token and went through the turnstile. He quickened his pace down the stairs to the downtown platform. Somewhere over his head, he figured, the agent on foot was frantically waving his partner over so that they could get together in the car and analyze their options. If one of them took the train he wouldn't have any backup. If both of them took the train they wouldn't have a car. The third option was to chuck it in, have a few drinks, get laid, and then file a report claiming that the subject went home and to bed. That's what cops would have done, so if one or both of these slick-as-sandpaper lawmen showed up on the train, that would clinch it. Feds.

The headlight of an approaching train hung over the track, motionless in the distance. It hovered a moment and then floated through the darkness of the tunnel, pushing the clatter of steel wheels ahead of it. A pair of Puerto Rican kids laughed at something and punched each other's shoulders, then leaned out over the edge of the platform to confirm the train. People beefed a lot about kids these days but these two looked okay. To tell the truth, most kids were okay. Chet Fiore believed that to be a fact. Hell, when Fiore was these kids' age, he had already been in trouble half a dozen times. And everyone he knew had been in and out of trouble at least as often. So how were things any different now?

The truth of the matter was that none of the stuff people said about the youth of today mattered. Because kids were kids. It was as simple as that. Chester Charles Fiore was thirty-five years old and he didn't have a single conviction on his record, except for some meaningless juvenile stuff, which was all off the record by now anyway. And when he was a kid he had been as bad as they come. So you never could tell anything.

Fiore couldn't remember the last time he had taken a subway, except for the fact it seemed to him it had only cost a buck. Which put it a long time ago. He got on a car near the middle of the train, and when he turned to look back at the platform he saw a man in a soggy black raincoat racing down the stairs and jumping into the first car just before the doors closed. One of the agents? It was possible. Give the guy credit, Fiore thought, and then put him out of his mind.

He waited a couple of stops and then dialed a number on his cellular phone. "Jimmy there?" he said when a man answered. In another minute Jimmy Angelisi, who had been his driver five years now and had been a friend of his ever since they were kids on City Island together, came on the line. "It's me," Fiore said. "I'm at Lex in the Forties. How's twelve-thirty?"

Jimmy said, "Twelve-thirty's fine," and that was the end of the conversation.

Cellular phones were worse than regular phones because anyone could listen. You didn't even need a tap. All you needed was a two-bit scanner anyone could pick up at RadioShack. But even with a regular phone you had to assume the worst. Anyone who did time because of something he said over the phone deserved every second he was in. It was the stupidity thing all over again. Fiore talked to his wife and his sister on the phone and that was it. Except once in a while for one or two sentences like this, which no one could understand.

Twelve-thirty meant wherever the train was supposed to be at twelve-thirty. Jimmy had a subway schedule and he'd know. Al Gianelli showed Fiore the trick when Fiore was just a kid. You take the train out to the end of the world and there's a car waiting for you. There's no car for the cops, of course, and that's the end of the tail. You tell them to have a pleasant night and you go about your business.

Fiore checked his watch. He still had a long way to go. Twelve-thirty would bring him out somewhere near Sheepshead Bay.

Which was perfect. Noel Garver lived in Brooklyn.

Wally Schliester knew he was screwed even before the train pulled in at Grand Central, which was the first stop it made. He had moved back a few cars until he could see Fiore through the glass in the next car and then he radioed his partner. "This isn't going to work," he said. "We're gonna need backup."

Gogarty had no interest in backup, partly because he knew he wouldn't get any and partly because he didn't like sharing anything with anyone. Especially something like this. A mug like Chet Fiore shows up at the invites-only birthday party of the teenage daughter of one of New York City's fanciest bankers. If you don't find that interesting, you're in the wrong line of work.

From his car, Gogarty radioed back, "It's gonna fucking work, *boychik*. Ixnay on the ackupbay."

Schliester was tired of being called *boychik*. Maybe he should have said something about it a long time ago, but Gogarty was a good partner. Schliester believed in letting things ride. Well, not all the time, but whenever you could. Besides, he was as fascinated as Gogarty with this curious development. He wanted to see what came next.

A few minutes later he radioed again to tell his partner that he was leaving Grand Central.

"See, nothing to worry about. I'm only a couple blocks behind," Gogarty said. "Bastard thinks he's slick. He's not that slick."

In fact, Gogarty was more than a couple blocks back. He was practically where he was the last time they talked. He had used the dome light and the siren to run the lights down Lexington Avenue, but he spun out still north of Grand Central when he had to jump on the brakes because a taxi ignored the siren and kept coming crosstown, cutting across the intersection right in front of him. Gogarty turned a full one-eighty on the ice and then sailed half a block down Lexington Avenue backward. No harm done. He enjoyed driving, and chasing after a subway train made him feel like Gene Hackman in *The French Connection*. Except that Hackman didn't have ice to deal with. So this was better, as far as that went.

Gogarty's theory was that Fiore was heading for Little Italy, that Schliester could follow him on foot when he got off the train and then stay with him until Gogarty made it down there to hook up with him. Then the two of them would be able to continue the surveillance while Fiore got careless because he was sure he had given them the slip. He got his car turned around even before it came to a stop, which was, it seemed to him, a totally mellow, even artistic piece of driving. In this sense, when he told Schliester he was only a few blocks back, he wasn't so much lying as making a rhetorical flourish because that's where he would have been if it hadn't been for that taxi. It didn't matter. He'd make up time the rest of the way.

Schliester, on the other hand, doubted very much that the subject was headed for Little Italy. Chet Fiore had more lackeys, servants, and lieutenants to do his bidding than the King of Mesopotamia on his best day, so he wasn't taking the subway for want of a ride. And he wasn't counting on outrunning anyone on the BMT local. Obviously he had a plan, and Schliester already knew it was a better plan than his because he didn't have a plan at all, just a jerk-assed ad-lib adjustment with no more thought behind it than scratching an itch.

This, more than anything else, was what surprised Wally Schliester about the federal Task Force on Organized Crime. They worked directly under a deputy U.S. attorney for the Southern District of New York and they had nice offices. Terrific offices, in fact, down on the East River waterfront practically in the middle of the South Street Seaport. But no one ever thought ahead of the game. Schliester's whole reason for taking a leave from police work and applying for a liaison assignment with the feds was to get away from the horse-blindered police mentality. Instead, he discovered in just a few short months that the only perceptible difference between the St. Louis Police Department he had left and the federal strike force he joined was that the strike force ate Chinese food instead of doughnuts.

Twenty minutes later he radioed Gogarty that his train was leaving the Canal Street station with Chet Fiore still on it. So much for Little Italy.

"Where's he going?" Gogarty radioed back.

"Somewhere else. Where are you?"

It took a minute for Gogarty's transmission to come back. He had to think about what he was going to tell his partner before he said anything. "All right, stay with him," he radioed back. "I'm right behind you."

More than half an hour later Schliester found himself coming up out of a subway station in the Crown Heights section of Brooklyn, where the stuff falling out of the sky was more like icicles than snowflakes. For what it was worth, he might as well have been back in St. Louis, on a wide boulevard lined with old, low buildings, none of them more than three stories high, with shuttered storefronts at street level. The only difference was that half the signs in the store windows were written in Jewish letters. He couldn't read a single one of them, but he knew perfectly well what they said.

They said, *Up yours, Wally Schliester.*

A message, in other words, from Mr. Fiore.

Who, the moment he came up out of the subway, stepped into a dark Mercedes that was waiting for him at the curb, idling with its lights off. Fiore looked right into Schliester's eyes and smiled at him. The car was moving the second the sonofabitch got in.

Schliester wasn't about to smile back. He looked around the intersection. A Chevy, five or six years old, idled at the light, waiting to take a left onto Utica Avenue. Schliester grabbed for his shield case and ran toward it. "Federal agent," he said. "I need your car."

This wasn't exactly hot pursuit and Schliester knew it. It was a routine surveillance, and nothing in the manuals permitted commandeering civilian vehicles for routine surveillance. On the other hand, they had Chet Fiore attending a banker's party, so maybe it wasn't routine after all. In any case, Wally Schliester was in no mood for fine distinctions. Not after that smug, self-satisfied, so-long-asshole smile. He was wet, he was cold, he had ridden a subway practically to the end of the line, and at the moment he wanted to make sure the well-dressed prick in the Mercedes had something to think about. He wanted more than that, but he would settle for that if he had to.

The kid behind the wheel looked like he was sixteen years old but Schliester figured that couldn't be true even though he didn't know how old you had to be to get a license in New York. The kid yanked on the door handle and slid over to the passenger seat.

"You're going to have to get out," Schliester said.

The kid said, "Are you nuts?"

Schliester could see the taillights of the Mercedes. He wanted to see more than that. He wanted to pull up alongside Chet Fiore and smile back. If that meant taking the kid with him, then that's what it meant. He got in the car and stepped on the gas.

"Are we chasing the Benz?" the kid asked.

"We're not chasing him," Schliester said. "We're following him."

"Cool."

Schliester hadn't been aware that kids still said *cool*. Maybe in Brooklyn they did. It sounded like something from the sixties, like something his parents would say. He reached for his radio and asked Gogarty where he was.

"Where am I? Where are *you*?" the answer came back.

Schliester turned to the kid. "Where am I?" he asked.

"Utica Avenue," the kid said. "He just turned onto Eastern Parkway."

"Who the fuck is that?" Gogarty wanted to know.

"Who's who?"

"Who are you talking to? You're talking to someone. Who is it?"

"I'm in a civilian car," Schliester said.

"Jesus Christ."

"Tell him you're in Crown Heights," the kid said. "And can the Jesus stuff."

Schliester started to repeat the message and then realized it was a joke. He looked over at the kid, who was wearing a yarmulke. "Sorry about that," Schliester said.

"No problem. Tell him to go east on Eastern Parkway. We're going west. That ought to pretty much cover it."

"Did you get that?" Schliester asked.

Gogarty said, "Yeah, but I'm nowhere near Eastern Parkway."

"Like where?"

"What does it matter? Get out of the car, I'll pick you up."

"Negative. I'm going to see where he's going."

He put the radio back in his pocket even though Gogarty was still transmitting.

"Is he supposed to be with you?" the kid asked.

"I'm supposed to be with him," Schliester said as he slid through the turn onto Ocean Parkway, the sideways drift taking him all the way across both westbound lanes of the divided roadway. Schliester could see the Mercedes well ahead and moving fast on the slick pavement. He eased down on the accelerator, but even this light touch was more than the bald tires could cope with. The wheels went faster but the car didn't. The back end wiggled from side to side, like a minnow.

"Hold it steady," the kid said. "It'll come around."

He knew his car. It came around, the back end lining up nicely with the rest of the vehicle, encouraging Schliester to try for a bit more speed. "Where does this go?" he asked.

"Goes everywhere."

"What's your name?"

"Aaron," the kid said. He didn't ask Schliester's name.

"If you've got a seat belt over there, I'd put it on, Aaron," Schliester said.

The parkway was flanked on either side by a narrow service road, separated from the main roadway by a tree-lined strip of snow-covered grass. The freezing rain was turning back into blinding snow that fell in heavy wet flakes. That was actually the good news because this stuff was easier to drive on than the sleet. The bad news was that Schliester couldn't see a thing. The Chevy's wipers left smeary streaks in front of his eyes, and even in the spots where they cleared the windshield, visibility was down to a block and a half or less.

"See him?" he asked.

"I think so," the kid said, and then he added, "For some reason the wipers always work better on the passenger side."

Wise for his years, Schliester thought. "Keep me posted," he said.

The last time he had seen the Mercedes, it was doing around fifty. So Schliester went faster.

Aaron asked, "Where are you from?"

"From?"

"Your voice," the kid said. "You don't sound like you're from around here."

"St. Louis."

"And you're chasing a guy in Brooklyn?"

"Following."

"All right, following. What kind of cop are you?"

"Dedicated and incorruptible," Schliester said.

The kid laughed. "No, I mean—"

"I know what you mean. You ask too many questions."

"Hey, it's my car."

"Do you work?"

"I'm in high school."

"Do you pay taxes?"

"No."

"Then you ask too many questions. Can you still see him?"

The movement of the car felt a little like one of those dreams where you're slipping through space and you can feel the motion except you're not going anywhere and nothing else is going anywhere either. He tried the high beams but the snow just threw them back in his eyes.

The road was straight and Schliester was able to close the distance to about a hundred yards.

"The guy in the passenger seat just looked back," the kid reported.

"That's all right," Schliester said.

The reason the guy in the passenger seat turned all the way around to look out the back window was because Jimmy Angelisi just said, "He musta got a car. He's right in back of us."

When Fiore saw the car back there he said, "Jesus."

"Want me to lose him?" Jimmy asked.

"No," Fiore said. "I want to take him home and meet the family. Yeah, lose him. What are you asking for?"

But Jimmy always asked everything. Which was sometimes a pain in the neck and sometimes comical but was better than if he didn't.

Jimmy threw a sharp right at Nostrand Avenue, then cut the wheel back the other way as hard as he could. The Mercedes slid through the corner and up onto the sidewalk of the service road, kicking up snow sideways so that it pelted the window at Fiore's shoulder like kids throwing slushballs at the car. There was a crunch as some part of the car clipped a bench at a bus shelter, turning it into kindling.

"I'm going to need bodywork," Fiore said. "That cocksucker."

The Mercedes righted itself and lurched back to the roadway. Fiore looked back and didn't see anything. "I think maybe that did it," he said.

Jimmy wasn't so sure. "Just hold on," he said.

He threw another right onto Rogers Avenue, which put the parkway out Fiore's window for a second, just long enough to let him see a pair of headlights making the turn at Nostrand Avenue.

Now they were streaking past little frame houses set shoulder to shoulder. Fiore's mother lived in a house like that her whole life, not here in Brooklyn but it was the same kind of thing out on City Island just north of the Bronx. She cluttered it with a million statues and trinkets and china tea plates in gaudy colors on counters and credenzas and little shelves built into the corners of the rooms, as though you could make a house bigger by filling it up. In other words, this was a depressing neighborhood just like the one he grew up in, and still lived in for that matter, and it would have been depressing even without a federal agent coming around the corner after him.

"Let's get the fuck out of here," he said.

"I'm trying but he's still there," Jimmy said.

"I didn't say you weren't trying."

"Then shut the fuck up. And don't worry about it. I know what I'm doing."

Jimmy Angelisi was the only person in the world who could tell Chet Fiore to shut the fuck up. They used to be just two kids together, and Jimmy more or less worked on the principle that they still were. So did Fiore. Once he had been told, by John Gotti himself, that it set a bad example, that a man in his position couldn't afford to let people see other people treating him with disrespect. But Fiore shrugged off the advice. He was comfortable with the relationship.

Jimmy hit the brakes again and then almost immediately jumped on the gas as he yanked the wheel through another right turn. This time he didn't hit anything, sliding through the turn as smooth as all those ice-skaters on television in their little skirts and their tight pants. Jimmy's wife watched ice-skating whenever it was on.

Well behind the Mercedes, Schliester had made the turn at Nostrand Avenue without hitting anything. "Look at that," Aaron said. "He wiped out the bench."

"Anyone waiting for the bus?"

"No."

"Then forget about it."

"I'll bet he doesn't forget," Aaron said. "They're cement at the bottom. I'll bet he's looking at five thousand dollars' worth of bodywork. A Mercedes, you know, they can't just straighten the panel. It's everything." And then he said, "He's turning again."

Schliester couldn't see Fiore's car but there was no reason not to take the kid's word for it. He tried to match Fiore's turn onto Rogers Avenue and almost lost it in the process. The back end came all the way around.

"I sure hope my dad's not looking out the window," Aaron said.

"You live there?"

"Right on the corner. Let's get out of here."

Schliester didn't have a chance to register a single thing about the kid's house but he had a pretty good idea what it looked like without seeing it. They all looked like nice enough houses, with little yards and some hedges covered in snow. The front rooms were all dark. It was well after midnight by now. If he had been out in a storm like this when he was Aaron's age, his father would have been pacing back and forth in the front room, looking out the window. "Hope I'm not getting you in any trouble, Aaron," Schliester said.

"No sweat," the kid said. "Watch out, he's taking another right."

The last turn put the wind across Schliester's bows and the snow was blowing sideways instead of right into him, so that he could see the taillights of the Mercedes up ahead. He was less than a hundred yards behind it. He saw the brake lights flash on and he saw the right turn at the same time Aaron did. "Got it," he said.

There was a light up ahead, red, where the road ran into Eastern Parkway again. All they had done was go around the block, but Schliester looked at this as a kind of moral victory. He had Chet Fiore going in circles, so at least the night wasn't a total loss.

Which is when it dawned on him that there was no real reason to be here. Whatever was supposed to come next after Chet Fiore's little visit to a banker's birthday party wasn't going to happen when Fiore knew he was being tailed. Maybe nothing was ever going to happen. Maybe Fiore went to high school with the guy. Maybe he went into the restaurant to take a leak.

Bullshit, Schliester decided. There were never innocent explanations. For anything. Ever. The whole thing needed looking into, and Schliester knew where to look, starting with the banker.

That was for tomorrow. Tonight was just for fun.

As the Mercedes came back to the parkway, Jimmy Angelisi had just a split second to register the looming shape of the bus coming from his left. A quick calculation told him he stood no chance at all of making it around the turn in front of the bus and no chance of stopping. "Hold on," he yelled, picking where he wanted the damn thing to hit him. Back end was better than front, so he hit the gas instead of the brakes, angling across the intersection the way a wide receiver cuts in front of the defense, giving away any possibility of making the turn but raising the odds that he could slice by without getting hit or at least hit bad, and then he'd worry about being in the wrong lane on the wrong side of the highway going the wrong way.

"What the fuck are you doing?" Fiore just had time to say.

What he meant but didn't say was *What the fuck does that asshole agent think he's doing?* It would have been better if no one knew he had gone to Blaine's party. All right, they knew. They couldn't make anything of it. It was a public restaurant. He was only in there ten minutes, maybe twenty. They'd raise their eyebrows and they'd shake their heads and they'd look for a connection and wouldn't find one. Because right now there wasn't one. The trick, of course, was to lose this guy before anything else happened. He was confident Jimmy could do that. It would be nice, too, if he could do it without wrecking a Mercedes with less than five thousand miles on it. He had taken a lot of shit about this Mercedes because the older men drove Lincolns and Caddies, and everything else was dismissed as either a piece of shit, a foreign car, or a foreign-car-piece-of-shit. There would be a lot of laughs on Mulberry Street if he got hit by a bus, which was looking more and more likely every millisecond.

Fiore checked back over his shoulder and the bus looked as big as the *Queen Mary*. He could see the bus driver's mouth moving in all kinds of curses, a black guy with a little mustache and big eyes and one of those bus-driver hats low on his head like he was an airline pilot or something, and his hand leaning on the horn, which sounded as big as a ship's horn when it went off practically in Chet Fiore's ear.

The bus kissed against the Mercedes a few inches behind the rear wheel, not a collision so much as a nudge, but it was like a hand catching your ankle when you're running at full speed. The car spun like a top, squirting across the oncoming lanes in three directions at once. There used to be a ride like that at Palisades Park. When there was a Palisades Park. In fact, Fiore and Jimmy had taken it together when they were kids. But there the similarities ended. The big Mercedes turned completely around at least three times and it might have been four or even five times. Inside, it felt like the spinning wasn't going to stop.

The bus stopped, though, and the driver threw open the door and jumped out onto the roadway to see what assistance he could render. He had never seen a car spin like that and wouldn't have thought it possible. He had seen them roll over onto their roofs and had seen them slide sideways, and once he saw a car do a complete somersault off an incomplete highway ramp and land on its wheels. The Mercedes was still spinning when the bus driver ran in front of his bus and started toward it.

A horn screamed from behind him and a rust-colored Chevy slid through the same intersection the Mercedes had come from, making straight toward him in a kind of slipping, sideways motion. It was like all of a sudden no one in the world knew what the word *ice* meant or how to drive on it. Where the hell were these people from? Hawaii? He leaped toward the protection afforded by the front of his bus, and the Chevy floated right past him, kind of easy and natural, the way drunks move when they're pretending they're not drunk.

"Oh, Jesus," Schliester said, doing things with the steering wheel that had no effect whatsoever on the movement of the car. He held his breath until they were past the bus driver.

Aaron looked back over his shoulder.

"I didn't hit him, did I?" Schliester asked.

"You're doing fine," the kid said.

The Mercedes stopped spinning. Its wheels had been turning the whole time, and now they bit pavement under the ice and the car lurched forward, westbound, which by luck was the direction Fiore wanted to go. The Chevy skated right to left directly in front of him.

"What the fuck was that?" Fiore asked.

"That's them, I think," Jimmy said.

Fiore leaned forward to look past Jimmy out the side window. "That's *them*?" he said out loud, marveling.

The thought passed through his mind that maybe these guys weren't federal agents or even cops after all. In which case they could have been absolutely anything. And they seemed to be pretty damned intent on what they were doing. "Let's get the fuck out of here," he said.

Fiore didn't carry a gun anymore because that's what he had Jimmy for, but right now he wished he had one.

Schliester's right foot was pressed so hard to the floor it almost went through. If he could have, and if it would have helped stop the Chevy from sliding across the highway, he would have jammed his shoe right through the floorboards and onto the roadway, the way bikers use their boots for brakes. He saw the Mercedes on his left-hand side, and then it was on his right. He saw it jump the divider and speed westward in the westbound lane while he was still sliding sideways westward in the eastbound lane. He feathered the brake even though the wheels were already locked. He knew he didn't have control of the car, but at least he had the illusion of control, which wouldn't last long unless the wheels started turning again.

They did. A moment ago he had been sliding and now he was driving again. He made straight for the divider, intending to take it the way Fiore's driver had done just a few seconds earlier. The

impact felt like all his teeth were coming loose, and his radio flew
out of his pocket. All four wheels left the ground at the same time
and then came back down one at a time. But the suspension held.
He couldn't afford to look over to his right, but he asked Aaron
how he was doing and the kid said, "So far, okay. But that's what
the guy said when he fell off the Empire State Building."

"What guy?" Schliester asked.

"Never mind."

In just the last few seconds the visibility out front improved
remarkably, even miraculously. The Mercedes was less than a quarter of a mile ahead of him. But all of a sudden there was something
that looked like an enormous cement building floating in the air
over the Mercedes and the Mercedes seemed to be driving right
into it.

"What the hell is that?" Schliester asked.

"Grand Army Plaza," Aaron said. "You better pray he bears
right."

"What's to the right?"

"Everything."

"What's to the left?"

"You'll see," Aaron said. "He just turned left."

The taillights were gone. Schliester streaked toward the looming mass of what turned out to be a triumphal arch at the entrance
to Prospect Park. Half a dozen roads seemed to converge at the
same spot. "Hard left," Aaron shouted.

"You see him?"

"No, but I know where he went."

Every kid in Brooklyn knew that the one place you could be
certain of getting lost was Prospect Park. If a gang was chasing you,
that's where you went. Or the cops. Or people you owed money to.
The roads snaked around as though they were going up and down
the sides of a mountain. There were a million paths and almost no
streetlights.

Jimmy Angelisi was in his element here. For a driver like
Jimmy, this was the equivalent of old-fashioned country hardball.
There were trees everywhere, left and right, forming a canopy over

their heads. There was darkness over the trees and in between them and off to either side of them beyond where the headlights cut a slender, almost insignificant hole through the middle of the night. The road itself virtually *writhed* under his wheels, twisting like a perch squirming in the air when you pull it out of the water. They were dropping down a pretty steep hill.

"This is gonna be good," Jimmy said. His left hand went to the dash and flipped a switch, and now the darkness swallowed whole everything it hadn't swallowed already.

"Chrissakes, turn them on!" Fiore yelled.

"It's all right," Jimmy assured him.

"Mother of Mercy!"

Fiore just had time to think that this is what a cockroach must feel like inside a shoe.

Schliester and Aaron both saw the Mercedes vanish at exactly the same instant.

"He cut his lights," Aaron said.

"I can see that."

"You gonna try it?"

"What the hell for? So he can't see me either? How far does this go?"

"All the way down," Aaron said.

Schliester hadn't realized until that moment how steep a grade he was on. What he did realize was that the Mercedes could be practically anywhere, off the road in the darkness, and that he was probably speeding past it at this very second. Or this one. Or this.

He knew he was licked, and so he eased his foot onto the brake and let out a long, slow breath.

"Yeah, you're right," Aaron said, conceding defeat with stoic maturity. "You'll never find him." Then he said, "Oh, shit!"

Because the road had just turned and Schliester didn't. It was an easy enough mistake to make. This part of the road, down at the bottom of the park, looked like the end of a ski jump. All the snow that fell higher up seemed to have washed down here, piling in soft, pillowy drifts that drew no distinction between what was road and what was path and what was neither.

Okay, no harm done. The Chevy simply stopped in a snowdrift like a kid jumping off the upper bunk into his father's arms. Schliester radioed Gogarty, and Gogarty radioed for a tow truck.

A half mile up the hill, Chet Fiore and Jimmy Angelisi weren't quite so lucky. Jimmy had pulled the Mercedes easily and expertly into a narrow little path that led to a pond, and then they both turned around to watch through the rear window as the Chevy sped past them. They knew it wouldn't be back. But when Jimmy tried to back out, the wheels refused to do anything but spin. They got out to look, and when they did, they could hear the G-man calling his partner on his radio. He must have gotten out, too. They heard him say, "How long?" and then "Jesus, a half hour! Well, just tell them to hurry."

Fiore wasn't about to call a tow truck until the police tow truck was gone. And it didn't get there in any half hour. It got there in an hour and a half.

Three in the morning was a hell of an hour to pay a visit, but it had to be done.

Maybe _bash_ isn't the right word for Jessica Blaine's long-awaited birthday party at Stasny's Friday nite. Maybe it is. No one's talking about it, but three teenage girls from three of N'Yawk's best families got thoroughly bashed in three private upstairs rooms.

Oh, let's not be so polite about it. They were raped.

Raped, you say? Why aren't we reading about this in the front pages of the paper? Why is it back here in Yours Truly's society column?

Because if you're connected the way Jeffrey Blaine is connected, you know how to hush these things up.

Noel Garver read that far and didn't read further. It was the millionth time he had read the piece since it came out of his printer and he wasn't sure he liked the tone. In fact, he knew he didn't like it. It was supposed to be outraged and it was snippy. Snippy was all right for last year's party, with little kids sucking the contents out of champagne bottles all night long. This was a different matter entirely. Rape is a felony and concealing a felony is a felony. For once Mr. Perfect had gone too far.

Garver, who had been pacing with the page in his hand as though it were a speech he was trying to memorize, flopped into the canvas-backed director's chair next to the bar and let his head roll all the way back until he was looking at the ceiling. He could hear Sharon Lamm's voice in his ear. *Why do you have such a hard-on for Jeffrey Blaine?* she asked.

He knew what the rest of her question meant, the part she hadn't bothered to say. Jeffrey Blaine was a nice guy, a regular guy. He was a decent fellow, a good chap. He was okay. Everyone said so and it might even be true. This was no Ivan Boesky, no barbarian at the gate. He didn't lead a fast life. Even this birthday party was no big deal after all. It wasn't like he pulled strings to close down the Lincoln Tunnel so he could hold the party there. It wasn't like he rented Yankee Stadium or Central Park. It was a restaurant, for Christ's sake. Just a restaurant.

Alone in his living room, Garver got to his feet and resumed his pacing as he made the effort to put his thoughts back together and figure out just exactly what the big deal was. He made himself another drink and then got back to the question at hand.

And then the answer came to him. It was one thing to be a shark if you acted like a shark. If you had long white conical teeth and a dorsal fin. Blaine was awfully fucking rich for a nice guy, a regular guy, a decent fellow, a good chap. Nobody hated Jeffrey Blaine.

So Noel Garver had to do it for them.

His toes still hurt from being outside so long but the whiskey was warming the rest of him. When the doorbell rang, he pressed the buzzer without asking who it was and opened the front door an inch or two.

While he waited for the elevator to come up, he gulped down the last of the whiskey in his glass and poured himself another. Noel Garver drank cheap whiskey because he didn't believe in wasting money on things like that. He grabbed the page he had left on the bar and let his eye run over it again. He didn't like it any better this time, but he was hoping that by leaving Fiore's arrival out of his account of the party, Fiore wouldn't give him any trouble about publishing it. "It's open," he said when he heard the knock on the door.

Chet Fiore said, "I hope you didn't waste your time writing anything, Mr. Garver."

Garver handed him the pages and asked if he could get him a drink. Fiore folded the pages without looking at them and slipped them into his breast pocket.

"This is on your computer, isn't it?" he asked.

"I didn't mention you," Garver said.

It was late, and after the fiasco in Prospect Park, Fiore wasn't in the mood for nice distinctions. "You're going to delete the file," he said. "I'm going to watch you do it."

5

"et me get this straight," Dennis Franciscan was saying. "You took a train to Brooklyn and you commandeered a civilian vehicle."

"I guess you could say *commandeered*," Schliester conceded.

Franciscan was standing up, Schliester and Gogarty were not.

"No," Franciscan said, "you don't have to fucking guess. I *did* say *commandeered*. Is this something you do a lot of in St. Louis?"

"I don't recall having done that in St. Louis, sir."

"Your answer interests me, Stanley," Franciscan said, slipping into his cross-examination mode. "Are you suggesting that commandeering a civilian vehicle is the kind of thing you might do but that might subsequently slip your mind?"

The only thing Franciscan knew about St. Louis was that the Cardinals played there, and the only thing he knew about the Cardinals was that Stan Musial used to play for them. So he had started calling Schliester Stan the Man the first day Schliester was assigned to the unit, Stanley when he was angry.

"No, I would remember that, sir," Schliester said.

"Then when you say you don't *recall* having commandeered a civilian vehicle, what you're really saying is that you never actually did anything so incredibly fucking stupid in your whole pathetic, misspent life. That's about right, isn't it?"

"Yes, sir."

"It's *about* right?"

"It's exactly right, sir."

"Don't give me that *sir* shit, Stanley. This isn't the fucking police department."

Franciscan turned around and walked all the way to the window. The sun wasn't even up yet. He had gotten up in the middle of the night and come into the office the minute the night desk called to tell him what happened in Prospect Park.

Schliester and Gogarty looked at each other, which they could afford to do with Franciscan's back turned. Schliester gestured with a movement of his head for Gogarty to say something. Gogarty shook his head. Schliester tried a more emphatic version of the same gesture. Gogarty rolled his eyes, which meant he was giving in. He took a deep breath and said, "That's not really the point, about the car."

Franciscan turned slowly. "That's not what point?" he asked. "It's the point I was making."

Gogarty wasn't the most assertive guy in the world, but if you rubbed him the wrong way, he started asserting. Franciscan had just rubbed him the wrong way. "And the point I was making," Gogarty said, getting up out his chair so that Franciscan would have to look up at him for a change, "is that we've been busting our asses trying to get something on Fiore and now we've got it. We've got him socializing with a very important Wall Street figure. I would say that connection is something worth knowing about."

"You would?" Franciscan walked over to his desk. He looked down at the report he had made Gogarty file before he would even talk to him and studied it much longer than necessary. Then he looked up. "Where do I see in this that you saw the two of them together."

"It was a private party," Gogarty said.

Schliester said, "Invitations only."

"Ah," Franciscan said, "you saw the invitation."

"Fuck you," Gogarty said.

Dennis Franciscan was nominally Gogarty's boss, in the sense that he was the head of the Organized Crime Bureau of the U.S.

Attorney's Office for the Southern District of New York and the man to whom Gogarty and Schliester reported. But he wasn't their boss in the chain of command, in the sense that he wasn't an agent. You could say *fuck you* to him in a way you couldn't to a ranking agent.

"Funny you should put it that way," Franciscan said without bothering to take offense. "Because it seems to me you've already fucked me fairly well. Getting me up at three in the morning is the least part of it. Explaining why my expense report is going to include a line about fixing a car we don't even own ranks a little bit higher."

There was a knock on the door and Greg Billings came in without waiting to be asked. Billings was an assistant U.S. attorney who wore the same suit to work every day for a week, Monday through Friday, then switched to another suit the next week. The agents kept track until the cycle started the second time. They concluded that he owned four suits. "We lucked out," Billings said. "Herskowitz signed a release."

Franciscan wanted to know who the fuck Herskowitz was.

"The kid's father."

"And what did this cost us?"

Billings pulled a piece of paper out of his pocket and unfolded it. "One thirty-seven eighty-eight," he said. "That's with tax."

"You paid the fucking tax?"

Federal agents can have the local taxes waived on federal business.

"It didn't seem like the kind of thing we wanted records on, Mr. Franciscan."

"Good thinking," Franciscan said grudgingly. He wanted Billings to leave, but the man looked down at the bill in his hands, studying it.

"They aligned the wheels," he said, "and they tightened the front-end struts."

"Do I look like I'm in the fucking used-car business? Why do I need to know this?"

The receipts quickly disappeared back into Billings's pocket. "No, sir. I just wanted you to get the picture. I think most of the damage was from before but I wasn't going to press it. We got off lucky."

Billings was a competent man. He was a lawyer but he thought like an agent. He covered his ass. Franciscan liked that. He just didn't want him in the room anymore. He waved Billings out and turned back to Schliester and Gogarty. "All right," he said, "we're going to forget this sorry little idiocy ever happened. No thanks to either of you two, it's dead and buried. Now get the hell out of my office and find yourselves something to do."

Gogarty and Schliester started for the door.

"And stay the fuck away from Chet Fiore," Franciscan added.

It was Schliester who turned around. "Wait a minute," he said. "This needs follow-up. We can't drop the surveillance now."

"We're not dropping it now," Franciscan said. "You two assholes dropped it last night. We're letting it lie there."

The two of them found Elaine Lester standing in the corridor when they came out of Franciscan's office.

"What?" she said. "He's not following up?"

She looked like someone who hadn't been to bed. Her hair was hanging kind of loose. Which wasn't a bad look for her.

"Do you even know what you're talking about?" Gogarty asked. He knew Lester's reputation in the department, but that didn't make him like her any better. He started to walk away and Schliester followed.

Elaine fell in step beside them. She had just finished a successful prosecution of half a dozen semicompetent non-Islamic terrorists who had come surprisingly close to killing an awful lot of people in, of all places, the Port Authority bus terminal. She worked as hard after the verdict as before and ended up with maximum sentences for all of them. Now she felt restless, and she was looking for something else to get her teeth into.

"I hear you had an interesting sighting last night," she said.

Gogarty stopped walking. "What the hell are you doing here at five o'clock in the morning?" he asked.

"I was notified," she said. "What's that got to do with anything?"

Notified? Elaine Lester had no business being notified. She probably bribed the night man to call her if anything happened. Give her credit. She was a go-getter. Gogarty just didn't like being what she went and got.

"Go back to bed, Elaine," he said. "If you're too horny to sleep, take my partner with you."

This time she didn't follow when he walked away. Neither did Schliester for that matter. "Fine with me," he said. "I've got nothing better to do."

She fixed him for a couple seconds with those blue eyes. Nice eyes, in fact. Very intense. Then she turned a hundred eighty degrees and marched back down the corridor.

For a lawyer, she had a damned fine ass.

Chet Fiore laughed when he heard Gus Benini's account of the goings-on in Crown Heights. Gus had a way with a story. Everyone laughed when Gus told one of his stories.

They were back in Seppi's on Elizabeth Street. Gus Benini usually had breakfast at home before he did anything in the morning. This was early for him. It was early for all of them.

"First the U.S. attorney shows up," Gus said, walking in front of Fiore's table. Gus never sat down. He said it made him nervous. He weighed only a hundred and thirty pounds and he was already as jumpy as a cat, hands flying everywhere, eyes everywhere, feet always moving. So nobody was inclined to press the issue, because if anything made Gus nervous on top of what he was like already, the man would have turned into a complete mosquito. He stood up even in restaurants. He never ate anyway, except at home, so it didn't matter.

"He says he wants to talk to the kid's father," Gus continued, "on account of the car's in his name. And he's got a ton of papers he brings with him. Which he can wipe his ass with because the Jew's not signing nothing till he talks to his rabbi. This guy's not a Jew for nothing, right? Okay, so the rabbi comes in, a hundred years old with a beard like fucking Castro. Now the U.S. attorney, it's this kid, the one that gave Billy Beans that hard time over those airplane tickets."

"Stafford."

"Right. Stafford. He starts getting nervous, on account of no one's signing a fucking thing and they're just talking this Jewish shit, he doesn't understand a word. So he calls in for help and they send him Billings. Like Billings is gonna know what they're saying, right? I mean, how dumb can you get? They got Jews all over the place in that office, but do they send a Jew? No, they send Billings. Anyway, he gets there, now it's two on two, two fed lawyers against the kid's father and the kid's father's rabbi. Which is the same odds it was when it started, so the Jews call in another couple rabbis. And these guys are older than the first one, and he was a hundred fucking years old."

"You said that already," Fiore said, teasing him.

The other guys around the table poked each other and nodded their heads and grinned because they knew what was coming next. Gus didn't like being interrupted. "Do you want to hear this or don't you?" he asked.

"Yeah, sure, sorry, Gus," Fiore said. The guys around the table laughed into their hands. Exactly the same thing happened every time Gus told one of his stories.

"Yeah, yeah, that's okay. I lost the train there," Gus said, circling the table to get his thoughts straight. "Anyway," he said when he found the train, "it's half the fucking morning and the Jews keep bringing in more Jews until it looks like a wedding or a funeral or something. I mean, Arafat should have been there, he could have cleaned up good. And this is all over a car that's still running."

"But the father signed the papers?"

"Sure he signed them. How many stupid Jews do you know? He got his car fixed up and it didn't cost him a cent, stuff that wasn't even broken, probably put a new stereo in it."

This wasn't true and Gus didn't have any reason to think it was true. It just made the story better. He smiled because he was pleased with himself. He had been asked to check into what happened last night and this was what he came up with.

"The thing is," Fiore said, picking his way carefully because no one ever liked to hurt Gus Benini's feelings, "what I wanted to find out was why those pricks were following me and what the hell they know."

"They don't know shit," Gus said. "Why would they know anything? What the fuck's to know?"

"I don't know, Gus," Fiore said. "That's what I wanted you to find out."

Gus shrugged his shoulders. He looked like a puppet when someone pulls all the strings at once. "They was just goofing, far as I can tell," he said. "In fact, they got themselves in trouble over it. On account of having to pay for the Jew's car. So it couldn't have been anything, right?"

It sounded right to Fiore. He had no idea how Gus Benini got his information and didn't care. That little detail about the agents getting in trouble was the kind of thing he looked for that told him whether Gus actually knew something or was making it up. Details tell the story.

"Jimmy," Fiore said, "get me a car."

"We can take mine," Jimmy offered.

"Just get me a car," Fiore said, "and get yourself some sleep."

Which was a good idea. They had been up all night and Jimmy Angelisi looked like a lump of cooked pasta.

6

They didn't get out of the restaurant until three. As they drove up Madison Avenue, Jeffrey announced that they were just going upstairs to change their clothes before making the one-hour drive to their country house in Bedford Hills.

"We're *what*?" Jessica asked in a voice that was almost a groan.

The prospect filled Phyllis with dread. The storm seemed to be winding down, but the roads would still be slick. Besides, she couldn't remember ever having felt this tired in her life. From beginning to end, the day had been blindingly exhausting. Even without the hideous way it all ended, she would have felt utterly depleted after so much preparation. Now she felt drained to the point of numbness. It was a brutal comedown for a woman who, toward midnight, could already imagine herself kicking off her shoes and stretching out on the bed in the most perfect dress she had ever owned, accepting the congratulations of her husband and the gratitude of her daughter. Highlights of the party would unspool in her mind like old family movies.

Instead, there was *this*.

"Why can't we go when we get up?" Jessica whined.

"Fine, then you talk to the *New York Times* when they call," Jeffrey said.

Phyllis glanced over to her daughter. She was a sensible girl with a surprisingly high reality quotient for a child of her age and upbringing, but she obviously hadn't let this particular reality sink in. What in heavens name did she imagine? That this was all going to go away like a bad date?

"I won't answer the phone, all right?" Jessica said.

Jeffrey didn't answer her because he didn't have to. He certainly wasn't going to let his daughter make any more decisions at this particular point in time. Eddie Vincenzo and his three friends said all that needed saying about her judgment.

Martin waited downstairs with the motor running while the three Blaines went upstairs to change into appropriate clothes. He was the fifth driver Jeffrey and Phyllis had hired in the last year. One was fired because the car reeked of alcohol and another because it reeked of marijuana. The other two quit because Phyllis ran them around like gerbils in a wheel, a thousand errands every day. The problem was that they talked to other drivers, who spent most of their time parked outside office buildings and restaurants with their hats low over their eyes. These comparisons inevitably led to the conviction that the best driving jobs involved the least amount of driving. And no errands. "I am driver," the Russian had announced when he gave notice. "If missus want, I take her to bakery." What he meant but didn't say was that it compromised the dignity of his calling to go into the bakery himself to pick up boxes of cakes and rolls, to go into Dean & Deluca's for grapefruits and pasta and salad greens, to deliver invitations door-to-door like a vacuum cleaner salesman.

Martin was a sullen kid, almost autistic in his silences. He had shrugged when Jeffrey asked him if he would mind doing errands and shrugged again when Jeffrey told him about the hours. His full name was Martin Luther King Junior Wilson, and he had written all of it, in tiny block letters, on his application. If the forty-five-mile drive from Manhattan to Bedford Hills in the predawn hours struck him as an excessive demand on his services, especially at the end of a day which began, almost twenty hours ago, with him ferrying the female Blaines around the city from florist to dress shop to hair salon, he gave no indication of it. He would be driving back to the city after he left them at the house. They used the Land Rover in the country. The big Jag always went back.

No one said a word on the drive up, which took well over an hour because of the lingering effects of the storm. The highway was reasonably well cleared but the local streets were a mess, and the long driveway to the house was covered with half a foot of crusty snow despite the best efforts of the row of white pines that stood shoulder to shoulder along both sides of the winding drive, canopying it all the way from the road practically to the front door of the house.

Jessica and Phyllis went straight to bed. Jeffrey watched Martin back the car down the drive in the ruts he had made driving in. The sound of the engine and the tires on the snow was absorbed into the landscape even before the car was out of sight. There is no silence like the silence after a snowstorm. In just a light windbreaker, Jeffrey waited on the front deck, watching and listening to the stillness. The sun wasn't up yet but he thought he could see a faint lightening of the sky to the east.

He didn't even consider going to bed. There was too much to think about. He had put everything on hold until he could get his wife and daughter out of the city and up here. Even on the drive up, he had kept his thoughts at bay. Now he had the world to himself and found, as he half expected he would, that he couldn't get that man out of his mind. *Fiore* he had said, hadn't he? Fiore. It was Italian for flower. Phyllis said he was a gangster and that certainly made more sense than Jeffrey's original supposition that he was a cop. Not that having a gangster walk in and take charge made any sense either. But that is exactly what the man had done. He had walked into the chaos as though he breathed chaos and lived for it. He assumed command with a sureness that took Jeffrey's breath away. The man instantly saw the ramifications of everything, tightened the screws, turned things the way Jeffrey wanted them turned, like a bottle genie in an expensive suit. Jeffrey had always been good at solving problems. Everyone he knew in the banking world was good at it. But this man didn't just solve them, he *made them go away*. The four boys vanished as though they had never existed. Amy Laidlaw whimpered when she saw her father, but she went with him. Laidlaw himself, who had stormed in like an avenging angel, clearing space before him with the sheer violence of his wrath, conferred quietly and privately with this stranger and then took his daughter home.

Why? That was the question. Why would a man like this Fiore, a gangster, if that's what he was, insert himself into the middle of a situation that had nothing to do with him?

Jeffrey knew, with that odd and awkward certainty that comes at random moments in one's life, that the answer to this question would be forthcoming soon. A few times in one's life, on unchosen occasions, a door will open and someone unexpected will step in, and one realizes with irrefutable clarity that what just happened was not in fact unexpected. In just this way, Jeffrey knew that Chet Fiore himself would bring the answers to all the questions he raised.

The cold air filled his chest. He could feel it expanding inside him; it seemed to sharpen all his mental processes. He watched as the sun, an unmistakable glow now just over the horizon, burned its way through the remnants of last night's storm. The willow at the bend of the brook bent with its burden of snow practically to the rippling surface of the water. Backlit, a dozen fine-lined birches in a stand where Phyllis had had the pines all cleared, looked black against a sky as pale and bright as water. As he walked around the corner of the house, his appearance startled a small flock of mourning doves and they scattered with a sudden whir of wings. Crows were massing on the trees beyond the lawn. A cardinal shrilled its two-note call over and over from the bare filaments of the forsythia.

The sound of a car crunching through the snow on the drive came as a kind of confirmation of everything he had been thinking and he smiled to himself. This was, after all, what he had been waiting for without quite knowing until now that he was waiting.

A Mercedes was easing down the drive toward the house.

Jeffrey waited.

The Mercedes followed the tracks Martin had made, slipping like an unsure skater. Chet Fiore cut the engine and got out of the driver's side. "I think we're going to be all right," he said.

• • •

Fiore looked around the kitchen as though he were appraising it. "Where's the coffee stuff?" he asked.

Jeffrey had no idea. Phyllis always took the coffeemaker out when she wanted to use it and then put it away. He never watched to see where it went.

"There's a little place in town, it's not bad," he said. "Maybe we should go there."

"I didn't come for brunch, Mr. Blaine," Fiore said. He started opening cabinet doors and didn't stop until he found an espresso machine, a coffee grinder, and glass jars of carefully labeled beans. "What do you like?" he asked.

Jeffrey walked away without answering, a toss of his shoulders indicating that anything would do. He crossed the kitchen to look out the back window.

Four deer were browsing on the bare branches of a stand of larch just beyond the lawn. They looked up, wary, as he came into their view in the window, their tails erect, their ears twitching to locate a sound that would tell them to run. They heard none, and Jeffrey remained motionless in the window. One by one they turned their heads and went back to their breakfasts. They were all males, young ones, judging by their frail and unassertive antlers. Grown males rarely travel together but at this age they have no need for the solitude that will be their lot for the rest of their lives.

In less than five minutes Fiore was standing by Jeffrey's side. "Espresso," he said, holding out a cup. "You don't do the whole steamed milk bit, do you?" he asked.

Jeffrey looked at the small cups of thick black coffee. He heard himself laugh and he said, "You make coffee, too. Is there anything you don't do?"

"No," Fiore said. "There isn't. This is a pretty place."

"We like it."

Fiore turned away, as though the banality of the response annoyed him. "We've got a lot to talk about," he said.

The living room was the showpiece of the house. The high,

slanted ceiling rose to a height of almost thirty-five feet at the center. Skylights cut in among the roof timbers gave the red cedar paneling of the room a warm, woody glow like firelight in the early morning. Staircases at both ends of the long interior wall led to a balcony that gave access to the upstairs bedrooms. Jessica slept upstairs. The master bedroom was on the ground floor because Phyllis wanted a bedroom that opened right to the deck and the yard beyond.

Jeffrey motioned his guest to the six-foot black leather sofa that shaped one of the two seating areas into which the wide room was divided. If Fiore registered the grandeur of the room at all, it didn't show in his face. He hadn't touched his coffee before but now he drained it in a gulp. "Who's here?" he asked.

"Here?"

"In the house. Who's in the house?" he said in a tone of dogged repetition, as though his simple question should have been answered already.

"My wife and my daughter," Jeffrey said.

"No servants?"

"No," Jeffrey said. "No servants."

Fiore nodded his acknowledgment. The preliminaries were over, the gesture seemed to say. Now it was safe to proceed. "I think the biggest part of your problem has been solved," he said.

"My problem?"

"Correct me if I'm wrong, Mr. Blaine. You gave a party for liquored-up minors, one of whom was raped, two of whom were sucking and fucking like seasoned pros."

"The staff was under clear orders," Jeffrey started to protest, but Fiore cut him short.

"I'm not talking about the staff. I'm talking about you. Did you call the police?"

"I thought you were the police. And then you said—"

Again Fiore cut him off.

"You know you've got to call the police on a thing like that."

"Right."

"And you called them?"

Jeffrey didn't answer. He looked at his coffee cup and then set it down, his mind sifting through the intricacies of this thing. He tried to find something he could grab hold of and he said, speaking slowly and carefully, the way he spoke at staff meetings, "I don't believe there's a crime here, Mr. Fiore. It was the girl's father who decided not to press charges."

"You've got a lawyer, don't you, Mr. Blaine?" Fiore asked.

"Yes, of course."

"And you trust him?"

"He wouldn't be my lawyer if I didn't trust him."

"Good. Then call him up. Tell him there was a rape. Ask him if there's a crime even if the girl's father doesn't want there to be. Ask him if you've got a problem."

This was a phone call Jeffrey didn't need to make. He knew the answer perfectly well. He had a problem. He had a lot of problems. "What are you proposing?" he asked.

"I'm not proposing anything," Fiore said. "I just came here to help you out. If you want to be helped out. Take a minute, think it over if you need to."

Fiore got to his feet and wandered to the wall under the balcony, which was lined with well-stocked bookshelves. There weren't a lot of doodads on the shelves, just books. His finger moved along the spines, taking in the titles, leaving Jeffrey to mull his options.

In fact, Jeffrey wasn't thinking at all, at least not in the way he always and invariably dealt with all the problems, business and personal, that came his way. He felt like a man who had been punched well below the belt. He recognized the feeling as cold, sweaty panic. He heard Fiore's voice but didn't catch the words. "Excuse me," he said, forcing his attention across the room.

Fiore turned to face him. "I asked you if you read all these books."

"Most of them I suppose, yes," Jeffrey said, his voice betraying his irritation at the irrelevance.

"It's all history, stuff like that," Fiore commented.

"History and biography mostly, yes. Why are we talking about books?"

"I'm just wondering," Fiore said, "if you learned anything reading all this history and biography."

"Are you making some kind of point?"

"You bet I am, Mr. Blaine," Fiore said, walking straight toward Jeffrey, who was on his feet now. "You don't get books written about you unless you're doing something worth doing. That means taking chances and that means sooner or later you get your nuts caught in a wringer. I'll give you killer odds right now, Mr. Blaine, that there isn't one of those people in one of those books that didn't pull his nuts out of that wringer when he got them caught. Do you hear what I'm saying?"

Jeffrey came right back at him, rising to a kind of indignation that just a moment ago he hadn't known he felt. "What exactly is your connection to all this?" he demanded.

"I told you. I'm trying to help you out."

"You cruise the city looking for good deeds to do?"

Fiore smiled. "Not quite. Stasny called. He said there was a problem."

"Why did he call you?"

"I own the place."

This was a possibility Jeffrey hadn't even considered. What did it change? His mind jumped through the permutations. "All right, Mr. Fiore," he said, "let's look at this the other way around. It's your restaurant and therefore your employees who gave those girls that liquor. It was you who sent the boys home and you're the one who talked to Amy Laidlaw's father. You're also the one who talked me out of calling the police. So it seems to me that you and I have the same kind of problem. If that's true, why don't you tell me what *you're* planning to do about it."

Fiore laughed. It wasn't a mocking laugh in the least. It was deep and rolling, the laughter of a man who gave every appearance of being genuinely amused.

"In the first place, Mr. Blaine," he said, and then seemed to change direction in mid-thought. "You know," he interrupted himself to say, "I ought to call you Jeffrey. That's all right, isn't it? Unless you prefer Jeff?"

"No, no," Jeffrey said.

"Jeffrey it is," Fiore said. "Okay, let's see what we've got here. In the first place, Jeffrey, there are very few people, very, very few who know I own that restaurant. Even fewer, none in fact, who can prove it. So that takes care of your first point. What was your next one? Well, they're all kind of the same. I sent the kids home, I talked to the father, I talked to you. But the funny thing is, Mr. Blaine—I'm sorry, *Jeffrey*—the funny thing is that I don't think there's anyone who remembers seeing me in that restaurant last night. Laidlaw sure as hell doesn't remember. Call him up. Ask him. He doesn't even remember going there himself. Because he had no reason to be there if his daughter wasn't raped, which we're all more or less agreed that she wasn't."

"All right," Jeffrey conceded, "we're all more or less agreed."

"That's you, me, Mr. Laidlaw, young Miss Laidlaw, those other two girls—"

"The boys of course."

"What boys?" Fiore asked with a sly smile.

Jeffrey returned the smile. "Admirable," he said.

"Fucking A. Admirable," Fiore agreed. "But I'd wipe that smile off my face if I were you because you're forgetting about Mr. Noel Garver of the *New York Post*. He swears he saw that Jewish chick with a young man's dong halfway down her gullet. He swears he heard Amy Laidlaw screaming and swears he saw her laid out on the floor in a pile next to her own underwear."

Jeffrey hadn't forgotten about Garver but he had permitted himself, over the last minute or two, to ease the reporter out of the equation while Fiore was going through his proof, showing how neatly it all might work out. Now the mention of Garver's name brought the dangerous little man back to the forefront of Jeffrey's consciousness.

"And he'll print it," Jeffrey said. Even to his own ears his voice sounded hollow.

If the story came out there would be an investigation. Jeffrey could deny it, of course, but lying to the police was a felony. The well-being of his family would be hostage to the first person at the party who broke ranks and told the truth. On the other hand, he could come clean the moment he was questioned about it. Except that doing so would leave him unable to explain his conduct on the night of the party, which amounted to nothing less than a conspiracy to conceal a major felony.

Fiore seemed to be reading his mind.

"You're probably dying to get in that slick red Land Rover of yours, haul your ass down to the Bedford Hills general store or whatever they call it, and see what's in this morning's *Post*. Am I right?"

Jeffrey didn't answer.

"Well, I've got good news for you, Jeffrey," Fiore said. "There's nothing in this morning's *Post*. No column. Not a word. Mr. Garver has very graciously agreed to hold off publication for a little while."

"Why would he do that?" Jeffrey asked.

"I imagine he figured it was in his best interest."

"Are you saying you threatened him?"

Fiore laughed again, but this time he let the mockery in his laughter show.

"You know I'm not saying that," he said. "If you know anything at all, Mr. B, you know for certain you didn't hear me say that."

All right, Jeffrey thought wryly, this gangster saved my ass. Saved it from what? An embarrassing scandal. What else? Nothing else. He dug a hole and we both climbed into it, and then he pulled it in after him. Magic. Alchemy. He changed an embarrassment into a felony, and now, right now, this minute, not one minute later, Jeffrey Blaine could either accept the consequences of that concealed felony or he could take whatever steps needed to be taken to walk away from them.

Later, when he looked back at the twelve hours that began the moment his daughter said *Daddy, I'd like you to meet Eddie Vincenzo* and ran until this moment, what surprised him most was how simple the decision seemed to be. If it was even a decision at all. Every act of his life to that point had been based on a clear and compelling, an uncomplicated and unproblematic sense of what was right and what was expected.

And it worked, hadn't it? He was a successful man.

But . . .

It was the same *but* that had sent a chill through his body at the party last night. *There is a sense one has, when one has everything, that everything is surely enough.* That's how it's supposed to work.

But it doesn't. It never has, it never does.

It seemed, he thought, so much simpler to be Chet Fiore than to be Jeffrey Blaine.

Before he could say anything, before he could even announce that he was accepting the terms of Chet Fiore's offer, whatever that offer might be, Fiore turned away, having heard a sound in the house, and Jeffrey's eyes turned, too.

Phyllis was standing at the far end of the living room. "Oh," she said. "Good morning, Mr. Fiore."

She was in a short nightgown that came halfway down her thighs. Her hair was tossed from sleep and her bare arms seemed to glow alabaster in the light from the skylight. She was conscious of how she looked as she walked across the room and extended her hand. "I hope there are no problems," she said.

Jeffrey kissed her on the cheek, conscious, too, of Fiore's eyes on her. She should have put something on. "We didn't wake you, did we?" he said.

And Fiore said, "This is a beautiful house, Mrs. Blaine. No, I don't think there are any problems."

He had a very charming smile.

7

Schliester and Gogarty went out for breakfast after getting their asses reamed and cleaned by Dennis Franciscan. Over pancakes and eggs, they decided that Franciscan's order to leave Fiore alone didn't extend to Jeffrey Blaine. There was no reason they couldn't follow up from that end, and if the questions they asked about Mr. Blaine involved Mr. Fiore, that still wasn't exactly the same thing.

They looked Blaine up and found out where he lived. Fifth Avenue, right across the street from Central Park. It figured.

The doorman popped through the door the moment they pulled to a stop. "Yes, sir?" he said.

Gogarty got out of the car. Schliester remained in the passenger seat.

"Just wanted to ask you a few questions," Gogarty said. "About one of your tenants. About some guests they might have had."

Jakob Beider's mouth went instantly dry. He was sixty-two years old. Three years ago he retired after thirty-five years at a rental building on the Upper West Side where the police were always asking the doormen about the comings and goings of the tenants. He hated it, being constantly caught between the cops, who made vague threats and accused him of being a bad citizen, and the tenants, who accused him of talking too much and made much more detailed threats. Jakob and all the other doormen knew better than to answer questions from the police, but the endless hassles wore him down. For years he had been looking for a better job but never found one, and so he put in for retirement the minute he had accumulated enough time for his union pension. After a year of doing nothing, he heard about an opening on Fifth Avenue in the Nineties, the kind of building that never got visited by the police.

Now here they were again. One sitting in the car, one on the sidewalk. Nothing ever changes.

"Could I see some identification?" Jakob said.

Gogarty tipped his head slightly, as though the question confused him. Slowly, like a man reaching for his wallet to pay a very large hotel bill, he removed a leather case from his breast pocket, flipped it open, looked at it himself a moment, and then displayed the contents. Almost as though the gesture were a signal, the second man got out of the car and came around to stand next to his partner. Jakob looked at the identification card Gogarty showed him. The man was a federal agent, not a cop. In thirty-five years, Jakob had seen more than his share of those IDs, too.

He looked up, into the agent's eyes, and said nothing.

"What's your name?" Gogarty asked. When they ask you for identification, you ask them to identify themselves.

"Jakob. Jakob Beider."

"And you've got a tenant named Blaine," Gogarty said.

"No, no tenants. This isn't a rental building," Jakob said.

Gogarty smiled but it wasn't a pleasant smile. "Choice of words, Gustav. Whatever you call them, there's a family living here named Blaine."

It didn't sound like a question, so Jakob didn't answer it.

"Yes or no?"

"The Blaines, yes."

"All right, Wilhelm, now we're getting somewhere. See how much better this is?"

Jakob didn't necessarily see.

"Have you ever seen this man visiting here?" Gogarty asked.

He took out a small photo of Chet Fiore. The picture was years old. Fiore appeared to be in his twenties.

Jakob looked at the picture and handed it back. He shook his head.

"That means he hasn't been here?"

"I do not know this man. This is all I can tell you."

For a moment Gogarty considered asking the doorman to ring up the Blaines' apartment. It might be fun to ask Blaine himself if he knew the man in the picture. But what would be the point? If there was anything worth looking into here, it would only serve to alert Blaine that it was being looked into. A good investigator is like one of those old-fashioned gods who is not allowed to meddle with human destiny, and Gogarty was a good investigator. Given the choice, he always chose to let things happen.

Schliester also thought of himself as a good investigator, although not necessarily as a god. He believed in asking the next question.

"What do you say we ring up the Blaines and ask them?" he said. "What do you think, Jakob? Think we might find out you're lying to us?"

The more Gogarty saw of this St. Louis kid, the more he liked him. The kid tended to go off half-cocked, but half a cock is better than none. He had style. And he wasn't always checking his watch. Gogarty had a partner once who couldn't wait for the shift to end. It was like being buried alive.

"You cannot do that," Jakob said.

"Oh, I've got a badge, Jakob," Schliester said. "I can do whatever I want."

Jakob liked this man. He didn't make fun of his name like the other one did. "No one is home," he said. "They come in last night, they go out."

Schliester raised an eyebrow. "They went out? In the middle of the night?"

"House in the country," Jakob said. "Somewhere. I don't know."

Schliester and Gogarty were thinking the same thing. It seemed like a funny thing to do in the middle of a snowstorm in the middle of the night.

But then, rich people did funny things.

· · ·

Gaetano Falcone made his home in a comfortable though far from lavish beach house in Orient Point on the north shore of Long Island, over a hundred miles out from the city. The backyard stretched to the water's edge. He liked to watch the birds that came to the seed feeders strategically placed around the grounds, cardinals and woodpeckers and nuthatches, ugly little starlings and brazen titmice that waited impatiently in the forsythia only a foot or two away when he filled their feeders. He especially liked the shore birds, the raucous gulls and the patient cormorants, the sandpipers who patrolled his beach on thin uncanny legs.

He lived as simply as he did because he believed that a man in his line of work was a fool if he called attention to himself.

Anyone who had any reason to know these things knew that Gaetano Falcone was the most powerful man in the New York underworld. Twenty years ago he united the families under his leadership. A whole generation of powerful young men like Chet Fiore grew up without ever knowing a day when the men to whom they reported didn't report to Gaetano Falcone.

Falcone liked Fiore well enough, although he didn't like the fact that he drove a foreign car. He was waiting in front of the house, feet planted wide, when a Mercedes rolled up and stopped only a few feet away. It was crimson red. Fiore's car was blue. Falcone looked at it with distaste, dispensing with the amenities of a greeting. "What? You traded it in already?" he asked even before Fiore was out of the car.

"It's a loaner," Fiore said. "There was a little accident. You're looking good, Mr. Falcone."

Falcone grabbed a handful of the soft flesh around his waist as though he were about to ball it up and throw it away. "Ah," he scoffed, "I've got to do something about this. The wife does exercises every day. If she gets any thinner people are going to start wondering what she's doing with a fat old man like me."

Fiore laughed because he was supposed to. He said, "I don't think so, Mr. Falcone."

"Come on," Falcone growled, "we'll go around the back, have some coffee, some fruit."

They walked around the house. There was no snow on the ground. The storm must have turned off somewhere before it got this far out on the island.

At the back of the house, in the middle of the sloping yard, was a spacious greenhouse that Falcone called his solarium. Part of it was set up with comfortable furniture, and the old man liked to entertain guests here. They could have entered through the house but he preferred the walk around the yard.

"How is this business coming?" he asked as soon as they were settled inside. He broke a macaroon in half and popped one of the pieces into his mouth.

"It's coming just the way we talked about, Mr. Falcone," Fiore said.

"This man Blaine, are you sure he's the right man?"

Fiore was sure. Blaine had listened to everything he had to say. No commitments were made, but he had listened. Yes, he was the right man.

He could have said this but he elected not to. He sipped at his coffee and then loosened his tie before answering. It was hot in here. "You put this thing in my hands, Mr. Falcone," he said. "Do you see any reason to question my judgment now?"

The pitch of his voice had to be absolutely perfect, because he was, no matter how one construed it, challenging Falcone's right to question him. It was a gamble on Fiore's part. He was betting that Falcone would elect to admire his willingness to take full responsibility.

The older man's eyes narrowed for a moment. "No," he said. "No reason to question."

He stood up and walked back to the glass wall. A few yards away, a thick hedge of wild roses lined a foot-high stone wall that protected the land from the beach and the water beyond.

Fiore joined him there. Far to their left a bright orange sun dove into the water, lighting it on fire. The sun set so early this time of year it hardly seemed there was any day at all. Which was more or less the way men like Gaetano Falcone and Chet Fiore liked it.

"This man is willing to help us?" Falcone said. "This is all I need to know."

Fiore considered carefully before answering. "He is," he said, choosing his words carefully. "We haven't talked about it yet, but he's interested. He's restless. Before he signs on, he's going to have to find the justification."

"However you have to do it," Falcone answered indifferently.

"Not just yet," Fiore said. "If he does it because he wants to, because he's rich and bored, I don't know how far I can trust him. I want him to have a better reason."

Falcone smiled and nodded. He had always admired Charles's thoroughness. Almost from the first time he met Fiore, years ago now, he had singled him out for advancement. The young man had imagination and he paid attention to the details. The two didn't come together in the same man very often.

"You do your experiments on this man," he said, "that's fine with me. Just so it comes out in the right place."

"Of course, Mr. Falcone," Fiore said.

"You understand how important this is, Charles. We can't keep going the way we've been going, hiding our money in suitcases."

It had been a long time since Falcone or any of his people hid their money in suitcases. Complex money-laundering systems did the work once done by pizza parlors and brown paper bags. But the money-laundering apparatus was the weak link in the food chain that fed the beast. Its capacity set limits on the business the families could do, and when those limits were exceeded, as they usually were, that's when the families became vulnerable, that's when arrests were made.

"It's a new century," Falcone went on, almost as though he were talking to himself.

If he was an old man by Fiore's standards, he showed no signs of it. Not in the strength of his arms, not in the reach of his mind.

Fiore smiled, enjoying and absorbing the sense of power that came off Gaetano Falcone the way the vast and reassuring hum of the ocean came off the waves that stretched in front of him out beyond the lawn and the wild roses and the stone wall.

Part Three

8

Jeffrey read the last paragraph a second time. He took a sip of his coffee and reached into his breast pocket for his pen. He uncapped it and wrote *This is unfundable* next to Roger Bogard's signature at the bottom of the report. He added his initials. The pen hovered a moment. He wanted to add, *Why the hell do we have a research department?* or *Did anyone check this with Research?* or even *Why am I reading this drivel?*

Every week at least two proposals came onto his desk that embodied absolutely no thought at all. The younger people in the department thought of themselves as visionaries, forever on the verge of discovering the next unexpected growth industry, the next Microsoft or Federal Express. They might as well have tried to fund a fleet of sailing ships to find the Northwest Passage. Sometimes the young people around him made Jeffrey feel prematurely wise, even though he was barely a decade older than most of them. His solid good sense, like a paradoxical kind of gravity, helped him rise quickly. He was barely thirty when he made his first million, thirty-five when he made partner. And he was still a young man with a long way to go, a long career that stretched out in front of him like a lit road.

On the other hand, while he didn't approve of the attitudes he saw around him, he didn't quite disapprove either. Greed, some people called it. But Jeffrey saw it as a kind of top-down energy, an unboundedness that he missed in his own life. He had only recently begun asking himself if there was something the matter with him. He knew that he wasn't a dull man, but more and more he felt that he had let himself become dull. Certainly he knew he looked that way to his daughter. Maybe, after all, he should be funding those fleets of sailing ships. Or even sailing on them, alone at twilight on the quarterdeck, eyes scanning the shoreline for that mysterious and elusive channel to another ocean.

He slipped the report into his briefcase and checked his watch. Eight-fifteen.

"Martin, please ask the doorman to ring up," he said.

Without a word, Martin got out of the car and went into the lobby. Through the heavy glass door Jeffrey could see him talking on the doorman's intercom, then handing it back to the doorman and returning to the car. He came around and got in behind the wheel. "Says she's on the way," Martin said.

Jeffrey stared at the lobby and took a sip of coffee. It was cold already. He drank it down and refilled it from the carafe. While he was doing this, the door next to him opened and Jessica said, "Slide over, Daddy."

He wondered whether he would have thought her beautiful if she hadn't been his daughter. He was able, at least now, to see her exactly the way she actually looked, tweedy and skirted, as innocent as the child he still believed her to be. She had her mother's fine bones and chiseled mouth, her mother's radiant hair. But she had his eyes, which lacked brightness and color and were too close together, and his awkward, gangling posture.

She reached out and took his coffee cup, then handed it back to him after he slid over behind Martin.

"Coffee?" he asked.

She shook her head, looked at his cup, and sighed. He knew that she disapproved of china cups in a car, but she had never explained her feelings except to say it was ridiculous. "Why is it ridiculous?" he had asked. "It just is, that's all," she had said. "I can't believe you can't see it."

The two of them had hardly spoken a word over the weekend.

Except for brief appearances at meals, at which nothing was said, Jessica remained in her room. Now, as the heavy Jag rolled down Fifth Avenue, Jeffrey broke the silence. "Do you have plans after school?" he asked.

She gave him a long, searching look.

"I don't know," she said.

"Well, if you don't know, then you don't have plans, do you?"

He could be so damned literal.

"Then I don't have plans," she agreed. "Happy?"

Jeffrey took a moment to formulate exactly how to put what he and Phyllis had decided he would say to her. "Your mother and I would rather you didn't go anywhere," he said.

"You'd *rather*?"

He rephrased it. "Come home right after school."

"I'm grounded?"

"In a manner of speaking."

"You wouldn't want to tell me why?"

"You don't know?"

"I'm asking. Is that a clue or what?"

"Don't get smart with me, Jessica."

"No, I really don't know," she said, drawing out every syllable and putting long spaces between the words. She could put more weariness and urgency into her voice than a woman six times her age should have been able to manage.

"Your mother and I are both very uneasy about—"

She didn't let him finish. Which was just as well. Sometimes lately, when sternness was called for and he tried being stern, he found himself talking to her as though he were dictating a memo, and he always regretted it.

"All right all right all right," she said. "You don't like my boyfriend."

"Am I hearing this?" Jeffrey said. "Do you really think it's a question of *liking* your boyfriend?"

Jessica came right back at him. "He didn't do anything," she said hotly. "If you remember, and I'm sure you do, he was downstairs with me the whole time."

Jeffrey didn't want to get into an argument on the subject. She knew perfectly well what the issues were. "Just give me your word that you won't see him and you can do whatever you want after school."

Trust was a keystone of the family. It had been clear to Jessica since she was old enough to understand the concept that her word would always be enough.

"I'll be home right after last period," she answered coldly, declining the offer. She leaned forward and said, "Let me off at the corner, I want to get something."

Martin said, "Yes, miss," and rolled to a stop.

She was out of the car before her father could get out a word of protest. He watched as she waved to a couple of girls walking toward the school. The curb was a lake of slush but she hopped it easily and raced into a convenience store at the corner. He felt a sudden tightening of all the muscles in his body.

"The Plaza, sir?" Martin asked.

Jeffrey's eyes were on the door to the convenience store, his mind on Jessica. It took him a second to realize that he had just been asked a question. "Yes, the Plaza," he said, and then, when the car started from the curb, he changed his mind and said, on an impulse that surprised him with its intensity, "Let's just wait a minute, Martin."

"Yes, sir."

The car slid back to the curb. A minute passed. Then another. Jessica didn't come out of the store. Jeffrey checked his watch, then checked it against the dashboard clock. They agreed with each other that it was eight-thirty.

"How long will it take us to get there?"

Martin did a quick calculation before answering. "Fifteen minutes," he said. Martin never guessed, approximated, or thought. His answers were categorical.

Jeffrey hated being late for meetings. He could say with assurance that he had never once in his life kept a client waiting. His fingers drummed on his knee. He wanted to get out of the car and march into the store, but if he did that, he would be telling his daughter he no longer trusted her, and once he did that, all bets were off.

Well, he thought, how was this any better? He was spying on her. Even Martin understood that. He tried to tell himself that he wasn't spying, that he was waiting for her the way you wait outside when you drop someone at their door until the light comes on inside. You can't drive off if the light doesn't come on, but that doesn't make it spying.

He reached for the door handle, then froze in that position as the front door of the store opened. But it wasn't Jessica. It was a tiny Puerto Rican woman with a shawl over her head.

"That's fine, Martin," he said. "We'd better go."

He turned to look in the store window as the car rolled past. He saw Jessica at the payphone in the corner. Why was she using a payphone? She had her cell phone in her pocket.

He knew the answer instantly. The bill came to him, with its carefully enumerated list of calls.

He bit at his lip and felt his face flush. He turned away, awkwardly conscious of having seen something he wasn't supposed to see.

It was strange, he thought as he settled back in his seat, that at her age she still let her father drive her to school. As she moved deeper and deeper into adolescence, she had taken to forbidding more and more of the favors and attentions she had always relied on, even insisted on, as a child. When she was younger he used to worry that they were spoiling her, but then he made up his mind that she was one of those kids who prizes her independence too highly to stay spoiled for long.

"Is Mr. Bolling here yet?" Jeffrey asked as Harold, the maître d' at the Oak Room, led him to his table.

"Yes, sir. Only a moment ago," Harold said. "Coffee for Mr. Blaine, please."

A waiter dashed off to get it. Clint Bolling stood up and extended his hand. "Hell of a nice party," he said. "Thanks muchas for the invite."

Jeffrey had almost forgotten that Bolling had been at the party. He must have left early, which was just as well.

"I'm glad you could make it," Jeffrey said blandly.

"What the hell," Bolling answered with a surprisingly loud laugh. "Beats sitting in a hotel room playing with yourself."

Obviously that was a joke, but Jeffrey didn't know the man well enough to know what kind of joke it was. He changed the subject and asked how he was enjoying his stay. For the next few minutes they talked about New York, the shows Bolling had seen and the ones he wanted to see. In both Norman and Dallas he subscribed to the symphonies but didn't like them much. He saw the road companies of all the Broadway shows and liked them better. "For a while there, I used to see *Evita* every time I came to New York. Then they went and made a damn movie out of it. I don't know anymore."

Jeffrey recommended a few shows and asked him if he was interested in hockey or basketball. "I have a box at the Garden," he offered.

"I'll tell you the goddamned truth," Bolling said, leaning forward as though he were about to confess one of the darkest secrets of his psyche. "I always liked baseball, always will. It's a real *game*, y'know what I mean. You catch the ball or you don't, you hit it or you don't. Hockey, I mean what the hell is that? Skating around on *ice*, for Christ's sake. Why would anyone do that? Basketball's okay if you like watching a bunch of tall rich niggers jumping up and down."

Then, apparently for the benefit of the waiter, a black man who was standing over his shoulder, he added, "No offense. I'm just an old country boy."

The waiter's face showed nothing.

Jeffrey made sure to address him by name when he ordered and reminded himself that an apology would be in order afterward.

They got down to business while they waited for their breakfasts to be served and then while they ate. Jeffrey had three funds in mind for Clint Bolling and laid out the pros and cons of each. Bolling didn't seem to be listening. He asked no questions. Each of the investment funds called for an initial buy-in in the twenty-five-to fifty-million-dollar range. "You call that a range?" Bolling said. "We've got ranges a lot bigger than that where I come from."

Jeffrey had no idea what he meant. It almost seemed as though Bolling had picked up on the word *range* simply to have something to say, like a man pretending he is keeping up with a conversation he really can't follow. But that made no sense. Despite his bumpkin act, Clint Bolling was a shrewd man, not likely to get confused by the preliminary details of an investment.

Yet there he was, plainly distracted, fidgeting around the edges of the discussion as though he wished they could get back to talking about Broadway shows. After a minute or two more, he plucked his napkin from his lap and held it over his plate like a dead bird. "Don't you go giving me three choices," he said, dangling the napkin as he got to his feet. "When a man wants a chunk of my money, I damn well expect him to put his balls on the line." He dropped the napkin on the plate. "You figure out your best offer and tell me what it is. Either I write you a check or sayonara. It's that simple. I've got to go to the can."

He walked off toward the front of the dining room, almost bumping into a man from the next table who got up when he did. The man from the next table seemed almost to be stepping in Bolling's footsteps as he followed him toward the restrooms.

The waiter appeared immediately. "Is your friend finished, Mr. Blaine?" he asked.

"My associate," Jeffrey corrected, to make it clear that Bolling wasn't a friend, "was insufferably rude. I'm very sorry, Brian."

"No need for that, sir," Brian said. "Shall I clear the table?"

"Please. And fresh coffee."

Jeffrey called the office while he waited for Bolling. He asked Jennie to get someone in research to run some numbers for him and have them ready for presentation to Bolling that afternoon. There were no messages for him. He half expected there would have been a call from Fiore. Something told him the man was as impatient as he was efficient, and that before very long he would want something in return for all that efficiency. A man doesn't take care of a problem in the middle of the night, drive forty miles in the morning before he goes to bed, make coffee, and ask for nothing. The call would come. Jeffrey was sure of that. What he wasn't at all sure of was what he would do when it did.

Bolling was in the men's room almost fifteen minutes. When he got back, Jeffrey started to tell him he would have workups on one of the proposals later in the afternoon but Bolling waved him off.

"Don't worry, we'll get around to all that," he said.

He didn't sit down. He was gone even before Jeffrey signed for the check.

Phyllis met Jeffrey at the door when he came home and brought him straight into her study. She closed the door and pressed the play button on her answering machine.

"Mrs. Blaine, this is Monica Seifert from the dean's office. There seems to be a problem here that I would suggest requires your immediate attention," a woman's voice said in such studied and precise diction that it sounded as though she were reading from a prepared statement. Monica Seifert taught honors math and was the school's top college-placement expert. "Jessica missed three classes this morning," the meticulously accented voice continued. "When I asked her about it, she said that she overslept. I would have to characterize the manner of her response as rude. And not really to the point, is it? If it turns out Jessica can't get herself to her morning classes, then I believe you and Mr. Blaine will have to take steps to get her here. Please feel free to call me at any time. I'm sorry to bother you with such problems. I assure you that if Jessica had been in the least amenable to dealing with the matter herself, this call would not have been necessary."

Jeffrey and Phyllis looked at each other over the machine. "I thought you drove her this morning," Phyllis said.

"I did."

He walked out of the room and down the corridor to Jessica's room. The door was closed. He knocked sharply. "Your mother and I want to talk to you," he said. "In her study. Put some clothes on and come there."

"Now?"

"Now."

He walked back to the study.

"If that child lies to me," Phyllis said. There was no second half to the sentence.

Two minutes later Jessica strolled into the study, emphatically nonchalant. The skirt she had worn to school had been replaced by jeans. She was still wearing the same top.

Phyllis said nothing. Jeffrey reached out and pressed the play button on the answering machine.

Jessica listened impassively until her father hit the stop button. Then she waited, glancing from one parent to the other. She said nothing. It was a contest, of course. The first one to commit to a position lost. Most of the contests in the Blaine household worked that way.

Jeffrey's hand hovered over the play button. "Do you need to hear it again?" he asked.

She considered her options for a moment. Her father knew enough to leave her very few. She had nothing to respond to except the voice on the machine.

"That woman is such a total bitch," she said. "I missed English, I missed social studies, and I missed health. They are not compulsory attendance courses, which she knows perfectly well, and I am acing every one of them. Which she also knows perfectly well."

"Your father took you to school in plenty of time, Jessica," Phyllis said.

"I just *told* you," Jessica moaned. "They are not compulsory attendance courses. Are you guys going to be at Yale every morning?"

"You're not in Yale yet, young lady. Your acceptance was conditional."

"Can we get real, please," Jessica groaned.

The letter welcoming her to Yale said that her acceptance was conditional on the satisfactory completion of her senior year. But all acceptance letters say that. It doesn't mean a thing. It was a mistake for Phyllis to bring it up because it gave Jessica something she could be right about when only a second before she had been completely in the wrong. She took advantage of the moment by turning to walk out.

Jeffrey let her get as far as the door. "Who were you calling this morning?" he asked. "On the payphone in the store?"

Jessica whirled to face him.

"What store?" Phyllis asked. No one heard her.

"Were you spying on me?" Jessica demanded.

"The store has windows, Jessica. I saw you on the telephone. With whom were you talking?"

"What are you talking about? What store? Why were you using a payphone?"

"You know something, Daddy," Jessica said. There were tears in her eyes. "Who I talk to on the telephone is none of your damn business."

"Jessica, you were calling that boy," Jeffrey said. Stating it as a fact.

"What payphone? What store?" Phyllis asked for the third time.

"He has a name," Jessica shot back.

"I'm sorry. I'm not that familiar with it. You just introduced me to him the other night. Eddie something. Am I right?"

"Maybe I didn't introduce you to him before because I knew the kind of shit I'd be getting."

"Exactly what kind of shit are we talking about?"

Phyllis said, "You called that boy from the party? And that made you miss three classes?"

She seemed to be lagging three sentences behind the conflict going on in front of her. Jessica looked at her and then back to her father.

"You know exactly what I'm talking about. He's not *acceptable*. He's not from a good family."

"When have we ever said anything to you about anybody's family?" Phyllis demanded, catching up, outraged.

"Because there was never anything to say, was there?" Jessica challenged. "Every boy I ever dated was perfect."

"And what exactly is wrong with that?"

"They were boring little preppies."

"Just because their friends aren't rapists doesn't make them boring."

"I am not going to have this conversation," Jessica said.

Phyllis looked at Jeffrey. She wanted his help. But she had turned the conversation in totally the wrong direction and there was no possibility of getting it back. He said nothing.

Jessica, who hadn't moved from the door, opened it now and walked out of the room.

"She asked me to drop her off at the store," Jeffrey explained needlessly. "There's a phone booth. She made a call."

"When exactly were you planning on telling me about this?" Phyllis asked.

She sat down at her desk, which was always Jeffrey's signal to leave.

The nice thing about a large apartment is that everyone has his or her own space. They wouldn't have to see each other until dinner was on the table.

9

I f the phone rang, there wouldn't have been anyone to answer it. All the little cubicles were empty and the aisles between them were full. It looked like one of those nature things, bees or something swarming outside the hive. *All those having business before the United States attorney for the Southern District of New York, hold your water. There's nobody home.*

Schliester looked at Gogarty and raised an eyebrow. Gogarty looked at Schliester and raised both eyebrows. Schliester couldn't top that, so he headed for the first informed person he could find, who turned out to be Greg Billings, who was wearing his gray suit with the faint herringbone pattern. He had five different ties he wore with it, none of which was right.

"What's up?" Schliester asked.

"You don't know?"

"How would I know?"

"We work for a living," Gogarty said, joining them. "We don't hang around offices trolling for gossip."

"What's up is Mr. Franciscan. More particularly his johnson."

Beryl Ross said, "That's not funny, Greg."

Beryl Ross was only a few months out of law school. She was famous in the office for never figuring anything out.

"Why is that of so much interest?" Schliester asked.

"I'm just guessing," Gogarty suggested, "but I assume it was up something it shouldn't have been up."

"Jackpot," Billings said, raising his hand for a high five. Gogarty took him up on the offer.

Beryl Ross scowled darkly and said, "Isn't it obvious that Mr. Franciscan has problems? Don't you think he needs our support?"

Billings said, "He needs a lawyer is what he needs."

At twelve-thirty A.M. Dennis Franciscan had been arrested in the lower concourse men's room at Grand Central Station in the course of performing an unnatural act with a much older man.

"Older?" Schliester asked.

"There's no accounting for taste," Billings said.

Beryl Ross said, "At least it wasn't a minor," and all three men looked at her funny and then agreed in chorus. It would have been wrong, Schliester suggested, to keep a child up that late.

Beryl groaned and shook her head and walked away. The three men took this as a signal that it was time for them to get serious.

"He resigned?" Gogarty asked.

Billings shook his head. "Nobody's said that yet, but yeah, he's got to."

"Who gets the office?"

"Up for grabs."

Interesting, Schliester thought. The Organized Crime Bureau was everybody's favorite and always had been. It was where Rudy Giuliani made his reputation, and Thomas Dewey before that. Dewey had a highway named after him. No one from any other bureau had ever had a highway named after him. Or even a street, for all anyone knew.

Elaine Lester walked up to the three of them and said, "I've got to talk to you."

Billings knew she meant the two investigators, so he walked away. Schliester and Gogarty followed her to her office. Her hair was loose, which it almost never was. She was wearing a plaid skirt and a blouse that could have been satin. How many women wear plaid nowadays? Schliester thought. But plaid skirts always look good on women with good bodies.

They followed her into the office and she closed the door. Gogarty looked around. "Jesus," he said. "You don't even have a window."

Elaine smiled exactly the way she would have smiled if she found him witty. She didn't. "I want your case," she said.

"What case would that be?" Gogarty asked.

"Fiore."

"We're not working Fiore," Gogarty said.

Elaine said, "The bullshit's over, boys. I know what you're doing. I know Dennis took you off the case and I know you're still working it."

Gogarty and Schliester looked at each other but didn't say anything. It was still her turn.

"Dennis is gone," she said. "His office has windows. I want it. I want your case."

"Because that will get you the office?"

"Because that will get me the office."

Schliester wondered whether it would be called Lester Road or Lester Boulevard.

Gogarty said, "Sorry, sister, there's no case," and walked away.

She saw Schliester looking at her. "What are you looking at?"

"I was wondering what you were doing for dinner?" he said.

Now it was her turn to walk away.

"All right then, lunch?" he asked.

Jeffrey found himself waking up every morning before the first glimmer of light made its way through the bedroom windows, which looked toward the East River and got the morning light. The first few times he woke up that early, he lay still, hoping to get back to sleep. When that didn't work, he got out of bed and padded about the apartment, making his own coffee and sometimes a few pieces of toast. The cook wouldn't be up for hours. He felt like a stranger in his own home.

If this feeling raised questions in his mind, he put them aside.

Not because he didn't want to deal with them but because he did. Jeffrey believed that the only way to deal with problems was to do something about them. If he wasn't comfortable at home, the answer was to be elsewhere. It was too late to ask why, and the why didn't matter in any case.

His new routine included a stop every morning at the corner of Forty-second and Park, where he got out of the car and bought a *Post* at the newsstand. He flipped the pages to the columns and looked for one by Noel Garver. If there was one, he read just enough to see what it was about. It was never about Jessica's party. So he threw the paper in the trash and got back in the car.

On Fridays he always ate lunch in the Partners Room on the twenty-eighth floor. The Partners Room operated pretty much like a gentleman's club except that most clubs pretend that gentlemen do not talk business at the table, whereas nothing else was ever discussed in the Partners Room at Layne Bentley. The room itself was an exact replica of the darkly wainscoted formal dining room at Lowthorpe, Everett Layne's ancestral home overlooking the Hudson at Cold Spring, just across the river from West Point. An immense stone fireplace large enough to roast a goat burned logs the size of telephone poles summer and winter.

Everett Layne himself sat at the head of the table for the Friday lunches, with the partners ranked to his left and right in descending order of seniority. Jeffrey, not only the youngest partner but the youngest in the one-hundred-and-thirty-year history of the firm, was separated from the gaunt old patriarch by a few dozen square yards of polished mahogany and a sea of throbbingly blue Limoges china and faceted Baccarat crystal that resolved the firelight into a thousand sparkling constellations.

Mr. Layne invariably set the agenda, which tended to be abstract and philosophical. "I was rather surprised to see in our midweek report . . ." he might begin, his reedy voice like an electrical hum in the air. Or, "Can anyone explain to me why . . ." Or, "Has it now become our practice to . . ." Discussions of principle, in other words, the questions arising more often than not from an incongruity of perspectives that measured the difference between the investment bankers of today and a man whose roots, if not his actual experience, went back to the days of Mellon and Astor. Although the old man harbored no illusions that his vision was shared by any of the men at the table, still he thought it important to keep his ideas alive. It was in fact all he did. At eighty-two, he came in only on Fridays.

From the very first time Jeffrey attended a Friday afternoon Partners Room luncheon, he hadn't been shy about speaking up. He was comfortable with the tone of high-minded abstraction, which felt as familiar as the Sunday dinners at home when his father held court in his worn gray suit. His father enjoyed raising large questions about life's larger issues. It was there, at his father's table, that Jeffrey learned to feel at ease in a world as thick with ethical options as the woods were thick with trees, tangled but far from trackless.

On this particular Friday afternoon, Jim Thornton cleared his throat to signal that he was about to speak. Thornton, whose grandfather on his mother's side was a Bentley, in fact the last Bentley to grace the board of Layne Bentley, managed to be both assertive and shy at the same time and within the firm was universally disliked for that reason. Even his simplest observation came out sounding sneaky and underhanded, as though he were trying to gain an advantage. Layne nodded in his direction.

"My reading of the prospectus," Thornton said, looking down, adjusting his silverware, "suggests that these people will be doing medical research in an excessively narrow range. When you get down to it, they've really got only one arrow in their quiver. Either they succeed wonderfully or they vanish without a trace. I don't see how we could feel comfortable steering A-list investors in that direction."

The prospectus in question was a proposal for a foundation to do leukemia research unaffiliated with any university or pharmaceutical company. There was a kind of quixotic desperation to the idea as well as to the style of the proposal that Jeffrey found appealing.

As if on cue, the old man turned from Thornton to Jeffrey, who was seated well below Thornton at the table. "Blaine?" he said, as though only Jeffrey Blaine could answer the objections just posed.

"They're working on leukemia, sir," Jeffrey said. "Jim's right, it's a long shot. But it's the sort of long shot you don't have to make excuses for if you lose."

Martins and Wynebrook, near Jeffrey at the bottom of the table, laughed mirthlessly, short snuffling laughs that could go either way, appreciative or derisive.

"Are we philanthropists now, Blaine?" Layne asked.

"No, sir," Jeffrey said. "But we service a great many clients who like to believe that they are."

It was at times like this that Jeffrey felt himself to be at home in his own element. More and more, the work bored him. His marriage bored him. But on Fridays, for an hour and a half at lunch, Jeffrey felt a sense of mastery, even of calmness, as though he were floating above the banking industry, seeing it whole, its touch of nobleness as well as the dark and tawdry secrets at its center. He had a sense of command, not the command of other men, which didn't interest him, but the command of himself and his whole world. A poem he read in college, he didn't even remember who wrote it, came back to him, haunting him now as it did even then with its sense of unrealized possibilities.

> *And we have been on many thousand lines,*
> *And we have shown, on each, spirit and power;*
> *But hardly have we, for one little hour,*
> *Been on our own line, have we been ourselves.*

Apparently satisfied with Jeffrey's answer, Everett Layne circled a finger in the air, a signal to the waiters to clear the soup bowls and serve lunch.

Layne said nothing further, and the conversation drifted in a dozen different directions. Jeffrey lost interest and found himself again thinking about the newspaper he had thrown away in the morning. The fact that no column had appeared or was going to appear obviously meant that Noel Garver had been threatened or bribed. He tried to form a sense in his mind of how such a conversation would go. Would it be lines from *The Godfather*? He didn't imagine that conversations like that took place in real life. The

Chet Fiore he met on the second floor at Stasny's, in the office at Stasny's, and in his own living room the next morning, never said anything directly. He made suggestions. And those suggestions instantly became reality, as though he created reality with his words and his will.

Jeffrey like to work the same way. It was better than giving orders—or maybe, he thought wryly, a better way of giving orders. The thought that he and Chet Fiore shared a common management style tweaked his curiosity, and he wondered if it could possibly be true. He tried to imagine himself approaching Noel Garver with the suggestion that he print nothing about what he had seen at Jessica's party, and couldn't quite make the scene come alive in his mind.

It must have been a bribe, he thought.

But he knew it wasn't. Bribery was a last resort, something for weak men who don't have any other way to make their wills felt.

He was suddenly gripped by a strange and urgent apprehension that was new to him, new and frightening. He felt as though his mind were transparent and that at least Everett Layne if not any of the others at the table could see straight into his distraction. He was eager for lunch to be over so that he could get back to his office and close his door.

"There's a Mr. Luisi on the line for you," Jennie said as Jeffrey returned. "Shall I take a number?"

He didn't know any Luisi, yet he knew that this was the call he had been expecting. There were times, random times, when the light on his phone lit up and he felt as though a warning light of some sort had been turned on in his brain. That light was on again.

"I'll take it inside," he said, hurrying back toward his office.

The moment he put the phone to his ear, even before he said anything, a surprisingly high-pitched man's voice said, "Do you know where Riverside Park is?"

"It's off Riverside Drive. In the Eighties. What is this about?"

Riverside Park wasn't what he had been expecting at all. Not that he knew what he had been expecting. Perhaps the name of a social club on Mulberry Street. Or an Italian restaurant.

"There's a car park just above the Ninety-sixth Street ramp," the voice said. "Four o'clock."

There was no reason for a clandestine meeting in Riverside Park, Jeffrey thought. For all he knew, Fiore wanted to talk to him about investing some of his money. Which was perfectly normal. Even if Chet Fiore was everything the newspapers said he was, and Jeffrey tended to believe the newspapers didn't report things about people unless they were true, still the man was entitled to invest his money.

As long as it wasn't undocumented cash, of course.

The more he thought about it, the clearer it seemed to him that Fiore couldn't possibly be calling him about anything illegal or even unethical. Fiore was no fool. He knew who Jeffrey Blaine was. He wasn't about to embarrass himself with an improper proposal.

These thoughts, like stray clouds on a darkening summer day, random and unsorted, piled on top of each other in such chaotic profusion that he actually had himself convinced that a meeting in Riverside Park wasn't in the least a signal of danger. He wanted to meet the man. He wanted to hear what he had to say. It was as simple as that. So he told himself that Fiore probably did all his business this way, habits of caution a second nature by this time, even where there was no need for them, even, for example, when he was meeting with a perfectly reputable investment banker for perfectly reputable purposes. It was odd, Jeffrey thought, how often our instincts of self-preservation work against us. There was every reason in the world for Fiore to be as open as possible about his legitimate business meetings. It would give anyone watching a sense of . . . well, *legitimacy.*

Jeffrey made a mental note to bring this point up to Fiore when they met. He smiled to himself at the thought that he was already proving to be a useful associate.

He buzzed Jennie and asked her to cancel and reschedule his afternoon meetings. Then he rang Martin on the car phone, told him he wouldn't be needing him, and sent him home to see if Mrs. Blaine had anything for him to do.

He left the office a little before three and walked crosstown for a few blocks before hailing a taxi. The cab dropped him at Ninety-sixth and Riverside, where he found himself on an overpass with the park to his left and the river and New Jersey beyond it. There was no parking lot in sight. Something must have been wrong with Mr. Luisi's directions, he thought. It didn't seem likely anyone would put a parking lot in the middle of a public park, and yet there didn't seem to be anywhere else it could be.

He realized that the street under the bridge he was standing on was in fact Ninety-sixth Street, and that it ran directly onto the West Side Highway. There were two gas stations down there but there didn't seem to be any way to get to them without going all the way around the block. He looked around. A woman with two leashed Rottweilers was going into the park across the street. As she bent to unleash the dogs, he called to her. She looked up and hurried away, keeping her dogs on their chains until she was out of sight.

There were buds on the trees already, a pastel wash of green. It was early for leaves, but it had been a warm spring. Perhaps the river brought them out early. It didn't seem there was any green in Central Park yet.

Or perhaps he hadn't noticed.

There was no one else around.

Jeffrey walked south to Ninety-fifth Street, then east a block, then north to Ninety-sixth. It took him almost five minutes to get to the gas station, and when he got there he realized he wasn't sure what he was looking for.

"Is there a parking lot around here?" he asked.

"Two on Ninety-fifth," the man said. "Right here and up on the other side of Broadway."

"Parking lot?"

"Garages, yeah."

"No, not garages, parking lots," Jeffrey said. "Isn't there one by the park?"

The man narrowed his eyes and seemed to weigh him for what felt like a long time. He wiped his nose with the back of his hand. "What is it you're looking for?" he asked.

"A parking lot."

"You want to park your car?"

"I just want to know where it is."

"It's on the other side of the highway," the man said. "But I wouldn't park my car there."

"I'm not parking my car. I just want to know where it is."

He let his annoyance show in his voice, which he realized immediately was a mistake. He was a stranger in this neighborhood, which seemed rundown and slightly on the sordid side.

"And I told you where it is," the man said sharply. "Other side of the highway."

He turned to a car that had just pulled in. The driver asked for a fill-up.

"How do I get there?" Jeffrey asked, hanging over the attendant's shoulder.

"Under the overpass. Stay to the right. Follow the signs for downtown."

"I'm not in a car."

"You're not in a car? Then what the hell—"

"Just tell me how to get there."

The man turned and looked at Jeffrey with undisguised annoyance. He set the clip on the pump control, took a rag off the top of the pump, and carefully wiped his hands. Then he walked out to the sidewalk. Jeffrey followed.

"All right," the man said. "You go under the overpass. You'll be in the park. You go over the fence."

"Over a fence?"

"A railing, a railing. You step over it. You're in the park. You walk north. You know which way north is?"

"I know which way north is."

"That's good, that's very good," the man said.

In the normal course of his life, Jeffrey wouldn't have tolerated being mocked by a gas station attendant. At the moment he didn't seem to have a choice. He thought about giving up the whole adventure and taking a taxi home, but he didn't think it would be a good idea to stand up Chet Fiore.

"You'll pass a playground. Oh, shit, that's not it. Forget every-thing I just said." He turned completely around and pointed toward West End Avenue. "Go up to the corner. A right, then another right. You're on Riverside Drive. Cross the street. You're at the park. No railing, none of that shit. You walk into the park. South, about a quarter mile, there's a path goes down under the highway, comes out at the river. Follow the path, then follow the river north. It's just past the tennis courts."

"Thanks," Jeffrey said.

The man nodded a grudging acknowledgment and went back to his duties in the station.

Five minutes later Jeffrey was in Riverside Park. He felt out of place wearing a business suit in the park. A few minutes ago the place had looked deserted, except for the woman with the Rottweilers. Now he could see eight or ten joggers and dog walk-ers. The grass was soft from rain.

Two men holding hands walked ahead of him, then turned down the path toward the river. Jeffrey followed them.

When he reached the river, the gay couple was gone. There were old men fishing here, some of them with two or three lines trolled out into the river, the butts of their poles wedged into the mesh of the fence that followed along the edge of the water. They kept their hands in their pockets, cigarettes jammed into the cor-ners of their mouths. There was, Jeffrey realized, an entire New York universe that he knew nothing about even though he had lived in the city for almost twenty years. He never would have imagined that people fished in the Hudson.

He passed a set of tennis courts as he had been told he would and finally saw what had to be the parking lot in question. Two yel-low cabs were parked there, motors off, the drivers nowhere in sight. Two rental limos were parked side by side. The drivers had takeout food they were eating on the hoods, their backs to each other. And there was a Mercedes.

Jeffrey walked to the Mercedes. Chet Fiore was sitting in the back seat. "Don't get in," he said when Jeffrey opened the door. "Let's take a walk."

He left his driver at the wheel, the engine running.

"Is all this necessary?" Jeffrey asked. Fiore was leading the way back down to the river.

"Who the fuck knows," Fiore said. "You want to find out it was and we didn't do it?"

He scarcely seemed the same man who had come to Jeffrey's house in Bedford Hills. There was a slurring of consonants, a flatness in the intonation that apparently Fiore could turn on and off at will. Which one, Jeffrey wondered, was the real Chet Fiore and which one was the act?

"It's an amazing river," Fiore said. "This time of day, the way the sun kind of falls on top of it."

"Yes," Jeffrey agreed. "Very dramatic."

Fiore looked at him as though he had just said something strange. "Did you ever try to think how much water goes down here every minute?" he asked. "Gallons, cubic feet, however you want to put it. Numbers you can't imagine."

Well, Jeffrey thought, here was the gangster-philosopher again. He had been offered the briefest glimpse of something else and instantly it was taken away, like a door that is quietly swung closed by an unseen hand as one passes in a corridor. He looked out over the water. It looked black and cold, breaking the late afternoon sunlight into gleaming dark shards. Here and there the wind, which had picked up in just the last few minutes, whipped the surface into white-topped waves. The day, which had seemed so warm and springlike when he left the office, carried reminders of winter in its winds. A tugboat pulling a heavily laden barge worked its way upriver, the barge low in the water. Beyond the river, the sun slipped behind the high-rises on the New Jersey shore, producing a dull and colorless sunset.

Fiore, too, was looking out over the water. Jeffrey waited, conscious now of the chill but far from sorry he had come.

"Let me ask you something," Fiore said without turning. "You invest money for people?"

"That's one of the things we do. We're not a brokerage, we're an investment bank."

"And the difference is?"

"It's complicated."

"I'm not a stupid man, Mr. Blaine."

Jeffrey forced a laugh. "No, of course not. I didn't mean that. I just wasn't prepared for an abstract discussion of banking on the banks of the Hudson River."

"You're not cold, are you?" Fiore asked.

"I'm fine," Jeffrey said, embarrassed about being cold, as though it were a weakness. "Let me put it this way. We service the investment community in pretty much the same ways a neighborhood bank services individuals."

"But on a larger scale."

"Vastly larger."

"And you keep records," Fiore said.

"Of course."

"Of everything?"

"Everything."

"That's good."

"It's required by law, Mr. Fiore," Jeffrey said. He didn't like the way he sounded, prissy and fastidious.

"I wouldn't ask you to knowingly break the law, Mr. Blaine. There wouldn't be much point to that, would there?"

He slapped Jeffrey on the shoulder in a friendly sort of way and the two of them walked back to Fiore's car. They talked about nothing on the way. Jimmy Angelisi got out to open the door for them.

They drove Jeffrey across town to his apartment. Fiore talked about the Knicks and the Rangers. Jeffrey had absolutely no idea what this meeting had been about.

The apartment was dark except for the lamp on the table in the foyer. The note from Phyllis tucked under the base of the lamp said that she and Jessica had taken the car up to the country house and that Jeffrey should take the train. He should call to let her know what train he was on so she could pick him up at the station. The note also said she called him at the office but Jennie said he had gone out and she didn't know if he'd be back. *She said she didn't have anything for you on her calendar,* the note said.

He cursed under his breath. Eight years ago there had been an affair, with all the attendant secrecy and recrimination. Ever since, whenever his time was unaccounted for, he worried about what Phyllis might be thinking. To make matters worse, he hadn't brought any work home because he didn't want to carry a briefcase up to Riverside Park. Now he would have nothing to do on the train.

He went into the kitchen, rummaged around for something to eat, finally settling for a few slabs of Gruyère and mustard on a thick slice of potato bread. He ate it standing at the counter. Carlos and Irena, the maid, would have gone to Bedford Hills with Phyllis and Jessica. Martin, he assumed, had been given the weekend off. He couldn't remember the last time he had been in the apartment when it was empty. The rooms seemed desolate and unfamiliar, and he felt again as though he were in a stranger's home.

The bookshelves in his study didn't offer anything that appealed to him for the train ride even though half a dozen unopened books he intended to read lay in a stack on a bottom shelf.

He turned off the lights and locked the door. He told the cab driver to take him to Grand Central but on the spur of the moment he asked the driver to stop when they drove past the Barnes & Noble at Rockefeller Center.

He wandered around inside for almost half an hour with no idea, really, of what he was looking for. He felt sickishly uneasy, almost the way he felt the time Dr. Lanz told him there was a suspicious lump on his colon but that it was probably nothing to worry about. That turned out to be case, thank heavens, although the news when it finally came did nothing to undo the wrenching weakness that entered his life with that first glimpse of his own mortality. He had a sense now that large parts of his life were coming unglued, although he wasn't quite sure why he felt that way.

Maybe it had something to do with Jessica, who still hadn't forgiven him for demanding that she give up her boyfriend. If she never said anything about it, that was only because she hardly said anything at all. Their lives at home were filled with silences.

He was disturbed, too, by his pointless and pointlessly clandestine meeting in the park with an organized-crime boss who had actually been a guest in his own house. Disturbed and disappointed. He had expected something a bit more dramatic, if not quite a Faustian struggle between himself and the devil over the ownership of his own soul, then at least an offer he *could* refuse. Instead, the gangster withdrew at the first suggestion that Jeffrey Blaine wasn't about to bend the law. End of story.

No, it wasn't. It couldn't be. Jeffrey's radar was too good to be fooled so easily. There had to be more to it than . . .

The answer came to him with the jolting clarity of a toe stubbed in the dark. It was so obvious he was surprised he hadn't seen it immediately. Chet Fiore hadn't dragged him up to the windswept banks of the Hudson River to chat about banking and then take him home. The only reason the meeting ended before Fiore asked a single significant question was that Fiore already had the answer to the only question that really mattered. Would Jeffrey Blaine come or wouldn't he?

Just by being there, Jeffrey told Fiore everything he needed to know.

And he told himself something about himself he hadn't known. He wanted to hear Fiore's proposition. He was interested. Next time Fiore got in touch, he wouldn't be so squeamish. *What is it you want?* he would ask straight out, and he would be ready for whatever Fiore's answer might be.

There was something thrilling in the thought. His nerves tingled. And when he found himself in the fiction section of the store, he had to pause for a moment to remind himself why he was there.

He picked up a Faulkner novel he had never read and leafed through it, testing to see if it piqued his interest. He put it back on the shelf and let his eye drift down the row of paperback spines in all the gaudy colors books sported these days. He drifted farther down the aisle and picked up a book by an author named Milan Kundera. That seemed more to the point. Faulkner was from his school days. Why go back? He knew nothing about Kundera but had heard the name. A picture of the man on the back cover of the book was reassuring, a thick neck rising out of an open shirt, a massive head that looked as though it were carved in granite.

"He's wonderful, isn't he?"

Her hair wasn't blond, but on the other hand it was too light a brown to be called brown. It was more the color of oak leaves in autumn, oak leaves on the ground, in profusion. Her eyes were dark, almost black, her lips full but pale. His first thought was that she was very beautiful, but he realized almost at once that in fact she wasn't. She was, however, dramatic, conveying a suddenness, an unexpectedness that took a man off guard, almost the way beauty does. It seemed to him, even in that first instant, that even if she were someone he knew, even if they had arranged to meet here, her entrance would have felt unexpected. Some women have this quality of endless surprise. She was about thirty years old, perhaps a year or two older.

"Sorry," he said, not quite certain what she had said.

"Kundera. Isn't he wonderful?"

"I don't know, really," he confessed. "I've never read him."

"Oh. Then that isn't the place to start."

She took the book out of his hand with an easy familiarity that surprised him, like the way your wife helps herself to something on your plate. She put it back on the shelf and handed him another. It was called *The Unbearable Lightness of Being*. The title sounded familiar.

"I'm being very presumptuous, aren't I?" she said.

"No. Not at all."

"Helpful?" she asked.

"Yes, helpful."

They both smiled awkwardly, and for a moment there was a silence that seemed to call for some response. On his part, he assumed. "I don't really read much fiction," he said. "I was looking for something to read on the train."

"This was written to be read on trains," she said. "I'm serious. Look."

She took the book back and flipped to a page very near the beginning. "'He had first met Tereza about three weeks earlier in a small Czech town,'" she read. "'They had spent scarcely an hour together. She had accompanied him to the station and waited with him until he boarded the train. Ten days later she paid him a visit. They made love the day she arrived.'"

She handed him the book again. "See?" she said. "Trains."

"Trains," he agreed. "Remarkable." There was another long silence. "Speaking of which, I've got to catch mine," he said.

"Me too," she said. "Don't let me keep you."

He hesitated but didn't know what else to say. So he thanked her and started to walk away. He got only a step or two before he stopped and turned back to her. "'Me too'?" he asked.

She looked puzzled.

"I said I had a train to catch," he explained. "You said 'Me too,' didn't you?"

She laughed. For a man so well dressed, well groomed, obviously self-assured and successful, there was a boyishness about him that surprised her, a delighted kind of surprise. "Yes," she said. "Me too."

"Grand Central, I hope. Not Penn Station."

"I believe you're inviting me to share a cab," she said.

"And a drink."

"I thought you had to catch your train."

"They run every hour."

In the cab they discovered they were taking the same train. She was going as far as Mount Kisco, and he was going to Bedford Hills, the next stop.

They went straight to the Oyster Bar at Grand Central without checking the board for the schedule. He had a Bushmill's and she had a San Pellegrino with a wedge of lime. He reached into the bag she had set on the table and slid out the book she bought. It was a novel by Doris Lessing. "Do you recommend her?" he asked.

"It's about justice."

"Are you a lawyer?" he asked.

"There must be other people interested in justice beside lawyers," she said.

"As far as that goes," he laughed, "I'm not even sure my lawyer is familiar with the term."

"But he's good at what he does?"

"Is there a reason you're not answering my question?"

"I am a lawyer," she said. She took her book back and slipped it into her purse.

"A criminal lawyer?"

"As a matter of fact I'm with the United States Attorney's Office."

He raised an eyebrow.

"Oh, come on," she said. "We don't all look like Rudy Giuliani."

Before he was mayor, Giuliani was a federal prosecutor.

"On the contrary, I was just thinking how *little* you look like Giuliani."

They both laughed.

"Aren't you going to tell me what you do?" she asked.

"It's too boring," he said.

"But it pays well."

"I suppose."

"Well enough for a house in Bedford Hills," she said.

Mount Kisco, where she was going, was a marginally white-collar bedroom community. Bedford Hills, just five miles farther up the line, was the start of Westchester County's horse country. The homes in Bedford Hills were much larger than the homes in Mount Kisco and used less often. They were weekend retreats.

On the train they talked about the train service in New York and famous trains in books, and about growing up in Mount Kisco, always just a little too far from the excitement of New York. When her station was announced she said, "This was all over a couple of books and we didn't even get to read them."

"I will," he said.

"Promise?" she asked.

It was a question that seemed to presuppose something.

"Promise," he agreed, making himself part of the implicit compact. *Com*plicit. That was the word that came to mind.

He watched her walking down the platform, and then the train was moving again and he took the book out of his overcoat pocket and studied the cover. Alone on the almost empty train now, he felt the edges of the despair he had felt in his empty apartment beginning to creep back over him, like a chill coming in through an open window.

He looked out the window and saw her walking toward the stairs. And then the train was out of the station and he couldn't see her anymore. He should have gotten her number. He hadn't even, for that matter, gotten her name. Elaine. He knew her name was Elaine. But that was all he knew.

No. He knew she was a lawyer in the U.S. Attorney's Office. How many Elaines could there be?

He opened his new book and started to read.

Elaine Lester stopped walking as soon as Jeffrey's train was out of the station. She stepped across the platform to wait for the next train back to Manhattan. It came in less than fifteen minutes.

She had the train almost to herself. On Fridays, early in the evening, the trains were filled with wives going to meet their husbands because they had theater tickets, dinner after the show, and then a late train back. And kids heading south to catch a band somewhere downtown, CBGB's or the Knitting Factory or a hundred other places, hanging by the train doors as if they couldn't wait to get to Grand Central so they could get out and grab a smoke. She knew all this because years ago she was one of those kids, although more often than not she just wandered the streets of the city when she got there, more interested in taking the pulse of the place than in anything any band might have screamed at her over a desolate splurge of guitar chords.

This middle-of-the-evening train was new to her, its emptiness new to her. A woman sat about five rows ahead, in a seat that faced backward. Why would anyone sit backward when there were empty seats all around? The woman was dark-skinned, Hispanic, pretty and precise, her hands folded on her lap, her eyes fixed on nothing. A maid? Definitely a maid. Not given the night off until after dinner was served.

Jeffrey Blaine, she realized, hadn't left her side once from the time they met in the bookstore until she got off the train in Mount Kisco. Which meant that he couldn't have called ahead, that there'd be no ride waiting for him at the station. The men all called home. *I'm on the eight-eleven, I'm on the nine-seventeen, I'm on the ten-twenty.* But he didn't call.

She knew perfectly well why a man would skip calling home.

An interesting man, this Jeffrey Blaine. Looking for a novel to read. Tentative and careful, as though a book asked a commitment of him. On the other hand, willing to experiment. Up to a point. There was a kind of simplicity to him she hadn't expected in the least. The way he came back looking for her, asking if she was taking a train. What train? And only then . . .

Thirty plus, closer to forty, and not quite sure how to ask a lady for a drink. He had to find an excuse for it. What train? The same train. Oh my, in that case . . .

Was it an act? He was a successful man, this Jeffrey Blaine. Wasn't self-assurance part of the package? It usually is. And yet he didn't seem self-assured. He seemed like a man who didn't know quite what he wanted. He looked uncertain. *Tentative*—there was that word again. He mocked himself rather than confess his uncertainty.

She smiled to herself. He had come back to find her, which saved her the trouble of finding him again. Better that way. Much better. How could he ever guess that she was following him when he was the one who went back for her?

For weeks she hadn't been able to get Chet Fiore's unexplained appearance at a banker's daughter's birthday party out of her thoughts. Gogarty and Schliester were off on something else; they'd dropped the ball. Wall Street and Mulberry Street—either there was nothing to it or there was a hell of a lot. Maybe Schliester was still thinking about it somewhere in the back of his mind, but he wasn't doing anything about it. And Gogarty's mind was all front. It didn't have a back.

Which is why she decided to see for herself what this banker was about. She wanted to get a look at him, and maybe ask the doorman a few questions. But she was a lawyer, not an investigator, and she didn't quite know what questions to ask. So she ended up leaning against the stone wall on the Central Park side of Fifth Avenue, trying to figure out what to do next, when a car pulled up in front of Blaine's building.

She didn't actually see it pull up. She heard it. What she heard was the doorman's voice. "Good evening, Mr. Blaine."

What she saw was a handsome man, blondish, a shade over or under six feet, getting out of a dark blue Mercedes. Younger than she imagined. Better looking. But with a straightness to his carriage that was exactly what she would have predicted. So this was Jeffrey Blaine, she thought.

And then she realized that the other man in the back seat of the Mercedes was probably Chet Fiore. She saw him for only a second, not enough to be sure. Maybe her imagination was playing tricks on her; there had been a Mercedes in Gogarty's report on the fiasco in Prospect Park.

She wrote down the tag number as the Mercedes drove off. She heard the doorman say, "Mrs. Blaine took the car up to the country, sir," and she realized that it was only by the merest luck that she saw what she had just seen. If god hadn't, as they say, dropped everything to make sure that not a single car, not a single truck, not a single taxi, not a single bus happened to be coming down Fifth Avenue at the moment the doorman said Blaine's name, she would have gone home.

Almost as soon as she decided that the man in the Mercedes couldn't be Fiore, she knew for an absolute certainty that it was. Too much had happened for this to be anyone else. Blaine's arrival just as she was getting ready to give up and leave, the window of silence on the street, the doorman's voice, her unimpeded line of sight into the car—it was all so perfect. It had to be Fiore. She was sure of it.

She walked half a block north, where she could still see the front of the apartment building but wouldn't be as conspicuous, and called the office on her cell phone. She asked Beryl Ross to run the tag number. "Don't call me back, just leave the answer on my voice mail," she said.

Beryl was the only person in the office to whom she wouldn't have had to explain.

A steady stream of cabs was dropping off a steady stream of visitors at Mount Sinai Hospital, just a block to the north, but she didn't want to take chances so she hailed one and ordered him to wait. She was ready when Blaine came downstairs.

She would have followed him to the train station if he hadn't made a stop at Barnes & Noble.

She would have said something to him on the checkout line if he hadn't come back to say something to her.

She liked the idea that he wasn't really what she had expected at all.

10

Wally **Schliester** bought himself a whole set of lightweight polyester suits, cut his hair so short his skull showed, and went to work. According to his business card, he was Frederick Linkletter, Senior Booking Manager and Special Assistant in the Exhibitor Relations Department at the Javits Center, the immense glass-and-steel egg crate of a convention center on Eleventh Avenue, a stone's throw from where the aircraft carrier *Intrepid*, bristling with fighter jets, protected the West Side of Manhattan from any and all comers. Only Mel Gottlieb, the Javits Center's personnel director, knew that Schliester was a federal agent, and Gottlieb wasn't about to tell anyone because the U.S. Attorney's Office had made it crystal clear to him that his tax problems would go away if and only if he gave his full cooperation.

Schliester planned to spend the entire summer under cover. Greg Billings asked him to take the assignment and he took it even though he didn't actually work for Billings in the sense that he didn't actually work for anyone. They were still waiting to hear who would replace the Cocksucker-in-Chief.

Schliester liked undercover work. It gave him a chance to mingle with people who weren't cops or agents or lawyers.

When Schliester came back from lunch on his fourth day on the job, he found a skinny man in a shiny suit walking back and forth in the corridor outside his office. Schliester recognized him

at once. Gus Benini. One of Chet Fiore's more energetic lieutenants. Which was hardly a coincidence. In Manhattan, most of
the crime that wasn't random was connected sooner or later to
Chet Fiore, who was connected in turn to Gaetano Falcone.

Benini was pacing back and forth like a shuttlecock on automatic pilot when he caught sight of Schliester walking toward him.
"Are you Linkletter?" he asked.

"That's right," Schliester said.

"Good, good. We gotta talk," the nervous little man said,
reaching for the nearest doorknob. "This your office?"

"Hey, slow it down," Schliester said, moving the man aside
with a subtle body block. He opened the door himself.

The office was state of the art, with a lot of glass and chrome,
like the Javits Center itself. "You say we've got to talk, that's fine
with me," Schliester said, slipping out of his suit coat, which he
tossed onto a glass table. "Let's start with you tell me who you are."

A tape recorder in a supply room in the subbasement of the
Javits Center started to turn. Gogarty grabbed his headset and
clamped it over his ears. The recorder was voice-activated.

"I guess you're new here, you don't know who I am," Benini
said.

"I guess I'm new here," Schliester agreed.

He walked over to the teak-and-chrome bar, a contraption so
elaborate that when Schliester first saw it he was reasonably certain
that it hadn't even been invented yet. "Something to drink?" he
asked. The bar had come into the Center with a computer show
and hadn't left when the show did. He pushed a button set into the
polished wood at the side of the bar, and a wooden door rolled
open without making a sound. The top shelf, which held eight
liquor bottles, slid forward. Schliester picked up a whiskey bottle.
A tray produced a pair of highball glasses. An ice bucket came up
out of the countertop.

"What the fuck did you just do?" Benini asked, bringing the
scent of garlic and marinara sauce right up by Schliester's shoulder.

"When you pick up a bottle, it gives you the right kind of
glasses."

"You're shitting me."

Schliester took the glasses off the tray, which withdrew into the innards of the machine. "Try it," he said.

Benini picked up a gin bottle as gingerly as if he thought it would electrocute him. The bar answered with a pair of martini glasses. "Ha!" Benini scoffed. "What if I wanted a gin and tonic?"

"You program it for what you like."

"What if there was four of us?"

"There aren't."

"It knows?"

"It knows."

"You're shitting me."

Schliester poured himself a drink. "You sure you don't want anything?"

Benini was studying the machine, wondering what it would do next. "Nah," he said. "My stomach's fucked. I know a guy would love to have one of these."

"They don't make them yet," Schliester said.

Benini shrugged, as though that didn't matter. "They made this one," he said.

"They made this one," Schliester agreed. "You were about to tell me who you are."

The ice bucket sank back into the countertop after Schliester dropped a pair of ice cubes into his glass. The shelf of bottles backed into the bar and the teak door slid closed.

Schliester moved around behind his desk and put his feet up. Benini started to explain something about an "arrangement" that had been worked out when the Javits Center first went up. "Before that, in fact," Benini said. "There was an arrangement on the construction."

"I like to know who I'm talking to," Schliester said.

"You're talking to me."

"And that would be—?"

"What, do you keep a diary or something?"

"Do you know my name?"

"Linkletter. Right?"

Schliester threw up his hands, as though that settled it.

Benini let out a long slow breath. "All right," he said, "it's Gus Benini."

"You didn't tell me who you're with?"

"I'm with you, asshole. Now listen and don't ask so fucking many questions."

For the next few minutes Benini walked back and forth in front of Schliester's desk, explaining the "arrangement." Schliester would give him a list of exhibitors. Benini would take it to his people and come back with the names of the ones he wanted contact information on. Schliester started to ask what he was going to contact them about but cut himself off. "I'm sorry. You didn't want so many fucking questions. Will there be a question period at the end?"

Benini stopped walking. "You're being funny, right?" he said.

It was just about the end of the day when Elaine heard that Greg Billings was being given Franciscan's job. She charged into his office ready for war, only to find his desk bare and his file cabinets already empty. Christ, how long had he known? How long had *everyone* known? And why was she just finding out now? She was furious. What made the insult even more galling was that Billings was the worst possible choice. He was a machine, and not even an interesting machine.

She reversed field, picking up speed as she neared what had been Franciscan's office. She heard voices and laughter, but they didn't slow her down, even though she realized a split second before she hit the door that she was walking in on a full-fledged party to which she hadn't been invited. A victory celebration complete with a plate full of misshapen stuffed mushrooms and stalks of celery in a glass and a pasty-looking dip that strikingly resembled dog vomit. Champagne. And beer of course, because this was really a beer-drinking crowd even though the champagne had to be there for show. A woman—Billings's wife—was the source of at least fifty percent of the laughter. Her head was tipped back, that's how hard she was laughing, but it came down because the other half of the laughter in the room stopped when the door opened. Silence spread through the room like drizzle.

"Elaine," Billings said through his biggest smile, "I'm so glad you could come."

Not so glad that you invited me, she thought. She said, "We've got to talk."

"Oh, we're going to talk. You're an important part of the team. Have you met my wife? Her name's Elaine, too."

The wife was walking toward them. She had two glasses of champagne in her hands, and she held one out for Elaine as her husband introduced them, telling the missus that Elaine was "probably the best attorney in the office."

Elaine took the glass and said, "You must be very proud of him." Even before Mrs. Billings could acknowledge how proud she was, Elaine said, "Not *going to talk*, Greg. Talk now."

Billings more or less waved his arm around and said, "Well, not *now* now. I've got this little party going."

"They'll do fine without you for a couple minutes."

He didn't want a scene, so he followed her out the door into the empty corridor. It was no wonder, he thought, that just about no one in the office liked her. Pedal to the metal, yeah, sure, but absolutely no sense of priorities. None.

"I want the Fiore case," she said.

He didn't see any reason why not but he didn't think being pushed into something one minute into his new job was the way to start, so he said, "Well, we've got the whole roster to work out."

What he didn't say was that he hadn't even considered inviting her to join his Organized Crime unit.

"Work it out however you have to work it out," she said. "I want that case."

He could hear laughter from behind the door and wanted to go back to his own party. "There's not much there, Elaine," he said.

She didn't say anything, which made him think he was supposed to. He thought a second, and then smiled. He had very small teeth, very neat and very white with little spaces between them.

"Oh," he said, justifying the smile, "you're thinking about that banker thing. It's just a rumor, you know. Nothing was ever connected."

Elaine didn't tell him that she had watched Jeffrey Blaine get dropped off at his Fifth Avenue apartment by Chet Fiore. And she didn't tell him she had drinks with Jeffrey Blaine. It was none of his business right now. When she made the case, he'd hear all about it.

"Yes or no?" she said.

"Whatever," he said. "Fine."

He invited her back into the party but she wasn't interested. Instead, she went back to her office and sent word to Schliester and Gogarty that she wanted to see them in the morning. Then she read all the reports the two of them had filed about Schliester's undercover work at the Javits Center and listened to all the tapes. It was a lot of wasted paper and a lot of wasted hours.

At Layne Bentley the partners thought of themselves not just as bankers but as gentlemen bankers. They kept gentlemen's hours. They were home for dinner every evening. Lately, though, Jeffrey found himself too restless to stay home after dinner. Jessica went to her room; Phyllis read magazines. He announced that he had work to do and went back to the office.

The hum of voices the minute he stepped off the elevator surprised him. It sounded nothing like what he was used to in the daytime, shrill and edgy, like a machine asking for oil. He followed the sound to the trading floor, where he found eight or ten of the firm's young traders working their clients on the phones. They led an almost secret existence in the firm, where they were routinely ignored, a sort of upstairs relative one doesn't talk about. None of them had ever made partner, and none ever would. They weren't gentlemen. It was that simple.

The traders knew it, but they were willing to come, young men out of Wharton and Harvard and everywhere else, because Layne Bentley had a name that meant something. They stayed only long enough to get their feet wet and develop a client list. The constant turnover, with each year's class cruder and louder, pushier and more demanding than the last, deepened the rift between the bankers and the traders, who formed an exclusive little club within the firm that boasted as its insignia their state-of-the-art running shoes and the designer jogging suits that they wore for a couple of quick miles around Battery Park City before they came back to the office, filling the air with the smell of their sweat, their takeout Chinese food, and the imported beer they drank straight from the bottle while they made obscene amounts of money chatting up far-flung clients so important they couldn't be interrupted during the business day even for the possibility of making one or two million dollars.

They commandeered the office's music system, which during business hours secreted standards and classics at barely audible levels but at night blared out new rock and old jazz, Green Day and Saturday Supercade, Bix Beiderbecke and Illinois Jacquet. Although the clients they screamed at on their phones were most often men in their fifties and sixties with conservative tastes, youth had so completely replaced probity as the quality one looked for in an investment counselor that the blazing thrum of the music, the occasional triumphant shout or roar of laughter in the background, served as a kind of auditory verification that these young men were offering the latest in cutting-edge financial instruments. To the extent that the young traders had social lives at all, they had them here in the office, mostly in the locker-room camaraderie they shared among themselves but also, more than occasionally, in the company of well-dressed, well-bred young ladies who used chopsticks or their fingers to pick morsels of Chinese food from the cartons, nodded their heads to the beat of the music, their heavily made-up faces wearing looks of cultivated, sensual boredom while their menfolk did business. There is not and never has been an aphrodisiac more powerful than closing an eleven-million-dollar deal.

The first night Jeffrey came by, one of the young men held up a carton of Chinese food, gesturing as he talked on his headset. Jeffrey declined the offer, but stood in the doorway for a moment and watched, picking up shards of conversations from around the room. He found he had more difficulty walking away than he might have expected. The young traders didn't offend his sense of himself as he imagined they would. They attacked the world with the head-down, reckless, and calculated ferocity of a ballplayer stretching a single into a double.

They were gone by ten-thirty. From his office, Jeffrey heard the abrupt end of the music and the laughter of voices on their way out. A few minutes later he began to hear the muted clatter of the night cleaning staff, an army of black and Irish ladies in nurses' shoes who would put the rooms back to order, dousing them with deodorizers that by morning would replace the smells of sweat, beer, and Cuban cigars with the gentler aromas of glades and forests. Except for the cleaning ladies, Jeffrey had the entire suite of offices to himself. It was a pleasant, domestic sort of feeling. In the quiet hours of the night, any man becomes something of a Magellan, staking a claim to all the unpeopled spaces his eyes come to rest on.

On the Internet it took Jeffrey only a matter of seconds to find a roster of lawyers in the U.S. Attorney's Office for the Southern District of New York. There was only one Elaine. Elaine Lester. The phone book had an E. Lester with an address on West Twenty-third Street. The number put it between Seventh and Eighth avenues. Chelsea. That sounded about right.

He wasn't ready to call her yet. It seemed like a big step. But he knew already that he would call. He wrote the address and phone number on a piece of paper and slipped it into his wallet.

With the computer winking back at him, awaiting his next command, he thought of looking up Chet Fiore to see what he could find out about the man. But that, too, seemed premature right now. Sooner or later Fiore would call, and sooner or later he would get around to asking Jeffrey to serve as his money launderer. Like alchemists looking for the philosopher's stone, gangsters were always looking for ways to clean money.

It was an impossible proposition. All money-laundering systems were the same, and they never worked. They didn't wash the money so much as they ran it through the spin cycle, in the vain hope that if they moved it fast enough and often enough, the trail would become untraceable. But the same technologies that made it possible to fly financial instruments at unprecedented speeds also made tracking the funds a relatively easy job for the authorities.

The irony, of course, was that venture capital, which was Jeffrey's field, was precisely the kind of high-risk investment capable of producing windfall profits on a scale that could do an enterprising gangster some good. But only, of course, if one knew the outcomes in advance . . .

Jeffrey sprang from his seat as if he'd just been hit with an electric current. He looked around as though he expected to discover he'd been dreaming, then down at his blank yellow notepad, as though it might contain some evidence of this remarkable . . . what? *Insight? Intuition?* Money, he realized, travels in dimensions of space and time, like particles in physics, like all material things. Moving it from place to place couldn't hide it, or hide it sufficiently. But moving it in time was another matter entirely.

He could feel his pulses pounding, so he got up and walked to the window. It was raining now. In Battery Park, a woman bent to let her dog off the leash. It ran across the grass, leaving big paw prints where it matted down the tall wet grass. The word that came to his mind was *evanescent*.

There had to be a catch, but he couldn't see one. Was it possible, he asked himself, that the answer could be so simple?

The door to his office was open and he hurried to close it, almost as though he were afraid his thoughts might be overheard if he wasn't careful enough.

He settled in back at his desk. There were a million details to be worked out, but he knew that the first step had just been taken.

· · ·

Wally Schliester had spent the night with a pretty girl from Kansas City who worked for a company that sold frozen steaks through the mail and over the Internet. She loved her job the way his father had loved being a baker and his uncle had loved his hardware store, all of which drove him crazy when he was a kid but didn't seem so stupid anymore. And she loved Kansas City so much that at one point he almost slipped and told her he was from St. Louis just to prove to her that at least in geographic terms they were on the same page.

Now, at eight o'clock in the morning, he was sitting with his partner in a corner office in the suite of offices the U.S. attorney maintained in the South Street Seaport complex. A full-rigged schooner dating from the nineteenth century, or the eighteenth, anyway some other century, was moored practically outside their window. Schliester cradled his coffee cup in both hands as he tried to explain to Gogarty how much he liked his job at the Javits Center. The work consisted for the most part of attending trade shows and the endless round of parties that went on before, during, and after them. He got to meet tons of different people from all over the country, and some from foreign countries, which he liked a lot. And he didn't have to get in their faces or bang them around, which was a part of police work he had never very much enjoyed. In another life he wouldn't have half minded doing something like this for a living.

Gogarty thought he was crazy. "Fine," he said. "Put in your papers if that's what you want. I'd go out of my goddamned mind with the fucking boredom of it."

"They practically throw broads at me just about every night," Schliester said. "How is that boring?"

Gogarty crossed his legs and put them up on the desk. With Gogarty this always signaled surrender in an argument. "Yeah well maybe that part's all right," he said. "The broads." And then he quickly added, "But I'll bet even that wears after a while."

The office door opened and Elaine Lester said, "What wears after a while?"

She had on one of those tailored suits that make a woman look like a man if she doesn't have the body for it. Elaine looked like a woman.

"Getting laid," Gogarty said.

Cops were always doing that, she had noticed. If you wanted to work with them, they made a point of treating you like one of the boys, only more so.

"I'll bet it does," she said. "Let's get serious."

She put her briefcase down on the desk. Schliester liked the way she looked from the back. So he stood up and said, "Good morning."

The reason he stood up was to show up his partner, who had only enough manners to take his feet off the desk.

Gogarty said, "Am I correct in assuming, since you ordered us to be here this morning, that you're taking over the case?"

Schliester said, "Congratulations," and offered his hand. She took it. Her skin was cool, her handshake firm, with none of the Dyke Death Grip so many women practiced.

"I'm taking over the *operation*," she corrected. "So far I don't see that there's a case."

Gogarty turned in his seat, his eyes just about level with her breasts. "Is that any way to say hello?" he asked.

"I didn't come here to say hello," Elaine Lester said. "I came here to find out what the hell you're doing with all the taxpayers' money you're using."

Gogarty stood up. He couldn't put himself on an equal footing with a woman when her tits were in his face. "Hey, what do you think?" he said. "You say hi to a guy like Gus Benini and right away he opens up a vein? This is a smart cookie, this isn't the Oprah show."

"No," she said. "It sounds more like Howard Stern. How many hours of Mr. Schliester's heavy breathing and Mr. Schliester pouring drinks for young ladies am I going to have to listen to?"

Schliester actually blushed. Of course he knew that everything said in his office at the Javits Center was taped, but sometimes in the heat of battle he forgot.

Gogarty said, "That's the very aspect of this investigation my partner and I were discussing when you came in. Gets you kind of horny listening to it, doesn't it? I know it does me."

"Something tells me you think that's funny," she said.

He said, "Something tells me you piss standing up."

Schliester put himself between the two of them before she could say anything. "All right, all right," he said. "This isn't going to work this way, so why don't we just pretend nobody said anything yet. Hi, I'm Wally Schliester. You must be Deputy United States Attorney Elaine Lester. I hear we're going to be working together."

She smiled. Not a bad smile.

"Tell me what you know about Jeffrey Blaine," she said.

Both of them looked at her like she had just dropped down out of the sky.

"He bought me a drink," she said. "I'll bet you'd like to know why."

The end of May brought Jessica's graduation from Brearley. Jeffrey sent his parents airline tickets, but he had to send Martin to meet their flight. He would have preferred for them to arrive in the evening, when he could have picked them up himself, but his mother came up with one excuse after another for not wanting to leave home "at all hours," so Martin ended up standing at the baggage claim area with a sign in his hands. He brought them back to the apartment, where they found a terse note from their daughter-in-law. *I've got committee meetings all afternoon. But make yourselves at home. Irena will fix whatever you want,* it said.

Gilbert Blaine wandered around the apartment with his hands in his pockets. "Are you sure this is where he lived before?" he asked.

They hadn't been to New York in almost ten years. They saw their son once or twice a year, usually for Christmas and a weekend in the summer, always in Massachusetts, because the senior Blaines were disinclined to travel. If there had been any way their grand-daughter's graduation could have been brought to them, they would have preferred it. Their lives were uneventful by design and had always been that way. The trenches were simply dug deeper now that Gilbert was retired. Twice Jeffrey had tried to send them on trips, one of them to England on the occasion of their fortieth wedding anniversary, and both times they came up with excuses not to go. The last time they were in New York, Jessica was in the third grade.

"She had it all remodeled," Winifred Blaine said. "Heaven knows I can't see the difference."

She thus managed, in a single sentence, to criticize her daughter-in-law for her extravagance, her husband for making too much of it, and her son for permitting it. It was what Jessica, if she had been there to hear it, would have called "Grandma's trifecta." The cause of her annoyance was less the remodeling than the fact that no one met them at the airport—a colored chauffeur certainly didn't count—compounded by the fact that no one was home when they got there. It didn't seem too much to expect that for one day in the year, in fact one day in practically ten years, her daughter-in-law could give up whatever it was she ran around doing all the time. Winifred drama-tized her irritation by declining the lunch the maid offered.

Carlos showed them to their room, where Winifred busied herself unpacking. It seemed odd to her that none of the servants was American. There were certainly plenty of Americans who could use a good job with a good family.

Gilbert wandered around inspecting Jeffrey's bookshelves, where he found a book he could settle in with on the straight-backed chair in the guest bedroom while his wife went about her business. He sat with both feet flat on the floor, the book held high in front of his chest because his eyes weren't what they used to be. He was a slender, even stringy man with rigidly erect posture, pale eyes, and pale skin. The resemblance to his son was striking, if one allowed for the addition of thirty pounds and the subtraction of thirty years, although neither Jeffrey nor his father professed to be able to see it.

The first one home was Jessica, who hurried straight to their room when Carlos told her they were there. She hugged her grandparents, who congratulated her profusely on her graduation. When she heard that they hadn't eaten she made them accompany her to the kitchen because, she said, she was starved. They glowed under her attention, like children, and the sour mood of the earlier part of the day had utterly vanished by the time Phyllis got home, gushing with apologies. She took them on a tour of the apartment, pointing out walls that no longer existed as though she expected them to remember the way it used to look.

"That's what I thought," Gilbert said. "I said that, didn't I, dear? I said, This isn't the same place they used to live."

"Of course it is," Winifred said. "That's what she's telling you."

"But it's different, that's my point."

Winifred shook her head as though her husband were being incredibly obtuse. "They took down some walls. It's the same place."

Gilbert fell silent.

A little later Martin drove them to a seafood restaurant in SoHo, where they met Jeffrey. He shook hands with his father and gave his mother the kind of hug one gives strangers. He knew enough not to offer more. Even at this, Winifred stiffened as though an embrace were something to be endured. Jessica looked away.

The small talk at dinner was mostly about Jessica, an endless and embarrassing stream of vacant reiterations on the theme of the pride everyone took in her. Graduating near the top of her class. Yale in the fall. Such a remarkable child. She did her best to stay gracious and to avoid grimacing. Meanwhile Martin made his way to the airport and back, where he picked up Phyllis's mother, who had flown in from Chicago for the graduation. She was able to join them at the restaurant in time for dessert.

Over brandies back at the apartment, Gilbert questioned Jeffrey closely about business matters. There was, to his mind, altogether too much speculation. It was unhealthy, and sooner or later a price would have to be paid.

"Investment *is* speculation," Jeffrey said.

"That's hardly the point, son," Gilbert said. "Things are out of control. That should be obvious, don't you think?"

Before Jeffrey could answer, Winifred Blaine said, "I'm sure Jeffrey knows what he's doing, dear," and then turned to Mrs. Armstrong. "My husband fancies he knows a great deal about these things," she said.

It sent a chill through the room, as though somehow the whole history of a long and unpleasant marriage had just been told in a single sentence, as though a lifetime of adverse judgments had been condensed into a single gratuitous sneer. Gilbert Blaine, who had been standing by the fireplace, settled into a chair, looking frail and diminished, although nothing in his posture changed.

"No, you're right," Jeffrey said, addressing his father, trying to salvage something of the moment. "There is a kind of recklessness."

Winifred smiled, as though she were touched by the gesture. "He always sides with his father," she said. "Thank heavens we live two hundred miles away. I don't imagine Jeffrey would have done so well for himself if he had to contend with his father's advice on an everyday basis."

Jessica got to her feet. "I have a couple calls to make," she said, and walked out of the room. She hated seeing her grandfather put down like that and she resented her father for not doing anything about it.

Mrs. Armstrong said, "That's such a lovely fireplace. It must be wonderful in the winter."

Everyone agreed it was lovely, and wonderful in the winter. It was a good note to end the evening on.

In the bedroom, Phyllis said, "I feel sorry for your father. Was it always this bad?"

It didn't seem to her it was.

"It was worse," Jeffrey said. "There used to be something at stake." Then he told her he had left some unfinished work at the office.

He thought of stopping by Jessica's room on the way out. *What could I have done?* he would have asked. But he knew it was pointless.

For as long as Jeffrey could remember, he had watched his mother grind his father into particles, and the bitterest aspect of it all, which Jeffrey recognized with a clarity that made delusion impossible, was that Jeffrey himself, simply by the act of being born, was the hammer she used to bludgeon the poor, meaningless man into something that would have been very like surrender if there had been anything worth surrendering. Like a creature in a laboratory, Jeffrey was designed to be everything his father was not. Every dollar Jeffrey made was one more confirmation of Gilbert Blaine's failure.

The doorman hailed him a cab, and Jeffrey gave the driver the address of the office. After a few blocks he asked the man to pull over at the next corner with a payphone. He had his cell phone with him but he didn't want to use it.

Out on the street he took the slip of paper from his wallet and then checked his watch. It was after eleven, almost midnight in fact. He dialed the number anyway.

He knew it was the right E. Lester the moment she answered.

11

Even before the doorbell rang, Elaine Lester felt that something strange, even dangerous, was about to happen. She wasn't quite sure why she felt like that, but the feeling was as vivid as the touch of a cold hand on her skin. This was part of her investigation, wasn't it? That's why she initiated the contact. And cleverly, too.

She leaned back against the door frame of her bedroom closet, holding the slacks she had just selected. She smiled, a contented smile—if she'd been asked to describe it she might have said *mischievous*. She had been like that as a child, always in trouble without ever being actually bad. It was odd that the distinct tremble of fear she felt now managed to coexist, side by side, with this comfortable feeling that was almost like serenity, as though one could be hot and cold at the same time.

She remembered, for the first time in years, that her mother used to say exactly that. She swam before the end of April in the pond behind their house, lap after lap in the frigid water, and afterward, when little Elaine, in her long blue wool coat, held up the towel for her mother to wrap herself in, she would ask, *Aren't you cold?* and her mother would laugh and say, *Well, yes, cold from the water. But hot from the swimming. You ought to try it.*

She never did. Maybe she was trying it now.

Slacks, she decided, were best. Not open to ambiguity. Caution was the watchword of the hour. The man was, after all, the subject of an investigation being conducted by her office. Not that anyone was doing any investigating. Certainly not Schliester and Gogarty. They should have jumped at the chance after the way they carried on when her perverted predecessor shut down their investigation into the Wall Street–Mulberry Street connection. But no. They were more interested in riding down the dead-end street of Gus Benini's shenanigans at the Javits Center.

Fine. She was conducting her own investigation. Some drinks, a conversation, and now a midnight phone call from Jeffrey Blaine. What could it mean? Her lawyer's mind ran through the possibilities. Consistent with innocence, consistent with guilt. Cottoning up to the U.S. attorney, whose office might someday be looking to prosecute? Or just a guy with a bad marriage?

She changed from one blouse to another and then back again. She put on shoes and then took them off because it seemed more natural to be barefoot alone in your own apartment after midnight.

What had she been doing when he called? He would ask. He would apologize for coming by so late. *I didn't get you up?* he would say, and she would have to have an answer. She turned on the television and found a movie. *No, I was up, I was watching a movie.* That would do nicely. She left the set on while she went to the bathroom to check her hair, then hurried back to turn it off because she wouldn't be able to say a thing about the movie.

The doorbell went off like an alarm, ending her confusion. "It's me," he said over the intercom, which seemed presumptuous, and she buzzed him in. He was at her door a minute later, offering her a shy, slightly awkward smile instead of the apology she expected.

"I read the book," he said.

Presumptuous again, expecting her to know what he meant. But she did.

She offered him a drink. "Whatever you've got," he said.

He followed her into the kitchen, where she uncorked a bottle of wine. Red. "You don't seem surprised," he said as she filled two glasses.

"That you called?"

"That I read it."

He had surprised himself reading it.

"Very little surprises me," she said.

"I never knew whether that's a quality to be proud of or ashamed of."

"That nothing surprises me? Proud, I would think."

"Good, then," he said.

They touched glasses and drank.

It was easy to think of her as a beautiful woman, although she didn't have the grace most beautiful women have. There was a quality about her that was in fact the exact opposite of grace. It would have been easy to imagine her at the craps table of a sumptuous casino, all eyes on her, all her chips riding on every roll of the dice. She had an intensity he had never seen in a woman before.

Standing in the dark kitchen, lit only by a shrouded bulb over the sink, they talked about the book through two glasses of wine. He had read it on the train, or in the car, or when he was tired of work and didn't yet want to go home. At first he found it hard to get into. There was a fevered energy to the lives in the story. So much uncertainty, he thought, and so much passion to the uncertainty. The characters were drawn in with pencil strokes, like a sketch, with such austerity in the lines that even their passions were austere. And yet he never felt tempted to put it aside.

What he didn't say was that he pictured her, the woman from the bookstore, the woman with him now, as Tereza. Not in Tereza's desperate and overheated passivity. Elaine Lester didn't strike him as passive in any part of her life. But there was an intensity to her movements and gestures that struck him as possibly no less desperate, though rather in a different way.

What she didn't ask was whether his wife thought it somehow out of character for him to be reading a Central European novel.

And then they were in the living room, eating shrimp the size of a fingernail out of an open can, passing the fork between them. He started to talk about his father, and she listened without answering. There was distance more than pain in his voice, as though he had put the pain away a long time ago. "I've never been able to protect him," he said.

She asked him why he thought that was his job.

"Because she uses me to batter him. She always has."

"And that's your fault?"

"Of course it is," he said.

What he didn't say, although she knew it without his saying it, was that his father haunted him like a ghost, just as he was haunted by the certainty that if he hadn't yet proved to his demanding mother whatever it was that seemed to have needed proving since long before he was born, then he never would.

There was no self-pity in his voice, which was low and soft, but certain, leaving no room for contradiction. She did the only thing she could. She reached across the table and touched the back of his hand, and the moment hung in the air between them like a palpable object, an ice cube melting in a dish perhaps, and they seemed for that moment to be waiting for it to vanish.

"I could use a cigarette," she joked tensely, "and I don't even smoke."

"I suppose it wouldn't do any good to offer you a cigar?" he asked.

She laughed.

He lit a slender cigar he took from the case he carried in his breast pocket. When he was satisfied that it was burning evenly, he handed it across to her, and she took a slow, tentative drag, barely closing her mouth, letting a small, perfectly rounded whiff of cloud float away, holding its shape as it rose toward the ceiling. She watched it drift away and handed the cigar back.

Neither spoke. He set the cigar across the shrimp tin and stood. She stood as well. Was he leaving? She wanted to stop him and wanted to let him go, conscious already that if he stayed, they would make love. And then she would betray him. She knew she'd be able to do it when the time came, and she trembled at the evil of it. They would become lovers, and she would be spying on him.

Well, that was the job, wasn't it?

He stepped toward her, and his arms were around her, while a thin trail of smoke rose listlessly between them, filling the air with its perfume. She pulled him to her and they kissed deeply, the same smoky taste in both their mouths. His hands moved down her back and under her belt, probing for bare skin.

They made love on the couch without undressing, and they said almost nothing when she walked him to the door.

With generations of headmistresses scowling down from heavy gilt frames around the balcony, the graduating class filed into an auditorium that had benefited only a few years before from a multimillion-dollar facelift. The seats were as comfortable as a Broadway theater, the sight lines perfect. Phyllis squeezed Jeffrey's hand the first time she caught a glimpse of her daughter in her cap and gown, then turned to smile at her mother. Jeffrey glanced at his parents to make sure they had seen her.

Renée Goldschmidt was valedictorian and Grace Tunney presented the class gift, substituting for Amy Laidlaw, who had been voted the honor by the members of the senior class. At the last minute Amy decided that she wasn't up to making a speech, and Grace agreed to do it for her. It was too late to correct the programs, which still had Amy's name.

The girls all knew what Amy was going through. None of them had failed to notice the change in her after the rape. She had never been one of the bubbly ones, but she had always been lively and fun and quick-witted. Now there were hollow silences in the spaces where Amy's contribution to any conversation might have come.

Renée and Grace gave lovely speeches, as earnestly optimistic about the future as young women of their social standing had every right to be. They pictured a world of eternal sisterhood, in which they would never forget one another while leading lives of dedicated, even impassioned concern for those less fortunate than themselves. The graduates listened absently, sorting memories in their minds as though they were preparing to paste them in books, while in the seats behind them their misty-eyed parents earnestly convinced themselves that yes or no, some or all of this might be true, but that what had to be true, above all these shining ideals, was that their daughters would always be young and would always be beautiful.

The graduation ceremony was followed by a brief reception on the patio which looked carefully out over the East River through the spaces between buildings. Lasting barely an hour, the reception marked the last time the graduating class would be together as a whole, and so it was tinged with a sort of prefabricated sadness, a nostalgia for absences not yet felt and moments not yet gone. Immediately afterward, three generations of Blaines and Armstrongs attended a buffet luncheon at the Goldschmidts' Park Avenue duplex for a dozen of Renée's closest friends and their families. Amy, who had been cheered when she accepted her diploma, sat next to Jessica the whole time, off in a corner, where she could stay away from both her mother and her father, who were in the same room together for practically the first time since their divorce. Neither had had the grace to decline the invitation.

And then it was over. As soon as the salads and spiced chicken and stuffed shrimp were replaced with cakes and cookies and a few more exotic desserts, Jessica seized the moment to make a quick round of good-byes. The four girls went off together, Jessica, Amy, Grace, and Renée. Phyllis took her mother and her in-laws home in a taxi while Jeffrey had Martin drive him back to the office, congratulating himself along the way for having steered his little girl safely through.

12

On a **Wednesday afternoon** late in June, Jennie buzzed Jeffrey in his office. "There's a man on the line. He wants to talk to you but he won't give his name," she said.

"Get a number. If he won't leave a number, forget about it," Jeffrey said, impatient at the interruption. He went back to the report in front of him but read only a few sentences before he found himself reaching for the phone.

"Listen," he said. "Are you still on with that guy?"

She was.

"Put him through," Jeffrey said.

He heard Jennie say, "Mr. Blaine just came in. If you'll just hold on a second," and then he recognized the high-pitched voice of the man who had called to set up his Riverside Park meeting with Chet Fiore.

"Do you know who this is?" the voice asked.

"Mr. Luisi."

"Good memory. Then you know who I'm calling for. He wants to meet you. There's a restaurant on Pell Street. China d'Or. That's *D*, *O*, *R*, with one of those little things in front of the *O*. Eight o'clock."

He sounded like a man who was about to hang up the phone.

"Wait a minute," Jeffrey objected. "Tonight's not good."

"I don't know nothing about that," Luisi's voice came back at him. "China d'Or. Pell Street. Eight o'clock."

The phone went dead.

As a matter of fact, Jeffrey and Phyllis had no plans at all that evening. Jessica was away for two weeks on Cape Cod with Amy and Grace and Renée, the last time they would all be together before they went off to their separate colleges in the fall. An evening home together with nothing to do had been Phyllis's idea, and she presented it with the elaborate premeditation she always brought to notions she picked up from one magazine or another. Even after all these years, she still believed there were tricks that could make a pallid and boring marriage better, the way spices perk up a soup.

Jeffrey asked Jennie to call home and leave a message for Phyllis, telling her he'd be late. The rest of the afternoon passed in a muddle of distraction. He stayed in the office until seven, and even called home at one point to give Phyllis an explanation about unexpected work. But she wasn't in. The maid had expected her earlier but didn't know where she was or when she'd be back.

So much for a quiet evening at home together. Even if he had been there, she wasn't.

He gave Martin the evening off and took a cab down to Canal Street, getting off at West Broadway and walking across to Chinatown. He found the restaurant easily enough. It seemed to him that the place used to have another name but he couldn't remember what it was.

He was early, so he walked around the block once before going in, promptly at eight o'clock. Fiore was already seated at a table near the kitchen wall. He nodded almost imperceptibly when he saw Blaine at the door.

"I'm joining that gentleman," Jeffrey said to the maître d', who followed him to the table with a menu, which he presented with a ceremonial bow as soon as Jeffrey was seated.

"Glad you could make it," Fiore said, offering his hand. "The food's okay here and they don't bother you."

"Do you own this place, too?" Jeffrey asked.

"Do I look Chinese?"

"No, but—"

Fiore cut him off. "Oh, that was a joke, right?"

"I guess so," Jeffrey said, but he wouldn't have been surprised if Fiore's answer had been yes. "What's this about?" he asked as he sat down.

"What do you think it's about?"

"You called me, Mr. Fiore."

Fiore studied him a moment before answering. There was an intensity to his black eyes that could be unnerving, and he had no scruples about letting his gaze bore in on a man with a directness that seemed almost an invasion. He held the look only a few seconds, while Jeffrey looked back at him steadily, refusing to back down or look away. Calculations were being made on both sides of the table. Then something like a smile played at the corners of Fiore's mouth and he said simply, "You remember Noel Garver, don't you?"

That's old history, Jeffrey thought. It's done with. He didn't see why it should be coming back now, months after the party. "What about him?" he asked, his voice so perfectly under control that none of his annoyance was audible there.

Instead of answering the question, Fiore took two sheets of paper from his breast pocket, standard typing paper, neatly folded down the middle. He handed them across to Jeffrey, who took them with what appeared to be a steady hand.

Across the top of the first sheet was some kind of computer coding, and then Garver's name.

A waiter brought a large platter of small chalky-white steamed dim sum buns. He said something to Fiore, or Fiore said something to him, Jeffrey wasn't sure which, and then he divided the buns equally between the two dinner plates. He was already gone before Jeffrey managed to pick his way through the typewritten pages.

The words on the pages might as well have been a bowl of alphabet soup for all the sense Jeffrey could make of them. His eyes jumped from one part of the page to another, grabbing for anything they could take hold of, picking out phrases here and there. He saw the word *rape*, he saw his own name in half a dozen different places. And Jessica's name. And Phyllis's. And Amy Laidlaw's and her father's. There was something about Amy's scream and something about the *assailants* being *spirited away.*

He put the pages down and looked across at Chet Fiore, no expression at all on his face, nothing showing in his eyes. "Congratulations," he said. "It doesn't mention you at all."

"You didn't think it would, did you?"

No. Of course not. That went without saying. Jeffrey acknowledged the fact with a kind of offhand shrug. "When is this going to come out?" he asked.

Fiore reached across the table and took the pages back. He looked at them to make sure they were in order, folded them along the creases, and put them back in his pocket before answering.

"It's not," he said.

"Why would that be?" Jeffrey asked, and then added immediately, in a voice that made no effort to conceal his bitterness, "Oh, that's right. You told me. It wouldn't be in his best interest."

Fiore was eating. He didn't even look up.

"Do you mind telling me the point of this little exercise?" Jeffrey asked.

"Don't you know?"

"It's a reminder. In case I've forgotten how grateful to you I ought to be."

"It doesn't help you evaluate the situation?"

"There is no situation, Mr. Fiore. You took care of the problem and it's gone. I appreciate that."

Fiore smiled like a man who appreciated being appreciated. But he said nothing.

"I suppose you're telling me that you could make this article appear as easily as you made it disappear. Fine. I'm telling you I don't give a damn."

He felt at the moment a boundless loathing for the man sitting across from him. It had nothing to do with the immorality of whatever steps Fiore had taken to silence Garver, nothing, really, to do with the power Fiore so blithely exercised over the press, over, it seemed, any part of the world he cared to control. It was Fiore's power over *him*, over Jeffrey, that rankled so deeply. It was the way he took action on Jeffrey's behalf without consultation, without asking whether or not he wanted these actions taken. He made Jeffrey feel small, insignificant, childish, in the way his mother always made him feel childish with her unasked-for generosities when he still lived at home, when he was in college, when he was just starting out for himself.

"That's good," Fiore said. "It shows strength of character."

"Why don't you get to the point?" Jeffrey challenged.

"Actually," Fiore said with a distinctly charming and somewhat boyish grin, "you make me a little nervous, Jeffrey. I'm not used to dealing with people like you."

"You may not be used to dealing with people like me," Jeffrey said, "but I don't make you nervous."

"You're being too modest," Fiore said. "I know a number of people who are considered *masterminds* at whatever it is they do. But frankly most of them aren't all that smart. So there's something a little"— His hand waggled as he searched for the word—"*daunting* about dealing with you. I don't really know you. I don't have a clear sense of what makes you tick."

"Can't help you there," Jeffrey said.

"No, of course not. So let's just move forward. You eat, I'll talk. The pork buns are terrific."

He waited until Jeffrey picked up a set of chopsticks. Was it possible, Jeffrey wondered as he started to eat, that any of what Fiore had just said was true? Did he really make this man nervous? It was possible, but it wouldn't be wise to count on it.

Fiore leaned back in his chair, slightly sideways, one elbow on the table, as he launched into a witty, almost light-hearted monologue spelling out exactly what he wanted. He needed a source of legitimate income through which he could funnel money he couldn't otherwise account for. "I've got businesses that are nobody's business and then I've got business businesses. I need a way to connect them," he said at the end, dropping his hands to the table.

It was Jeffrey's turn.

He could have said that he had worked out the solution already, in late-night sessions at the office, but he chose not to. The temptation was there, no question about it. He was here because he was drawn to the man as much as he was drawn to the idea, drawn not merely by the seductive force of Fiore's charm but also by the seductive force of his power. He wasn't afraid of Fiore. On the contrary, he understood without even having to think it through that if he joined forces with Fiore, a portion of that power would be his.

But now, faced with the man and the moment, he held back, looking across the table at Fiore with a bitterness and resentment he hadn't realized he felt. Chet Fiore had studied him, analyzed him, run his experiments, summoning him here, summoning him there, testing, probing, driving a pin through his body as though he were a curious insect fated by his rarity to be skewered to a velveted board. At that moment it dawned on Jeffrey Blaine with startling clarity that Fiore had been far too ready to exploit the chaos at Jessica's party. He had to have known in advance that sooner or later the girls would be taken upstairs, that sooner or later one of them would scream, that the boys were to do whatever it took to produce the scream that would bring Chet Fiore onto the scene to restore order. He didn't see how Fiore could have done it, but he was sure it had been done.

"I can't help you," Jeffrey said, setting his napkin on the table. "I'm not a broker. We don't do stock trading."

He started to get to his feet.

"Don't be in such a hurry," Fiore said. "Let's think about this a little more."

"I don't have to think about it," Jeffrey said.

Fiore's expression didn't change.

"All right," Jeffrey said, "let me give you a crash course in reality. How much money do you envision this thing producing?"

Fiore figured that in a couple of years he would like to be clearing forty million a year.

"You don't have to lowball me, Mr. Fiore," Jeffrey said. "You wouldn't be going through all this if you were just talking about forty million. But that's fine, let's take your number. You want forty million dollars to come down the laundry chute. Okay. If I had a crystal ball I could turn a hundred dollars into a thousand by lunch, ten thousand by the next day. It snowballs. Forty million is no problem. In fact, I thought you'd say more. The point is in six months I could have any number you want."

"With a crystal ball."

"Exactly. But it wouldn't help anyway. You can make anything happen on paper as long as you keep those papers in your pocket. But you don't want them in your pocket. You want records. And the SEC monitors records. When a hundred dollars turns into forty million they investigate because that's a tip-off that the wheel is rigged. They call it insider trading. You're trying to be discreet but you're running a red flag up their pole. A five hundred percent return on investment won't wash. Even a hundred. Maybe once or twice, but not on a steady basis. You could get away with a fifty percent return but that means your initial investment has to be around eighty million. I take it you don't want to do that."

"I'd have to tell them where the eighty million came from," Fiore said.

"Which defeats the whole purpose."

Fiore didn't change expression. But he reached out a hand and grabbed Jeffrey's wrist so hard it made Jeffrey's eyes water. His fingers probed in among the tendons as though he were trying to pry them loose from the bone. "Listen to me," he said softly, leaning forward, not relaxing his grip, "I don't want to hear the problems. You're smart. Figure something out. I'm sure you can do it."

He smiled pleasantly as he released Jeffrey's wrist, as though he hadn't realized how forceful his grip had been.

Jeffrey returned the smile, trying to ignore the force he had just been shown, willing at least for the moment to accept the smile at face value. "There's nothing to figure out," he said. "You figured it out already and it doesn't work."

"Make it work."

"How?"

"I don't know that," Fiore shrugged. "But I know you can do it. Take a couple days if you have to. Get back to me."

Jeffrey shook his head. "It can't be done," he said. "If you want to tell Noel Garver to publish his damn story, go ahead and tell him. I'm telling you this won't work."

Fiore studied him a moment without speaking. He knew that Jeffrey wasn't bluffing. "You want to be a tough guy," he said at last, "go ahead. Get out of here."

He poured himself some tea, as though Jeffrey were gone already.

Jeffrey got to his feet and reached into his pocket for his money. He put two twenties on the table.

"Keep it, genius," Fiore said. "Dinner's on me. Give my love to your wife. And your pretty little daughter. When does she get back from the Cape?"

A thousand alarms clanged in Jeffrey's ears, and the surge of adrenaline that rushed through his body hit him so hard he could hear the pulses in his temples. He leaned forward, his knuckles on the table, his face close to Fiore's.

"How do you know where my daughter is?" he demanded.

"Was it a secret? I didn't know that," Fiore said, smiling again. There was an edge of nastiness to the smile that hadn't been there before. "I was talking to Eddie," he said. "You remember Eddie Vincenzo, don't you?"

"Are you telling me he's with her?" Jeffrey said, his voice far too loud. Around the dining room, heads turned.

"Hey, she's in love with him," Fiore purred, and then, more quietly, confidentially, he said, "Eddie says she's got a cunt like candy."

Jeffrey's left hand flashed out and grabbed a fistful of Fiore's shirt. His right hand, balled into a fist, pulled back and started forward. But before he knew what happened, two men from the next table—they must have been Fiore's men but he hadn't noticed them before—grabbed his arms, yanked them down, pulled them behind him with expert and excruciating pressure.

Waiters rushed forward from different parts of the room.

"It's awright, it's no problem," one of Fiore's men growled.

The waiters held their ground.

"He's okay, he's not going to be trouble," Fiore said levelly.

The two men let go of Jeffrey's arms.

"You tell that slimy bastard to leave my daughter alone," Jeffrey said in a voice that carried through the whole dining room.

"Hey," Fiore grinned, "right now it's the other way around. She can't get enough of him. But maybe he'll drop her. Sometimes that happens, you know. Let's see how things work out with you and me."

In the mornings, the Goldschmidt home in Truro lay shrouded in a fog that hung over the ocean like a blanket. This was Amy Laidlaw's time on the beach, when the whole gray world was all her own, the sky the same gray as the water, the same gray as the sand. In a few hours the sun would burn through the fog, and every pebble on the beach would cast a stark shadow. By then she'd be back in her room, waiting sleeplessly for the other girls to get up.

The hardest part of being here was that Jessica and Renée and Grace had all made a pact to ignore the difference between who Amy was and who she had become, treating her with the elaborate and hideous kindness people lavish on terminal invalids. They would coax an almost hysterical enthusiasm into their voices as they suggested something to do for an hour or two of an afternoon. Even a walk into town to the little shop that made its own ice cream elicited shrieks of enthusiasm that would have done a roomful of preschoolers proud. They sensed her withdrawal, the unfathomable aloneness that grew inside her like a tumor, and they were intent on seeing her through it as though it were something that would go away.

There was a line from *Hamlet* she couldn't get out of her mind. A month and a half ago they put on the play at Collegiate, with Brearley girls playing the female parts. *O how weary, stale, flat and unprofitable seem to me all the uses of this world.* Justin Riggan played Hamlet beautifully. The way he said that line just broke your heart.

Weary. Stale. Flat. And unprofitable. That was what she thought as she lay in bed every morning waiting for Renée and Grace and Jessica to get up. A set of unconnected adjectives digging into her brain like pebbles in a shoe.

The worst part was that her friends were all squabbling among themselves. They'd go off out of earshot, and then they'd come back wearing tense, artificial smiles, exactly like her parents fighting with each other before the divorce and pretending they weren't. Amy knew perfectly well what the girls were arguing about. Eddie Vincenzo had followed Jessica to the Cape, and she was sneaking off just about every night to see him. These few weeks were supposed to have been just the girls together and they resented it. They're probably telling Jessica that she's being disloyal to me, Amy thought. That having Eddie around was a reminder of what happened.

In fact, Amy didn't have a problem with Eddie, or even with Georgie, whom she was never going to see again anyway. Her problem was with her father, who made her feel like a total tramp. He hadn't even been going to let her come to Renée's house on the Cape at all. She heard her mother fighting with him on the phone about it. When she picked up the extension phone in the TV room, they kept talking about her even though they knew she was on the line. Her father said she shouldn't be allowed to go off unsupervised. Her mother didn't even defend her. She just said she wouldn't be unsupervised because Renée's mother would be there, and her father said, *Renée. Right. That's the one that was giving her boyfriend a blow job in the next room.* Amy hung up the phone and cried. She knew that her father would win because he always won. She was going to have to spend the whole summer locked up in that awful house in Maine with him, which would be like prison except that in prison there were other prisoners.

About two days later some guy showed up at the apartment and made her mother sign for something that turned out to be a subpoena, and Amy's mother got on the phone with her father in his office, and when she didn't come out for a couple hours Amy went into her room and found her lying on the bed crying. Her father was going to go into court and take away custody because she was an unfit mother.

The next morning Amy went down to his office without calling him first. He made her wait almost two hours outside his office.

His secretary obviously didn't know what was going on because she kept asking questions about what Amy was going to do in the summer and whether she was excited about graduating and starting college in the fall. This was a week or so before graduation. She talked the way someone talks to a kid who is going to Disney World for the first time.

Amy finally got to go in and told her father she was there to suggest a compromise. She said she would spend the summer with him in Maine the way he wanted if he would let her have a couple of weeks with her friends on the Cape. It was the last time they'd have a chance to be together because they were all going to different colleges.

The only reason he accepted the offer was because he checked his calendar and found some things he didn't want to give up in the first two weeks in June.

Once they were all together on the Cape, it wasn't anywhere near as wonderful as it was supposed to be. And then one night Renée's mother happened to call them on the car phone while they were out and somehow she figured out that Jessica wasn't with them.

Clarissa Goldschmidt taught sociology at NYU and had written an important book about adolescent boys. She was short and she had thick legs and a voice that sounded like something being dragged behind a car. She waited until all four girls were down for breakfast the next morning, and when she served the first order of pancakes, she said, "I want one of you to tell me what is going on."

The girls looked at each other as though they were baffled by the question.

Mrs. Goldschmidt said, "Maybe you need a couple minutes to think about it. That might be a productive use of your time."

She went back to the stove and poured some more batter onto the griddle. When she came back to the table with more pancakes on the platter, she sat down and said, "Let's put our cards on the table. I'll go first if that makes it easier for you. Last night I called you in the car. You said you were on your way home. When I said something to Jessica, it was instantly apparent that Jessica was not with you."

Jessica didn't wait for the other girls to lie for her. "I was with my boyfriend," she said levelly.

"Who is?"

"His name is Eddie. You don't know him."

"No, but I'll wager your parents do."

Amy felt her nerves tighten, like someone twisting another turn into a rope. She felt sorry for Jessica.

When no one said anything, Mrs. Goldschmidt said, "It's certainly none of my business whether you have a boyfriend, Jessica. I don't really want to be a chaperon, but I can't help thinking that if you need these three sidekicks covering for you while you run off to see this particular boyfriend, then it's not something I want to permit on my watch."

She asked Jessica to give her word not to see him again while she was staying at the house.

Jessica's eyes went down to the plate in front of her for just a second, and then she looked up and her eyes were fixed on Mrs. Goldschmidt's eyes with so much intensity it was almost scary. It wasn't anger and it wasn't resentment and it certainly wasn't hatred. It was just intensity, stripped bare of any content, the way a person can be beautiful without having, say, beautiful eyes or beautiful hair or a beautiful mouth. And this was beautiful, in a way, Amy thought. She wished that just once she could look at her father the way Jessica was looking at Mrs. Goldschmidt now, and she knew that she'd never be able to do it.

"I can't give you my word about that," Jessica said.

The upshot was that the four of them were grounded, but late that afternoon, while Mrs. Goldschmidt was working on a paper in the back room she used as a study, Jessica went out the front door and walked into town by herself. She didn't tell any of them she was going.

For some reason she didn't understand, Amy started to cry when she heard Renée tell Grace that Jessica was gone. She felt as though she didn't have a friend anywhere. She knew Jessica and she understood Jessica. Jessica was like a sister to her. She didn't *know* these other two girls at all. Not like that.

It was crazy, but she couldn't stop crying, and they went off and whispered together and then they left the room. She knew they were going to get Renée's mother, so she ran down to the beach because she didn't want to face Mrs. Goldschmidt right now.

She sat out on the beach with her knees pulled up to her chin, and she managed to make herself stop crying. She was just watching her shadow move on the sand, as though she were the hour hand of a sundial, when Grace and Renée came and sat next to her. They told her they called her mother because they were worried about her and they got her answering machine. So they called her father.

Which was exactly the same thing that happened the night of the party.

She ran into the water and they had to pull her out, and they practically had to sit on her on the sand.

They told her her father was coming for her, but she knew that wasn't true. He was *sending* someone.

It would serve him right, she thought, if she jumped out of the car while it was going over the Sagamore Bridge. Which is what separates the Cape from everywhere else.

As soon as he left the restaurant, Jeffrey walked around the corner onto Mott Street. He looked over his shoulder to make sure Fiore's goons weren't following him and then he took out his cell phone and called home.

"Where have you been?" Phyllis asked immediately.

He could have answered by asking her where she had been for that matter, but he really didn't care. "Never mind that," he said. "When's the last time you talked to Jessica?"

"What's wrong? What happened?" she asked, instantly alarmed.

"Nothing happened," he said doggedly. "When did you talk to her?"

"This morning. No, it wasn't this morning. Yesterday," she said. "What's this about, Jeffrey?"

"I'm downtown. I'll be home in half an hour. Call her and tell her she's got to come home in the morning. We'll send her a ticket."

"I wish you would tell me what this is—"

"Just do it," Jeffrey said, cutting her off. "I'll be home in half an hour."

He could hear her still demanding an explanation, but he clicked the phone off and put it back in his pocket.

He had to walk down to Canal Street to find a cab.

He felt the way he imagined people feel when they learn they have a disease that is going to change the rest of their lives. Not cancer, not something that kills them. Paralysis. Deafness. Blindness. Something like that. He felt no anguish, no pain, just an overwhelming sense of loss. And a numbness that at least for the time being made anger impossible.

Phyllis must have heard the elevator because she opened the front door even before he got there.

"What is this about, Jeffrey?"

He knew it wouldn't have taken any time at all to answer her but he didn't. "I'll tell you in a minute," he said instead. "Where's Carlos?"

He didn't wait for an answer but hurried straight back to the kitchen and down the corridor behind it to the maid's room. Carlos lived in the maid's room. The maid was a day worker who came in the morning and left after dinner.

Phyllis followed him.

He knocked on the door. When Carlos opened it, he was wearing a shirt and tie and was slipping into his jacket. "Sir?" he said.

"I'm sorry to bother you so late," Jeffrey said. "I'd like you to call whatever airline flies to the Cape. Order a prepaid ticket for tomorrow morning in Jessica's name. It will be from Hyannis, I assume. A morning flight, after nine if they can, so she'll have time to get to the airport. But if it's got to be earlier than that, then make it earlier."

"Yes, sir."

Jeffrey walked back into the kitchen and poured himself a glass of scotch. He was going to need it to fill Phyllis in on all these developments. The two of them had never once mentioned the birthday party after it was over. He had never told her the purpose of Fiore's visit to Bedford Hills the morning after the party, and she never asked.

He asked her if she wanted a drink.

"I just want a goddamn explanation," she said. "How long are you going to draw this thing out?"

He walked into the living room and sat down. Phyllis remained standing.

"When Amy was raped at the party —" he began.

"I doubt very much that she was raped," Phyllis interrupted.

He didn't bother responding, didn't care whether she meant that nothing had happened or that whatever happened wasn't rape. "Do you remember the man who showed up and more or less took charge of things?"

"You mean Mr. Fiore," she said.

"Right. Fiore. And there was a reporter there. Noel Garver. Fiore made sure he didn't write anything about what happened."

"How could he do that?"

"He's a gangster, Phyllis. You're the one who told me that."

Phyllis stiffened and walked away from him. She didn't like being made to feel stupid. She sat down and carefully crossed her legs. "What does any of this have to do with our daughter?" she asked, her voice icy.

He told her about his dinner with Fiore. About the unpublished article Fiore had shown him, and about Fiore's claim that the boy from the party was with Jessica at Truro.

"I don't see how that's possible," Phyllis said. "She's staying with the Goldschmidts."

"What did she say when you talked to her?" Jeffrey asked.

"I didn't talk to her. She was out," Phyllis admitted. And then quickly added, "But that doesn't mean anything. She didn't go up there to sit in the house all evening."

Jeffrey didn't tell her what Fiore wanted from him, his price for their daughter. And she didn't ask.

• • •

Jessica's plane was due in at LaGuardia at ten forty-five. They hadn't spoken to Jessica, but Phyllis talked with Clarissa Goldschmidt around midnight and Clarissa assured her she'd have Jessica on the plane. Clarissa said she was sorry to be breaking up the group. "They're like sisters," she said, but in fact she was thrilled to have the girl go and already had been considering calling the Blaines when they called. She asked if anyone was ill and Phyllis told her it was nothing like that, just that something had come up and they needed Jessica at home.

Phyllis hung up the phone certain Jessica would call to protest but the phone didn't ring until seven-thirty the next morning, and then it was Clarissa calling from her cell phone to say she had just dropped Jessica at the airport.

Jeffrey canceled all his morning appointments and had Martin drive him to the airport. Phyllis had a hair appointment and a New York City Ballet board luncheon and didn't go with him. "I really don't need to listen to her lies," she said. "I'm sure I'll get to hear them when I get home."

"She doesn't lie," Jeffrey said. "She won't do what we tell her, but she doesn't lie."

He checked the monitor inside the terminal. Her plane was due in five minutes. After a whole night to think about it, and the drive to the airport, he still wasn't sure what he would say when he saw her. Oh, yes, he would let her know unequivocally, and without any discussion of the matter, that she wasn't to see Eddie Vincenzo anymore, and he would let her know how angry he and her mother were over the deception.

Well, perhaps *deception* wasn't quite right. She hadn't told them she was seeing the boy, but she hadn't told them she wasn't either.

The display on the monitor changed, announcing that her flight was in. He went as far as the metal detectors, which he couldn't pass without a ticket. But he could see down the long corridor leading to the boarding gates. After a few minutes a stream of incoming passengers started toward him from one of the gates. He tried to pick out Jessica but couldn't see her. She'd probably be the last one off the plane, just like her mother, never missing a chance to dramatize her displeasure. In another minute even more people were milling in the corridor, emerging from another gate, this one closer to him, blocking his view. A steady stream of people walked toward and past him. An elderly man stood at his shoulder, waving to someone down the hall. "Wonderful. She looks wonderful," he said to no one in particular.

There was no sign of Jessica.

The phone in his pocket rang and he pulled it out quickly and put it to his ear, knowing whose voice he would hear. This was no call from the office. "Yes?" he said, trying to ignore his premonition.

Jessica's voice came at him. "Daddy, it's me," she said. There was something tentative in her voice, yearning. She sounded like a kid.

"Where are you?" he asked sharply.

"Never mind that," she began, but he cut her off immediately.

"Yes, I will mind that. Where are you?"

"Daddy, I'm not coming home now," she said.

He imagined she was in a phone booth somewhere on Cape Cod. He imagined Eddie Vincenzo standing beside her, coaching her. She never had been good at doing toughness or determination, but she was trying.

"This isn't subject to discussion," he said. "You've still got the ticket. Use it on the next flight. I'm at the airport. I'll wait here."

"Daddy, I am eighteen years old," she said.

"I'm well aware of that, Jessica. I was at your birthday party, if you recall. Along with your boyfriend and his nice little pals."

"I am not going to listen to this," she said.

He knew he was going about it the wrong way. He wasn't bringing her any closer. But he didn't know how to reason with an unreasonable child.

"You don't have to listen to anything," he said. "You just get on that plane."

There was only silence at his ear. She had hung up.

It took Martin less than twenty minutes to get from the airport to midtown Manhattan. Jeffrey virtually leaped out of the car in front of Stasny's, hurried around to the service entrance, and rang the bell he found there. The waiter who answered the door, in shirtsleeves, his tie unknotted around his neck like an imitation of a lounge singer, was the one who had been at the door the night of the party, the one who left the door unattended so that Noel Garver could slip in.

"Where's Stasny?" Jeffrey demanded.

"Is he expecting you, Mr. Blaine?" the man asked.

There may or may not have been a touch of insolence in his tone. Jeffrey stepped past him, using his hand to push the man aside, and marched down the corridor that led to the kitchen. Half a dozen sous-chefs and sous-sous-chefs were at work with whisks and sharp knives, slicing, stirring. Two older men were scanning vegetables and cuts of meat as though they were reading them for omens. The moment they became aware of a stranger's presence, all motion in the kitchen ceased. The knives seemed to hang in the air, the whisks hung poised between strokes. The eyes of the entire staff locked on him like the eyes of watchful dogs who weren't used to company. The waiter who had opened the door for him was still at his shoulder, silent, like a shadow.

There was no sign of Stasny but the door to his office was closed. It opened just before Jeffrey got to it, and Stasny stepped out, in his suit coat and tie, smelling of cologne. "Ah, my friend," he smiled, "it is good to see you."

Jeffrey hadn't been back to the restaurant since the party. He didn't return Stasny's smile.

"How do I get in touch with Fiore?" he asked.

"Fiore?" Stasny asked, as though he had never heard the name. He pronounced it *fey-or-ee*.

"You don't have to pretend with me," Jeffrey said. "He told me he owns this place."

"That is as it may be, monsieur," Stasny said, moving through the kitchen as he spoke. He stopped at the shoulder of a young man slicing leeks into half-inch lengths. "No, no, I have told you. You pull as you cut. The ends must be rough. So."

He took the knife from the young man's hand and demonstrated with two deft slicing moves. Then the blade swept the sliced leeks off the cutting board and into a garbage pail. He handed the knife back.

"I want to talk to him. Now," Jeffrey said.

The young man started over with a handful of leeks he removed from a wooden crate.

"Monsieur Fiore," Stasny said, "is not such a man one picks up the telephone and calls."

"You sure as hell knew how to call him the night of the party," Jeffrey said. "What happened? Did he give you a number where he could be reached when the girl screamed?"

"Very clever, Jeffrey. You're getting the hang of this thing."

Fiore's voice coming from behind Jeffrey startled him.

"And you knew I'd come here looking for you when she wasn't on the plane, didn't you?" Jeffrey said.

"Of course. Where else would you look? You can make us something for lunch, can't you, Erill?"

Two minutes later Jeffrey and Chet Fiore were seated at a table for two in the middle of the otherwise empty dining room. The waiter who had let Jeffrey in filled their glasses with a white wine neither of them had asked for. His tie was knotted now, his jacket on.

"Let me explain something to you so we don't misunderstand each other," Fiore said. "She wasn't kidnapped. She is where she is by her own choice."

"I'm sure you and your young friend had something to do with that."

"I'm sure you're right," Fiore agreed.

"I want her back," Jeffrey said. "Now."

Fiore tasted his wine and scowled at the glass. He shook his head with an air of resignation. "I'll bet people pay a hundred and a half a bottle for this dog piss," he said. "You want to know the truth? Nobody knows anything about anything. And the less they know, the more they pretend they know." And then, holding up his glass and raising his voice, "Excuse me, could you get us something else over here?"

The young waiter practically ran across the room with another bottle of wine and another set of glasses.

"Where were we?" Fiore said, back to Jeffrey. "Your daughter, yes. And you were showing me how smart you are, how much you've figured out. Let me see if I've got it all. You figured out that I more or less knew there was going to be trouble. You figured out that I arranged for Stasny to call me when it happened. And you figured out that I've been talking to Eddie Vincenzo wherever he is with your daughter right now. Oh yes, and you also figured out why I'm here now, which is to meet you. That's all very good. Now let me ask you something. The last time we talked, correct me if I'm wrong, you said go ahead and tell Garver to publish his damn story. You said that, right?"

Jeffrey didn't answer.

"Since you're so good at figuring things out, Mr. Blaine," Fiore went on, as though he hadn't expected a response, "did you give any thought at all to what the fuck I would do after you said that?"

His voice had turned suddenly sharp. It was the change itself, the unexpectedness and the completeness of it, that was more alarming than simply the fact of the cold, controlled anger it revealed.

"I want my daughter back," Jeffrey repeated, conscious now that he was having trouble getting the words out.

Fiore smiled and nodded his approval of the second bottle of wine. The waiter withdrew, backing away from the table.

"Oh, you'll get her back," Fiore said. "Not necessarily as good as new, but that's the way it is with kids. You know that."

"When?"

Fiore made an elaborate shrug. "It's summer. She's sowing some wild oats. I wouldn't worry about it. It's not like she called you and told you she's running off with the guy. It's not like she said she's dropping out of college, she'll see you in some other lifetime."

"Is that a threat?"

"Mr. Blaine," Fiore said, "it would be nice to think she's too bright to throw her life away over a putz like Eddie Vincenzo, who thinks he's going to be a made man when this is all over."

"I don't care about Eddie Vincenzo's future. I care about my daughter."

"Good. Have you given any thought to what we talked about last night?"

He half expected Blaine to tell him he hadn't had a chance, that Fiore had given him too much to worry about these last sixteen hours. But Jeffrey answered with a simple "Yes."

He knew the moment he said it that there would be no turning back, but that didn't concern him. Because he also knew that once he took the first step he wouldn't be interested in turning back. He wouldn't do it on Fiore's terms. He would do it on his own. He knew he could produce millions of clean green dollars for the man, and when he had shown he could do it, he would get his daughter back.

Once he had her back, there would be time enough to settle scores with Mr. Fiore.

He felt a rage building in him that was unlike anything he had felt before. It felt good in a way. He had never imagined that rage could put things so clearly in focus.

Part Four

13

Eddie Vincenzo was beginning to think it was a stupid idea taking the girl to New Orleans. It was hot as hell. The air was so clotted with moisture you could hardly see through it. They walked around for a little while on Canal Street and Bourbon and St. Charles, listening to the jazz that came from inside dark and cool-looking clubs. They went into three or four of them and had drinks in each, but neither of them had any interest in the music, so they left when the sweat on their bodies began to dry.

The girl had one hell of a body.

On the other hand, she bitched all the time. About the heat, about being bored, about their lack of plans. She was eighteen years old and she probably never had a second in her life when she didn't know what came next. All of a sudden she walked away from all of it. Flew away, in fact. Eddie was hoping she wouldn't come unglued.

He suggested another stop for another drink but Jessica opted for a walkaway cocktail from the window counter of a bar they were passing. Even the heat at this point seemed preferable to more clarinets and saxophones.

They were drinking rum, a different concoction at every place they stopped, rum and pineapple juice, rum and cranberry juice, rum in some kind of sugar syrup that carried the liquor to her brain so fast she could feel it moving up through her neck, her jaw, her lips, her eyes, the back of her skull. The one constant was the crushed iced that made the drinks as creamy as milkshakes.

She rolled the cold beaded plastic cup across her forehead and smiled with relief. She dipped her fingers into the slush and popped a dripping snowball into her mouth just long enough to suck the juice and liquor out of it. She spit the compact little ball of ice into her hand and then put it under her shirt, between her breasts. If she were a skillet it wouldn't have melted faster, forming a dark wet circle.

"That is so fucking sexy," he said.

She looked down at herself. "If you like women with three nipples," she said.

She reached into the cup for more of the drink and this time she grabbed Eddie's belt, jerked it forward, and dropped the ice ball down his pants.

He yowled melodramatically, swore vengeance in Sicilian, then poured a quarter of his own drink into the palm of his hand, squeezed his fist around the ball of ice, and grabbed the elastic waistband of her skirt with his other hand. He jammed his fist down there. He felt the cotton-candy fluff of her hair before he got to the delicate lace of her panties, and then he was under her panties where it was hot and wet, and he deposited his little ball of ice and patted it home.

All this was happening on a public sidewalk on St. Charles Street. A middle-aged woman gasped audibly and nudged her husband. But he laughed a pleasantly Midwestern laugh, more attuned to the innocence of the thing than the depravity his wife saw. Others watched, numbly expressionless, as though Eddie and Jessica were a team of clever mimes put there for their amusement.

Jessica didn't resist. Her eyes were locked on his, slate gray on black, her thin lips taut, waiting for the sensation as the coldness of his hand moved down her belly. When it came, more delicious than anything she had expected, she reacted with a convulsive shudder that started deep inside her body. Pinning his hand there, she pulled him to her, pressed her face against his, sighed like a woman in ecstasy, and then slowly and carefully poured the rest of her drink down the back of his pants. This time she earned the enthusiastic laughter of a dozen spectators. Three women, thirty-ish, vacationing together, broke into applause.

Eddie whirled toward them, indignant. His face turned red and his eyes darkened momentarily, warning anyone who might have noticed, though no one did, that he was a dangerous man to insult. And then, abandoning menace as quickly as he had summoned it, he ended the moment with a deep dance-recital bow.

Earlier, when they checked in at the Lafayette, their room was as hot as an oven, stoked by the subtropical sun burning through the French lace curtains on the tall balcony doors. The bellboy dialed the air conditioner all the way up and pulled a heavy curtain over the lace, blocking the sunlight. But the hotel was old, the room old, the air conditioner old. Jessica doubted it would do much good. Eddie shrugged off the complaining and talked her into going out for a walk until the room cooled down.

Now it turned out she had been right about the superannuated air conditioner. Her sullen petulance returned the instant Eddie unlocked the door and she was hit by a wave of tepid air which hadn't been improved much for having been stirred. She headed straight for the bathroom, closed the door behind her, and turned both taps of the tub all the way on. Then she peeled off her sticky wet clothes and lay down on the cool porcelain of the tub, waiting for the water to rise around her.

Even over the roar of the water she could hear Eddie talking to someone on the phone. She couldn't make out anything he was saying, but the thought that a quick and rootless boy like Eddie might have parents he was calling struck her as utterly unlikely. Kids like the kids she knew did that, but Eddie wasn't in the least like any of the kids she knew. With whom, she wondered, was he checking in?

She stepped out of the tub and put her ear to the door. She heard him say, "I don't know, a couple days maybe, whatever you want." She heard him say, "She's driving me fucking crazy. Because it's hot, that's why." And then he said, "What about Vegas? At least they've got fucking air conditioning." Then she didn't hear anything for almost half a minute and she hurried back to the tub.

The water was warmer than she wanted it, so she turned off the hot and left the cold running. It came halfway up her thighs now, washing the stickiness of their ice war off her genitals. She touched herself, rubbing herself lightly with her fingertips, and wished that Eddie would come in.

He did, easing the door back without knocking, moving to the side of the tub, looking down at her. He was still in his clothes, which smelled of rum, but she could see the bulge in his pants that she put there.

"I was just thinking about you," she said.

"Good I hope."

She didn't ask him about the phone call. "Okay," she said coolly.

As he knelt on the floor next to the tub, he noticed the wet footprints on the tile. A series of quick calculations raced through his mind, and his eyes followed the trail of the footsteps to the bathroom door. So she was in the tub and she got out. She went to the door. While he was on the phone. He didn't like that.

"Just okay?" he asked.

"Well, maybe a little better than okay," she said.

He bent low over the lip of the tub and kissed her between her breasts, where the water hadn't reached yet and she still tasted of sweat and rum. He moved his kisses slowly down her body and she raised her hips to him so that he could have his fill of her without drowning. She made a soft, low moan of pleasure because she liked what he was doing and wanted him to know it.

He reached toward her face with the hand he had been holding himself up with, felt her cheek, felt her turn her head to kiss his fingertips, licking them as though he were an ice cream cone. His hand moved on, to her ear, tangling in her hair. And then, with no warning, he was pushing down hard on the top of her head. If she had been braced for it she could have resisted. But she wasn't, and the pressure forced her head down into the water and she choked on it. If he thought he was being funny, he wasn't. He didn't even give her time to take a breath.

Her head flailed like a fish at the end of the line, except that a fish fights for the water and she was fighting for air. His grip tightened and for the first time in her life, really, she was afraid.

Her legs kicked. Both hands grabbed for his hand. Christ, he was strong. She couldn't move his hand, couldn't get herself free of it, couldn't breathe.

She thought in another minute, no, less than a minute, she would drown. She tried to turn, to roll over on her side so she could push herself up, but she couldn't move. She felt like she was crying under the water.

And then his hand was gone and she pushed herself, gasping, out of the water, sitting up, coughing and choking.

Eddie looked at her with his big Eddie grin.

It took forever until she could say anything, and then she said, "That's wasn't funny, Eddie."

"No shit."

He was still grinning, like a little boy peeking into the girls' dressing room. She couldn't think of anything to say.

"You went for a little walk," he said.

She didn't know what the hell he was talking about.

"What were you, listening?" he said.

He pointed toward the door. She looked and saw the footprints, saw the big puddle of water next to the tub from her thrashing.

"I was just wondering who you were talking to," she said.

"I was talking to who I was talking to," he said. "Is that any of your fucking business?"

"No, Eddie," she said, because she knew right then that it would be dangerous for her to say anything else.

Later he went out to score some coke. She didn't go with him because she had no interest in leaving the room, which was finally growing cooler as the sun sank. And because she didn't want to be with him right now. She was afraid when he said he was going out that he wouldn't let her stay behind by herself, but he just said, "Fine, I'll be back."

She cried when he left and she thought about leaving so that he'd find an empty room when he got back. But somehow that seemed like it would take more strength than she had right now. So she lay down on the bed and waited.

She had never done coke, in part because it didn't interest her, in part simply because the kids she hung with weren't into drugs much beyond an occasional joint when someone else supplied it. She was proud of her abstinence even though it had cost her nothing. But she sat up on the bed when Eddie came back with the coke and crossed her legs, yoga-style, and smiled at him when he showed her what to do.

It was Jeffrey's idea that he and Fiore take separate flights to Oklahoma City. He didn't want a record of them traveling together. He flew straight in from New York and Fiore came by way of Dallas but got there first. He waited for Jeffrey at the gate, unaware that the man standing opposite him was the man he had come to meet. Jeffrey introduced them, saying simply, "This is Chet Fiore. He's involved in the proposition I mentioned."

Fiore said he had to make a phone call. Jeffrey offered his cell phone but Fiore declined. He went to a phone booth only a few yards away.

Clint Bolling kept his eyes on Fiore's silk-suited back. "Your friend looks like a hood," he said, keeping his voice low.

Jeffrey said, "He is."

Bolling didn't say anything as he processed Blaine's terse response to what had been on his part simply a harmless little ethnic joke. Blaine must have been joking, too. The guy couldn't really be a gangster, could he? On the other hand, Blaine didn't strike Bolling as the kind of man who kidded around, certainly not about a thing like that.

So that left two possibilities. Either he hadn't heard right or this New York guinea was exactly what Bolling's New York banker said he was.

So be it.

Both men had brought only light overnight bags, which Bolling insisted on carrying, slinging the straps over his shoulders like bandoliers. He led the way to his metallic blue 4Runner, parked in a remote parking lot a good twenty-minute walk from the terminal. "They didn't have parking spaces in Oklahoma?" Fiore asked as they trudged across the melting macadam.

Bolling laughed but declined to explain that he had put it in the long-term lot to save a buck or two on the parking.

Along the way, Jeffrey peeled off his suit coat and slipped off his tie, neatly folding the tie before sliding it into the breast pocket of the coat. Fiore kept his coat and tie on, despite the Oklahoman's invitation to "make himself comfortable."

"I'm always comfortable," he said.

For all practical purposes, this ended conversation for the rest of the hike. Fiore contented himself with taking in the scenery, which was essentially an endless plain of dry, flat land that stretched beyond the airport to the horizon, shimmering like a bleak, waterless mirage. Fiore, who had spent his whole life in New York, except for one week of what was supposed to have been a two-week vacation in Europe with a twenty-year-old actress, had never seen anything even remotely like this.

Jeffrey sat in the back seat as a courtesy to Fiore.

At the parking lot gate Bolling asked for a receipt for the two and a half dollars the parking cost him. He folded the slip when it was handed to him and inserted it at the center of the thick roll of bills he had taken from his pants pocket to pay for the parking.

He glanced over at Fiore, who was looking at him like he just farted.

"I always get receipts," Bolling said. "For everything."

Fiore didn't say anything.

"You don't?"

Fiore answered with a flat "No," as though this stranger had asked him a personal question he had no business asking.

Bolling glanced to his right, checking out either his passenger or the side mirror as he changed lanes. "I can understand that," he said, and then added, "I guess there's something to be said for not wanting a whole lot of paper keeping tabs on what you're doing and where you go."

Fiore turned his head slowly. "Are you trying to make some kind of point, Mr. Bolling?" he asked.

"No. No point," Bolling said.

"What is it you want to know?"

"When I want to know something I'll ask."

Jeffrey watched the two of them from the back seat. He could have said something to turn the conversation in a different direction and end the macho testing process going on in front of him. If he had been on his way to a normal business meeting with Fiore and Bolling, he would have done so. He was a master at facilitating the relationships he wanted to see flourish. But in this case it didn't particularly serve his purposes for these two to like each other. There are situations when distrust is as good as trust; in the end they pretty much come to the same thing. So he said nothing, letting the tension of the moment play itself out on its own.

Which it did quickly enough. Bolling's eyes went back to the road and Fiore's to the scenery.

"It's something, ain't it?" Bolling said, with a wave of his hand that took in everything outside the car. "What you see is what we've got. Soil so thin a chicken can scratch through it. A man doesn't have to live here too long or think about it too deep before he comes to the conclusion that sometimes even god fucks up."

"It may be thin soil but it's got oil under it," Jeffrey said from the back seat.

Bolling looked at him in the mirror. "That's true enough," he said. "But you can't farm oil. You can't use it to water your stock. All it's good for is making sons of bitches like me rich. Everybody else around here is just about dying."

Fiore thought he understood. "Your people were farmers," he said.

"Yeah," Bolling said. "Were."

Well beyond the city, perhaps twenty or thirty miles out, where the land was all gray with dust, with here and there a few head of cattle listlessly picking their way among the brown weeds, a sudden oasis materialized beside the road. An immense green lawn, well watered, immaculately tended, as smooth as a pool table, stretched back easily three hundred yards from the opposite side of the highway. Stately shade trees, poplars and oaks and elms, rose above the plain in dense groves, punctuating the flatness. A double row of maples flanked both shoulders of a long drive leading back to a sprawling one-story building so densely surrounded by shrubbery that it looked almost like an underground bunker. Jeffrey knew enough to know that these trees were not part of this landscape. They had to have been trucked in at great expense.

"My office," Bolling said laconically, letting the dreamlike splendor of the site do its own talking.

And then it was gone and the land was brown again. There had been no sign at the head of the drive. Apparently the people who did business with PetroBoll could be counted on to know it when they saw it.

Bolling punched a single digit on the tiny keypad recessed into the hub of the steering wheel. In a moment a woman's voice said, "Yes, Mr. Bolling?" She sounded young.

"Any messages, Doll?" Bolling asked.

"Mr. Jeffers from Getty. He went on about how he wants you to call him back."

"Well you know that's not about to happen. Anything else?"

"Nothing you don't know about, Mr. B. Wilson's still walking around like his dog died, waiting on you. What time are you going to be in?"

There was a comfortable Texas drawl to her voice, as though the words had a hidden melody.

Bolling said, "You tell that scapegrace if he wanted to talk to me so bad he should have been out on the highway. I just drove past."

"Sir?" She sounded puzzled.

"I'm taking Mr. Jeffrey Blaine and his associate out to the house. What I want you to tell Mr. Jarrett Wilson is that I pay him all that money to figure things out himself."

"No, sir," she laughed pleasantly, "you don't want me telling him that."

"Love you, Doll," he said, and pressed another button on the keypad.

"Colored girl," he said, glancing across to Fiore. "But damn, she knows more about the business than I do."

Bolling's home, another fifteen minutes east on I-40, mirrored the office complex on an only slightly smaller scale. The trees and lawns were visible from the interstate.

The 4Runner pulled off the highway onto a county road and then turned immediately onto the shaded drive. Even in the closed car, Bolling's passengers could feel the drop in the temperature outside as the greenery sucked the heat out of the air.

They passed a sizeable pond, perhaps two acres of shimmering water surrounded entirely by evenly spaced shade trees. The drive went on another half mile and then the house was visible before them, low and close to the ground, sprawling in all directions as though new wings kept growing out of it like a plant spreading roots. They rolled to a stop in front of the main entrance. Bolling left the engine running and got out of the car. A Mexican in jeans and a Western shirt peeled himself away from the soccer game he was watching on the television in the carport, settled his hat on his head, and loped toward them to take the car. Bolling greeted him in Spanish, then got the bags out of the back and led the way to the house.

Two shallow steps rose to the railless deck that edged the front of the house like the running board on a vintage car. A massive oak door carefully worked with Mayan-style carvings opened easily at his touch despite its enormous weight. Bolling stepped back to let his guests precede him inside.

The foyer was large and bare, except for a pair of ancient seven-foot wooden benches, their seats uneven with wear, the armrests at either end worn to a warm, rounded polish. Bolling's first wife acquired them in Southern California. They were the pews from an eighteenth-century Spanish church that had fallen down from neglect. Bolling, who gave prodigiously to religious charities, had been approached to contribute to the church's restoration. He took María with him on an inspection and she fell in love with everything inside the church, the fragrant woods, the fragrant leather. So Bolling made them a proposition. He would build them a new church on the very site, in exchange for which his wife would be allowed to choose what she wanted from the furnishings of the old church.

The young priest and the elderly parishioners debated the proposal for weeks. What they wanted was the restoration of their beloved Church of San Junipero Serra. But they had been able to raise very little money for the work, largely because most of the philanthropies they approached assumed that the Roman Catholic Church had tons of money. Which it did, of course, but not for impoverished Mexican churches south of San Diego practically on the Mexican border. Though old, the church was considered to be without artistic merit. Its name appeared in none of the guidebooks to Southern California.

A delegation of parishioners came to the motel where Mr. and Mrs. Bolling were staying. Their priest announced that they were happy to accept Mr. Bolling's generous proposal. But the parishioners looked grim and sorrowful, the way a woman might look when she is constrained to accept a marriage proposal from an unattractive man she doesn't love. They took some consolation from the fact that María Bolling was Mexican.

In the end, all she took from the church were these two pews, which, Bolling joked from time to time, cost him two and a half million dollars apiece. But he never regretted the expense. When María died two years later, he had the pews moved to the foyer, where they would remind him of her every time he came into the house.

Between the two pews, a large double doorway opened into a sunbaked central courtyard. Jeffrey and Fiore followed Bolling through the door and straight across the courtyard, where a pair of stone lions bellowed water from their mouths, and entered a long corridor flanked on both sides by closed doors and decorated with watercolors and hanging tapestries. There appeared to be eight guest rooms in this wing. Bolling stopped at the last pair of doors, where he handed Fiore and Blaine their bags.

"I think you'll find everything you want," he said. "You probably didn't bring bathing suits but there's a couple in the dresser. You might want a swim. Take as long as you want. I'll be at the pool. We can talk there."

He turned and retraced his steps down the corridor.

"The *pool*," Fiore said with an odd, ironic emphasis.

"I'm sure we'll be able to find it," Jeffrey answered. "Do we need to talk before we talk to him?"

"I wouldn't know, General," Fiore said. "This is your show."

He opened the door and disappeared into his room. Jeffrey followed suit, entering the room on the opposite side of the corridor.

The decor was surprisingly spare and simple, although there were half a dozen charming lithographs and oil paintings on the walls depicting rural Mexican scenes.

After a brief inspection of the room, Jeffrey stepped to the floor-to-ceiling window and found himself looking out at the swimming pool and its surrounding patio of beige tiles. A woman lay on a chaise. Although her face was averted, it seemed to Jeffrey that she was very young, in her early twenties at most. She had long jet-black hair that flowed over the edge of the chaise almost to the tiled floor. Her body was tanned the color of the Oklahoma earth. She was bare-breasted, her breasts rising in rounded shallow mounds, soft and full. It was hard to tell with her lying on her back, but it seemed to Jeffrey she was very generously endowed. He felt the tension in his loins that told him he shouldn't be looking but couldn't bring himself to back away. His lips felt dry and tight, the thrill of her nakedness mixed with a stinging sense of mortification, as though he had just been caught looking in a window like a common voyeur.

Jeffrey turned from the window and moved away. He put his bag on the bed and began to unpack, filled with a strange feeling he had never been aware of feeling before, a sudden and inexplicable consciousness of the power he commanded. For an instant, more like an impulse than a thought, he felt himself drawn back to the window. He would stand there openly until, inevitably, she turned and saw him. He would hold her eyes with his, challenging her to make something of his presence.

But of course he didn't do that. He didn't even permit the idea to form clearly in his mind.

He found bathing suits in the bottom drawer of the dresser as promised, men's and women's suits in a range of sizes and styles.

He went into the bathroom to change, taking a handful of the bathing suits with him.

The bathroom turned out to be as opulent as the bedroom was simple. The space was lined on two sides with floor-to-ceiling mirrors. A woman's vanity table displayed a comb-and-brush set with inlaid pearl handles worked with gold as well as a shallow cut-glass bowl. A hair dryer, thoughtfully plugged into the wall, hung from a hook attached to the glass. The toilet and sink were on the opposite wall. A set of glass doors rising above a marble sill separated this area from an even larger space that featured a Jacuzzi the size of a double bed sunk into the floor. A shower head was mounted in a bracket well away from the tub. The outer walls of the bath area were glass. Beyond them the emerald lawn stretched for only fifty yards or so until it ended abruptly in parched bare earth dotted only here and there with clumps of stubborn-looking weeds.

It wasn't until he had undressed and selected a modest suit instead of one of the skimpy Speedos that he noticed the small silver spoon on the vanity table next to the glass bowl. He lifted the cover of the bowl and saw that it was filled an inch deep with snowy-white cocaine.

The perfect host, he thought, replacing the cover.

He checked himself out in the mirror—it was impossible not to; he was surrounded by mirrors—and liked what he saw. Although he hadn't done much to stay in shape since college, except for an occasional squash or tennis game when business dictated, or when he was teaching Jessica to play, he was still lean and trim, perhaps a little softer around the middle than he would have liked but with very little else to betray the creeping advance of middle age.

He realized when he thought about tennis with Jessica that this was the first time he had thought about his daughter since the day she called him at the airport to tell him she wasn't coming home. Actually thought about her, that is. He had thought about her absence and about her defiance and had even tried, in an abstract way, to calculate how vastly different their relationship was going to be when she returned. But this wasn't the same as thinking about Jessica herself.

He found a beach robe in one of the closets and slipped it on.

He knocked on Fiore's door and Fiore opened it, dressed as he had been before, minus the jacket and tie, his only concession to the pool party their host apparently had planned for them.

"Jesus," Fiore said with mocking disapproval as he looked Jeffrey up and down.

When Jeffrey and Fiore got to the pool, the black-haired woman was in the water swimming laps with a steady, powerful crawl, her arms pumping with the easy rhythm of a machine, her legs knifing the water so smoothly she hardly seemed to disturb it as she passed. Bolling was seated in a chair next to the chaise where she had been lying. He got to his feet and pulled two other chairs around to his, then sat back down and asked them if they wanted anything to drink. Without waiting for their response, he called over his shoulder, "Rachel, come here. There's some people I want you to meet."

The glass in his hand was beaded with condensation. He took a long drink.

Without breaking the steady pulse of her stroke, she swam to the side of the pool near where they were seated, coming to a rest only when her hands caught the lip of the drain channel. She tipped her head back in the water and used her hands to smooth her hair back from her forehead. She was almost unnaturally beautiful, her features perfect the way the simplest of sketches done with the fewest possible lines can be perfect, her eyes as black as her hair, her skin glistening, dark and wet, her lips full and red. She put her palms on the surface of the patio and raised herself from the water, slowly, effortlessly, shoulders and bosom and belly rising up out of the water like an apparition rising into view. She had put on her bathing suit top at some point since Jeffrey had watched her through the guest room window.

Now she stood before them, water sheeting down her body, and Bolling said, with no further explanation, "Rachel, this is Mr. Blaine and Mr. Fiore. Rachel."

Her hand was cool, her grip as firm as a man's. The bottom of her suit wasn't skimpy. Smaller suits are seen every day on beaches everywhere. But the fabric was thin and fine and tight, molded to her body so provocatively that it outlined the mounded folds of her sex. As Fiore got to his feet to shake her hand, his eyes lingered for a long time at the top of her thighs. When he looked up, her eyes were looking back at his, bold and direct, demanding his attention for a long moment that seemed pointedly to exclude the other two men at poolside. She heard Bolling say, "You want to see what they want to drink?" and so she said, "He's having iced tea but you could have anything."

Jeffrey said, "Iced tea would be fine." Fiore said nothing, merely nodding his concurrence.

She walked away.

"She's very beautiful," Jeffrey said.

Only then did Fiore's eyes come off her retreating figure. "She is," he said. "Tell her to put something on."

For a moment Bolling seemed not to have understood his guest. He looked at Fiore as though he were about to ask a question. And then he got to his feet and hurried from the patio.

"Who the hell is she?" Fiore asked.

Jeffrey shrugged. "His daughter, I suppose. His wife's dead. She was Mexican. I don't know," he said.

In a moment Bolling returned carrying two glasses of iced tea. The woman didn't return.

"I hope you don't take anything in it," he said, handing them their drinks. "What is it we're supposed to talk about?"

From this point on, Jeffrey did the talking, with Fiore listening as intently as Bolling. The proposal was as new to one man as it was to the other. Jeffrey started by explaining that venture capital was, among all investments, a uniquely high-risk, high-yield proposition. Large sums of money were sunk into start-ups for new enterprises. Investment banking firms like Layne Bentley, Jeffrey's firm, raised this capital by in effect soliciting subscriptions to huge multimillion-dollar funds. This allowed them to reduce the risk to individual investors by providing start-up money for a variety of enterprises from a single fund. An investor who put twenty million dollars into a fund, for example, might find his money parceled to as many as half a dozen different enterprises. Conversely, a start-up that required capitalization of eighty or a hundred million dollars—and in many cases the figures ran far higher than that—might draw money from four or five different funds.

Jeffrey explained all this as carefully as if he were teaching a class in elementary economics. The point, of course, was to smooth out the bumps on what would otherwise be a very choppy ride through the all-or-nothing countryside of venture capital, where some investments literally vanished without a trace while others multiplied like rabbits in heat.

Neither Fiore nor Bolling asked any questions and Jeffrey moved on to the specifics of his proposal. He made no effort to disguise or conceal its purpose. They would start with three funds of approximately twenty million dollars apiece. Bolling would be the principal subscriber in all three, Fiore a secondary subscriber in only one of them. To put the matter simply, investments would be surreptitiously moved from one fund to the other, depending upon their returns, so that two of the funds would bear a disproportionate share of the losses while the third, in which Fiore had his money, would consist almost exclusively of winners.

Jeffrey's explanation was peppered with detailed examples so that both men got a clear picture of what would happen. When he was finished he asked them if they had any questions and he knew what Bolling's question would be.

"What's in this for me?" the Oklahoman asked.

"I think you know the answer to that already," Jeffrey said, and then proceeded to explain the consequences. The aggregate return on the three funds would be exactly the same with or without these artificial manipulations. Fiore's account would show immense gains, Bolling's offsetting losses. "Mr. Fiore," he said, "has no interest in getting any of the money, so you get to keep all of the profits even though they appear on his books. You get cash and a tax write-off for paper losses, he gets taxable profits."

"This is money laundering," Bolling said flatly.

Fiore stiffened. He hadn't expected Blaine to propose anything so transparent, and he couldn't at the moment imagine how the banker was going to answer what seemed to be an obvious challenge.

Jeffrey didn't hesitate. "That's exactly what it is," he said.

Bolling was quick enough to see how he gained from the enterprise. He knew how to add up a column of numbers. A paper loss of say twenty-five million was worth easily ten million in tax savings. An untaxed cash gain of say forty million was worth, say, seventy to seventy-five. What Blaine was offering came very close to a hundred percent return on his investment. But he thought he saw a flaw in the logic. "That's cute," he said, "but you're solving his problem by making it mine. I'm left with a pile of cash I can't account for."

Jeffrey laughed. He had a warm, ingratiating laugh. "Yes," he said, "but your problem isn't as complicated as his. You're certainly right about one thing. What we're talking about wouldn't make sense if you were the only person we were approaching. The fact of the matter is four people can each hide ten million dollars far easier than one person can hide forty. We're talking about manageable amounts of money here. I have people who can help you with that end of it."

Bolling nodded and was silent for a long time. "What if I say no?" he asked.

"You won't," Jeffrey said.

A heavyset woman in white linen appeared at the edge of the patio and announced that lunch was ready.

"I'm working on the assumption," Schliester said, "that this deal sucks."

Gus Benini's voice got high and shrill. "What the fuck are you talking?" he said. "We're taking care of you."

Schliester smiled and shrugged. "Well, that's the thing," he said. "My mother takes care of me, so I don't really need you for that. On the other hand, she cut off my allowance, so let's talk money."

In a funny way, Benini liked this guy. Because he was always

202 • **Philip Rosenberg**

saying things like that. Not the asking-for-money part. That was
no good. Benini didn't like being asked for money. But it was the
way this kid put things. You couldn't help liking him.

They were walking along the West Side waterfront, a few blocks
up from the Javits Center, a few blocks below where the *Intrepid* was
moored. For the past few weeks they had been going out for walks
whenever they had anything to talk about. Which meant that
Schliester had to wear a body wire. The first time Benini suggested a
walk, Schliester and Gogarty hadn't been prepared for anything like
that. The office was bugged but Schliester's person wasn't. And this
turned out to be the meeting at which Benini laid out what he wanted
from Schliester and how much he would pay for his services. They
didn't get a single word of it on tape, which meant they had to rely on
Schliester's notes on the meeting.

Elaine Lester wasn't very happy with them. Like all prosecu-
tors, she wanted everything on tape. She wasn't crazy about the
whole Benini thing anyway. It would be, at best, an indirect way to
get at Chet Fiore. More likely, if it worked at all, it would net only
a minor player in a minor racket. It was what Schliester and
Gogarty were doing when she took over, and they insisted it was
worth pursuing. Well, she thought, if she couldn't get them off it,
at least she could make them make it work. "From now on," she
announced, "you wear a wire. It's the only way."

Schliester shrugged; that was fine with him. But Gogarty had
objections. He held up a finger, wagging it in his schoolteacher
mode. "Not so fast," he said. "Mr. Benini isn't taking walks for his
health. If he's afraid the office is hot, he's going to look for a wire.
And if he finds one, it's game over."

Elaine turned to Schliester. "Did he do that?" she asked. "Did
he check you for a wire?"

"Of course he didn't," Gogarty said, not letting his partner answer.
"But that was only because he knew my man here wasn't expecting to
go outside. Next time he will be, so next time Benini's gonna check."

Elaine considered the possibility a moment and then turned
back to Schliester. "Your call," she said.

Schliester took no time whatsoever to think about it. "No problem," he said.

Gogarty muttered a string of curses under his breath. Later, when the two agents were alone, he let his partner have it. "*Your call*," he said in a mocking falsetto. "You know what that means? It means, 'Gee, Agent Schliester, let me see your balls.' And you, *boy-chik*, you just laid them on the table."

Schliester laughed. "If she wants my balls she can have them," he said. He saw the expression on Gogarty's face, so he added, "She's got a nice ass for a lawyer."

The next morning a technician named Wilson Something or Something Wilson came to the office with a sample case full of equipment. This wasn't the old-fashioned stuff where they tape a transmitter to one part of your body and a microphone to another. It was James Bond stuff. There was jewelry for women, cufflinks and a wristwatch for a man, a little notepad, one of those little palm-of-the-hand computers, and a ballpoint pen that was a complete self-contained radio with a microphone and transmitter inside. On top of that the pen actually worked. You could write with it. Schliester chose the pen.

"You got yourself all in a lather for nothing," he told his partner. "This is amazing shit."

Nobody east of the Mississippi said things like *got yourself in a lather*. Gogarty wondered how long it would take this kid to talk like he came from around here.

It turned out that Gogarty had been right about one thing. The next time Benini and Schliester went outside for a walk, the skinny little gangster insisted on patting Schliester down for a wire. He even made him empty his pockets, but all he found was a wallet, with Schliester's New York driver's license, Social Security card, and a few credit cards, all in the name of Frederick Linkletter, some folding money, some change, an address book, and a ballpoint pen. The time after that Schliester emptied his pockets the minute they were out of the building. They were standing on Eleventh Avenue. "Aren't you going to feel me up?" Schliester asked.

Benini glanced around at the steady stream of traffic flowing south on the avenue, and at the pedestrians making their way into the Center, where a housewares show was in progress, and then proceeded with a perfunctory frisk. His heart wasn't in it.

"That's it?" Schliester said. "I look forward to this all week and I don't even get a decent hand job?"

Benini said, "Shut the fuck up," and Gogarty, listening in with headphones and a tape recorder in a locksmith's van with Jersey plates parked just below Thirty-second Street, laughed so hard the coffee he was drinking came out his nose.

After that, there were no more frisks.

Now all of a sudden this kid, who until this point was tops in Benini's book, the best contact man he had ever had, was spoiling things by asking for more money. "Look," Benini said, "you're getting a couple of bills a week for absolutely nothing. What's the matter with you?"

"What's the matter with me," Schliester said, "is that I'm not stupid. If you give me three bills before I even ask for anything, then it's got to be worth more than three bills."

"How do you figure that?"

"Because you're not stupid."

"Right," Benini said.

"Right," Schliester agreed.

Benini looked at his shoes. He wasn't quite sure what they had just agreed on.

Schliester, on the other hand, looked up at the deck of the immense aircraft carrier looming eight stories over their heads. "Can you imagine the balls on a guy who would actually land a plane on a boat?" he said. It was his way of telling his partner where he was. Gogarty liked to keep track of those things.

"They're fucking heroes," Benini said. "How does five bills sound?"

"I don't know. How much do you take off these guys?"

Benini looked at him like he was crazy. "What do you wanna know for?" he said. "You wanna be my partner all of a sudden?"

"I *am* your partner," Schliester said.

"Bullshit," Benini said.

Schliester stopped walking. "No it's not bullshit," he shot back angrily. "That skinny Korean with the stereo systems came into my office pissed, ready to start the Korean War all over again, says you took ten K off him."

"*K?*"

"Oh right, I forgot, you guys still say *G's?* You sound like a fucking George Raft movie."

Benini ignored the crack. "He's fucking lying," he said.

"Hey, one of you is," Schliester said with a shrug and a little bit of a grin.

Benini's face turned so red with rage that Gogarty, in the van, could practically feel the heat coming off the man over the radio transmission. You don't tell guys like Gus Benini they're lying because they have an overdeveloped sense of honor. But before Benini had a chance to express himself, Schliester switched gears. "Now if you're telling me it wasn't ten, I'll take your word for it. But if he's telling me ten, then it sure as hell wasn't five and it wasn't six. The point is he wanted to go to the cops and I talked him out of it."

"All right," Benini conceded, his voice still sharp from the anger he was trying to get over. "That's worth something. You did good."

"No," Schliester said. "It's not worth *something*. It's worth a cut. Because the next guy maybe he won't come to me at all. Maybe he'll go straight to the cops. And he's not going to know who you are or where to find you. But he's sure as hell going to tell them where to find me. Now I wouldn't tell them anything because that would be stupid and we both agreed that I'm not stupid. But I am going to end up with a lot more aggravation than I can justify for three or four bills a week, which, if I wanted it that bad, I could make tending bar."

It was just about the longest speech Schliester had ever made in his life, and certainly the longest anyone had ever made to Gus Benini, who didn't have the attention span to listen to long speeches. The nervous little man took a couple seconds to think it all over, walking around in a circle in front of Schliester. Who gave him some time but not enough. When he thought Benini was ready to listen to more, he said, "Ten percent. And I throw in helping you pick the marks because I've got all their paperwork and I know who's good for how much."

Which is how Gus Benini and Frederick Linkletter became partners.

14

She knocked on Jeffrey's door first. He pulled on the ter-rycloth beach robe just before he opened the door and noticed the brief flicker in her eyes, like a shutter clicking open and closed behind a lens, that told him she had come to the wrong room. But her smile was ready in an instant. She was wearing a pool robe herself, and her hair was wet. The robe came only to the top of her thighs. Sexuality radiated off her the way hot land shimmers light.

"I was at the pool and I saw your light," she said. "Is there anything you want?"

"Everything seems to be fine," Jeffrey said.

She turned to go.

Jeffrey hesitated in the doorway, his eyes on her as she started away from him, wondering what would happen if he asked her to come back. She would turn back to him. She would come into his room. He was sure of that. He could almost hear her name forming on his lips and he could feel the urgent pull of desire. What the hell was happening? he asked himself. First the affair with Elaine Lester. Now this. How old was she? Twenty-five? Less. Certainly less.

It took an effort of will to step back from the door and close it, but he had never been short of will. He closed the door but stayed right there, just on the other side. Listening. He didn't hear a sound. Was she barefoot? It seemed to him she was. And the hallway was carpeted. Or was it? No, it was a wood floor, polished wood, dark and aged. Even barefoot, she couldn't have walked away without his hearing. Then she was waiting, too.

He saw his hand, as though it were someone else's hand, reach for the doorknob. And then it stopped, and his brain told him why. She wasn't waiting for him to open the door. She wasn't waiting for him at all. He could sense her presence only a few feet away in the midnight stillness of the house. His breath seemed to ratchet through his chest like the last raindrops dripping off the eaves and so he held his breath to keep from giving himself away. A few seconds passed. A few more. And then he heard the faint rap of her knuckles on the door across the hall.

He turned away and walked across the room to the window, where he could look out at the pool, rippled with a night breeze, lit now only by the moonlight. He cursed himself for still being too much like the goddamned banker he had been as recently as yesterday. He had felt, from the moment his plane took off from LaGuardia this morning, that a new part of his life had begun. Whatever he had been before this moment, he was something else now, someone else now. So he cursed himself for not taking this woman when she seemed almost to be offering herself. Right now Chet Fiore wasn't telling her there was nothing he wanted. Chet Fiore wasn't sending her away. In his mind's eye he could see Fiore stepping back from the door, inviting her in. He could see her moving into the room. And then, as he saw Fiore turn to her, the woman in the moonlit room wasn't Rachel Bolling, it was Phyllis. Fiore's eyes on Phyllis. In her nightgown. In the Bedford Hills living room. Fiore's eyes examining her long legs, the tousled flow of her hair, the cling of the silken fabric on her hips.

Nonsense, of course. He was jumbling things together, Fiore and his wife, Fiore and his daughter, Fiore and this young woman his daughter's age, or at least more his daughter's age than his own.

Maybe, he told himself, it was going to take a little time for him to figure out exactly how to go about being this new person he had become.

But he didn't doubt for a moment that he could do it.

Or that he wanted to. The one thing that was clear was that he was once and for all irrevocably finished with that young man who set off for New Haven so many years ago, harnessed to the burden of generations of Blaines and Tripletts, a burden that stretched far back into a horse-drawn, gaslit past. Consideration for others and ruthlessness with himself—that was the formula he had been bred to use, pushing himself to success, ingratiating himself with those around him. And what did it get him? A magnificent apartment on Fifth Avenue, yes. And, yes, a beautiful home in Bedford Hills. Also a wife he didn't love and a daughter who ran away from him at the first opportunity.

He was sick of it all.

He smiled at the outline of his image that looked back at him in the window glass and told himself that he was going to enjoy being an outlaw.

The ceiling swung in a stately arc, bridging her nose, so close there wasn't room for her head in the room. No, that couldn't be. It was silly. No room in the room. Of course there was room. There was always room. She started to giggle.

And then there *really* wasn't room because her own voice, cackling like a hen, filled the space like marshmallow goop floating under the ceiling, coating the walls, caulking the cracks, white caulking because they called it white noise, smoothing into the walls, coating them even though it was too hot for a coat. Or even a shirt.

Naked on the bed, she watched the flow of her voice while the cold conditioned air pecked at her skin.

Eddie floated somewhere in the space above her, somewhere between her voice and the ceiling. His hand looked as big as a clown's hand. Except that clowns have big feet, they don't have big hands. But she couldn't see his feet, so that must mean he was standing on the floor.

Shit, he was big.

It was scary, him being so big, and his hand so big. Like a clown's hand.

It felt so soft she wasn't sure she could feel it at all. But she tasted blood and she felt that her mouth was crooked, so that her top teeth and her bottom teeth weren't in line with each other and wouldn't meet, wouldn't ever meet again.

She tried to make them meet.

He drifted in and out of focus, and she asked herself where the blood was coming from. It was warm blood.

And then he hit her again going the other way, so she closed her eyes and didn't see anything else.

Well, she said, I shouldn't have done that. But it wasn't clear what it was she shouldn't have done.

At least it didn't hurt. Except for the taste, bloodtaste, she didn't feel it at all.

Across the hallway from Jeffrey's room, Chet Fiore answered the knock on his door, barefoot, bare-chested, wearing only the slacks he had worn to dinner that evening. He didn't need to open the door to know who had knocked.

He had gone to Blaine's room after dinner, where the banker outlined a plan to assure that Bolling would come to the right conclusion about their proposal. All it would take was a few phone calls on Fiore's part.

Fiore made them, using Blaine's cell phone. There was a telephone in the room, of course, but he didn't want Bolling to have a record of the numbers he called. He was careful because he didn't trust cell phones. He didn't identify himself by name, and his end of the conversation was so guarded it sounded to Jeffrey as though he were talking in code.

He turned off the phone, handed it back to Jeffrey, and went back to his own room to wait for the knock on the door he knew would come when the rest of the house was asleep.

She didn't say anything when he opened the door because she

didn't have to. She didn't ask him if there was anything he wanted because she knew there was.

She stepped past him, moving into the room. He closed the door without a sound and slowly, quietly, turned the dead bolt. He watched as she looked around, taking in the room as though she had never seen it before. Everything he had brought with him— clothing and toiletries, perhaps a book, perhaps some papers, for she knew that this man and his friend had come on some sort of business—had been carefully put away, so that the room bore no sign whatever of his presence there. As though he was not quite real, she thought. The bed didn't appear to have been disturbed. The television wasn't on and hadn't been when she knocked. She knew he had been waiting.

She arched her back and the robe slipped down her body like a caress. He moved to her with no particular sense of need or urgency. He put his hands on her shoulders and turned her around, letting his eyes take in her nakedness as though she were some- thing he was considering buying.

His indifference had always been his special gift to women. They took it as an index of his power, and also, in a sense, as an index of their own power. His coolness and distance freed them for a sexual relationship that for once wasn't simply the product of the sweaty importunings of a man.

He put his hands on her hips and waited, motionless, silent, and faintly smiling while she undid the top button of his pants. Her hand reached inside, past the hardness of his penis to cup his balls in her palm. Her other hand opened his zipper with one smooth pull. His pants fell to his ankles. His hips were narrow like a girl's, his butt small and taut. Her lowered eyes studied him. The fingers of one hand prowled his skin while her other hand slowly and gen- tly massaged his testicles. She moved her hips so that the head of his penis nestled into the thick tangles of black hair, as dense as the most intricate of nests. Then, when she was ready, she guided him into her with her hand, her lips parting wetly to welcome him.

He hadn't moved all this while, and neither of them had spo- ken, but now he took a step forward, driving her backward, and then another and another until her spine was pressed against the wall. He arched his back, ramming his hips forward, skewering her to one point in the wall like a butterfly in a case, hair tangled with hair, bone grinding bone. He moved slowly in a circular motion, not releasing the pressure at all, not thrusting in and out, but rubbing, rubbing, rubbing, a steady, insistent rhythm that went on and on, endless and powerful, until her eyes misted and closed and her perfect white teeth bit so hard into her lower lip that she might have drawn blood. Her breath came in quickening gasps and then stopped entirely. Her body went slack and limp, and he realized she had been standing on her toes, hips thrust out to meet his, because now he fell out of her, still hard and straight, as the taut sheath of her inner muscles that had gripped him so tightly seemed to melt away like snow in the spring.

"That was for you," he said, the first words either had spoken to the other. "How about my turn?"

She nodded her head in a weary but ready acquiescence.

She walked to the bed and lay down on top of the covers, spreading herself out for him, legs open wide, arms reaching toward him. She sensed intuitively that he was one of those men who wouldn't touch her sex with his hand and so she touched his, guiding him again into her. The tension of her muscles was beginning to return, but still she clamped her thighs together, knowing that after the overwhelming experience of two minutes before, it was the only way she could be as tight for him as she wanted to be.

He took her with a brief and relentless ferocity that lasted barely half a minute, but half a minute that felt as though if it went on any longer he would churn her inside out.

His body sagged against her chest and then he rolled over and lay on his back. It seemed to her that they were both asleep.

The next thing she knew, she felt his hand brush the hair from her forehead and his lips were at her ear and he whispered, "You have to go."

She opened her eyes, bringing the room and the night, the memory of midnight's passion into focus. "What time is it?" she asked.

"Quarter to two."

She stretched languidly and smiled up at the face looming over hers. "I can stay if you'd like," she said.

"No bed checks?" he asked.

"No."

He smiled. His front teeth were uneven, rotated slightly, a bit like the blades of a propeller, and the imperfection gave his smile a boyish sort of charm. "I'll tell you one thing," he teased lightly. "If you were my daughter, there'd sure as hell be bed checks."

Her arm pushed him gently to the side and she was on her feet. She moved to the middle of the room, where her robe had fallen, and put it on, belting it around her waist. Then she turned to him, standing over him where he lay naked on the bed, his head pillowed in his hands as he watched her.

"I'm not his daughter," she said. "I'm his wife."

Phyllis was just getting into bed when she heard the telephone ring in Jessica's room. The first few days after Jessica was expected back from the Cape it rang often. Once or twice she answered it, even though she knew when she picked it up that she would have to confess that she didn't know where her daughter was or when she would be back. Most of the time, though, she just let it ring. The calls dwindled and then stopped. Sometimes Phyllis wondered if Jessica was in contact with any of her friends or what, for that matter, they knew about her whereabouts.

Tonight, though, because the ringing startled her, because it was so late, and because she was alone, she felt a sudden impulse to talk to whoever wanted to talk to her daughter. She darted across the bedroom and ran, naked, to Jessica's room, where she lunged for the phone. "Yes?" she said.

There was silence, and then a girl's voice said, "Oh. Mrs. Blaine. I guess Jessica's not there, is she?"

Phyllis recognized Amy Laidlaw's voice. She had always sounded younger than Jessica's other friends, and tonight she sounded even younger still, like a child.

"Amy, do you know where she is?" Phyllis asked.

"No," Amy said. "But she calls you, doesn't she? Could you ask her to call me?"

For some reason Phyllis was suddenly and acutely aware of her nakedness, as though there were something obscene about standing here in her daughter's room like this. She dropped her hand to cover the wispy triangle of sand-colored pubic hair, inexplicably arousing herself with the light touch of her fingertips brushing her hair, lighter than the touch of any man.

"Once in a while she calls," Phyllis confessed, making a focused effort to keep her sudden confusion from revealing itself in her voice. The calls from Jessica were all brief. Just to say hello and that she was fine. She never stayed on the line long enough for Phyllis to ask any questions. "I'll be glad to give her the message," Phyllis said. "Are you home?"

Amy gave a number with a 207 area code. That would be Maine. So she was with her father. Phyllis remembered Jessica telling her that Winston Laidlaw refused to let his wife have the Maine house. "As though she wanted it," Jessica had said, but didn't elaborate. What Phyllis couldn't remember at the moment was the last time she had seen her own daughter naked. Sometime in her early teens, it seemed, the girl had become intensely fastidious about showing herself. Once, when Jessica was fourteen or fifteen, Phyllis walked in on her in the bathroom when she was drying herself after a bath, one foot up on the toilet seat, one heavy, dangling breast flattened against her leg as she bent forward, drying her calf with the towel. She turned away quickly, wrapping the towel around herself, and Phyllis laughed and said, "You don't have to be shy, Jessica. I would have killed for breasts like yours when I was your age."

She saw her daughter's shoulders turn scarlet, and after that she heard the turning of the lock whenever Jessica took her bath. (And yet, she remembered only now, puzzled by the paradox, Jessica swam nude in the Bedford Hills pool until Jeffrey put a stop to it.)

Heavens, Phyllis thought, *why am I thinking about this nonsense now?*

"I'm sorry," she said aloud. "Could you give me that number again?"

She found a ballpoint pen and a piece of paper in the table by Jessica's bed. Amy repeated the number. "Please," she said, "you won't forget to tell her."

Her voice sounded so small and plaintive that Phyllis asked her if she was all right.

"Yeah, I'm fine," Amy said. "I am. Really."

Phyllis looked at herself in the mirror after she hung up the phone. She touched herself again, this time on purpose, this time to finish what she had started by accident. She watched in the mirror as her finger slid between her lips. In her mind she heard the word *cunt* and in her mind it was Eddie Vincenzo's voice, even though she could only vaguely remember what his voice sounded like, a word or two as they were introduced at the birthday party, just enough to shape a permanent memory of that crude Bronx accent, the *d*'s and the *t*'s so heavily dentalized. He was saying the word to Jessica, whispering it in her ear, praising her cunt, praising the softness of her cunt, praising the strength of it.

Jeffrey had no words for his wife's sex. *You,* he would say. *You feel good,* he'd say. *Oh, you're wet,* he'd say. *Let me play with you.* In his mind, no doubt, he was avoiding offense, but in the end it seemed as though he made no distinction between Phyllis Armstrong Blaine and those few square inches of moist flesh between her legs.

Fuck you, Jeffrey Blaine, she thought. *Fuck you.*

Chet Fiore got out of bed and showered quickly, washing the smell of her off him. He had just buttoned his pants and taken a fresh shirt from the closet when he heard the sound of a car engine outside, something powerful, humming like a truck. He heard the wheels grinding slowly along the gravel of the drive. Outside lights came on, which he correctly assumed were part of Bolling's security system. He heard the car door and then a house door and then eager but indistinct voices squabbling in Spanish. He thought he heard footsteps inside the house and then Bolling's voice. He slipped on his shoes and walked to the door, opening it just as Blaine opened the door opposite.

Clint Bolling hadn't been expecting any visitors. When the motion sensors along the front drive detected the four-by-four approaching the house, a red light flashed in the east-wing room where Miguel, the gardener, handyman, and general-purpose security guard, slept. When the sensors continued to receive input after fifteen seconds, a buzzer sounded next to Miguel's bed. Bolling had been asleep and didn't hear the car come up, but when the outside lights came on, he became aware of them in a dreamlike sort of way. He stirred and felt Rachel's reassuring presence in the bed beside him, and knew somehow that she hadn't been there long. But that didn't matter. It wasn't unusual for her to come and go in the night. She was often restless at night, not coming to bed until dawn, spending the night reading or painting—she had a studio in the east wing—or writing endless letters to her three sisters in Mexico City, Vera Cruz, and San Vittoria. Even after sex she often got out of bed to spend the hours of darkness by herself.

She didn't bother to pretend she was asleep. "What is it?" she asked in a whisper.

"Just the alarm," he said. "Miguel will take care of it."

He reached under the covers and put a hand on her thigh. Her legs were like steel. When he met her two years ago, when he married her a month and a half later, she had been a bit on the plump side, full-breasted, full-hipped, voluptuous. Her endless swimming had done wonders for her body, but in truth he preferred her the way she had been. Every ounce of muscle she added made him feel that much older.

"I like your hands," she said. "You have nice hands."

He was about to answer with a kiss when he heard Miguel's voice outside. He propped himself up on his elbows to listen. Despite the open window—on the hottest as well as on the coldest nights Bolling slept with at least one window open—he couldn't make out the words, but he was reasonably certain Miguel wasn't the sort of man to engage in conversation with a stray buffalo.

He got out of bed and slipped on a pair of jeans and his boots. "Let me check this out," he said. "Stay here."

When he got to the front door he found Miguel aiming a shotgun at the chest of Rafael Ordoñez, a surly, muscular man who wore two handguns in shoulder holsters openly displayed outside his shirt. Miguel knew perfectly well what business this man came on although he had never been told, for what could such a man be except a drug dealer?

"Where is he? Get him out here," Ordoñez mumbled with his usual rudeness. "I didn't drag my tired ass all the way out here to go back with what I came with."

He wasn't in the least intimidated by Miguel's shotgun.

Bolling stepped forward quickly, before the confrontation in front of him ended in a show of force Miguel couldn't possibly win, even with a shotgun.

"What the hell are you doing here?" he asked.

"Your help's getting out of line," Ordoñez snarled. "I brought you the stuff."

"He's got a name, he's not out of line, and I didn't order any 'stuff,'" Bolling said.

Ordoñez looked down at his lizard-skin boots. "Yeah, you did," he said.

"I'm afraid there's been a mistake," Bolling said.

"Hey, amigo, nothing to be afraid of. I give you the shit, you give me thirty grand. That's what I was told to do, that's what I'm gonna do."

Rafael Ordoñez was a highly paid and ostentatiously visible mule who worked for a Jew in Oklahoma City who in turn operated under the protection of an organized crime family headquartered in Tulsa. Their connections into the local police departments, sheriffs' offices, and even state police command posts in Oklahoma and northern Texas were so secure and so pervasive that Ordoñez could afford to advertise his trade as publicly as he did.

"You go back and tell that little hymie you work for I don't want to see your ugly face around here unless I call him and ask him to send you," Bolling said.

"He says you did."

"No, that was me."

The voice came from behind Bolling. Fiore's voice. He was standing in the front door. He posed there for a moment to let the impact of his unexpected appearance register, and then he strolled down the two steps from the deck and across the walkway to join the others. The banker was right behind him. Miguel stood only a few paces away, his shotgun still nervously at the ready.

"Who the fuck are you?" Ordoñez asked.

"That's none of your business, is it?" Fiore said. "Are you going to get the stuff or do I have to climb up there and get it myself?"

He stepped past the two men to the four-by-four and reached for the handle of the rear door on the passenger side.

"Get your fucking hands off my wheels," Ordoñez snapped.

Fiore had turned his back to them when he reached for the door, and now, when he turned to face them, he had a gun in his hand, a small-caliber automatic pistol. In New York he never carried a weapon. He always had people around him who did that for him. And he hadn't brought this one with him from New York. It had been delivered to him at the Will Rogers Airport while he was waiting for Blaine and Bolling to arrive.

"I take it that means you're going to get the stuff yourself," he said.

He opened the door and held it open for Ordoñez, who came forward warily. It is not normally a part of human nature to walk toward the open end of a gun that is pointed at one's breastbone.

Fiore didn't move aside because he didn't want to lose sight of what Ordoñez was doing with his hands when he reached into the vehicle. This meant that the drug dealer had to sidle past him, practically bumping up against him to get to the door. If Ordoñez had been dealing with a lesser man, he might have thrown a shoulder into him and made a play for his gun. But something told him this gringo knew how to use that thing in his hand and wouldn't be reluctant to do so. Something told him he was being suckered into exactly such a move, which was reason enough not to do it.

There was a plastic picnic cooler on the back seat. Ordoñez

removed the top and came out with a small package tightly wrapped with the dark green plastic of a standard garbage bag. It was a bit smaller in all dimensions than a conventional fireplace brick.

"Good," Fiore said. "Now what do you say we all go inside where we can talk?"

The meeting adjourned to a library in the west wing of the house. Fiore put his gun away. Miguel stationed himself at the door with his shotgun, feeling far more confident after having seen the stranger in the tailored shirt force Ordoñez to do his bidding.

"Somebody mind telling me what the hell is going on?" Bolling asked, directing the question to Fiore.

But it was the banker who answered.

"I would have thought," Jeffrey said, "that a man's relationship with his narcotics supplier had to be confidential. It should be, don't you think? Because that's an area where you're very vulnerable."

Bolling looked at him guardedly. He was beginning to understand the subtle but rather appalling message he was being sent. "Go on," he said.

"No, that's all," Jeffrey said. "Just a simple observation."

"What's the point?" Bolling sneered. "That one guinea can pick up the phone and call another guinea who calls a Jew who calls this punk?"

"Something like that," Jeffrey agreed. "It's interesting, don't you think, the way these guineas help each other out from one end of the country to the other? I guess that's why they call it organized crime."

Bolling didn't say anything.

Jeffrey said, "You've got a very dangerous habit. You ought to consider giving it up."

"I'll consider it."

"That gives you a lot to consider tonight."

Fiore hadn't expected a performance like this from Blaine. It was Blaine's idea to reach out to Bolling's coke connection. It was Blaine's idea to demonstrate that being two thousand miles away in Oklahoma didn't get Bolling very far away at all. He came up with the ideas and now he was handling the scene all by himself. Christ. It was hard to square this with the guy who needed someone to pull his balls out of the fire the night of his kid's birthday party. One way or another, he could see already, he was going to have his hands full with this guy.

Bolling's eyes narrowed. Earlier in the evening he had made up his mind that he wasn't going to accept their offer. The illegality of it was just about the only aspect of the whole thing that appealed to him. Maybe it would do something to bring back the wildcatter's thrill he hadn't felt in years as his business flourished beyond anything he had ever imagined. But he had a rule that said that anything he got involved in had to be on his own terms, and that wasn't in the cards with any proposal brought to him by Jeffrey Blaine and the slick dago he was working for.

Now he realized that turning them down wasn't an option.

Unless he didn't mind ending up dead on the bathroom floor with a coke spoon in his hand.

The house in Belfast, Maine, was old and square, three stories tall, fastened to a rock that loomed over the ocean like a dark lighthouse. Amy hated the house and had always hated it, not just because the ocean below it was so cold and hostile, not just because it was an austere, unfriendly place, like something out of Hawthorne or Stephen King, but because her parents had never spent so much as a single happy weekend there, even in those summers, so hard to remember now, that always began with a wan and forlorn hope that their marriage would mend itself.

From infancy through the sixth grade Amy had come here every summer with her mother, leaving New York with all the joy of two civilians packed off to an internment camp by an occupying army. Two or three times one of her little school friends came up to visit for a week or so, flying up with her father, who visited on weekends. But all of them hated the place as much as Amy did and none of them ever came a second time. One Wednesday, during the summer Amy turned eleven, her mother called for a taxi that took them to the train station. She didn't lock the doors on her way out, or even close them. She left half a dozen lights on. After an endless train ride with a thousand stops to Boston and a thousand more to New York, mother and daughter arrived home well after midnight, where they received a chilly reception. Two months later, the week before Labor Day officially ended the summer, her parents were officially filing for divorce. Amy hadn't been back to Maine since.

Until this summer.

Her father spent his time on the telephone conducting business while Amy passed her days either on the porch overlooking the water or in her room, where only the sound of the waves dulled her father's high-pitched, obstreperous voice. Sometimes he cooked dinner, sometimes she did. They shopped together for food because, as he hinted more than once, he was afraid she might debauch herself with one of the bag boys at the supermarket if he let her go into town by herself.

In the evenings they played board games. She knew that she was going out of her mind.

Weary. Stale. Flat. Unprofitable. Hamlet said. Hamlet wished that his *too too solid flesh would melt thaw resolve itself into a dew.* Not dew. *A* dew. Why *a* dew?

So that you could tell the dew that used to be him from the rest of the dew. That was a beautiful thought. Not mixing with everything else. Still himself.

A note said that in the second quarto the word is *sullied,* not *solid.* O that this too too sullied flesh would melt. *Sullied* means dirty.

That made sense, too. That made a lot of sense.

Keats, who knew that he was dying, wrote, *I have been half in love with easeful death.*

Amy called Jessica but Jessica wasn't home. Mrs. Blaine sounded confused. She didn't know where Jessica was. But that was nice for Jessica because there is something warm and snuggly, as cozy as a secret, about no one knowing where you are.

Amy smiled when she thought about that. She imagined Jessica all curled in on herself.

She was still smiling when she fell asleep because she knew that the sun would come up very soon and she wanted it to be light when it happened. She knew she would feel the sun on her closed eyelids and she would wake up. *But look, the morn, in russet mantle clad, walks o'er the dew of yon high eastward hill.* That was from *Hamlet,* too. In Maine the sun came up out of the sea, not over a hill, but still the lines were perfect. They had *dew* in them again, the dew that Hamlet is going to become.

She walked out to the edge of the rock and looked down at the ocean.

Which looked so cold and inviting that she didn't even have to think about it before she dove in.

15

The next time Jessica called home she was more talkative than she had been all summer. She told her mother she had gone to a Kinko's and used one of the store's computers to get onto Yale's Web page. She registered for all her classes online.

Phyllis could scarcely conceal her excitement. All summer catalogues and letters from the college had been piling up with no one to answer them. This phone call was the first time she was able to feel confident that Jessica would be coming home and would be going to school. It all sounded so *normal* it made it easy to forget for a minute that her daughter had become, in fact, virtually a stranger.

Phyllis forgot to give her Amy's message until the two of them had said good-bye. She remembered as she was hanging up the phone and shouted Jessica's name. Twice, three times.

"Yeah? What?" Jessica said, putting the phone back to her ear, annoyance in her voice.

"I almost forgot," Phyllis apologized. "Amy Laidlaw called a few days ago. She wants you to call her. She sounded like it was important."

Of the four inseparable friends, Amy and Jessica were closest. Still, all Jessica said was, "Yeah, all right," and she said it in a tone that left some doubt that she would call.

"She's not home, she's in Maine."

Phyllis gave her the number.

That night Jessica took her mother's breath away, and her father's, too, walking into the apartment as if it was the most normal thing in the world, as if she had just gone out a half hour ago for a slice of pizza. Phyllis and Jeffrey were sitting in the living room with guests when it happened. She just leaned in through the doorway and said, "Hi, I'm home," and then disappeared in the direction of her bedroom.

They were both on their feet at once. As soon as Jeffrey came home that evening, Phyllis told him about her phone call from Jessica and they both agreed that it seemed to mean she was planning on being back in time for school. They certainly didn't expect her to show up the very same day.

"Our daughter's been away," Jeffrey said. "You'll have to excuse us."

The guests, Chloe and Bill Todd, smiled and said they understood perfectly, although Phyllis could tell from the way Chloe glanced over to her husband that she really didn't understand at all.

Phyllis hurried back to Jessica's room while Jeffrey saw them to the door.

"Let me look at you," she cooed enthusiastically as she came through the door Jessica had left open.

Jessica turned around and seemed almost to strike a pose, putting herself on display for inspection, turning her head to the side, holding her arms out in a way that seemed to mock the moment.

Phyllis stopped right there, not quite sure anymore that she was supposed to rush forward and give her daughter a hug. She wanted to, but she also wanted Jessica to rush to her. Posing like that, making a joke out of it, Jessica seemed to be saying that she didn't want an emotional scene.

Well, Phyllis thought, she was certainly well tanned. Her hair was wild and ruined, but that was to be expected. "Oh, honey, I am so glad to see you," she said.

Jeffrey knocked on the open door and stepped in. Jessica had spent the long flight from Las Vegas dreading this moment.

"Welcome home, baby," her father said.

He noticed the bruise on her cheek, a faded circle of discoloration, when she turned to face him, but before he could say anything about it, Jessica took a deep breath and said, "Amy's dead. Her funeral is tomorrow. I think you and Mom ought to go."

Her face looked like a stone mask, rigid and emotionless. Her eyes were locked on her father's, but when he took a step toward her, all the muscles of her body seemed to melt at once and she fell into her mother's arms and let her mother hold her while she cried. All that was left for Jeffrey was a superfluous hand lying on her shoulder, offering little consolation.

The service was held at a Presbyterian church on Broad Street at the very southern tip of Manhattan, barely a block and a half from Winston Laidlaw's office. It wasn't the family church, to the extent that the family had a church at all. They weren't even Presbyterians. Their only connection with the Broad Street church, if you could call it a connection, was that Winston Laidlaw married his second wife there, a marriage that ended bitterly about two weeks short of its first anniversary.

"For god's sake, Winston, she was never there in her life," Carla Laidlaw pleaded when she was told of the arrangements. "Why does she have to be buried out of a church where she's a complete stranger?"

Grace Tunney was waiting on the sidewalk for Jessica when Martin dropped her off with her parents in front of the church. The two girls ran to each other and hugged each other and cried together on the sidewalk while mourners filed in around them.

As he stood at the curb with Phyllis, giving the girls room for their grief, Jeffrey realized that his daughter was eighteen years old and until this moment had known nothing at all about death. His parents were both still alive. Phyllis's father died when Jess was just ten, old enough to understand, perhaps, except that he had been so vacant and diminished the last three years of his life that Jessica, like Phyllis herself for that matter, seemed hardly conscious of a loss. Amy's death was different. It was real.

Grace said, "Her mom called me last night. Yesterday. No, it was at night. She asked me to say something at the service. She thought it should be you but she didn't know where you were, none of us knew where you were, she didn't know you were going to be here. I can do it, I guess, but it really should be you."

Jessica said, "Yes."

She hadn't slept all night, or if she had slept, it was so fitfully that she wasn't aware of drifting into sleep or drifting back to wakefulness. She watched the numbers on the clock by her bed change, and it seemed to her she had seen them all. Before going to bed she spent what felt like hours with her parents, the three of them sitting together in the kitchen enveloped in a large and aching silence. Phyllis asked at one point how Amy died, and Jessica looked at her with burning red eyes before she said, "She killed herself. All right?"

Jeffrey and Phyllis had both known that would be the answer, which is why Jeffrey hadn't asked and hoped Phyllis wouldn't ask either. He didn't want to hear her say it, and when she did, the words went through him with the sharpness of a physical pain. He was, in a way, almost as innocent of death as his daughter, certainly of death like this, without disease, without accident, without any of those mindless workings of fate that were the hallmark of every form of death he knew. There was intention here, not accident. Intention on Amy's part, of course. But her father, too, had willed her death, and before that Fiore, and even Jeffrey himself. The chain stretched back through a handful of choices and abdications of choice, reaching back to the night of Jessica's party and forward to—where?

The end of the chain wasn't in sight, but as Jeffrey sat with his wife and daughter in the silence of the night kitchen, and again now as he stood on a sidewalk outside the ancient stone church, he saw with devastating clarity that if tiny Amy Laidlaw's death was the first fatality to grow out of his connection to Chet Fiore, it wasn't going to be the last. And he saw, as clearly as one sees one's own reflection in a mirror, that once he accepted this fact—and there was no choice in the matter, accepting or not accepting—then any alteration of the course he had chosen for himself became irrelevant.

Jessica knew already, without even having to think about it, the kinds of things she wanted to say. *We all loved Amy,* she wanted to say. *We just didn't love her enough. She was hurt so badly these last few months. She called me, and by the time I called her back she was gone. Maybe if I was less caught up in my own life, maybe if I loved her more . . . Maybe if her father eased up on her a little, if he let go of his own indignation and held her up and gave her strength when she needed it . . . Maybe if her mother just said, "Amy, stay with me, lean on me, we'll fight this thing . . ." None of us did any of the things that had to be done to save her. So let's not make this pretty and gentle, let's not let ourselves off with sad thoughts about a beautiful flower that wilted early, because that's just a load of crap and we all know it. Everybody says we're here to think about Amy, but let's not think about Amy. As though she was in this thing all by herself. Let's think about ourselves. Because we're the reason we're all here now.*

She took her place in the church, sitting with her friends, filled with bitterness, her eyes locked on the casket in front of the pulpit. Her parents slipped into a pew a few rows back. Carla Laidlaw sat with her own family, two brothers it seemed, judging from the resemblance, and their wives. The minister ascended to the pulpit and commenced to deliver one of those awful eulogies compiled out of carelessly gathered notes. Not of word of it sounded like it had anything to do with Amy. The restlessness in the congregation spread like fog, and then like water, visible and then audible as his voice droned on, a slither of dresses, a slither of suits, a slither of shoes sliding on the worn wood floor.

"I think at this time," he said at last, gathering all the wandered attention back to him, "it would be appropriate to hear something from Amy's friends. Because friendship was so important a part of Amy's life." He looked down at his notes and said, "Jessica Blaine was close to Amy and she'd like to share some thoughts with us. Jessica."

As Jeffrey watched his daughter rise from her seat and move into the aisle, he was filled with an immense pride that she, of all those here, had been chosen to say what needed saying. She had no patience with pretense or abstraction, with china coffee cups in the back seat of a car, no patience for things that weren't true or didn't matter. She would scandalize everyone here if she was moved to do so, and he could see in the set of her shoulders as she started toward the pulpit that she was moved to do exactly that. Whatever her faults—rebellion and self-absorption and willful blindness when it suited her—compromise wasn't one of them. For Jeffrey, on the other hand, compromise was both his strength and his weakness as well as the center of his being, and he thought with a feeling almost like joy how good it was that his daughter wasn't like him in that.

His eyes were fixed so intently on his daughter that he didn't see Winston Laidlaw get up from his seat, didn't see him moving toward her until he was practically in front of her only a foot or two to the right of the gleaming casket. The man's face was a shocking scarlet, so lurid it seemed for a moment that a seizure wouldn't be out of the question. He hissed some words at Jessica through tightly clenched teeth, his voice so low that Jeffrey, only a few rows back, didn't hear a thing even in the stillness of the church. But those in the first and second rows obviously heard because they turned and looked at one another, and they were troubled looks.

Jeffrey rose and felt Phyllis's hand on his arm. He looked down at her. "Please," she said, an inaudible but intense whisper.

He glanced back at Jessica and saw Carla Laidlaw hurrying toward her ex-husband. "I asked her to speak," she said, and her voice carried through the church with remarkable urgency.

Laidlaw said, "Go sit down. Both of you."

Jeffrey didn't hear what Jessica said, but when Laidlaw put a hand on her, Phyllis's plea didn't matter anymore. He strode quickly down the aisle while Phyllis clasped both hands over her face, dreading the scene that she knew was inevitable now.

Even before Jeffrey reached the three of them, Laidlaw whirled toward him. "Get out of here, Blaine, and take her with you," he roared, no longer interested in preserving even a semblance of propriety.

Jessica turned to look at her father, with Laidlaw's fingers biting painfully into her upper arm. How, she actually wondered, was her father capable of summoning such glacial calm at a time like this?

In fact, for Jeffrey it wasn't like that at all. His calmness required no effort on his part, seemed almost literally to descend on him in response to the tension of those around him. "Please take your hand off her," he said.

Laidlaw tightened his grip. Jessica winced and raised her arm to relieve the pressure, and for a moment she was certain that in another second the two men would be fighting right there in the church. Carla Laidlaw said, "For god's sake, Winston."

"Just get her out of here, get out of here," Laidlaw growled. "A little decency, Blaine. This is a family thing."

"Your wife asked her to speak," Jeffrey said. "And I asked you to take your hand off my daughter."

The minister took a few steps toward them from the height of the pulpit and then a few steps back, confused and indecisive.

With sudden and unexpected violence, Laidlaw flung Jessica toward her father as though she were a small thing. The heel of his hand rammed into the small of her back, shoving her forward as she lurched awkwardly in the space between them. Jeffrey caught her, unnecessarily, as she righted herself.

"She'd be alive if it wasn't for you," Laidlaw screamed, "you and your tramp daughter."

The words hit Jeffrey like a blow and Jessica like something worse than a blow, as though something wet and lifeless and disgusting had been slung in her face. But where Jeffrey's expression didn't change in the slightest, Jessica turned pale and her whole body trembled like someone in a high and dangerous fever.

"That's not true," she gasped. "It isn't true." In an instant so brief and so intense it barely registered in her consciousness at all, registered only as a moment of sickening confusion, she felt as though she were Amy plunging toward the cold, hard wetness of the rocks and ocean far below, lucid, almost serene in her awareness of the perfection of her escape from this man. "She was afraid of you, afraid of going to you," she said, remembering her last intimate conversation with her friend, the two of them sitting on the bed in the low-ceilinged bedroom on the Cape.

Laidlaw lurched forward a stride and his hand flashed out, open-palmed, but Jeffrey, reacting almost before it actually happened, reached up and caught the man's wrist. His mind ratcheted back a few months, as though this were a scene he was seeing for the second time, except that in the earlier time it was his own hand being caught, not exactly like this, from behind.

Jessica turned and bolted away from them, the hard soles of her shoes ringing on the hard wood floor as she raced up the aisle. She slung open the doors, letting in a wave of sunlight, and disappeared into it.

All through the church people were crying as bitterly as though they had just learned at this moment that Amy was dead, crying and wailing, something almost biblical in the ostentation of their grief and confusion. And the minister was babbling ineffectually into his microphone, his words voiceless and unnatural, floating down to them from speakers mounted high above the pulpit, something about reconciliation and forgiveness and god's mercy.

Jeffrey realized that at some point while Jessica was still racing through the church, he had released Laidlaw's hand.

"She's telling you the truth," he said, because he knew with as clear a certainty as if he had spoken with Amy himself that his daughter couldn't possibly be wrong about something like this. "If you can't live with it, god knows I wouldn't blame you."

The minister talked about hope and compassion and the healing of god's hand as Jeffrey turned and followed his daughter's path up the aisle, calm in the knowledge that he was ready to bear his own part of this particular burden.

Phyllis joined him in the aisle and walked with him out of the church, followed by more words from the minister about the wisdom and forgiveness and inscrutable ways of a god who, in the final analysis, had had nothing to do with any of this.

Jeffrey was lying when he told Clint Bolling there would be other investors in the scheme. He said it because it would help secure the Oklahoman's cooperation but he had no intention of involving anyone else in his plan. The more people who knew what was going on, the more dangerous it would be, and Jeffrey had no intention of running any more than the absolute minimum of personal risk. Indeed, once the working plans were all in place, he wouldn't need even Bolling's cooperation. But for the time being, until he was sure the system would perform the way he meant it to, until all the bugs were worked out, he needed a silent partner who could be counted on to keep quiet if any irregularities appeared in his investment accounts.

The first order of business after returning from Oklahoma was to find someone inside Layne Bentley to do the computer work that needed to be done. Finding the right man involved a search through the firm's personnel files. He couldn't examine them during business hours without raising questions about whom he was recruiting and for what purpose. But he had already established the practice of going in late, so no one would ask questions if he continued to do so.

He spent the hours until the traders left for the night meticulously charting the movements of prices from one night's closing to the next. He sorted and resorted them until he had the optimum arrangement for his purposes. He felt like a man who can suddenly see through walls, look into people's minds, visit the future at will, and come back at will. He knew, of course, that these powers were an illusion. He could see into the future because he had discovered a trick that allowed him to transform the past into the present whenever he needed to do so. The thrill, he realized, was in the illegality itself, in the magnitude of the crime he was committing. Anything less brazen would have been merely clever. It still would have been what management classes at school called "thinking inside the box." Jeffrey was out of the box. He had soared clear of the gravitational pull of all planets and systems. He was weightless and free.

When the office was finally empty, he would make his way to the records room and pull out an armful of personnel files. He took them back to his office and lit a cigar as he began to study them. Sometimes, when he had done as much of this research as he cared to do for the night, he went to Elaine's instead of going home.

There was no night doorman. He rang the bell and she buzzed him in without even asking who was there. Upstairs, her door was open and she had gone back to bed. He joined her there. There was a desperate intensity to her lovemaking that he had never experienced with any woman. And he hadn't failed to notice that having a lover in the U.S. Attorney's Office might come in handy if his involvement with Fiore ever began to unravel. He had heard once that a good burglar always locates the back door before he begins his search of an apartment so that he knows how to get out in case anyone comes home. He doubted it would come to that, but if it did, he would give them the gangster.

When Elaine's alarm went off in the morning, she found the bed empty. He always made it home before Phyllis woke. If she knew what time he came in, she never said anything about it.

The routine continued night after night as he searched the personnel files. He was looking for someone who knew the software system inside and out. More than that, he wanted to be able to read greed and ambition in the man's file.

The file of a young man named Gabriel Enriquez fascinated him from the moment he started reading it and he kept coming back to it night after night. Enriquez was the son of formerly wealthy Cuban refugees. His father had been an eminent surgeon in Havana, his mother an interior decorator whose client list included the best families on the island. The couple stayed on in Cuba after Castro took power. It wasn't until after the Bay of Pigs invasion in 1960 that they fled to Florida in a sixteen-foot fishing boat. Apparently they had had children in Cuba and apparently these children, if they were still alive in 1960, remained behind. According to an autobiographical memorandum included in the file, Gabriel Enriquez himself didn't know the fate of these brothers or sisters, didn't know even how many of them there had been. In Miami Enriquez's father found work as a limo driver. If his mother worked at all, there was no record of it. Dr. Enriquez was over fifty, his wife forty-five, when they embarked on a second family, first a girl and then, a year and a half later, Gabriel.

It wasn't merely the family history, with its legacy of expropriation and resentment, that interested Jeffrey. At seventeen Gabriel left his mother, father, and sister in Miami to attend Columbia College on a scholarship. He graduated near the top of his class and then earned an MBA from Wharton before going to work on the trading floor at First Boston. He stayed there less than a year, went back to school for a second master's degree, this one from NYU with a concentration in advanced mathematics and computer sciences. What especially piqued Jeffrey's curiosity was the timing of the young man's departure from First Boston. He left in March although he didn't begin his studies at NYU until the following September, which suggested that he hadn't quit to go back to school. One would have to guess he was fired, and one would also have to guess that the reason for the firing had been expunged from the First Boston records or Layne Bentley never would have hired him.

When Jeffrey went to look for Enriquez in the small suite of offices where the firm's internal computer programs were written, he found a dramatically handsome young man an inch or two over six feet tall, with ink-black eyes and ink-black hair that fell well below the soft collar of his open shirt. He was the only member of the software division in pressed slacks rather than jeans. Jeffrey introduced himself and invited Enriquez to be his guest for dinner at the Yale Club that evening. "That is, if you're free tonight," he added.

Enriquez pondered the invitation a moment, as though there were some aspect of the proposition he didn't quite understand or trust. His voice was surprisingly soft, unaccented but with the faintest trace of Spanish in the gentle rhythm of his speech when he said, "No, I am free, quite free. What time?"

"Seven," Jeffrey said.

Enriquez nodded his approval. He didn't ask any questions about the purpose of this meeting, although it was clear that his lack of curiosity wasn't due to shyness. On the contrary, there was an almost impudent directness in the way he looked straight into Jeffrey's eyes.

"I'll see you at seven," Jeffrey said, and then added, "They require jackets and ties."

Gaetano Falcone was not a patient man but it was a hard-and-fast rule with him that he never under any circumstances let his impatience show. He tended to smile when he was angry and to appear calm when he was agitated, and so now he leaned back on the soft, overstuffed couch and put his stockinged feet up on the coffee table, crossing his ankles. His hands were folded almost beatifically across his gut, but Chet Fiore knew the old man well enough to recognize the signs. He had no illusions about his standing with Mr. Falcone because he knew how dangerous illusions can be. He was like a son to Mr. Falcone, but in fact the old man had a son with whom he hadn't spoken in years.

Fiore let his fingers curl around the dark, heavy ceramic of his coffee mug, so thick he could scarcely feel the warmth, and waited for Mr. Falcone to speak.

"You're going to have to tell me, Charles," Falcone said softly, in the tone of a man speaking on matters of no consequence, "why is this taking so long?"

"Is it?" Fiore asked with his most boyish smile. "Considering what we're asking for, I don't think it's taking long at all."

"It's proceeding? This is what you're telling me?"

"Of course it's proceeding," Fiore said.

Falcone studied his fingernails a moment. He had been working in his garden. It always seemed strange to him that the earth should be called *dirt* because, in fact, there were few things cleaner than the soil. Everything came from the soil.

"This banker is cooperating with you?"

"He is."

"You put a little pressure on him? Through his family? That's my understanding."

"There's no pressure anymore, Mr. Falcone," Fiore said. "There was. It's been removed."

One hand rose from the man's ample belly and a finger waggled back and forth in warning. "In that case, I advise you to be careful," Falcone said. "There are few things more dangerous than an honest man when he puts his honesty aside."

Gabriel Enriquez was waiting on the sidewalk on Vanderbilt Avenue when Jeffrey's car pulled to the curb a few minutes after seven. Jeffrey told Martin he wouldn't be needing him before nine. The car, though, remained at the curb while Jeffrey crossed the sidewalk to greet his guest, offering his hand. Enriquez was wearing a lime-green shirt under a Bill Blass blazer that looked to be a few years old, probably a relic of his days on the First Boston trading floor.

"Does he just sit there all night?" Enriquez asked, gesturing toward the car.

"I wouldn't know," Jeffrey said.

"Boring job."

"I don't pay him to be entertained."

Jeffrey had reserved one of the small dining rooms on the second floor, where the door could be closed for privacy. Although the room contained only a single table, it had its own well-stocked bar as well as its own sideboard for china, glassware, and silver. Albert, who had already been at the club for decades when Jeffrey started coming years ago, poured drinks while Gabriel Enriquez glanced quickly at the simple placard that served as the club's dinner menu. The date appeared at the top, with an explanatory legend under it reminding diners that the items listed below were available *in addition to the usual fare*. There were no prices and no indication of what the usual fare might be.

When a glass of scotch was set in front of the young man, he tossed his menu aside. "You're familiar with the place," he said. "I'll let you decide."

"No preferences?" Jeffrey asked.

"None."

"I suppose that's an admirable quality," Jeffrey said.

Enriquez smiled. He had large, even teeth. "It's not a philosophy, Mr. Blaine," he said. "It's simply a convenience."

Jeffrey ordered tossed salads, the confit of duck, and roast lamb with shallots for both of them. He wrote the orders on the small pad that lay beside his place setting and Albert claimed it the moment Jeffrey set down his pencil. "I'll be back presently, Mr. Blaine," he said, closing the door as he left.

"I'm surprised," Jeffrey began, "that you haven't asked me what this is about."

Gabriel shrugged his broad shoulders. "You'll tell me when you want to tell me," he said indifferently. "I assume that's what you're going to do now."

"And you weren't curious?"

"I didn't say that."

"I'm aware of what you didn't say. That's why I'm asking."

Gabriel reached for his whiskey glass and then changed his mind and took a sip of water instead. "Look," he said, "everything about this is like some kind of test. So you tell me, what's the right answer? If I don't ask you anything, I lack curiosity. If I start asking questions, I'm not a good soldier."

"And you want to be a good soldier."

"I *am* a good soldier."

"Good," Jeffrey said. "So far you're passing the test."

Gabriel's dark eyes looked back at him, patient and unsmiling. The young man was as prickly as a porcupine, which didn't make Jeffrey like him particularly but seemed to be a desirable quality for the purpose at hand.

"I've got a few more questions, if you don't mind," Jeffrey continued. "Why did you leave First Boston?"

The petulant, slightly amused annoyance that had characterized all of Gabriel's reactions to this point turned into something sharper, more like anger. "What the hell is this about?" he shot back immediately, even defiantly.

It was exactly the answer Jeffrey assumed he would get. If, that is, he had read the man correctly.

"What I am about to propose to you, Mr. Enriquez, is completely illegal. Before I make that proposal, I want to be sure you're the right man."

"I'm the right man," Gabriel said, without the slightest hesitation.

The door opened as Albert arrived with a large wooden salad bowl. Working at the sideboard, he tossed the salad with a pair of clumsy-looking wooden spoons, adding oil and vinegar as though he were baptizing the greens, then dusting it all with a few pinches of herbs he took from a small covered wooden bowl. He served out two portions, which he delivered to the table. There was enough salad left in the bowl for four more people. He offered them freshly ground pepper, left the pepper mill on the sideboard next to the salad bowl, and withdrew. "Thank you, Albert," Jeffrey said just before the door closed, the first words either man had spoken since the waiter came in.

"All right," Jeffrey said. "This part isn't a test. I don't want you to say anything. I want you to just listen."

Gabriel nodded his acquiescence, picked up his fork, and began to eat.

Jeffrey explained that he needed someone who could enter the company's computer to move investments from one fund to another as well as to manipulate investments within the individual funds, switching them when necessary from one account to another. The computer's timekeeping functions, which allowed it to automatically put time and date stamps on all transactions, would also have to be bypassed so that the surreptitious changes could be predated to the dates of the original transactions they replaced. All of this, Jeffrey said, was the easy part.

Gabriel raised an eyebrow and shrugged as though he were amused by Jeffrey's judgment about what was easy and what wasn't.

"Fine," Jeffrey conceded. "I don't know if it's easy or it isn't. And I don't care. The bottom line is this. I have no interest, none whatsoever, in anything you can do or claim you can do unless you can also provide me absolute assurance that you can do it in a way that leaves no trace of the original transactions."

Gabriel considered a moment and then nodded. He wasn't

committing himself, merely leaving open the possibility that it was doable.

"No trace of the records," Jeffrey repeated, "and no trace of the software program you use to do all this."

Gabriel nodded again, still waiting for his signal to respond. Jeffrey picked up his salad fork. "All right," he said. "You've heard the proposal. Say anything you want."

"Questions or statements?" Gabriel asked.

"Either."

"Question. Are we talking about embezzlement?"

"Is there a reason you need to know that?"

"If I get involved in something, I need to know what it is."

Jeffrey weighed the answer. He had intended to tell the young man as little as possible, but the idea seemed at the moment rather overwrought and melodramatic. Enriquez's question was a legitimate one. "No," Jeffrey said simply, "it's not embezzlement."

"Money laundering, then," Gabriel said matter-of-factly.

There was no hint of a question in his voice this time. He said it as though it were an obvious conclusion from the rather vague outline Jeffrey had presented to him. If it wasn't just a lucky guess—and Enriquez didn't strike him as the sort of man who made guesses—then there were only two other possibilities. Either it was the result of a remarkably quick analysis, for there were at least as many forms of fraud as there were legitimate transactions. Or Gabriel Enriquez had already been thinking about exactly the same sort of scheme himself.

Gabriel took Jeffrey's silence as a confirmation. "Statement," he said. "The company software has safety protocols built into it to prevent the kind of thing you're talking about. I wrote some of them myself and I know how the others work. They're surprisingly easy to get around. Kid stuff, really."

Jeffrey nodded.

"Statement," Gabriel continued. "There are paper records. They would have to be located and destroyed."

"They'll all be my accounts," Jeffrey said. "The paper records come to me."

"There isn't a master copy?"

"There is. It comes to me first."

"Then you don't have a problem there."

"Where do I have a problem?" Jeffrey asked.

"Queuing," the young man said. His explanation was detailed and technical. It had to do with the basic operating system of the computer that told it where to store new records on the system's data-storage media. "Think of an old-fashioned paper ledger book," Gabriel said. "Imagine on Thursday morning you want to go back and change something you entered on Tuesday. You carefully erase the numbers and the date, you change them so now it says the transaction didn't happen until Thursday. That's okay as far as it goes, but isn't that record going to look funny sitting there with Thursday's date in the middle of a page filled with things that happened on Tuesday?"

He held up a finger to forestall an interruption and went on with his lecture. "Now a computer isn't quite that simple but it isn't that much more complicated either. It puts new records in the first available space it finds. If you delete something, it doesn't really erase it. It just makes the space it was in available for other things. Do you have a computer at home?"

"Yes."

"Did you ever lose something and have to look through the disk to find it?"

"No."

"Well, if you did you'd find a terrible mess. Three items from your date book, half of one of your kid's homework assignments, one or two of your wife's recipes, the other half of the homework, some records from your checking account. If you sat down and typed in the Gettysburg Address, you'd find eighty-seven different things between *four score and seven* and *this hallowed ground*."

"Wouldn't that make it difficult for anyone to notice that records were out of order?"

"On your home computer it would," Gabriel agreed. "The trouble is the firm's software almost never deletes anything. You make a transaction, a record is created. You cancel the transaction, a new record is created recording the cancellation, but the old one isn't deleted. You see the problem?"

Jeffrey saw it. "Too much order, not enough chaos. Is there a solution?" he asked.

Gabriel finished his salad before answering the question. "Sure there is," he said. "We've got to provide our own chaos. I go in tonight and I create about a thousand files. Pure junk. Big ones, little ones. And then one by one I start erasing them. I keep adding, I keep deleting. Within a week, the records are going to be far too random for anyone to know when they were entered. Magic, isn't it?"

For the first time in weeks Jeffrey Blaine smiled because he felt like smiling. It *was* magic.

16

Wally Schliester liked wandering around the convention-hall floor when he had nothing better to do, which was most of the time. He liked gadgets and gizmos of all kinds. It was like visiting the Future Pavilion at the World's Fair every day, better in fact, because the exhibits were changing all the time, he didn't have to pay to get in, and he wore an ID badge on his breast pocket that made him seem like an important man at the Convention Center. Serving girls were always rushing up to him with hors d'oeuvres while he inspected television sets you could hang on the wall in a picture frame and barbecue grilles that lit themselves and put themselves out and told you when the steaks were done. He saw a clock that set itself every day, accurate to one-ten-thousandth of a second, and he wondered why anyone needed to know the time like that. He saw computers that took dictation and robots that would serve drinks at a party and then vacuum the room when the guests were gone. When he asked, he found out that some of the things he was looking at didn't really exist. The proprietors of the booths told him they were just prototypes, which meant something very scientific to them but to Schliester simply meant that these things were more or less like Pinocchio. Maybe they'd be real someday but they weren't real now.

Of all the things he saw, the one that stopped him dead in his tracks was a microphone so small you could practically wear it on your nose and still no one would see it. There was a poster-size blowup of an article from *Scientific American* at the front of the booth. Schliester stopped to talk to the guy manning the booth, who was a bodybuilder type from Encino, California. All the seams of his suit looked like they were being stretched.

"This thing really exists?" Schliester asked.

The man laughed and introduced himself. His name was Loren Bannion but his friends called him Banny, "like Manny with a *b*," he said, presenting his card. "You're looking at it. Of course it exists."

Schliester felt stupid for asking, since he obviously was looking at it. "I thought maybe it was a prototype," he said to get himself off the hook.

Banny shook his head. "It works on the same principle as a telescopic array," he explained in a geeky way that didn't match very well with his square, muscle-bound body.

Schliester didn't think he could call anyone Banny but he wanted to hear more. "What principle would that be?" he asked, getting over his shyness about pegging himself as an imbecile. It had probably been years since Loren Bannion had talked to anyone who didn't know what a telescopic array was.

"Radio telescopes," Banny said. "For picking up signals from deep space. For years they kept building the dishes bigger and bigger but there's only so big you can build them, right?"

Schliester nodded knowingly. It *seemed* right.

"Okay," Banny said, warming to the subject. "Then someone figured out that if you put a little dish here and a little dish there, like twenty miles away, and another one twenty miles beyond that, and you hook them all up, it's exactly the same thing or almost exactly the same thing as if you had one dish sixty miles across. Unimaginable. But it works. So now they've got these arrays stretched across the Andes and they've mapped the whole southern sky all the way out to Christ knows where. They're picking up signals from hundreds of millions of years ago."

"Ago?" He was losing Schliester again.

"Time, distance, it's the same thing," Banny said. "The further out in space you go, the further back in time."

Schliester was going to have to take his word for that part of it. "So you're telling me you can record something someone said yesterday?" he asked cautiously.

Bannion laughed. "That's good," he said. "I'll have to remember that one."

Apparently that hadn't been his point. Schliester laughed, too, to show that he enjoyed a good joke as well as the next man. "I'm sorry," he said. "I must have left my brains in my other suit. What does this have to do with microphones?"

"Yeah, right, okay, I got you," Bannion said. "The thing is, these single-cell microphones, they're virtually molecular but they're not very sensitive. I mean they tell you there was a sound but that's about it. On the other hand, you can string them together—arrays, see what I'm saying? You spread a couple thousand of them out on a desktop and all of a sudden the whole desktop is one gigantic, incredibly sensitive microphone that's going to pick up a mosquito's footsteps. Hey, you mind getting us a couple of those shrimp things?"

He pointed to where a young lady in a microskirt was working the crowd with an immense platter. She disappeared around the corner, down another aisle.

Schliester promised to be right back. He caught up with the girl just in time. Her plate was almost empty. "How about I put you out of business?" he said, helping himself to the last four shrimp and a little specimen cup of cocktail sauce.

"Oh, I'll get more," she said in a tone of earnest reassurance. She was a pretty little thing who obviously took her work seriously. That was nice to see.

Banny and Schliester divided up the shrimp. While they were eating, Banny whipped out a tape recorder, hit rewind, then play. Schliester heard himself saying *How about I put you out of business?* and the girl saying *Oh, I'll get more.*

"Jesus," Schliester gasped. "Where was the mike?"

Bannion plunged a couple of meaty fingers into the outer breast pocket of Schliester's suit coat and came out with the business card he had given Schliester only a few minutes before. He handed it over and Schliester held it up and studied it like a man looking for an image of the Holy Virgin in a stain on a tablecloth. As far as he could see, it was just a business card.

Bannion explained that the paper stock was embedded with hundreds of microscopic microphones, chained together with invisible wire and powered by the kind of metallic batteries used in something he called smart credit cards. A transmitter so thin and flexible it could be woven into the paper the way metal threads are woven into paper money completed the technology.

An hour and a half later Elaine Lester called on Mr. Bannion and presented her credentials. If these things were anything like she had been led to believe, she said without explaining who had led her to believe it, the U.S. Attorney's Office would be interested in testing the capabilities.

Bannion grinned and explained that he had some interesting hardware but the card-bug she was talking about wasn't on the market yet.

"But you have them?" she said.

He placed a call to the home office in Encino and he got the answer Elaine Lester wanted to hear. She signed a paper and he gave her three cards. The batteries were good for a month. They had Loren Bannion's name on them. She asked for blank cards instead and she got them.

Any printing process that didn't use heat could do the printing, he told her.

In the few weeks between Amy Laidlaw's funeral and the start of the fall term at Yale, Phyllis witnessed a major change in her daughter. She saw it in her eyes, which sometimes came to rest in odd and empty corners of the room. Not that she was sad or morose all the time. But the sadness was there, even when it was invisible. And with the sadness came a new recognition of her parents, an acceptance of them, perhaps because she needed them, perhaps simply because of their shared complicity in Amy's death. It made Phyllis feel closer to her daughter than she ever felt before.

On the other hand, this newfound intimacy between them put demands on Phyllis that she wasn't prepared to accept. It didn't make sense, because for years she had yearned for a relationship with her daughter that would be free and familiar, a fantasy of friendship and trust. But when it came it frightened her, and she realized that Jessica had been much easier to deal with at a distance. Missing her was better than being with her. The weeks between the funeral and the start of Jessica's freshman year dragged on like a torture for Phyllis.

She sat through the meeting of the New York City Ballet Outreach Committee, listening abstractedly to the presentation of proposals for bringing the art of the dance to public schools in the poorer parts of the city. Two dancers from the company had been invited to the meeting, a girl scarcely older than Jessica, stick thin, as flat-chested as a boy, and a muscular young man in a tight tank top that he wore like skin. Neither was particularly articulate, but they managed to convey some of the excitement of their visits to schools on the Lower East Side, in the Bronx, and in Spanish Harlem, where they staged demonstrations and then invited seventh and eighth graders to participate. They actually managed to convince at least a few young boys that there was nothing faggy about a job that consisted in significant part of holding and handling women's bodies.

Phyllis envied them. She couldn't remember a time when she had felt that kind of enthusiasm about anything. Certainly not now, and probably not at their age either.

She knew that Jeffrey would be at the office late, but after the meeting she took the precaution of phoning home and telling Carlos that she would be having dinner with friends. The cook should wait to make something for Mr. Blaine when he got home.

It was five o'clock when she left Lincoln Center but the sun was still high in the sky, bathing everything in warm, syrupy light. She decided to walk instead of taking a cab. She walked quickly, flowing past the dense streams of people on their way home from work. In her mind they were merely stray objects drifting in the flow of a wide and stately river, while she, with her long strides and the steady drumming of her heels on the pavement, was a sleek scull propelled swiftly forward by powerful strokes.

At the hotel, she took the elevator up to the fifteenth floor, not drawing her room key from her bag until she was at the door. She let herself in and poured herself a scotch from the bar that was kept locked next to the squatty little refrigerator in the room's comically inadequate kitchenette. She drank the scotch as she undressed and was naked by the time she finished it. She rinsed the glass, discarded the little single-shot bottle, and went to the bathroom to brush her teeth. Then she got in bed to wait.

She touched herself between her legs so that she would be ready for him when he came. But she was thinking about the girl dancer, who giggled nervously as she talked, shy no doubt about expressing herself other than with her body.

She closed her eyes and took a deep breath. She didn't know what time Jeffrey came in last night. She remembered waking up a little after one and he wasn't home. She knew he was having an affair and had known it for months, from the time she saw him reading a novel she knew he would never read. Years ago there were little clues like that, the first time it happened. Back then she used to cry every time he was out and she didn't know where he was. Now it was different. Because she didn't give a damn. It was hard to see just what men saw in sex that gave it so much importance. She enjoyed sex as much as anyone, she assumed, but not to the point of losing one's perspective.

As she lay on the stiff hotel sheets that smelled like hospital sheets, she thought of telling Jeffrey *I'll give up mine if you give up yours,* and wondered whether he would see the humor in the proposal. Yes, of course he would. Jeffrey had his faults, but an inability to be amused by life's more interesting ironies had never been one of them. Not until recently in any case. He seemed somehow to have changed over the last few months, distant from her, distant from himself. Certainly a new girlfriend could be the cause of the difference. Or the result. The thought made her question whether she had been changed by her affair in any way, but she couldn't see that she had.

It was a depressing thought. If she was still the same woman she had always been, then what exactly was the point of this whole complicated business?

Yale was like nothing Jessica had ever experienced. There was an intensity to everything that happened there, to everyone around her, that almost literally left her gasping for air. She was just barely managing to keep up. Her classmates argued passionately about absolutely everything, an interpretation of a few verses from Ezra Pound's *Cantos* or a chapter of *Bleak House*, an attitude about Freud or Marx or Woodrow Wilson. They argued about science and literature, music and history. They argued over beers at a local tavern called The Rectory and then continued the arguments until sunrise in their seedy little dormitory rooms with eighteenth-century plumbing and nineteenth-century wiring. Or was it the other way around? as the local joke went.

They were ironic about everything except themselves. They worked hard to create and preserve the myth that their lives had always been exactly what they were now. They wanted the world to believe, and came to believe themselves, that they had spent their high school years in a fever of intellectual excitement, because each of them knew that admitting anything else would have amounted to a confession that one was in some sense an impostor, that one didn't belong here.

It took Jessica almost a month to get up enough courage to ask her roommate Barbara, a lanky, athletic girl from Boulder, Colorado, "Do these kids seem as weird to you as they do to me?"

"Weird?" Barbara asked, guarded, as though she didn't want to commit herself until she had a clearer indication where this was going.

"Like they're not real," Jessica said.

Barbara took a long time before answering, weighing what was at stake in whatever answer she gave. But she liked this New York girl, who made friends easily but wrapped herself in a cocoon of silence that gave nothing away. If there was a sadness there, and

Barbara thought there was, it wasn't a sadness she imposed on those around her. She kept it to herself. And so Barbara decided to answer truthfully.

"Yeah," she said, and then added, with more emphasis, "It's like they're making themselves up. *I fake it, therefore I exist.*"

They laughed with delight at the secret that they alone, of all their classmates, saw through the charade, and at the sense of relief it brought them. It made it possible for them to lead double lives, delving as deeply as they cared to into freshman life but able to withdraw into the comfort of their shared secret whenever they needed to.

Eddie Vincenzo showed up one Thursday night toward the end of September. He simply knocked on the door of Jessica's dormitory room and waited until she opened it.

She hadn't expected she would ever see him again. They had almost said as much when they parted in the Las Vegas airport the day he put her on a plane to go home for Amy's funeral. Not that they talked about themselves that day. He kissed her hard and wrapped his arms around her, one hand on her ass, pulling her tight against him, as though the pressure of his body could somehow vanquish her tears for Amy. They hadn't said a word about the future, which in that moment simply ceased to exist.

Now here he was, grinning that wonderful grin, as though it were still summer and they were still somewhere far away. "You look great," he said. "This place must agree with you."

She invited him in and introduced him to Barbara as "a friend from New York."

"You mean you knew real people in New York?" Barbara teased, cocking her head as she studied Eddie with an openness he wasn't used to from a girl. He half expected her to tell him to turn around so she could get a look at him from the side and the back. He didn't like that crack about *real people* even though he wasn't sure what it was supposed to mean. There was no real and not real to it. Nobody shits flowers, whether they go to college or not.

Jessica laughed and said, "It means she likes you."

Eddie didn't see how it meant that but didn't much care one way or the other. He knew even before he got to New Haven that he wasn't going to like the people he was going to run into there. "What do you say we get something to eat?" he suggested, looking around at the room, unimpressed. It was a dump. What was so goddamned great about Yale anyway? There was nothing special about it as far as he could see, and he felt like he had gotten a pretty good look.

They took Eddie's car, with Jessica giving him directions as he drove. When they got out of the car they were in the parking lot of a dim-looking restaurant on the main drag of some one-street town about fifteen miles from New Haven. He looked around and said, "What do you think? Is this far enough away?"

She felt guilty and embarrassed, ashamed of herself and ashamed that he had been able to see through her so easily.

For almost two months Eddie hadn't been able to get Jessica Blaine out of his mind. She wasn't like any of the girls he knew. Maybe the kind of money she came from had something to do with it, but he liked to think it wasn't that simple. He had never spent so much time with one girl in his life. It was like being married or something. Except that he still didn't know her, whereas the girls he knew you knew inside out by ten o'clock the first night you were with them. With Jessica it was like there was a door in her mind that kept closing and opening, closing most of the time, opening only once in a while, and never long enough for him to get through.

She was crazy about him. He knew that with absolute confidence. But that was the part that messed up his mind. Because normally when a girl is crazy about you it's like one of those poker nights when everything comes up straights and flushes and three of a kind. You can't lose for winning. With Jessica Blaine it was like playing a game with wild cards he didn't know about, and that was what stayed in his mind after she left him in Vegas and after he got back to the city. She wasn't even around and she was messing up his head.

So here he was, eating some kind of shrimp that came on a metal plate so hot it was still sizzling, and feeling the simple thrill of being with her again, feeling that strange hot coolness that radiated off her like glints of sunlight off water on the hottest day of the hottest summer anyone could remember. The feeling was

exactly everything he had expected, and so was the fact that absolutely everything she said or did pissed him off.

After dinner they found a motel on the road back to New
Haven. There were maybe eighteen or twenty units and only one
car in front of any of them, which made sense because nobody with
any options would stop at a place like this. What didn't make sense
was why the place was still in business.

They weren't bad little rooms, though, bigger than you might
have expected, with pretty furniture and pictures on the walls with
little night lights over them. It was hard to imagine whose idea that
little touch might have been. It sure as hell wasn't the guy who
rented Eddie the room, a cross-eyed geek who seemed half unconscious and needed a shave.

Eddie went into the bathroom to take a leak and when he came
out Jessica had almost all her clothes off. He thought when he
looked at her that she still had an incredible body, as though he had
been expecting to find that she had gotten old in the couple
months since the last time he saw her.

After they made love, he laid out a couple lines of coke. He
knew she liked it better when they did the coke first but he didn't
want to make it easier for her.

"You didn't tell me you had that stuff," she protested. She was
just teasing him but it didn't come across as teasing. Or if it did,
Eddie wasn't in the mood for being teased.

"Make a difference?" he said.

She was standing naked over the little table where he laid out
the coke. Once she had her clothes off, she walked around naked
all the time. Eddie didn't know any other girls who did that. He
always put on his pants when he got out of bed.

"You don't think it does?" she asked.

"I'm asking you."

When she turned to him, there was something about her eyes,
like she was looking at him from a long way away. Then she turned
back to the coke without answering him—which she had to know
from months of experience was absolutely the surest way there was
to piss him off.

He slapped his hand down on the table hard, scattering the white powder like it was so much talcum. "I asked you a question," he said.

"What question was that?"

Her voice didn't give an inch. She knew everything that was going to happen next, and she didn't give an inch.

"I asked you if having this shit makes a difference."

"That all depends, doesn't it?" she said.

"On what?"

"On whether you just happened to be passing through New Haven or this is going to be a regular thing."

"We're not fucking married, y'know," he said.

"I didn't say married. I said regular thing."

"I know what you said."

"And?"

"And what?" he snapped, turning her to face him, stepping into her so that she had to back up. "You don't get in the sack if you don't get your stuff? Is that what you're saying? Unless there's some kind of *regular thing*?"

"Don't be stupid," she said.

His hand caught the side of her face with enough force to send her sideways onto the bed.

He stood over her with his hand raised to hit her again. There was a purple mark on her cheek already. If he hit her a couple more times she'd cry. And then he'd hold her. And then they'd get in bed again. But he didn't want any of that to happen, so he dropped his hand and said "Fuck you, Jessica," and turned around and grabbed his shirt and walked out of the room.

She didn't move even when she heard his car start and even when she heard the tires squealing on the gravel.

No big deal, Eddie thought as he drove down the empty road, looking for some sign that would tell him which way he was supposed to go. She'd have to call for a cab. So what?

She had plenty of money.

Plenty.

17

They met on the outdoor observation deck of the Staten Island ferry at two o'clock in the afternoon. A gentle breeze stirred the smells of the sea out of the Verrazano Channel like soup in a stirred pot.

Fiore was leaning with his back to the bow rail, the salt wind feathering his hair. "How much longer is this going to take?" he asked. "People are asking questions, I've got to have answers."

It was the first time Fiore had ever allowed himself to acknowledge that he himself had people he answered to. Jeffrey filed the information at the back of his mind for safekeeping. He had no idea what use he could make of it, but thoroughness was second nature to him, a part of his banker's instincts. He felt the pleasure a methodical man always feels when he is in possession of a fact in the afternoon that he hadn't owned in the morning.

"We should be ready to do something next week," Jeffrey said. "I'll need a hundred thousand dollars."

"Cash?"

"No. Not cash. Good clean money with a mother and a father and a birth certificate. There's no sense doing this if you won't be able to answer a few direct questions about where it all started."

"Don't lecture me," Fiore said, embarrassed at his mistake. He had known they would have to start with clean money. That was the whole point. "I'll have a check for you. One week. Right here."

"Not here," Jeffrey said. "My office."

Fiore scowled darkly and turned completely around to look out over the water. "Is that a good idea?" he asked.

Jeffrey smiled, although Fiore wasn't looking at him. "Of course it is," he said. "I'm your investment banker. When you're conducting legitimate business, you don't do it in parking lots or in the middle of the river."

It was the second time in less than a minute that the banker talked to him the way you'd talk to the slow kid in class. He kept his eyes on the water and nodded an acknowledgment. "Fine," he said. "Your office."

That night Jeffrey ate dinner at home and then went back to the office. He bantered with the young traders for a while, picking up an education in their end of the business. They wore headsets with microphones at their lips, like astronauts, not simply because the technology amused them but because it seemed to be a point of pride with them to do as little as possible with their hands. They had their shoes off, their feet in sixty-dollar socks up on their desks, computer keyboards in their laps. They were expansive in their answers to Jeffrey's questions and would have been even if he hadn't been a partner in the firm. They were gracious with their time, not because time wasn't money but because they so conspicu-ously had so much of both. Jessica, Jeffrey was certain, wouldn't be impressed with their scatological humor or their hands-free phones.

He retired to his own office around ten o'clock to catch up on some reports. A little before midnight Gabriel Enriquez came in, wearing unpressed slacks and a V-neck sweater with no shirt under it. "What do you say we kick the tires and take her for a spin?" he said, flashing his electric smile.

Jeffrey looked up from the report he was reading. In a few min-utes he had been planning to go to the computer room to check up on Enriquez. Now he didn't have to.

The traders and the cleaning staff were gone by this time, and Jeffrey followed Enriquez to the computer room, a silent and air-less alcove behind locked doors at the far end of everything.

Explaining what he was doing as he worked, Enriquez used customized cables and a specially installed port on a customized laptop to tap into the mainframe that contained Layne Bentley's database. He had taken the precaution of buying the hardware out of town and paying cash for it. There were no records of anything.

"There are no available read-write ports on this thing," he said, "because it's not designed to accept input except through the dedicated channels. But it's got a tape backup system that's supposed to write only. I'm going in through there."

He went on to explain that the system contained what amounted to a burglar alarm designed to shut the machine down if it detected an attempt at unauthorized entry. "That's the beauty of going in through an output port. The guards aren't watching."

Jeffrey, who knew very little about computers, was always surprised at how clearly the young man explained everything. "Like smuggling a handgun *off* an airplane," he suggested.

Enriquez glanced back over his shoulder and nodded his appreciation. "Exactly," he said.

The door was locked behind them.

As Gabriel completed the cable hookup and switched on his computer, Jeffrey could feel his pulses pounding in his temples like a drumbeat. He had to make a conscious effort to breathe normally. He was already a wealthy man; it wasn't the prospect of more money that excited him. It was the very real likelihood, the certainty in fact, that in the next few moments he would cross over into a country where he had never traveled before, a country from which, if everything went according to plan, he would never have to return.

He leaned over Gabriel's shoulder to study the screen of the laptop computer, but all he saw was a stream of numbers flashing by far too fast to be read. He knew they would have conveyed no meaning to him even if he had been able to read them.

"What it's doing right now," Gabriel said, almost as though he had read Jeffrey's mind, "is reconfiguring the port. As soon as it's done that, we can get in."

"Kind of exciting," Jeffrey said.

"Not really," Gabriel answered laconically. "Not yet anyway. There—we're in."

The words, Jeffrey knew, were nothing but standard computer jargon but he felt as though he were literally *in*, as though he had just stepped through a door into a cold and brightly lit room filled with gleaming and complicated appliances, a room so bright that he cast no shadow and was completely invisible.

A simple menu appeared on the screen, with half a dozen lettered choices. It looked crude and primitive, lifelessly monochromatic compared with the lively and complex color-coded screens generated by the firm's software. He didn't recognize anything on the list.

Gabriel began typing at the keyboard, and with each keystroke another menu appeared and disappeared, some of them vanishing even before the machine had time to complete them. Finally, the screen showed him something he was able to recognize, the names of the fourteen firms that composed what Jeffrey referred to as the Branford Fund. It was named for Branford Technologies, an Atlanta metallurgy firm that was the chief beneficiary of the moneys poured into the fund. The company held patents on a dozen different alloys of exotic metals combined with plastics and exotic metals combined with ceramics. Clint Bolling was heavily invested in the Branford Fund.

The name of another fund in which Bolling had money appeared on the screen as Gabriel clacked away. A moment later an old dot-matrix printer, banished years ago to this inaccessible outpost, clattered to life behind Jeffrey. The sudden noise startled him. Panicked him, in fact. It couldn't have been worse if the door to the room suddenly flew open and Everett Layne was standing in the doorway demanding in his courtly way to know what Jeffrey Blaine was doing in this place at this hour.

"Sorry," Gabriel laughed, "I should have told you I was going to do that."

Jeffrey let out a long, slow breath as Gabriel got up from his chair and stepped around him to get to the printer. With a flick of his finger, he separated the pages of the continuous form paper as they emerged from the machine. There were only two of them, reporting Bolling's holdings in the two funds. He passed them to Jeffrey.

In terms of format, though not in the quality of the printing, they were identical to the reports Jeffrey regularly received. They were dated two days ago, and Jeffrey was familiar enough with the details of the Oklahoman's holdings to recognize that half a million dollars had moved from the second fund to Branford.

"You created a predated transfer," Jeffrey said, impressed.

Enriquez smiled. "I did better than that," he said. "This runs all the way back to his first buy-in. As of now the money was always in Branford. No matter how you look it up, that's what you'll find."

Jeffrey nodded because he didn't trust himself to say anything. By tomorrow he would feel comfortable about passing invisibly through solid walls. Right now it was still too new to him.

He waited while Gabriel restored the original records.

Phyllis was asleep when he got home.

If you want to know what the word *tedious* means, try conducting a police investigation sometime. Not the kind where you dig around at a crime scene looking for clues, sorting out what looks important but isn't from what doesn't but is. That kind of work was at least vaguely interesting—or so Schliester assumed, although in fact he had never done it. His own experience tended to be in the kind of police investigation where you get in someone's face and bang his head against the wall until he tells you what you want to know. This was interesting, too, but it numbed the soul.

No, what Schliester was thinking about when he used the word *tedious* was the kind of undercover work where you methodically build a case. That's a great word, *methodically*. It means doing the same thing over and over and over. Catching someone like Gus Benini in a shakedown is nice but not nearly as nice as catching him in two shakedowns. Three is better still. At four even the prosecutor begins to concede that Mr. Benini is looking at some legal problems that could soon complicate his life.

"How much trouble does this little prick have to get into before we reel him in?" Schliester asked Elaine Lester.

They were in a bar way up on Broadway around Columbia University. It was eleven o'clock. They had taken to meeting at night to discuss the case, always in dark, out-of-the-way taverns in neighborhoods where neither of them, Schliester especially, was likely to be known. Gogarty wasn't invited. When Elaine showed up for the first such meeting and noticed that Schliester was waiting by himself at a corner table for two, she knew even before she sat down that he was going to put the make on her.

Except he didn't. In fact he didn't even come close, didn't give it so much as a half-hearted try. The same thing happened the second time, except that Elaine made up her mind in advance to bring up the subject herself if he didn't. She liked Schliester, and she was having the most confused and conflicted feelings she had ever had in her life about her deepening involvement with Jeffrey Blaine. Was he or wasn't he the subject of an investigation by her office? Well, yes. Well, no. Schliester and his partner insisted they weren't investigating him. Lord knew she had asked them to, so where was the conflict? There was none. There wasn't a single report in a single file anywhere in the office that contained so much as a shred of credible evidence of anything wrong there. Besides, she was absolutely certain that if, in fact, there was a connection between Jeffrey and Chet Fiore, it was her intimacy with Jeffrey that offered the best possible chance of finding it.

She knew that when the time came, if it came, she would be able to step back and smile and tell him, sorry but she had a warrant for his arrest in her purse. Sometimes she actually imagined the scene, which had a strange power to excite her. He would shrug and smile, a wan and wistful smile that made her wonder what games he had been playing while she was playing hers.

No, she had no reason to want to get out of her relationship with Jeffrey Blaine. All she needed, she told herself, was a breath of air. And right now Wally Schliester seemed like a good way to get it, in fact the only possible way that presented itself.

But first they had to talk about the case. "Wally," she said, answering his question, "it has nothing to do with quantity. You know that. Quality."

"What quality?" he objected. "A shakedown is a shakedown."

She took a deep breath and explained carefully. On Benini's first deal they didn't have anything on tape. That made the case weak. Yes, all the conversations with Benini after that were recorded. But what good was his shakedown of the Korean, who was back in Korea and wouldn't return to the States to testify? Elaine also doubted very much that the jeweler from Wisconsin or the contact lens guy would testify. They were rabbits, with just enough imagination to form a vivid conception of the underworld assassins who would be coming after them if they gave a statement to the police. So what did that leave? One case on which, maybe, if they got lucky, they would have a witness.

"Except we don't need any goddamned witnesses," Schliester said. "We're not taking him to court, we just want to lean on him."

She finished her drink and gestured for another. "He's got lawyers, Wally," she said. She had taken to using his name a lot after hours. In the office she never called anyone by name. "If we don't have credible witnesses, then we don't have a case we can put him away with. In which case his lawyers will tell him to keep his mouth shut."

He could see the logic. You needed less evidence to send a guy to jail than you needed to let him go. He said exactly that, and she said, "Always," and the two of them laughed like two kids in on the same joke.

She waited until her drink came, and then she said, "Is it my turn to ask you a question?"

"It was," he said. "Too bad you used it up for that."

She made a face. She was really kind of pretty an awful lot of the time. He nodded for her to go ahead.

"How come your partner's not here?" she asked.

He nodded thoughtfully. "That's a good one," he said.

"Could it possibly be because he's an asshole?" she asked.

"He doesn't think that much of you either," Schliester said, "but no, that's not it."

"In that case," she said, "the other possibility that comes to mind is that we're meeting just the two of us because you want to seduce me."

"My," Schliester said, "don't we think a lot of ourselves."

Elaine looked up over the rim of her glass with just her eyes, keeping her face down. "If I told you I have good reason to, what would you say?" she asked.

"Something clever," he said. "Like, *Hey, baby, you wanna fuck?*"

They couldn't go to her apartment because Jeffrey sometimes showed up unexpectedly after staying late in the office. So they went to his. Which wasn't in the least what she expected his apartment would look like. It wasn't cramped or cluttered or implacably adolescent. It was small, but it had furniture someone actually had gone out and *bought*. None of the prints on the walls bore the images of athletes. There were old views of New York, from the days when there was a wall at Wall Street, and photographs dating from the era when horses drew streetcars over cobblestones.

"I owe you an apology," she said as she looked around.

He didn't ask why, and she assumed it was because he knew what she meant.

The minute he put his hands on her, she was surprised at how simple it seemed.

Not that it *was* simple. She had just added cheating on her married lover to the mix. How was this making her life less complicated?

In the morning, while he was showering and she was still in bed, the idea came to her of setting Gogarty up as one of Benini's marks. Schliester liked it.

He wasn't as crazy about the fact that this was the kind of thing she thought about in bed in the morning.

Chet Fiore still lived with his wife in a little house on City Island three blocks from his mother. He bought it just after he got married and he lived there in the sense that sooner or later he showed up to sleep there almost every night. His wife's name was Virginia, Ginny, and she was a City Island girl who never really wanted to live anywhere else. For this reason, and others as well, she was never troubled by what might have seemed, to anyone watching, a rather lonely and isolated life. The truth was that she wasn't lonely in the least. She had a cadre of girlfriends from her high school days and she saw them constantly, for shopping, for cards, for endless cups of coffee in the spring and the fall and the winter, for iced tea and cakes in the pretty little backyard lapped by the ocean all through the summer. Her friends were all married, while Ginny was, for social purposes, effectively single, so that she functioned more or less as a spinster aunt, a confidante to her friends' children and an odd place setting at dinner parties. Still, as the wife of Chet Fiore, she was entitled to and received enormous deference in the tiny community. She was satisfied with her life in a way few women are.

When she and Chet were first married, they planned on having children, but two second-trimester miscarriages and then a disastrous surgery eliminated that possibility. A few months after the surgery she asked her husband to consider adopting, but he shrugged his shoulders and walked out of the room. She never asked again. He came home when he came home, and that was enough for her.

Being alone as much as she was, she could have had affairs of her own. She never did. Her sexual needs were minimal, and she experienced them not as passion or desire, but only as a vague restlessness that crept over her from time to time. She had only to move next to him in bed, to touch him, and they would make love, and then the restlessness would go away. If she had been asked, she would have said that she was happily married and that her husband loved her.

And he would have said the same thing.

He tended to sleep late, waking at ten or eleven. He usually made himself breakfast—he enjoyed doing it—and then Ginny joined him for coffee. They sat together and talked at the kitchen table for half an hour or so, until Jimmy arrived to take him to the city. Mostly, Fiore listened while she talked about things she was planning to do with the house, or about his mother's health, which was deteriorating steadily. She had round-the-clock nurses now, and Ginny made it a point to see her every day. Ginny was a good daughter-in-law, and that was one of the things Fiore prized about her. She was a sensible and intelligent woman with clear and well-formed opinions on a wide variety of issues. Fiore enjoyed listening to her. If it wasn't for Ginny, he sometimes thought, his brain would rot away from lack of exercise. In the city he was considered an intelligent man, but Fiore himself never felt that his dealings with the mobsters above him or below him called for much intelligence at all.

Until the thing with Blaine. That was different. Even in the privacy of his own thoughts he would never call it a stroke of genius, because he had too much respect for intellectual accomplishments to ever think anything like that. But it was sure as hell a clever piece of work. Every detail had been carefully worked out, from the moment he picked Blaine's name off Erill Stasny's client list. The carefully orchestrated chaos at Jessica Blaine's birthday party, followed by the application of more pressure on Blaine through his daughter, had all worked perfectly. Blaine put up a good show of resistance until his daughter disappeared, but Fiore suspected from the very start that it was only a show, and he grew more certain of it as their partnership deepened.

The man he met on the Staten Island ferry a week ago was hardly the same man who dithered around so ineffectually on the night of his daughter's birthday party. Fiore knew that no one changes that much that quickly. There was only one way to explain it. Something buried got unburied. But it had to have been there all along.

The situation would bear watching. A man like Blaine, trying on his new life, getting the feel of it, could be ruthless and reckless at the same time. Like a storm.

Fine, Fiore thought. A storm is never a problem if you dress for it.

On this particular morning, as on many others, Jimmy joined Fiore and Ginny for coffee and pastry. "Call Blaine, see if he can meet me this afternoon," Fiore said, and Jimmy took his coffee cup to another room to make the call. He got the man's secretary, who put him on hold while she buzzed her boss. Then she came back on the line. "Sorry to keep you waiting, Mr. Angelini," she said. "Mr. Blaine says this afternoon will be fine. How is two o'clock?"

Angelisi didn't bother to correct her on the name. Two o'clock, he said, was no problem.

A minute after she hung up the phone and noted the two o'clock appointment on Jeffrey's calendar, his assistant was standing in Jeffrey's office. Her name was Jennie and she had been with him almost three years. She was a bright young woman with a quick and intuitive understanding of Jeffrey's complex business. She read every report submitted to him by his staff; like a monk poring over sacred texts, she studied the marginal notes with which he responded. When she didn't understand his thinking, she got books from the firm's library on the eighteenth floor or downloaded articles from business journals.

Still, for all her maturity, she had the disconcertingly girlish habit of standing pigeon-toed, clutching a memo pad in both hands in front of her skirt whenever she came into Jeffrey's office. It made her look like a junior high school student at that perplexing stage in life when a girl is too tall to be child and too awkward to be anything else.

"Excuse me, Mr. Blaine," she said. "You just made an appointment with a Mr. Fiore."

If it was a question, Jeffrey didn't know what the question was. So he said nothing and waited.

"Is that who I think it is?" she asked.

Jeffrey smiled at her carefully. He had known that sooner or later he was going to have this conversation and would have brought it up if she didn't. He wanted her to have answers in case others in the office had questions, and he wanted it clear that he was not keeping Fiore a secret. "Do you mean is he a gangster?" he said. "The newspapers seem to say he is. He's never mentioned it to me."

Her face flushed and her hands grappled with the memo pad, wringing it back and forth.

"That's all right, you did well to ask," he said. "He's not the sort of man one expects to see here. But he has money to invest, and as long as it's not undocumented cash . . ."

He left the sentence unfinished. Jennie nodded, satisfied with her boss's probity, and backed out of the room, looking forward to the arrival of the well-known gangster later in the afternoon.

Chet Fiore stepped off the elevator promptly at two o'clock. He was wearing a light gray Armani suit that followed the lines of his lean, taut form like the sculptured draperies on a statue. He looked like anything but a gangster, and when he gave his name to the receptionist at the front desk, she misunderstood it as *Fury* and didn't recognize him. She said that Mr. Blaine's assistant would be out for him in a minute. It wasn't much more than that before Blaine's girl—she said her name was Jennifer—came out to claim him, but even that minute was long enough for him to take in what he could only describe to himself as the grandeur of these offices. He surprised himself, not pleasantly, with random and uninvited thoughts about the shape his own life might have taken if he had made a different set of decisions after his grandfather died. He greeted the girl with a distant and somewhat abstracted smile. "I kind of figured Blaine would have a good-looking assistant," he said.

She blushed the way girls do who aren't used to compliments, and lowered her eyes with a fleeting look of annoyance because she knew it wasn't true. By the time a girl is sixteen she either knows she's pretty or knows she's not. Jennifer had a good body and took care of herself, but she knew that she was plain.

"Mr. Blaine is having lunch in the Partners Room," she said.

"I can wait," Fiore said.

There was a kind of boyish deference in the way he said it that took her by surprise. It made her wonder about all the things she had heard about him and read in the papers. The Chet Fiore of her imagination would never say anything like *I can wait.*

"He told me to take you up," she said.

If the reception area impressed him, the Partners Room filled him with something almost like awe. Not the awe one feels in the presence of castles or cathedrals. This was different. What came into his mind when he stepped into the room was an image from when he was a kid playing ball. There was an Irish kid—he could see that pale, flat face as though it were there in the room with him—and this kid could throw the ball from deep in the hole at short as flat as a bowling ball rolling down the lane, like a missile, no trajectory at all. That was the kind of awe he was feeling now. Here he was, Chet Fiore, reputed to be one of the most powerful men in New York. And maybe he was. Yet this man Blaine, who was nothing really, just one of a thousand bankers, or twenty thousand for all Fiore knew, was having lunch in a room with a fireplace big enough for a man to stand in and the kind of wood paneling on the walls that belonged in a mansion.

Blaine got to his feet when he saw Jennifer and Chet Fiore crossing the room toward him. He was having lunch with a young guy with bad skin and an expensive-looking suit that still managed to fit him badly. "Chet Fiore, Roger Bogard," Jeffrey said. "I hope you're joining us for lunch."

The two men shook hands. Bogard had very small hands.

"A cup of coffee maybe," Fiore said. He felt awkward about confessing that he had just had breakfast barely an hour ago.

Bogard remained on his feet and said something about "getting on that research" right away. "Pleasure meeting you, Mr. Fiore," he said.

"Don't let me chase you away," Fiore said.

"On the contrary," Bogard said. "I shouldn't have been sitting here this long."

On the contrary, Fiore thought. He hadn't known that people actually said things like that. He watched the young man follow Jennifer across the room and then took the chair on Blaine's right that had been vacant before. Blaine signaled the waiter for coffee, which came immediately.

Jeffrey, in fact, had drawn out his lunch with Bogard on purpose, because he wanted Fiore to be seen. A few days earlier he had taken the precaution, at the weekly staff meeting, of personally raising the question of the propriety of opening an investment account for Chet Fiore. Did Layne Bentley, he asked, want a person of Fiore's "background" on its client list? By asking the question, he kept others from asking it. He pointed out that the account would be quite lucrative, and he was sure it would be possible to demand incontrovertible evidence that any funds invested with Layne Bentley came from legitimate sources. The partners, of course, endorsed his thinking.

Fiore looked around at the other men at other tables. They were all older than Blaine. "This is a hell of a room," he said.

"Does it make you nervous?"

Why did he ask that? Fiore was certain he didn't look nervous. He surprised himself when he said, "A little maybe. We're kind of out there in the open. I'm not used to that."

Jeffrey smiled at what he took to be a rather surprising naivete on Fiore's part. "You want to be out there in the open," he said. "That's the point."

"I suppose," Fiore conceded.

Jeffrey got to his feet. "Let's talk in my office."

In the elevator, Jeffrey said, "You're going to have to get used to a whole new way of thinking. No one who has funds they can spend in public doesn't spend them. Buy a yacht. A big apartment. A Van Gogh for that matter."

Fiore liked the sound of that. A Van Gogh.

There was a desk at the far end of Blaine's office with a couple of stuffed chairs facing it, but Jeffrey directed his guest to a couch that looked like it belonged in someone's living room. Not Blaine's probably, at least judging from the furniture Fiore had seen in the guy's country house. This thing was just a sofa, big and comfortable in an old-fashioned way. The girl had followed them in and asked if they wanted anything to drink. Fiore shook his head, declining for both of them. She withdrew without another word, pulling the door closed behind her.

Jeffrey drew two slender cigars from a wooden humidor on the table next to the couch and offered one to Fiore. "I assume you're ready to go forward," he said.

Fiore reached into his breast pocket and took out an envelope. He drew a paper from the envelope and passed it across to Blaine. "One hundred," he said. "That's right, isn't it?"

Jeffrey had made up his mind beforehand that if Fiore tried to give him cash, which he was told not to do, or even a check, he wouldn't accept it. Unless, of course, Fiore could provide rock-solid documentation of the source of the funds it was drawn against. But this wasn't a check. It was a letter of credit on the letterhead of a commercial mortgage division of the Chase Manhattan Bank.

Jeffrey looked at it and then up to Fiore, expecting an explanation.

"I took out a loan. On the restaurant," Fiore said. "You wanted clean money. It doesn't get any cleaner than that."

"No," Jeffrey agreed. "It doesn't."

Then he explained what would happen with the money.

Fiore didn't listen. Details bored him when they were other people's business.

18

t took only a week for Chet Fiore to double his money. Jeffrey could have made it happen even faster but he didn't want to do anything to call attention to the account, even though he knew the risks were minimal since the amounts involved were so small. But they wouldn't stay small for long, and it was a good principle to err on the side of caution. Besides, he wanted to keep Fiore's expectations reasonable. The next few months were going to be like training a puppy, Jeffrey thought, amusing himself with the notion. When you give him a biscuit, it's not a good idea to let him know you've got another one in your other hand and a few more in your pocket. You want him grateful, not distracted.

Jeffrey had a check drawn in the amount of one hundred thousand dollars payable to the Mid Atlantic Restaurant Association, a nonexistent company that would be created solely for the purpose of receiving and clearing these checks. Its name was similar but not identical to the Atlantic Restaurant Company, the company in whose name Fiore had opened his Layne Bentley account. Gabriel Enriquez taught him how to draw the check to one name on the company computer and then alter the name before the check was printed.

Exactly one week after Fiore opened his investment account, he and Jeffrey met again, this time in a Thai restaurant overlooking the immense central hall of the newly refurbished Grand Central Station. Fiore, who was usually as punctual as a schoolteacher, walked through

268 · Philip Rosenberg

the dining room twenty minutes late. A glass of Cabernet was waiting at his place, and a platter of hors d'oeuvres gave off the provocative and mysterious scent of lemongrass. Fiore apologized for being late but offered no explanation. Something told Jeffrey that the man had just stepped out of a shower, which could mean either a midmorning love affair or a workout in the gym but in Fiore's case meant only the former. He had a lean, well-honed body, but he didn't work at it.

Jeffrey accepted Fiore's apology without comment and invited him to help himself to the hors d'oeuvres. At the same time he took an envelope from his breast pocket and removed the Layne Bentley check. He passed it across to Fiore, who looked at it and set it down on the table. "Nice," he said. "Now what?"

Jeffrey surprised Fiore by taking the check back and returning it to his pocket, but Fiore realized his mistake at once. Blaine wouldn't be giving him any money. Fiore had plenty of money but no records of how he got it. Now he had records.

"Tomorrow," Blaine said, "you deposit one hundred thousand dollars to the Atlantic account. Your bookkeeper records it as a payment from Layne Bentley. The minute she does that, it's clean money. And you've still got an account with us with a little over a hundred thousand in it."

"What happens to the check?" Fiore asked.

Jeffrey studied him a long time, letting his silence be his answer, letting it draw a straight, crisp line right across the middle of the table between them.

"Something tells me it doesn't go to the cowboy," Fiore said.

"Let's keep this simple," Jeffrey answered. "I don't ask you where your money comes from, you don't ask me where this money goes."

The original idea, as Jeffrey outlined it to both Bolling and Fiore when the two New Yorkers were in Oklahoma, was that Fiore would be credited with receiving the money while Bolling got the cash. But there was something so decisive and final in the way Blaine slipped the check into his pocket, something so clean and complete in the gesture, that Fiore knew immediately that the rules of the game had changed.

"Are you telling me he's out of the picture?" Fiore asked.

Jeffrey carefully set down his knife and fork and refilled both their wine glasses. "There's something I want you to think about," he said. "It's an old game, a riddle really. It used to show up from time to time in business school textbooks. Feel like playing?"

Fiore didn't answer. His eyes remained locked on Jeffrey, waiting.

"Here's the situation," Jeffrey went on. "Imagine ten pirates. They find a treasure chest with a hundred gold coins in it. They've got to split it up. Ten apiece seems fair but these men are pirates. They're not interested in fairness. Each one wants the most he can get. Is there some logic that dictates something other than an even split? Well, let's see, they say. They come up with a method for deciding what to do. Here's the method. The biggest, baddest, toughest pirate, the one with seniority, gets to go first. He makes a proposal, any proposal he wants. If he gets at least half the votes, his proposal carries and the treasure is divided up the way he suggests. But, and it's a big *but*, if the other pirates vote him down, they throw him over the side and the next guy in line takes a crack at winning the hearts and minds of his colleagues. Got the picture?"

Fiore nodded but said nothing.

"Take all the time you need," Jeffrey said. "You're the biggest and the baddest of the pirates. What do you suggest we do with the treasure?"

"And you're telling me it's not ten apiece?" Fiore asked rhetorically, like a man talking to himself. There's always a trick to riddles like this. He knew that much.

"I'm not telling you anything," Jeffrey said.

Fiore didn't like playing games but he did enjoy watching how they played out. He held up a finger for silence and tried to think it through. But he didn't even know how to get a handle on a problem like this. After a moment he gave up and shook his head. "I know you're going to tell me the number one pirate makes out like a bandit. But you're going to have to tell me how."

"Don't give up so fast. Let's see if we can work it out," Jeffrey said. "The trick is to simplify. So let's start with the simplest case. Let's say there are only two pirates left. The first eight are already shark food. It's down to you and me. You're tougher, so you make the proposal. What will it be? Fifty-fifty? Or do you think you can do better?"

Fiore swirled the wine in his glass and watched for a moment as the blood-colored liquid caught and twisted the light from the sconces behind him. Then he looked up with a big, boyish grin as the answer came to him. It was like being in school again. "I get a hundred, you get nothing," he said.

"Is that reasonable?" Jeffrey asked.

"There's only two of us and I only need one vote," Fiore said. "All for me, nothing for you. All in favor raise your hands." He raised his hand above his head. "The motion carries."

Jeffrey laughed at the demonstration. "Good. Very good," he said. "Now back up a little. Three pirates and pirate three has to make a proposal. He knows what's going to happen if he gets thrown overboard because he can figure out what you just figured out. Which is that you get everything and I get nothing. He needs two votes. What does he do?"

This time Fiore did his thinking out loud. "He's not going to get my vote no matter what he does, because I get all of it if he gets voted down. But you'd get nothing if it comes down to that, so he offers you one buck and you take it. Ninety-nine for him, one for you, the two of you vote for it and I'm screwed."

"All right," Jeffrey said. "Now you see how it works. You can go back to the sixth pirate and it's the same principle. Just keep backing up like that and you get to the winning answer, which is ninety-six pieces of gold for the head pirate and one apiece for the four guys he bribes to get him the five votes he needs."

"Clever," Fiore said evenly. It bothered him that he hadn't been able to work this out without Blaine's help. "But what's the point?"

Jeffrey gestured to the waiter. "My friend and I aren't having dinner," he said. "Just the check please." The waiter hurried off.

"The point," Jeffrey said, "is that there aren't any losers. Five pirates get nothing but they had nothing to start with. Four pirates end up one gold piece ahead, so they're happy. And the tenth pirate makes out like a pirate. He gets very rich very fast, but nobody's complaining."

"We're the tenth pirate?" Fiore suggested. "Is that what you're saying?"

The waiter returned with the check and Jeffrey signed his name at the bottom of it. "We made a deal with our friend in Oklahoma. The profits go on your books, the losses on his. Except there aren't any losses when the markets are going up. Investments are coming through all over the place. I cooked the books and he still made money, just not as much as you."

"So we *are* the tenth pirate," Fiore said, a wide smile cracking his face. It was the first time Jeffrey had seen him smile like that, an *expression*, not a gesture. Until this moment everything about the man seemed calculated. His smiles, his scowls, his words were all chosen as instruments of control. This smile was different. It came from somewhere inside and had reference only to himself.

"Actually," Jeffrey said, with something almost like a laugh, "I think we may be all ten pirates. We may be all the pirates there are."

Fiore laughed out loud with the sheer triumph of the moment. He reached out, clasped Jeffrey's hand, and pumped it effusively, two men closing a deal. And what a deal it was. So simple. Generations of men from Capone through Gotti to Falcone had looked for this El Dorado and never found it. But here it was, stretched out in front of them like a new continent. He felt as though he were holding a flagstaff in his hand, driving it into the earth. And he could see in Blaine's eyes and feel in the pressure of the man's hand that Blaine was feeling exactly the same thing.

"We did it," he said. "We really did it."

He sounded like a kid.

After that, they went their separate ways. As he walked under the vaulted, star-studded ceiling of the magnificent terminal, Fiore stopped suddenly. The smile fell off his face and his eyes darkened, lit from inside with their usual fire. Because he realized that if there were only winners and no losers, like Blaine said, and if they didn't need Clint Bolling anymore, like Blaine said, then Bolling was just a loose end that ought to be tied up.

• • •

Phyllis was on her way to a committee meeting at the Metropolitan Museum, a committee she found herself on without knowing why. It was a wet day and she was dying for a cup of tea, so she ran into the cafeteria, her heels clattering across the tiled floor like dice rolled from a cup. She splashed hot water into a paper cup, threw in a tea bag she took from a little enameled box in her purse, and waved to the black woman at the register. She had no time to stop. She was already late for the meeting.

"That's fine, Mrs. Blaine," the cashier called back. "You take care now."

As Phyllis hurried toward the door, she heard her name and turned. It was Sue Tunney, Grace's mother, and she was getting up from a table where she had been seated by herself, a sketchpad open in front of her. She was wearing jeans and a plaid shirt and looked more like a child her daughter's age than a woman of Phyllis's.

She had never fit in well with the mothers of Jessica's classmates and consequently received very little sympathy when her husband left her, even though he behaved shamefully, buying a palatial house on Long Island and ostentatiously installing his mistress there without even bothering to separate from his wife. None of the class mothers stood by Sue or called to offer their support. She didn't belong to their world, which wouldn't have been a problem in and of itself if only she hadn't let it be known that she didn't care to belong to it. Japanese women, Irish women, even native-born Americans of no social distinction at all managed to fit in quite nicely. The doors of the best homes were open to any woman willing to stand patiently in the hall until she was invited in. The only unforgivable sins were smugness and self-sufficiency, the sense that one could walk in without being invited or walk away without being diminished.

Sue Tunney fell in the later category. She had no use for them, and so they made sure to have no use for her.

And yet here she was, dressed like an art student, calling out to Phyllis as though they were the best of friends, as though they had arranged to meet here for tea.

"Oh, hi," Phyllis said, offering a plastic smile. "I'm late for a meeting. I've really got to run."

Sue fell in step beside her. "I'll walk with you. I was just wondering how Jessica was doing."

"Thriving," Phyllis said.

"How can you tell?" Sue laughed. "They don't even talk to us." And then, realizing she had been presumptuous, she added, "Unless yours does."

"Not really," Phyllis conceded, in a tone that suggested she was agreeing out of generosity but in fact had an excellent relationship with her daughter if the truth were known.

She had reached a bank of elevators in a somewhat hidden recess. Sue, who spent a great deal of time at the museum, had never realized there were elevators. "Grace tells me Jessica's still seeing that boy," she said. "I was surprised."

The elevator door opening behind Phyllis might as well have been a chasm opening in the earth. She felt as though she might fall in. She managed a wan smile but felt a twitch at the corners of her mouth. "She hasn't mentioned any boys," Phyllis said. "What boy would that be?"

Sue paused for effect, smiling unpleasantly, as though she were enjoying this. "From the birthday party," she said. "I'm sure you know the one."

Phyllis stepped back into the waiting elevator. She sensed the doors closing on her from both sides. "She sees whom she wants," she said, trying to make it all sound fine. "She's never given us cause to meddle."

Hot tea spilled over onto her hand as the elevator started to rise. She passed the cup to her other hand and shook the pain away. It wasn't clear which one she hated most at that moment, smug Sue Tunney, who certainly seemed to get a kick out of breaking this little piece of news. Or Jessica. Who had all the morals and good sense of a cat in heat. *Just like her father,* Phyllis thought. *She thinks with her crotch.*

· · ·

Jeffrey had no trouble reading the shock on his daughter's face when she opened the door to her room and saw him standing in the corridor. She was wearing panties and a loose shirt that hung halfway down her thighs. She flashed a smile and said, "Hi, Daddy," with a show of enthusiasm.

He heard someone moving in the room behind her. "Who's there?" he asked.

He saw the dark flicker of annoyance in Jessica's eyes. "Barbara, wait a second. My father wants to check you out," she called out without turning back. And then, as she stepped back from the door, she said, "She's not dressed, Daddy," in a tone one might take with a child.

Barbara was standing no more than eight feet away on the far side of the tiny room. She was wearing tights but the spandex top of her exercise suit was in her hand. She brought both hands up to her breasts to cover them.

"Hi, Mr. Blaine, it's good to see you," she said.

She stepped toward him, and before he even realized what she was doing, she offered him her hand, uncovering herself with careless and insolent bravado. She stood like that a moment, one small but perfect breast pointed straight at him, the other covered by the dangling fabric she held in her left hand.

"Daddy was afraid I might be with a boy," Jessica said. "Satisfied?"

"Put something on," Jeffrey said sharply.

The girl smiled knowingly and turned away to pull her shirt over her head. He could smell the sweetness of her sweat.

"You, too," he said to Jessica.

He let her choose the location for their talk. All he wanted, he said, was somewhere they could get a sandwich and wouldn't run into too many of her friends. Half an hour later they were sitting opposite each other in a corner booth at a dirty sandwich shop that did mostly takeout business.

"I assume you know what this is about," he said.

"You drove all the way up here to tell me," she said. "Why don't you just do that?"

She opened her sandwich and busied herself picking off the pieces of lettuce that had too much dressing.

"I can't believe you're seeing that boy again," he began. "Don't tell me you've forgotten what happened at your birthday party."

"Eddie had nothing to do with that," she protested sullenly, without raising her eyes.

"Yes. He did," Jeffrey said with toneless emphasis, a simple declaration of fact.

Her eyes came up to meet his, bright and defiant. "He was with me," she said, countering fact with fact. "He didn't even go upstairs at all."

Her father probably thought all the girls were virgins and all the boys were like Georgie Vallo.

"Let me ask you something," he said. "What do you remember about that night? Starting with the moment you heard Amy scream."

She wished he hadn't mentioned Amy and so she made an effort to recall the night only in an abstract way, just as words, without playing it back in her memory.

"Everybody ran upstairs," she said. "And then her father came. We went home. And then we went up to the country."

"Do you remember a man who showed up? He talked to Amy and he talked to Amy's father?"

She remembered him. Dark-eyed and handsome. "Yeah, who was that?" she said. "He took over like he owned the place."

"He does," Jeffrey said. "Now listen to me and don't say anything. You're not going to like what I tell you. But you know I wouldn't lie to you."

Everything inside her felt as though it had just tied itself into one suffocating knot, and for a moment she was actually afraid she was going to be sick right there at the table. She bit her lips together and held her breath and waited. She had no idea what he was going to tell her, but she felt as though she already knew every word, as though the two of them had played exactly this scene before. Even though she couldn't remember how it turned out, she knew it turned out badly.

"Jessica," he said, speaking slowly and carefully, "everything that happened that night happened on purpose. The man's name is Chet Fiore. He's a gangster. There was something he wanted me to do. So the girls were attacked and it was covered up and I let myself become part of the cover-up. That's a felony, and that was the hold he would have on me, to get me to do what he wanted. That boy took you away this summer for the same reason. He works for Chet Fiore."

Tears streamed down her face and her shoulders heaved with violent, convulsive sobs. She shook her head vehemently and tried to speak, just "No, no, no," but no sound came out. She knew her father was telling the truth as fact after fact jumped into her mind like the sequence of images in an out-of-control nightmare. She suddenly remembered that Mr. Stasny knew Eddie. *You are enjoying, Ms. Blaine? And you, Edward?* the little man asked, looking straight at Eddie. Edward. He called him Edward. And then there was the fact that the boys somehow knew that there were rooms upstairs. And the fact that the rooms just happened to be open. And the phone call Eddie made from the hotel room in New Orleans, and others like it in Las Vegas and all along the way. And even the money, for that matter. Eddie had money for everything.

Her ears were roaring like a waterfall and she didn't even know if her father was still talking. She lurched from the table and ran blindly for the door. Jeffrey followed slowly, giving her a little time.

He found her by the car, her face buried in her arms, which rested on the roof. It was possible that she was crying so bitterly because she loved Eddie Vincenzo, but he doubted that she did in any serious way. Being used like that would hurt just the same whether she loved him or not, and there was nothing he could do about her pain except offer a little comfort. He came up behind her and put a hand on her shoulder.

She whirled to face him, her tear-red eyes gleaming with rage. "Don't you touch me," she screamed, "don't you dare touch me."

He pulled his hand back, hurt but not wanting to hurt her further.

She hesitated only a fraction of a second. "You want to know something, Daddy?" she hissed, hating him at that moment with all the passion in her body. "I went down on Eddie Vincenzo. You want to know something else? I fucked Eddie Vincenzo all over the country. I did coke with Eddie Vincenzo. You knew what he was, you knew why he wanted me, why he was using me, and you didn't say a goddamned thing. What gives you the right to try to save me now?"

The truth of her accusation stung more sharply than the bitterness.

"You're still seeing him?" he asked.

"No," she said. "But not because I stopped. I give myself away cheap. Don't you know that?"

"Don't do this, Jessica. Don't talk about yourself like that."

"He stopped coming to see me. He stopped calling. I thought, fuck you, I'm better off rid of him. But y'know what, Daddy? I think if he calls I'll meet him somewhere. Maybe we can get it started again. And he *will* call. Y'know why, Daddy? Because your little girl gives great head."

He felt his body tense and he knew a feeling he had never known before. He wanted to hit her, to slap her across the face and then see the wide-eyed hurt in her face. He had never hit anyone in his life, certainly not his child, but already he could feel the tension and movement of the muscles of his arm, as though he had done it already. He stared into her face, looking for the features of a little girl he hadn't seen in years. And he found them. In the mouth, in the eyes, in the precious precision of her chin and her nose. He used to call her Jess.

He said nothing. He waited. And when she said nothing, he said, "Come on, baby. I'll drive you back to your dorm."

"I'll walk," she said, and turned to walk away.

He knew better than to stop her.

When she reached the corner, she turned back to him. "That thing Mr. Fiore wanted you to do, Daddy," she said. "Did you do it?"

"We don't have to talk about that, Jess," he said, and she knew that he had.

She smiled, a wan, sad smile. "Good," she said. "At least someone got what they wanted out of all this."

• • •

Rachel Bolling wasn't sorry she married him but that still left a great many things she could be sorry about. She missed her village in Mexico and she missed her sisters. She loved her husband but she was no more a part of his life than a chicken is a farmer because it lives in the farmyard. She liked having money because she had been poor her whole life. She enjoyed being able to send money to her mother and to Ariana, the one sister who hadn't married well. She liked her swimming pool. She liked the feel of fine clothes against her skin.

When she was first introduced to Señor Bolling in San Vittoria, her life was an endless party from the time she woke up in the afternoon until she went to bed at sunrise. It was a party before she met Señor Bolling, and he kept the party going.

Now she didn't even like getting high anymore.

She painted pictures of her life in the village where her mother still lived, even though she hadn't been happy there as a child and wouldn't dream of returning. There was always a child in the pictures, a little girl, naked, breastless, wide-eyed, watching the village life as it unfolded, the way Rachel watched it now in her mind's eye. She drew from memory because the pictures in her memory were sharper than anything she saw with her eyes.

She was twenty-five years old and she thought to herself sometimes that already she was older than she would be when she was an old woman.

Tonight, the painting on her easel displeased her. She sat before it for a long time, trying to understand why this should be so. The figures were wrong, she decided. Tonight they seemed for some reason to be people she didn't know, strangers who didn't correspond to anything in either her memory or her imagination. And the village was wrong, too. The mountains closed it off, as though everyone in the village were trapped there forever like a parrot in a cage. In truth, as well as in the picture in her mind, the village included the mountains the way it included the sky.

She thought for a long time about how she could fix this, and when she knew that she couldn't do anything about it, she turned off her light and drank the last of her coffee by the moonlight that slid in through the open window.

She checked to assure herself that the alarm hadn't been set and walked out to the pool. It was October and the air pinched at her skin, because every night this sterile land surrendered the warmth it had gathered in the day. No wonder nothing grew out of land like this.

She pulled her dress up over her head and threw it aside, then plunged naked into the pool. In an instant the chill of the water drew from her body the stifling heat that had accumulated inside her studio while she was studying her failed painting. She swam back and forth twenty laps that made her arms tingle with the strength in them. She could feel the moon moving across the sky above her, and when she was finished swimming—she knew that it was twenty laps, exactly twenty, although she hadn't counted them—she lay on her back to feel the moonlight on her skin.

She climbed out of the water and pulled her dress over her head, letting the soft cotton dry her like a towel.

She didn't turn on a light in the bedroom. Her husband, who often snored, was sleeping so quietly she couldn't even hear him breathing. She dried her hair with a towel in the bathroom and left her dress there. She climbed into bed gently, so as not to disturb him, and settled her head on the pillow before she reached out her hand to rest it on his back. She knew the instant her skin touched his that he was dead.

He was the temperature of the sheets.

She felt the breath freeze in her body, so that she couldn't have cried out even if she had been willing to let herself. She had known that someday this would happen, and she knew why it happened.

She looked at him in the moonlight. This man built churches. He was a good man. His eyes were open. His mouth was open, too, and his tongue hung out. His lungs had stopped, she thought, before his heart did. Her own father died exactly the same way, suffocating in his sleep from the damned *coca*.

She closed her eyes and turned her face away. But she lay there till morning, crying to herself because she hadn't loved either one of them enough.

19

"ood morning, Mr. Blaine," Jennifer said, handing Jeffrey
his messages. "You ought to take a look at this clipping."
He was calling her Jennifer these days because she
finally got up the nerve to tell him she preferred it to Jennie.

He glanced through the messages and handed them back.
There wasn't anything there that needed his attention. The clipping was only half a dozen lines from an inside page of the
Oklahoma City *Sentinel*. It announced simply that Clint Bolling, of
PetroBoll, had died in his sleep. No cause of death was stated. A
family spokesman, whoever that might be, was quoted as saying
that he hadn't been ill.

He told Jennifer to hold his calls and went into his office. He
had no trouble locating the online *New York Times* archives and
calling up every article they had on Chet Fiore. He hadn't the
slightest doubt that Fiore was responsible for Bolling's death and
he wondered if he would find anything in the newspaper files that
would help him understand how a man's mind came to work the
way Fiore's did. It was a display of power like nothing Jeffrey had
ever seen, for he had never before met a man for whom will and
deed were synonymous. Fiore had no further need of Bolling and
so Bolling ceased to exist. It was as simple as that.

As he read through the articles about Fiore, Jeffrey noted that
they followed a predictable pattern. An article would mention that

the District Attorney's Office or the U.S. Attorney's Office or a state or federal grand jury was looking into Fiore's involvement in one racket or another. Fiore was invariably identified as a rising young star, handsome and articulate, in a crime family headed by a man named Gaetano Falcone. Three or four more articles in the next week or two would give promising follow-ups on the progress of the investigation. And then Fiore's name would drop from the papers for six months, nine months, as much as a year, when he would appear again as the subject of a new investigation into a new set of charges. Somewhere in each series it was always pointed out that Fiore had never been convicted of a crime, or even arrested.

Jeffrey found much more interesting material in a lengthy year-old article from the *Times* Sunday *Magazine*. The piece began with a scathingly satiric account of the U.S. attorney's frustration with the chronic press leaks that torpedoed every one of its investigations into Fiore's activities. Assistant U.S. Attorney Elaine Lester was quoted as saying that in most cases press leaks result from an improper relationship between a reporter and someone in the prosecutor's office. In Fiore's case, however, the leaks were spread out with almost obsessive evenhandedness among the four New York dailies. "Eeny, meeny, miney, and mo," she called them. The same problem plagued the District Attorney's Office. No source for the leaks had ever been found.

Jeffrey read the passage again but couldn't tell if it meant that Elaine had actually worked on one of the Fiore investigations. Was the world really that much smaller than he imagined? He doubted it, took a moment to think through the implications, and then read on.

He learned that Fiore grew up on City Island, the son of a sanitation worker and grandson of an immigrant fisherman. As a young man, Charles—his birth certificate gave his name as Charles Chester Fiore but at some point he reversed the order of the given names—was apparently an outstanding student, so bright that he won admission to Stuyvesant High in Manhattan, the city's most elite and demanding public high school. In fact, he attended Stuyvesant for three years before returning to City Island to graduate from the high school there. The records at Stuyvesant gave no

indication of academic or disciplinary problems, leading the author
of the article to conjecture that the change in the young man's
plans might have had something to do with the death of his grandfather during the summer before Charles's senior year. The old
man's boat went down in a storm under circumstances at least suspicious enough to have prompted City Island detectives to open a
file on the incident, but the investigation went no further than that.
At the time, and indeed until quite recently, the fish markets of
New York had been completely under mob control.

Reading on, Jeffrey learned that Fiore was married but was
never seen in public with his wife. He got his female companion-
ship from a series of attractive actresses and models, each one his
exclusive companion until she was replaced by the next, a pattern
the writer drolly characterized as *serial bigamy*. Nothing at all was
known about his wife. In addition, there were rumors that couldn't
be substantiated about an earlier marriage that resulted in a child
and ended in an annulment.

The remainder of the article detailed Fiore's rise to power
under the wing of Gaetano Falcone, an old-school mobster who
united New York's underworld under his command after a series of
bloody purges in the early 1960s and who still ruled the scene,
through deputies like Chet Fiore, from his seaside estate in Orient
Point on Long Island. Shortly after Fiore appeared on the scene,
three gangsters reputed to be the mob's enforcers at the Fulton
Fish Market were found dead under an elevated section of the
FDR Drive. Although the police never made a connection, the
writer of the article speculated that this triple assassination was
Chet Fiore's revenge for his grandfather's death.

Jeffrey turned off the computer. He had read enough.

Traffic crawled out of the city and then gradually thinned as
Martin and Jeffrey made their way east. For the last sixty miles they
made good time, but still it took more than two and a half hours to
get to Orient Point. The village itself consisted of only a few stores

and a gas station. Martin pulled into the gas station away from the pumps and Jeffrey got out of the car. The sun had set already but night hadn't yet taken hold. It was just after seven.

The gas station attendant was a skinny man with stringy blond hair and a barbed-wire tattoo around one of his biceps. "Help you?" he asked, wiping his hands as he approached.

Jeffrey said that he was looking for the home of Gaetano Falcone.

The attendant sized him up with a long look that took in not only the thousand-dollar suit and the sixty-dollar haircut but the car and the colored chauffeur as well. Definitely not cops. Anyway, cops wouldn't ask for directions at a gas station. Or maybe they would. He didn't much care. He thought of asking the well-dressed guy if he had business with Mr. Falcone, just to sound like he was doing the right thing, but he figured the old man had his own bodyguards and didn't need his help.

"Just follow the shore," he said. "Stone wall with a gate, mile and a half, maybe three-quarters."

Jeffrey thanked him and walked back to the car, with the attendant's eyes following him the whole way. He relayed the instructions to Martin as he got in and then glanced back as Martin rolled forward to pull out of the station. The attendant was jogging back to the office. Probably to put in a call, Jeffrey figured. That was fine.

As they drove out of the tiny town, they passed immense estates on both sides of the road. Shielded from sight by forests of scrub pine, the houses, with one or two exceptions, couldn't be seen from the road except for a few lights that managed to pierce the greenery, but the distances between the driveways gave a good indication of the size of the properties. Because of a rise in the land, the ocean wasn't visible from the road but the salt smell of it thickened the air.

A mile past the start of a chest-high stone wall, an immense iron gate rose as predicted to a height of perhaps twelve feet. The gate was set back from the road about ten feet, so that visitors could pull off the road while they waited for it to be opened. A considerate touch, Jeffrey thought.

So were the two men in dark suits who stood on the other side
of the gate, confirming Jeffrey's guess about the gas station attendant. They looked enough alike to be father and son, which in fact
they were. The older man opened a door in the gate and stepped
through. Jeffrey rolled down his window but didn't get out.

"This is private property," the man said.

Jeffrey held out a business card. "My name is Jeffrey Blaine,"
he said. "I'm an investment banker. I'd like to speak with Mr.
Falcone. Please tell him that I handle the Atlantic accounts."

The bodyguard took the card and studied it a moment, turning
on a flashlight to read it, as though he expected to find additional
information there. His name was Sal and he was called Big Sal to
distinguish him from his son, Little Sal, who stood three inches
taller and outweighed him by forty pounds.

"He's not expecting you?" Big Sal said, phrasing it as a question.

"No, but I'm sure he'll want to see me. If this isn't a good time,
tell me when to be back and I'll be back."

Big Sal considered the offer and answered with a grunting
sound. He clicked off his flashlight and walked back through the
door in the gate, which his son dutifully closed. The two of them
vanished from sight.

A motor of some sort started nearby, and then a golf cart,
which had been hidden by the stonework, bounded onto the pine-
speckled gravel drive, heading away. It had only one occupant, the
father, so apparently Junior was still lurking somewhere on the
other side of the gate.

The drive was flanked on both sides by skinny, stunted pines,
the only thing that would grow in the sandy, alkaline soil. The golf
cart bounded comically down the path, bearing the squat, comical
body of the bodyguard. Unfortunately for Big Sal, it's impossible to
appear formidable in a golf cart, and so he had to accept the indignity of looking like an oversized, loose-jointed puppet as he
bounced down the lane until, about a hundred yards away, he and
his cart outran the reach of Jeffrey's headlights and disappeared
from sight.

Fifteen minutes passed. It was possible, Jeffrey realized, that he had misunderstood. Not that there was anything either to understand or misunderstand. Falcone undoubtedly operated in a world of almost telepathic communication, where messages didn't even have to be sent to be received. Perhaps the elder bodyguard's departure alone in the golf cart meant that Jeffrey was supposed to leave, with Bodyguard the Younger remaining behind just to make sure that he did. And to shoot him if he tried to crash the gate. He decided to give it another ten minutes and checked his watch.

Before the ten minutes were up, the gate swung open with a whir of well-oiled machinery. Little Sal, two hundred twenty muscular pounds of him, stood in the glare of the headlights. He approached the car on the passenger side even though Jeffrey was seated directly behind Martin. He gestured for the window to be rolled down and Martin complied. Leaning in through the open window, he said, "Yeah, he says it's okay. I'll ride up with you." He had skin like a road in need of repaving. He was no more than twenty years old.

He tried the door but Martin had taken the precaution of locking them all.

"Let him in, Martin," Jeffrey said.

Martin hit the switch and the young bodyguard slipped into the front seat. "Yeah, okay," he said.

Martin eased the car through the gate, which swung closed behind them.

"My name's Sal," the young man said. "There's rabbits and stuff running around. You gotta take it kind of slow."

Jeffrey thought about Lenny in *Of Mice and Men*. He wondered if Sal patted the rabbits.

The drive wasn't nearly as long as Jeffrey had imagined it would be. There was a turn to the left at about the point where he had lost sight of the golf cart, and the trees ended abruptly about fifty yards beyond that as the land rose in an immense clearing, with the sea behind it. The house itself was situated on the highest point of land, an attractive, old-fashioned house, large but without pretension. Light washed out from the neatly ordered rows of casement windows, the curtains all drawn back, suggesting that the occupants enjoyed the surroundings during the day and found no reason to close themselves off from the night.

The elder bodyguard was waiting for them in front of the house. "Pull up where my father's standing," Sal instructed.

Sal the Elder said only, "He stays out here," when Jeffrey got out of the car. He meant Martin.

Jeffrey followed Sal up the short flagstoned walk to the front door. Well-tended beds of rust-colored chrysanthemums, pale dahlias, and dull red sedum flanked the walk, dying back, at the end of their season. A few months ago the area must have been a blaze of color but now it wore the sad and forsaken look of fading flowers. Myrtle beds did their best to keep the illusion of summer alive. Possibly this was the handiwork of a well-paid gardener, but something told Jeffrey otherwise. Someone in the family tended this garden.

Gaetano Falcone stood waiting for him in the front foyer, a round-faced man with large, soft hands and a soft, paunchy body that still gave evidence of the hardness underneath. He was wearing a sport shirt and rumpled pants. Jeffrey, who had expected to be ushered into a darkly paneled office where the godfather would be waiting for him behind an immense desk, said only, "It's good of you to see me, sir."

"If you came all the way here, I can at least offer you hospitality," Falcone said. "I'm not aware of these accounts you mentioned to my associate."

Falcone, of course, was being cautious. He could have had Jeffrey searched for a recording device but it was simpler and less offensive to say nothing.

"I understand," Jeffrey said. "I didn't come here to talk to you about the accounts."

Falcone studied him quizzically for a moment. "We eat early, I'm afraid," he said. "My wife has theories on these things, so we've already had dinner. But come, we'll find something."

He turned and led the way past the main staircase and through a door to a short corridor that led to a spacious kitchen. He threw on the lights as he entered and made straight for the immense stainless steel refrigerator. He took out cardboard baskets of blue-berries and raspberries, as well as a cantaloupe and a honeydew melon. "If you want coffee, hit that button," he said, indicating a coffeemaker that stood at the end of the long slate counter in the middle of the room.

Jeffrey declined.

"Good," Falcone said. "It's not good for you, too much coffee. You're an investment banker but you don't want to talk about investments."

It was an invitation for Jeffrey to get to the point of this meeting while his host busied himself rinsing the blueberries and raspberries.

"No, I wanted to talk to you about my daughter," Jeffrey said, choosing his words carefully. Falcone's denial of knowledge about the Atlantic accounts put him on notice that he had to be circum-spect in what he said or Falcone would end the conversation with an abrupt denial. "In the spring she became involved with a young man named Eddie Vincenzo. He wasn't interested in my daughter, Mr. Falcone, he was interested in gaining access to me on behalf of the people he works for."

"I don't need the details, Mr. Blaine," Falcone said, tacitly acknowledging that he knew them already.

"Fine, then I can shorten the story," Jeffrey said. "I was given assurances that this man's involvement with my daughter would end if I complied with the wishes of the people he worked for. That hasn't happened."

"Do you know for a fact that this young man is still seeing your girl?" Falcone asked.

He added a few slices of the melons to the bowl.

"So I'm told," Jeffrey said.

"And you have no control over your daughter?"

"I do now," Jeffrey said. "I've spoken with her. She understands the situation."

This was the right answer. Falcone had little sympathy for modern parents who believed in the possibility of fixing their chil-dren's problems without fixing the children.

He divided the fruit into two serving dishes and set them on the counter along with spoons and a cut-glass sugar bowl. He spooned sugar onto his own helping. They ate standing up.

"Let me understand," Falcone said. "You didn't drive all the way out here because you want me to save your daughter from this boy, did you? You've already taken care of that."

"That's right," Jeffrey said. "I have taken care of it."

"Then this is about settling a score," Falcone said, with no particular intonation expressing either approval or disapproval.

"That's right," Jeffrey said, even though Falcone's statement hadn't been a question.

The old man's shrewdness didn't come as a surprise to Jeffrey. You don't get to be who Gaetano Falcone obviously was if your eyes don't look straight to the heart of the matter. What else, Jeffrey wondered, did this shrewd old gangster see? Did he see that Jeffrey's problem was with Chet Fiore more than it was with Eddie Vincenzo? Did he understand that Jeffrey Blaine had driven almost the length of Long Island to let Gaetano Falcone know that Falcone's protégé, if that's what Fiore was, had failed to live up to his word and had insulted the family of Falcone's banker?

Yes, Jeffrey was certain Falcone understood all of this. And Jeffrey wanted him to understand it. There was a boldness to the move, because it posed a question Falcone would be forced to answer in his own mind. How many men did he have who could do what Chet Fiore did for him? And how many Jeffrey Blaines? If Jeffrey was right in his calculations, Falcone would come up with the only reasonable answer.

Falcone nodded his head and walked with his ambling shuffle to the kitchen door. The man who had met Jeffrey at the gate, the older one, the father, was standing in the corridor off the kitchen as though he had been there all along, as though, in fact, he was always there. Falcone conferred with him briefly, his back to Jeffrey, making no gestures that Jeffrey could see, his words inaudible. Then both men turned and walked in opposite directions, Falcone returning to the kitchen.

"I understand what you're telling me, Mr. Blaine, and I'm glad you came to me," he said, offering his hand. He picked up the two bowls and carried them to the sink. "The matter has been taken care of to your satisfaction," he added as he turned on the water to rinse the bowls.

Jeffrey had Martin drop him off on Fourteenth Street and Third. He walked across to Elaine Lester's apartment, cutting through Union Square. The area teemed with people his daughter's age, maybe a few years older, milling about with the indiscernible purposefulness of ants on the march.

Elaine was asleep when he rang her bell. She buzzed him in and went back to bed as she always did, leaving the front door open. She didn't come awake until he was in bed beside her. He kissed the back of her neck and let his hand drift down past her breasts and over her belly. She rolled over onto her back and turned her face to him. "Why do you always take so damn long?" she said.

"I'm in no hurry."

She said, "I am," and they made love, each taking care of the other with the patience of long-term lovers. She fell asleep afterward and didn't wake up until she moved in her sleep and sensed that he was no longer at her side. He was getting dressed in the dark when she opened her eyes. She turned away.

He sat on the bed to pull on his socks and shoes. When he saw that she was awake he said something about seeing her name in the *Times*.

She seemed surprised. "Why was I mentioned in the *Times*?" she asked.

"It wasn't recent," he said. "About a year ago. In the magazine section. I found it on the Internet."

Now she rolled over to face him. She never liked watching him get dressed. That was the worst part of having an affair with a married man. Not the leaving. Getting dressed. Because it meant that he was gone already even though he was still there, so that she could feel the presence of his other life palpably in the room beside them, like a leering intruder.

"Why were you looking me up on the Internet?" she asked.

"Not you," he said. "Chet Fiore. He's a client. I'm handling some investments for him."

Her mind didn't feel clear. She couldn't make herself understand why he was telling her this. So she said nothing.

"But you probably knew that," he added over her silence.

She didn't answer his question, if it had been a question. Instead, she said, "It's a small world, Jeffrey."

He knew that it wasn't.

Before he got up, she put her arms around him. Their unspoken rule was that she wouldn't ask him to stay, but there was no rule against asking without speaking the words.

He lay back, resting his head on her breast, while she drew pictures with her fingers in his hair.

They made love again, and this time when she fell asleep she didn't wake up to hear him leave.

The voice said, "Eddie."

Eddie didn't recognize the man, so he kept walking.

The man fell in step beside him, so Eddie stopped. "You want me?" he asked.

"You're Eddie Vincenzo."

It wasn't clear if it was a question or not. If it was, Eddie wasn't in the mood for answering questions. The guy was a couple inches taller than Eddie, bigger across the chest. But not so big that it would be a problem if he meant trouble. Eddie had a six-pack in his hand, in a paper bag. He was going home, and Georgie and some friends were coming over. They were probably going out after that; the six-pack was for until they figured out what they were going to do.

Eddie started to walk again and the man said, "I'm talking to you."

It wasn't until he turned that Eddie saw the second guy leaning against the door of a car parked at the curb. If they were cops, they were supposed to identify themselves, but there were a lot of wiseasses who never bothered with things like that. Eddie had run into his share. His mind raced through the possibilities of why a couple cops might want to talk to him and couldn't come up with anything in particular. "What?" he said.

The man said, "You always like this? A person wants to talk to you, you act like it's the end of the fucking world."

"It's not the end of the fucking world. I don't know who the fuck you are, that's all."

"If that's all, the name's Joey."

Joey held out his hand. Eddie didn't take it. Joey said, "See what I mean?"

Eddie said, "Look, I got stuff to do. You wanna get to the point?"

"Mr. Falcone said he wants to talk to you."

Jesus, Eddie thought. The idea that Mr. Falcone wanted to talk to him took his breath away. He didn't think that Mr. Falcone even knew who he was. "Why didn't you say that?" Eddie said.

Joey said, "I did say that, just now. Am I going too fast for you, kid?" But he kind of smiled when he said it and the two of them walked over to the car, where the second guy was still leaning against the door. He opened the front door and Eddie got in. Joey got in behind the wheel. The other guy got in back.

Eddie didn't know if he was supposed to ask any questions, so for a while he just sat there without saying anything. They drove down to Canal Street and across Canal and onto the bridge to Brooklyn. When they turned off at the first exit on the Brooklyn side, Eddie said, "Where are we going?" He didn't see any harm in asking.

That's when he felt something around his neck and realized he had made a big mistake. It wasn't piano wire or anything like that. It wasn't going to cut right through his throat. It was more like a scarf all twisted up or a piece of rope. He reached up and tried to pull it off him, because it was choking him, but the guy was holding on too tight and there wasn't a fucking thing Eddie could do about it. He tried to wedge his fingers in, just enough to give him a chance to breathe, and he realized that whatever it was felt kind of rubbery. It came to him, one of those stupid things that pops into your mind that doesn't do you the least bit of good, that it was a hunk of electric cord.

He thought for a second that he was putting up a good fight but he knew at the same time that he wasn't really putting up any fight at all. Nothing he did, twisting one way and the other and kicking around with his legs, was helping him in any way. But he was so caught up with it that he didn't even realize that the car was stopped.

All of a sudden the door opened and the pressure on his windpipe went away, leaving him free to cough his head off. Joey was standing in the open door. He reached in with two hands and dragged Eddie out onto the street.

Eddie landed on his back. The son of a bitch kicked him right in the ribs. Fuck! It felt like he was wearing steel-tipped boots. The foot went right into his bones with enough force to break everything there. And then the bastard said "Get up," and the second guy was pulling him to his feet.

Which told Eddie that this was going to be the worst thing that ever happened to him in his whole life. All Eddie could do was hope that he passed out as soon as absolutely possible.

Joey punched him a few times, in the face and in the ribs, which hurt like a motherfucker because of the kick. And then Eddie saw that the other guy had a knife in his hand, and he wanted to cry. Whatever this was about, it didn't require a knife. Eddie wanted to tell him, *You don't need a goddamned knife.*

Joey said, "Pretty boy, aren't you? Is that what the girls like?"

What girls? Eddie didn't know what the fuck he was talking about.

Joey said, "Think they're gonna like this?"

The knife was so sharp Eddie didn't even feel the blade on his face. But he felt the blood running down his neck and into his shirt. First on one side, then on the other. He thought he was being skinned alive. He managed to get his hands up, and when the knife cut his hands and his arms he could feel it just fine.

He felt something hit him on the back of the neck and then he was on the ground again. He was starting to pass out. He could feel his own blood in a puddle his face was lying in.

Joey said, "Just a warning, kid. Man wants you to leave his daughter alone."

Then he got kicked again, this time right in the cheekbone. It felt like his head was going to come off. He managed to get a hand up by his face to keep it from happening again, and the guy stepped on the back of his hand. Hard. Grinding.

"Got the message, kid? Next time there won't be nothing left," the man said.

Eddie could hear the bones of his hand breaking. And then he didn't hear anything at all.

Phyllis took a deep breath and waited for sleep to come back. When it didn't, she turned onto her back again and lay there looking up, letting her eyes adjust to the darkness. She heard a bus shift gears as the light changed down on Fifth Avenue, and wondered about the lives of people who took buses at three o'clock in the morning. If that's what it was. She could have turned to look at the clock, but she really didn't want to know.

It was never dark in the city. Even this many stories up, light from the street lamps climbed the sides of the building and oozed in through the windows. Light like moonlight, pale and wasted.

She threw her feet out of the bed, angry with herself for not being able to find her way back to sleep. It isn't because Jeffrey's not here, she told herself. It just happens sometimes that a person can't sleep.

She stepped into her slippers and pulled on her robe and found herself tiptoeing down the corridor, as if there was someone not to wake. She caught herself and changed her stride to a normal walk.

Gin or whiskey? she asked herself. Whiskey seemed more sociable, but she wasn't in a sociable frame of mind. Whiskey was for when you have someone to talk to. So she poured a few fingers of gin into a tall glass, ice cubes, tonic. She sliced a wedge out of a lime, squeezed the juice into the glass, and watched the juice spread around like smoke. She dropped in the wedge with a ceremonial flourish and stirred the whole thing by swirling the glass in her hand.

She drank it down at once, like it was medicine. Jeffrey always made the drinks, and she didn't realize how much gin she had put in until she was already mixing herself a refill.

Refill. That sounded social, too. *Bartender! Have a refill here*, with just the right wave of the hand. She practiced the wave in the empty room, saying the words to herself. That's what they should have, she thought. A bartender. Fire the maid and hire a bartender.

Wouldn't Jeffrey be surprised.

Jessica had never been so frightened in her life. She stood on the corner of Orange and George, just a couple blocks south of campus, exactly the way she had seen Eddie do it. She imagined everyone she saw was an undercover police officer. Eddie was always the one who did the buying. He would go out, and then he would come back with the stuff, knowing where to go even in cities where he was a stranger. She asked him once, and he said, "Hey, you just look around." Sure, she thought. *Look around.* But don't you have to know where to look?

If he hadn't taken her with him once, leaving her in the car while he got out to conduct his business, she never would have imagined that this was where you go. Orange and George.

She wished she remembered what the man Eddie dealt with looked like. She should have paid more attention. He seemed young, very young, she remembered that, and he was taller than Eddie, but she hadn't really looked because she was frightened just being there. He was black but that didn't help because everyone on the street here was black.

She didn't even know how much the stuff cost.

She thrust her hands deeper into the pockets of her windbreaker, clutching the bills she had just gotten from the ATM in the student center. She had made up her mind when her father told her about Eddie that she wouldn't see him again. She even made it her business for most of the next week to be out every evening, staying in the library until it closed at midnight, so that she wouldn't have to deal with him if he came by or called. But he didn't come by and he didn't call, and with each passing day her anger mounted as she felt more and more used and misused.

No one on the street looked at all familiar. She scanned the intersection, up the street and down, then stepped around the corner onto Orange Street to look both ways again.

"Temple, babe," a deep voice said practically in her ear.

She jumped back in alarm, whirling around. A heavyset black man with a shaved head had just passed behind her. It must have been he who spoke, but he gave no sign of it as he hurried away from her, walking quickly with a flamboyantly athletic precision to his gait.

She wasn't even sure what he said or what it meant. Maybe, she thought, he was just talking to himself. And then she realized he had said *Temple* and Temple was a street near here. It ended at the campus. Yes, that made sense, she thought. These people would have to move around, to keep ahead of the police. He was telling her where to go.

She hurried to the intersection of Temple and George, not even thinking about how conspicuous she must have looked to be delivered such a message by a stranger.

She saw the boy she was looking for from half a block away. Even by the dirty yellow light of the streetlight, he wasn't hard to recognize. She quickened her pace.

"I need some stuff," she said. (Why did she say *need*? It made her sound like a drug addict.)

His insolent eyes ran the length of her body and then back up to her face. He didn't look more than fifteen years old, except for those eyes, which were an old man's eyes, shallow and indifferent. "I don't know what you need, kid," he said, "but I'm betting I ain't got it."

She thought of half a dozen things she could have said but heard herself simply saying, "Please."

This time his eyes stayed on her face and he seemed to be asking himself a question. Then the answer came to him and he said, "You're Eddie's chick, right?"

She felt a surge of anger. Her face burned with it, and she wanted to tell him that she was not Eddie's *chick*. She was not Eddie's anything. Eddie was out of her life. She was here because she found her way here herself. Did that sound like anyone's goddamned chick? But before she could say any of this, a voice in her head stopped her and she realized that she had to swallow her dignity and smile and say *Yeah, that's right, I'm Eddie's chick*, because he wouldn't sell to a stranger.

"Eddie got stuck in the city," she said. "He asked me to pick it up."

Inside, she boiled with outrage that that arrogant Italian bastard hadn't even had the decency to call. He was finished with the assignment, so of course he didn't call. *Eddie, we've got a job for you. Get with that dumb little cunt and fuck her silly till we tell you to stop. You think you can do that, Eddie?* And her own father never even warned her till it was over. He was as bad as the lot of them, working out his own damned salvation while Eddie Vincenzo, that egotistical little prick, turned her into a complete fool. *He got stuck in the city.* The words scorched her ears like a scream.

"Cool," the kid said. "How much you want?"

"I've got a hundred dollars," Jessica said, pulling the bills out of her pocket.

Even to herself she sounded like a little kid plunking her change on the counter to see if it was enough for an ice cream cone.

"Christ, bitch, put that away," the kid snapped, actually slapping at her hand as though he were shooing a fly. She jammed her hand back into her pocket.

"C'mon," he said.

He turned with the crispness of a soldier doing a drill, a startling movement in someone so loosely strung together, and walked toward the entrance of a small apartment building just a few paces up from where they had been standing. He didn't even glance back to see if she was following.

She was.

The tiny lobby had a rank, cabbagy smell. Very little light from the street penetrated here, and the single fixture in the ceiling wasn't working. The space was only a few feet square, with a bank of about a dozen mailboxes on one wall, a graffiti-covered tile wall opposite it. A door, sprung on its hinges, led inside.

She took the money out again, and this time he snatched it out of her hands, counted the five twenties, and stuck them in his pocket. He turned around and opened one of the mailboxes without using a key. He took out a plain white paper envelope and handed it to her. "Awright, get outta here," he said.

She thought she ought to look in the envelope, to make sure she wasn't being cheated, but at the same time she thought she had better just leave.

It took her no more than five minutes to reach the edge of campus. She didn't run, but she felt like she was being chased the whole way. She stopped to calm the pounding in her chest, and then felt a sudden rush of confused thoughts. What if Barbara was there when she got back to the room? In fact, she would be. She was always in by this time.

Well, in that case, she thought, any ladies' room in any building on campus would do just fine. At any given moment, she remembered, eighteen percent of the freshman class was stoned and another twenty-one percent was drunk. A friend of hers named Aubrey came up with those numbers one night when a bunch of them were talking over hamburgers in the student union. He made them up in a long, hysterically funny monologue that sounded like the text of the latest study of student behavior. According to Aubrey, twenty-seven percent of female freshmen were virgins, but the figure dropped to eight if you counted sex with other female freshmen.

For some reason the numbers all stuck in Jessica's mind.

The idea of going to a ladies' room didn't appeal to her. It was like drinking out of a bottle in a brown paper bag. She smiled to herself, amused at the notion that Jessica Blaine was too good for that.

Yeah, right.

She ended up on the grass behind the chapel. There was a nice little maple tree there, and a hedge that marked off the borders of the useless space. She sat on the ground with her back against the maple and took the envelope out of her pocket.

She used a rolled-up index card. Which seemed a very Yale thing to do.

This stuff was supposed to make her feel better but it didn't. It made everything sharper, which it wasn't supposed to do.

The stone wall of the church seemed to throb like a membrane, systole and diastole, pumping like a machine. And the clouds above the maple circled like a pinwheel.

She took another hit, hoping for something that didn't happen and wouldn't happen.

She ran through the list of people she hated.

Eddie Vincenzo.

Jeffrey Blaine.

Jessica Blaine.

She lay on her back and cried while the church walls powered the still world with their endless pulsing. She could hear them now. *Thwump-uhhh, thwump-uhhh, thwump-uhhh.*

Eddie Vincenzo. Amy Laidlaw. Jessica Blaine.

Eddie   Vincenzo.   Amy   Laidlaw.   Jessica   Blaine.

Part Five

20

The night before Clint Bolling's funeral, a captain from the state police called on his widow. He presented a business card instead of a badge. He had a thick, unkempt mustache but wore a dress uniform that managed to convey a sense of considerable dignity despite his sagging, basset-hound face, and he carried his hat before him as though he were in church. His name was Loving, a strange name for a man of his calling, for any man.

"Ma'am," he said, "the toxicology report showed a considerable amount of cocaine in your husband's bloodstream."

She had known it would, so she said nothing.

"Ma'am," he said, "I just saw a draft of the report. It's not final."

"This cocaine did what?" Rachel asked. "It caused his heart to stop?"

"No, ma'am. There was strychnine, too. Sometimes it's put in cocaine."

"For what purpose."

"To kill someone, ma'am. It doesn't take much."

She didn't say anything for almost a full minute while she considered this information. She turned and walked away from him, and she kept her back to him until she was ready to respond. Then she turned to him.

"But his heart did stop, didn't it?"

"Yes, ma'am," Captain Loving said.

"Then why can't your reports simply say that?" she asked. "That his heart stopped?"

"Yes, ma'am," he agreed. "Heart failure. That's why I wanted to talk to you. It seemed to me you ought to know the truth."

"This is the truth," she said. "His heart stopped."

Captain Loving looked down at the hat he held in front of his belly.

"You're very kind," she said.

The state police were invariably kind to local boys who stayed home and made the kind of money Clint Bolling made. Even, she thought without bitterness, when they married Mexican girls half their age.

Captain Loving came to the funeral.

Rachel watched her husband's coffin descend into the dry, bare ground out beyond where the grass grew, so false and green, on the tended part of his estate. His first wife lay beside him, and Rachel watched as the workers filled the hole, shovel after shovel. Then she turned away and walked back to the house, closing the doors behind her, permitting none of the guests inside, even though they had come from Dallas and Houston and Norman and St. Louis, and of course the entire workforce from PetroBoll—his people, all of them, none of hers, because she had yet to notify her mother or her sisters that her husband was dead. She didn't want condolences from anyone. She wanted to be alone in the house, where the earth-colored walls offered the only comfort she was willing to accept.

And so the cooks, who had prepared a lavish spread of fresh bread and local game and cheeses and salsas, carried their tables to the back patio by the pool and set them up there, under umbrellas to keep the sun off the food. Rachel remained in the master bedroom all afternoon, pacing with long restless strides until the last of the guests was gone well after sunset and silence settled over the house like a warm, slow wind.

For almost two weeks after the funeral she stayed in the house alone, except for the servants. Some people from the company came for the first few days, but when she made it clear to them that she wanted nothing, they stopped coming. Day by day the silence in the house grew until it was like the silence of the desert, simply a natural fact. She took her meals by herself, entering the dining room with a place already set and the food already served. Except for the fact that the food was eaten, no one in the house would have known she had come out of her room.

When she felt she was ready, she sent for Miguel and asked him to book her a flight to New York. She wanted to meet this man Blaine again. She wanted to rip his heart out with her hands.

When she got to Blaine's office, the obnoxious girl at the front desk told her to wait please and someone would be out for her and she agreed to wait, even though she should have said, *No. This man Blaine, this banker, this partner in your company, killed my husband and I do not choose to wait.*

She wore a short black skirt and a black silk blouse with no jewelry. Her stockings were so fine that the rich earth color of her skin shone through them, glowing the way her hair glowed. Her face was expressionless, with the abstracted look of an Old World Madonna, distant and self-contained. Her hands were knotted in her lap.

A few moments later she was in an office that one was supposed to think of as a living room, as though this woman who was in reality the man's secretary was to be thought of as his wife and there would be wine and canapés and conversation with interesting guests until dinnertime. It was a lie, this office that pretended not to be an office, and she despised it, and so she declined the young woman's offer of something to drink.

The young woman left. From beyond the door Rachel heard telephones ringing, a strange and sterile chirping as though the machines wished to conceal the fact that they were telephones.

Her strength and the bitterness that fueled it blazed in her heart the moment Jeffrey Blaine stepped through the door. "Mrs. Bolling," he said, striding toward her across the muted patterns of the carpet, "I'm so sorry. I would have come."

"Cocksucker pig," she hissed, and would have spat if he were closer.

Jeffrey stopped in his tracks, shocked, momentarily off balance. He had no idea how much she knew, which made it all the more imperative that he be careful. She blamed him for her husband's death. That much was clear. Nothing further.

He reached out a hand toward her and kept his voice smooth. "You'd better sit down, Mrs. Bolling," he said.

She remained standing. "My husband is dead," she said.

"I know," he said.

"Strychnine," she said. "Did you think nobody would know this?"

The color fled from his face, and even his eyes seemed to dim. His lips were parted, slackly, and for this reason the moment seemed to shock her as much as it did him. Was it possible he *hadn't* known about the strychnine? She could see in his face that this was so. She could see it in his confusion. And this confused her because she would have sworn he knew. Desperately, she wanted Jeffrey Blaine to have known, because if he hadn't known, then there was no way for her to keep her hatred intact.

"It happened exactly the way you showed him it would happen," she said.

In his mind he could hear Fiore's phone call to the drug dealer, could hear again that strange coded language Fiore spoke. Fiore made the call and that ugly South American made the delivery. Jeffrey knew almost nothing about how drugs worked and found himself wondering how quickly one knows if one has taken a poisoned dose of cocaine. Or if one knows at all. The answer mattered only to the extent that it mattered whether or not Clint Bolling knew, in his last conscious minutes, that he was being murdered.

"Sit down," he ordered in a tone that left her no choice.

She dropped back onto the sofa. He moved a chair, close enough already, even closer and sat facing her.

"If your husband died from poisoned cocaine," he said, "that's because he used cocaine. It has nothing to do with me."

"Why did you come to our house?" she asked. He could hear the confusion in her voice. "What were you doing with my husband?"

"I handle some of his investments."

"It was something illegal," she protested. "He didn't want to do it. He wouldn't have done it if you hadn't threatened him."

"I imagine you believe that, Mrs. Bolling. I don't think anyone else will."

"I'm not going to the police, if that's what you're afraid of," she said.

"I'm not afraid of anything," Jeffrey said, and she knew that he wasn't.

Her lips trembled. His assurance was so complete, his earnestness so convincing, that she found herself doubting everything. Jeffrey watched as tears formed in her eyes and began to roll slowly down her cheeks, leaving tracks the way raindrops leave tracks on a dirty window.

He let her sit for as long as she felt like sitting, neither of them speaking. When she stood to go, he walked her as far as the elevator and would have accompanied her downstairs if she hadn't asked him not to. She said she had a car waiting.

Before returning to his office, he took a detour to the computer section. Gabriel Enriquez was by himself, so Jeffrey was free to get right to the point. He asked the young man to familiarize himself with the Bolling account and to learn as much as he could about Bolling's finances. "I want you to fly out to Oklahoma City next week," he said. "See what help you can be to the widow."

He went back to his office and closed the door after telling Jennifer he wasn't to be disturbed. He unlocked the bottom drawer of his desk, which was deep enough for file folders, the only drawer of the desk equipped with a lock. He took out his notes on the Bolling transactions. These were his own copies of the instructions he hand-delivered to Gabriel Enriquez, directing the alterations in the accounts. Gabriel always destroyed his copies as soon as he completed the transactions. But Jeffrey kept his. They were the chips he would cash in if it ever became necessary for him to cooperate with an investigation.

He went over them carefully, analyzing each transaction, satisfying himself that there was no trouble Bolling's widow could make even if she had a mind to. The trail of illicit transactions was so perfectly hidden, covered over by unimpeachable records, that it would have been impossible for anyone, even if they knew what they were looking for, to find anything.

He couldn't help admiring the perfection of the scheme. Money grew under his hands the way fire spreads in dry leaves. A hundred thousand dollars became two, became four, became eight. Not so neatly as that, of course. He made sure there were no traceable patterns. As Fiore opened a third, a fourth, and a fifth account, Jeffrey made each of them behave in its own way. One would cash out regularly, in spasms of greedy profit taking; another left the gains to multiply; while a third grew fatter and fatter by plowing its profits back into new investments. Sooner or later they all produced checks that wound up on Fiore's books but in Jeffrey's pocket.

He formed a series of offshore corporations in the Bahamas and the Cayman Islands and let the money drift its way there. There was no hurry. He had hardly even begun to think of the things this money could buy. He remembered a farmhouse in Normandy where he and Phyllis had stayed for an idyllic three weeks when she was pregnant with Jessica. They bicycled across the countryside during the day, and in the evenings the two of them repaired to the immense kitchen, where they cooked preposterous dinners. The baby, they joked, would be born speaking French. He wondered if the house was still standing. It would be nice to own it, he thought, and promised himself he would look into it. And there were a hundred other things like that he could buy, things he had never known he wanted because they weren't part of the life he had mapped out for himself.

Money, he was discovering, has a dimension he had never so much as suspected. In a strictly literal sense, there was nothing he could buy now that he couldn't have bought before. But the money he earned before wasn't for the sorts of things he was thinking about now. There is a money of the body, which pays for things with which one surrounds oneself, and a money of the heart. And a money of the hidden self.

In the depth of his reverie, the sound of the telephone came at him vaguely, like the nebulous ringing of a phone in a dream. Annoyed at the interruption—he had explicitly told Jennifer to hold his calls—he hurriedly gathered his papers, patted the edges even, and jammed them back into the folder, as quick and furtive as if the phone had eyes. He returned them to the drawer and locked it before he pressed the button on the intercom to put Jennifer on the speaker. "What is it?" he asked sharply, letting his irritation show.

"Your wife's on the line, Mr. Blaine. She said it's urgent," Jennifer said.

He clicked her off and pressed the button for the lighted line. "What?" he said brusquely. "I'm in the middle of something."

"I'm in the car, I'm on the way down there." Phyllis's voice sounded tense, tinged with hysteria. "Jessica was taken to the hospital."

All of a sudden his skin stung and the muscles of his body tightened under it, as though he had fallen into a cold bath. He grabbed the phone from its cradle, which automatically cut off the speakers. "What happened? What's the matter?" he asked sharply.

"I don't know, I don't know anything," Phyllis wailed. "I can't talk now. I'll be there in five minutes."

The phone went dead at his ear. He dropped it back into its cradle as he got to his feet. He felt unsteady. Why the hell couldn't she have told him anything? *I can't talk now*, as though her turmoil and confusion were the first issues to be dealt with. His daughter was sick or in an accident, and he had no way of knowing anything until his wife pulled herself together enough to let him in on it.

Jennifer look up, alarmed, when he came out of the office. It was the look on his face. She had never seen him like that.

"My daughter," he said. "She was taken to the hospital. I'll call as soon as I know anything."

He hurried down the corridor and pushed through the door into the men's room. He stood for a moment with both hands on the sink and took a deep breath. In the silence it seemed to him he could hear his heart beating, so he turned on both taps full force to drown out the sound in a rush of noise. Water splashed against the basin and onto his suit.

He slowed the taps and let his hands dangle in the water for a moment, just for the coolness. Then he cupped water into his hands and lowered his face into it. He heard the door open and grabbed a towel off the stack.

"Oh, Jeffrey." It was Roger Bogard. "I wanted to talk to you," he said. "That Didier thing, the leukemia research, they've got management problems. The whole thing's starting to go soft."

Most of the junior people on the staff called Jeffrey Mr. Blaine even though he had asked them not to. Roger wasn't one of them.

"It'll have to wait until tomorrow," Jeffrey said. "I've got to go out. Family problem."

"I'm not sure it can wait," Roger said. "We could get stuck holding the whole thing."

He didn't ask about the family problem. It was as though he hadn't heard that part. But that was Roger. In fact, that was virtually all of the younger people in the business. Whatever native instincts for personal connection they may or may not have been born with had been trained out of them, and Jeffrey sometimes wondered what the office would be like when these people became the next generation of partners.

"Get together with Elizabeth," he said. "Work it out. If it's not going to turn itself around, withdraw the offering. You make the call."

Roger looked uncomfortable and lowered his head. They made good money, these children; they swaggered around like overwhelmingly important people and wrote up reports that sounded as though they had inside information from god himself. But they ran like mice for a hole whenever real responsibility was thrust at them.

"I think we'd want you to sign off on it before we did anything like that," Roger said, studying his shoes.

"Well, that's not one of the options right now, Roger. You make the damn call," Jeffrey said.

It felt good to let the anger show in his voice. He flung the towel into the hamper as he pulled the door open.

Downstairs, he didn't have to wait more than two minutes before the car pulled to the curb in front of him. He slid into the back seat next to Phyllis. "All right," he said, even before Martin had them moving, "tell me exactly what you know. She called?"

"Her roommate."

"What did she tell you?"

His voice sounded harsh even to himself, but he knew that she was going to have to be walked through the whole thing step by step, debriefed the way astronauts and soldiers are debriefed, or she would leave out things he should know.

Phyllis took a deep breath and held it while she tried to order her mind, sorting out what needed to be said in what sequence. "All right," she said at last. "She said Jessica was taken to the hospital this morning. I talked to her again after I talked to you, and she talked to the doctor in the meanwhile. She's not in danger. Stabilized, she said. She couldn't wake her up this morning and she was having trouble breathing."

"Do they know why?"

"Barbara thinks she was using drugs."

Jeffrey didn't say anything for a long time. He had considered the possibility of drugs as long ago as her disappearance with Eddie Vincenzo. Not because he had any evidence, but because it seemed like the sort of trouble two kids vagabonding around the country were likely to get into. Then, after she came back for Amy's funeral, in the few short weeks before she left for Yale, she seemed to him both tense and listless, sometimes in alternation, sometimes both at the same time. It made him wonder.

Phyllis said, "It doesn't make sense. I just can't imagine Jessica ever using drugs. It's not like her."

"Apparently it is," Jeffrey said.

"Goddamned son-of-a-bitch cocksucking faggot dwarf," Schliester shouted as he slammed the door and threw Gus Benini against the nearest piece of furniture. Which didn't even rattle as Benini bounced off it like a ping-pong ball, that's how skinny Benini was. He landed practically in Schliester's arms.

"What the fuck?" he said.

"What the fuck?" Schliester shot back at him. "You're asking me what the fuck? I ought to stick that coat rack so far up your ass it comes out your ears."

Benini actually glanced over to the coat rack, as though he had better get a handle on what it was going to feel like when it went in. "Jesus," he said. "What happened?"

Schliester stayed right in his face, his hands all over the skinny little man's grubby suit. "What happened, asshole, is I had cops here."

"Cops?"

"All over me. They wanted to know about a shakedown. You wouldn't know anything about that, would you?"

Benini shook his head like this was the most baffling thing he had ever encountered. "What would they want with you?"

"That's what I asked them."

"Yeah?"

"They weren't answering questions. They were asking them. Seems one of our clients got shaken down. You're supposed to shake a little harder, pal. You're supposed to shake hard enough that they don't dial 911."

"They say who?"

"The knife guy," Schliester said.

The "knife guy" manufactured handmade triple-tempered hunting knives in a barn in Wisconsin. He was famous all over the world, and he had a booth at the Javits Center's hunting and fishing exposition. Actually, the real knife guy had stayed in a hotel room somewhere south of Times Square while Gogarty impersonated him for Benini's benefit.

Benini looked confused.

"That bastard must have known I gave you his name," Schliester said. "What the fuck did you tell him?"

"I didn't tell him shit," Benini said. "What did you tell *them*?"

"The cops? I told them I didn't know anything about it. I told them to let me know as soon as they found out anything. You fucked me good. I could lose my job over this."

Benini walked in little circles around the office. Apparently he was thinking. He stopped walking and said, "Don't worry about it. They were guessing. They don't know you're involved. As long as you don't tell them anything, we're all right."

Schliester looked like he was going to cry, running a complete and instantaneous transformation from anger to fear. He wished Gogarty were there to actually see it instead of just getting the audio from the room bug. "What do you mean *all right*? I could lose my *job*," he wailed.

"They're guessing, they're guessing," Benini tried to reassure him.

"Yeah, but they're guessing *me*," Schliester whined.

Benini was in a hurry to get out of there. He hated whining. It made him sweat all over and tightened up his stomach so that he felt gassy and uncomfortable. "Just keep your mouth shut," he said, slipping sideways toward the door. "I'll be in touch."

"I don't want you in touch," Schliester moaned at the door as Benini disappeared through it. "I'm gonna lose my fucking job."

He walked over to the door and watched Benini, who walked like a rooster, speeding away like a man who had to go to the bathroom bad. Then he closed the door and said, "He's on the way out. You ready, partner?"

In the van on Eleventh Avenue Gogarty received the message. He was ready. So was the backup team they had borrowed for the afternoon because someone had to pick up the tail at the beginning while Gogarty waited for Schliester to come out to join him in the van.

In just a few seconds Benini was climbing into his car, which he always left under the No Parking sign at the bus and taxi dropoff in front of the Center. The backup team eased out to follow in a yellow cab, and Gogarty picked up his cell phone and dialed Schliester's office.

"You missed your calling, *boychik*," he said. "You should have been an actor. He's gone. You ready to rumble?"

Schliester hurried outside and jumped into the front seat of the van as his partner pulled in to pick him up. Gogarty was laughing and quoting his favorite lines from Schliester's performance. "I'm gonna lose my *jo-o-ob*," he moaned over and over in a singsong falsetto. "Please, Mr. Benini, I'm gonna lose my *jo-o-ob*."

"I didn't say *please*," Schliester said, and they both laughed.

They made radio contact with the backup team and got their location. When they had Benini in their sights, they thanked the backups and sent them home. Schliester fiddled with the controls on a radio receiver he took out of the glove compartment and hooked the receiver into a tape recorder he set on the floor between his feet. He plugged in a set of headphones and put them on. He wasn't getting any signal but that was no surprise. Benini wouldn't be talking to himself in the car.

"What if it doesn't work?" Gogarty asked.

Schliester was sure it would work.

"You're sure you gave it to him?"

Schliester had had no trouble palming the card into Benini's breast pocket while he was manhandling the guy. The theory was that even if Gus found it at some point he wouldn't think it was more than a business card, and he wasn't bright enough to wonder why he had taken the man's business card. He'd probably figure he just did. Anyway, it didn't matter, as long as he didn't find it until after he went running to Chet Fiore to warn him that the cops were closing in on the Javits Center operation.

A case is like a chain. One link connects to the next to the next to the next. They had Benini wrapped up like a mummy. One more link and Fiore would be part of the package.

Benini went straight down Seventh to Grand and then turned east again. In Little Italy he parked at a fire hydrant in front of a restaurant on Elizabeth Street. When Benini slammed the car door, the sound of it over the headset practically punctured Schliester's eardrum.

"It's working," he said as he turned down the volume.

Gogarty found a place to park around the corner and put on a second set of headphones. They heard Benini say, "Is he here?" They didn't hear an answer but Benini said, "Where the fuck is he?" so they settled in to wait.

It would have been better, since Fiore wasn't there yet, if they could have parked on Elizabeth Street and eyeballed him going in so that later they would be able to verify his voice on the tape. But that would have been too risky. Two men in the front seat of a van would have been kind of obvious. On the other hand, there were always cops and agents all over Little Italy, monitoring wiretaps in one place or another. They were part of the scenery. The locals didn't get too excited because there wasn't anything they could do about it anyway except watch what they said on the phone. Which made for an interesting standoff, the feds and cops brazenly monitoring taps on telephones on which nothing was ever said.

Room bugs, of course, were another matter. Ever since John Gotti got put away because agents actually managed to plant a room bug in the social club where he did business, which was a first at the time it was done, the interesting people were suddenly as careful about the rooms they were in as they were about their telephones. The Gotti case made it a good time to be in the security business, because anyone who knew what he was doing could clear a few grand a month for every room he guaranteed clean, which might be as many as a dozen rooms for a single client, counting restaurants, social clubs, apartments, and mistresses' apartments. Rooms were swept every week, and no one ever found anything for the simple reason that, after Gotti, no one tried it again. There was no sense putting in bugs that you knew would be found and removed. In that sense, the security people working for the mob and the cops and agents working against them became mirror images of each other, sweeping for microphones that weren't there and monitoring phone conversations that didn't take place. Agents with college degrees called it symbiosis. Cops with high school diplomas called it a circle jerk. Everybody stayed busy and no one got hurt.

A supersensitive microphone on a business card that a Fiore lieutenant brought into the place himself was going to change all that. Wally Schliester was sure of it. He and Gogarty were about to make law enforcement history.

They waited an hour, and all they got for their trouble was Gus Benini chirping like a cuckoo clock every fifteen minutes, asking *Where is he?* and *Where the fuck is he?* and *What do you mean you don't know?* Gogarty went out to pick up some food and came back with a couple plates of lasagna, a couple orders of garlic bread, and a couple salads. It was a known fact that no one who partnered with Gogarty ever went hungry.

"No Chianti?" Schliester asked.

"Fuck you," Gogarty said. "You want, I can go back and pick up a couple of beers."

Finally they heard what they were waiting to hear. It was Jimmy Angelisi who spotted Fiore the moment he walked into the restaurant. "I told you he'd be here," he said. "Wait here a minute." And Gus said, "You'll tell him I've got to talk to him, right?"

A little while passed and then they heard Chet Fiore saying, "All right, Gus. What is it this time?"

The two agents looked at each other with grins a mile wide. They could hear every word. "That's our man," Gogarty said.

Benini said, "Someone went to the cops. They came around asking Linkletter a lot of questions."

Fiore had never heard the name Linkletter. He never bothered Benini about details as long as things were running the way they were supposed to.

"Who's Linkletter?" he asked.

"My man," Benini said.

"Say *Javits Center*," Schliester coached him under his breath.

"The kid at the Javits Center," Benini went on, almost as though he had heard. In the van, Schliester and Gogarty exchanged high fives. "He's the one what's giving me the names," Benini said. "I'm keeping him out of it. Some asshole from Michigan or something, one of those states around there, he sells knives. I took six grand off him and he went to the cops. They went to the kid."

"Linkletter?"

"Yeah. Linkletter."

"Is he a stand-up kid?"

"So far he's a rock. But he's scared. He thinks he's going to lose his job."

"Why do you give a shit whether he loses his job?"

The question confused Benini. Right. Why should he care if Linkletter lost his job? There was a long silence, long enough that Schliester and Gogarty might have started to think their microphone had stopped working if they hadn't heard a steady drone of background noises from the restaurant. And then they heard Fiore's voice again.

"Listen to me, Gus," he was saying in a very level tone, like a man talking to child. "First thing, you shut it down."

"I thought I'd slip the kid something," Benini suggested. "A grand, y'know, something like that."

"I could get myself a nice set of speakers," Schliester joked.

"You're not listening," Fiore said. "Shut it down. You give him something, that's just going to tell him you're scared and that's just going to make *him* scared."

"Hey," Schliester said, "that's my money you're talking about."

Gogarty had to laugh. Everything the St. Louie kid did cracked him up.

"This isn't a problem, Gus," Fiore said. "We shut it down, we'll find something else for you, that happens all the time."

"Yeah, I know, but . . ."

"You did the right thing, Gus. As soon as you saw a problem, you came to me. If the cops had any line on who you are, they wouldn't have bothered with this kid, whatever his name is."

"Linkletter."

"No," Fiore said firmly. "It's not Linkletter. It's not anything. He doesn't have a name. Because he's not important. If he's worried about his job then he's not very worried. He's more scared of you."

"He just about fucking strangled me," Benini protested. The thought struck him that his boss might be missing the point.

"That's good," Fiore said. "He got mad, he acted a little crazy. Now he's got something to think about. He's going to think about it all night, Gus. He's going to wake up in the middle of the night just thinking about all the things that could happen to a nice kid like himself if he starts laying his hands on important people like you. He's going to get out of his bed and get down on his knees and say a long and very serious prayer so that maybe, if god's in the right mood, Gus Benini won't send someone to disconnect his legs. He made a mistake and that's going to scare him, and so he's going to promise himself not to make any more mistakes. You're all right, Gus. You did the right thing. Go home. Don't worry about it."

"You're sure?"

"I'm sure, Gus," Fiore said.

In the van, they could almost hear Fiore's hand coming to rest on Benini's shoulders. That's what his voice was like, smooth and reassuring. Schliester thought it was too bad Chet Fiore didn't have any kids because he sounded like he would make a great father.

And then he heard a voice he didn't recognize say, "Can I talk to you, Mr. Fiore?"

The voice had that hushed quality that comes with urgency. "Who's this?" Schliester said. Gogarty shrugged his shoulders.

"Just a minute, Georgie," they heard Fiore say.

Schliester said, "Georgie?" and Gogarty said, "Georgie Vallo. Minor punk."

"It's Eddie, Mr. Fiore," the voice that belonged to minor punk Georgie Vallo said.

"What about him?"

"Who's Eddie?"

"Could be a couple guys, I don't know," Gogarty said.

"Somebody beat the shit out of him. He's in the hospital. Been there a week, week and a half."

Fiore said, "Are we finished, Gus?"

He was inviting Benini to leave. Benini said, "Yeah, I guess so. You don't want me to do nothin', right?"

If Fiore answered, it wasn't audible in the van. Schliester and Gogarty could just barely hear Georgie Vallo say, "They fucked him up real bad," and then they didn't hear any voices for almost a minute. Then they heard a voice call Benini's name and Benini said, "Hey, later maybe. Take care of yourself," and they knew from the sounds around the voices that he had left the restaurant and was out on the street.

"Not a bad night's work," Gogarty said.

"Not bad at all," Schliester agreed.

He turned off the tape recorder and unplugged his head-phones.

It would be nice to know who Eddie was and what he did to get himself majorly hospitalized.

The woman at the information desk looked up Jessica's name on her computer and sent them to the fifth floor. When they got off the elevator, Barbara was already hurrying toward them from a waiting room just across from the elevators. "Okay," she said, as though one of them had asked a question, "she woke up and she's okay but she's back asleep now. Not unconscious, just asleep."

She took them to the room.

Phyllis gasped when she saw her daughter. There was a slack-ness to Jessica's face that made her look like a middle-aged woman. There was sweat on her forehead and her hair stuck to it darkly.

"The doctor said maybe you should just let her sleep," Barbara suggested as Phyllis practically ran across the room to the bed. "He said he'd be back to talk to you in a little while."

Jeffrey moved up beside his wife and the two of them stood there looking down at their daughter, side by side like figures on a wedding cake. With her fingertips, Phyllis brushed the hair back from Jessica's brow. "Jeffrey, she's cold," she said.

He had been about to stop her from touching the girl because the doctor said she should be left to sleep. But now he reached down to feel for himself, lightly touching Jessica's cheek. She wasn't *cold*, at least not in any alarming way. Her skin was cool and damp, that was all. Phyllis made it sound like she was touching a cadaver.

"We have to get her a blanket," she said. "Do you think there's one in the closet?"

She hurried to the closet and opened the door. There were no blankets.

Barbara said, "I'll get one, Mrs. Blaine," and left the room. She came back in less than two minutes with a scratchy, mustard-colored blanket. Phyllis helped her spread it out over Jessica, whose eyes remained closed.

Half an hour passed. Jessica sighed in her sleep and rolled onto her side. Her eyes opened, and then she blinked with the effort to keep them open when she saw her mother sitting by the head of the bed.

"You can sleep, baby," Phyllis said.

Jessica answered with a wan smile that seemed to require a certain amount of effort, as though this were all she could manage. "That's all right," she said.

Her voice sounded dry and scratchy. Phyllis asked her if she wanted something to drink, and then Barbara ran off to fetch some juice.

Jeffrey said, "How do you feel?" and she seemed to take a moment to locate him in space.

"Okay, I guess."

Phyllis asked her what happened, and Jessica answered by asking if they had spoken with the doctor.

Jeffrey stood up and walked to the window to look out. Jessica's evasiveness was all the answer he needed. She hadn't tried to kill herself. It was just a drug overdose, plain and simple. He felt his hands knotting into fists and he had to fight off the impulse to turn and tell her how stupid she was, how reckless, how . . .

But he knew perfectly well it didn't matter in the least what he said. If she was still playing games, answering questions with questions and readying her lies, she wasn't prepared to deal with any of the realities of the situation. On the other hand, she had her wits about her. That was good. He made up his mind right then that they would take her home as soon as the doctor gave his permission. She certainly wasn't going to be permitted to continue the life she had been leading.

He could hear Jessica and Phyllis talking in hushed voices, but he had little interest in whatever it was they might be saying. He didn't turn from the window until he heard the door open.

Barbara stepped in carrying a glass of apple juice. The man with her wore a hospital tunic. He looked to be no more than thirty years old, dark-skinned, with yesterday's shadow of a beard.

He introduced himself as Dr. Agarath. "You're Jessica's parents?" he asked, and then, not waiting for an answer, addressed Jessica. "I see you're awake. That's good. How are you feeling?"

Barbara deposited the juice glass on the table by the bed, mumbled something about waiting outside, and hurried from the room.

"I don't know how much Jessica's told you about her problem," the doctor said.

"She hasn't told us a thing," Jeffrey answered brittlcly.

The doctor took a moment to appraise the sharpness in the father's voice, a moment that was long enough for Jeffrey to reach his own conclusions about the young physician. He knew what was coming. A lecture on understanding that drug use was a treatable illness. Jeffrey listened and nodded, as he was expected to do, as Phyllis did.

When the doctor asked if they had any questions, Phyllis asked him if he thought Jessica was addicted to cocaine.

"I'm glad you asked me that," Dr. Agarath said, in the tone of a man who is in perfect agreement with himself. "We've found, that is, the medical community has found, as our understanding of these problems deepens, that addiction isn't a very useful model. It doesn't tell us anything. We say this one is addicted, this one is not addicted, and it has no bearing on the outcome."

"Outcome?"

"Recurrence. Relapse."

"I see," Phyllis said, although it hardly seemed likely that she did see. It all sounded like a speech the doctor had given before, honing the sentences with repetition until he convinced himself that all those idiotically nested clauses meant something. There was a kind of singsong lilt to his recitation, which was probably no more than the lingering traces of a Pakistani or Indian accent. It added to the sense of ritual performance.

"And you, Mr. Blaine. Do you have any questions?"

"She seems to be alert," Jeffrey said. "Is there any reason we can't take her home this afternoon?"

Jessica's eyes locked on his. She knew what he meant by home. She looked surprised. What had she expected? That they would drive her back to her dormitory? If she was prepared to argue the point, she was not prepared to argue it in front of the doctor, and so she looked away, as though whatever was going to be said between these three people didn't concern her.

The doctor agreed that there was no reason to keep her. He wanted to let her have lunch and then do a blood test. It would take only an hour or so to get the results, and if they were what he expected, she would be free to go. He suggested that she enroll in a counseling program and then excused himself, after shaking hands with Jeffrey and Phyllis as well as his patient.

"I'll do that," Jessica said, trying for a preemptive strike even before the doctor closed the door on his way out, "I'll sign up for a counseling program. They have—"

Jeffrey didn't let her finish. "You'll sign up for one in New York," he said.

"That's ridiculous. I'm in the middle of the semester."

"I'll talk to the dean," Jeffrey said. "Maybe you'll be able to try again next semester. Don't bother to say anything. It's not subject to discussion."

It seemed to him, as he looked back over eighteen years of raising a child, that she had never before been confronted with a situation that wasn't open to discussion. That was undoubtedly a mistake, but not a mistake that was going to happen again.

While Jeffrey went to talk to the dean, Phyllis and Barbara went to the dorm and packed a few bags with some of Jessica's things. When they got back to the hospital, Jessica was waiting for them in the corridor. "They said you're going to have to sign me out," Jessica said, taking the red Louis Vuitton leather bag from her mother. "I'll get dressed."

She had tried to sign herself out but wasn't allowed to. It was ridiculous. She wasn't a child.

Phyllis went to the nurses' station, where they directed her to an office, while Jessica returned to her room to get dressed. Her mother's choices of clothing were appalling, a pair of powder-blue frocks that Jessica didn't even remember owning, let alone bringing to New Haven. It was a fucking joke. Her mother must have imagined that if she left the hospital looking like something from a Girl Scout handbook, then the reason she was in the hospital would no longer be true.

She didn't bother with makeup or even with her hair, which was wildly disorganized. When she was dressed she carried her bag out to the corridor and set it down. There was no sign of her mother, and for a moment she weighed the possibility of sneaking out while her mother was stuck filling out forms in some office. She didn't have a penny, or even her wallet with her ATM card. Packing a few practical things like that was beyond her mother's capabilities.

She was still weighing her options when her mother suddenly materialized beside her. "The blood tests were just fine," Phyllis said. "Why don't you get ready and we can go?"

"I am ready."

She knew her mother meant her hair.

Phyllis bit back the impulse to say anything and picked up the leather bag.

"I can get that," Jessica said, but she made no move to take it from her mother's hand.

Phyllis said, "That's all right, dear."

Two of the nurses said good-bye to Jessica as she walked toward the elevator with her mother. They both called her *dear*. Jessica wanted to scream. Her mother said "Thank you" in that pointed way mothers fulfill the neglected courtesies of their children.

"They weren't talking to you, you know," Jessica whispered harshly when the elevator doors closed behind them.

"No," Phyllis said, "they were talking to you. But you declined to answer."

"Because they're a pair of condescending, supercilious bitches."

"They were just being polite, dear."

"If one more person calls me *dear*, I'm going to scream."

"Go right ahead, dear," Phyllis answered as the elevator doors opened on the ground floor lobby.

Jessica glared at her, shook her head, but didn't scream.

Martin was waiting on the other side of the revolving door. He came forward to take the bag as Phyllis preceded her daughter through. "Hello, miss," he said softly when Jessica came out.

Jessica liked Martin. He was the only servant her parents ever hired that she did like. She smiled faintly and lowered her eyes, embarrassed that he should be here now, that he should know, as he inevitably did because her parents talked about *everything* in the car, the whole story of her hospitalization. She wished he wasn't here.

Martin led the way to the car. There was a circular drive in front of the hospital. An abstractly prayerful statue with upraised steel excrescences that were meant to suggest arms rose from a bed of gravel and crushed stones that filled the center of the circle. Parking lots flanked the drive to either side, extending along the hospital's north and south wings. The car was illegally parked at the far side of the circle.

"You know this is ridiculous," Jessica said. "I am not some god-damned drug addict."

"Lower your voice!" her mother shot back in the riveting whisper that had always commanded instant obedience in Jessica's childhood.

A pair of young doctors in scrubs looked at them, then looked away. A woman hurried by, dragging a child by the hand.

"I will not lower my voice. I am not a drug addict. And I don't give a damn what you and Daddy worked out without even thinking about it or discussing it with me. I am *not* going home. If you fixed it so I can't go back to school, I'll fix it back. Or I'll stay here without going to classes. Do you like that better? That will be great, won't it? I'll bet you didn't think of that in your planning."

She didn't even wait for a reply, but turned instantly and bolted down the drive, running with reckless abandon, away from Phyllis, away from Martin and the car.

Phyllis watched her run for a moment and then said, "Please get her, Martin."

The prospect of having to physically restrain his employer's daughter filled the shy young driver with an unbearable sense of dread. "Ma'am," he protested, "I can't just—"

"Martin," Phyllis cut him off, "get her."

Jessica was already halfway down the length of the south wing when Martin started after her. Even in stiff shoes, he began closing the distance quickly. She cut to her right, into the parking lot, and he matched her, forty yards behind. She wove her way, dodging among the parked cars, a zigzag that would bring her out to the street. Martin kept to a straighter path. A few right angles brought him into the same lane she was in only a couple dozen yards behind.

All through the lot, people stopped, turned, followed their progress with alarm, a young black man chasing a white girl, a recipe for disaster in a town as racially divided as New Haven. Martin knew it, and he called Jessica's name, hoping she would stop before anything happened.

She heard his voice and glanced back. *Why was he doing this?* she thought bitterly. *Why was he taking her mother's side?*

She kept running, knowing with perfect certainty that she couldn't outrun him, that there was no reason at all to keep going, except her rage at her parents and her stubbornness.

From somewhere in the lot, somewhere behind both of them, a man's voice called, "Hey! Leave her alone!" and a woman's voice called, "Someone! Stop him!"

Martin was only five yards behind Jessica, almost close enough to touch her. This wasn't part of his job. It wasn't hard for him to imagine a gun being drawn, and a shot fired. He didn't even *want* to catch her. It was none of his business, what these people did. *I tried, some people stopped me*, he could tell Mrs. Blaine. She could see with her own eyes that he tried. What more did she want?

He was just behind her shoulder when a different man's voice called, "Hold it there, son," grim and commanding, and Martin knew this was a cop's voice at the very second he reached out and caught Jessica's wrist on the backswing.

Her momentum carried her forward as she spun back toward him and a car slid into the aisle ahead of her and she lurched into it.

"No!" she screamed, so breathless she was afraid she hadn't made a sound or only a sound so faint that the cop wouldn't hear her as he leaped into the aisle behind Martin, gun drawn, three cars back.

Martin flung his hands into the air, praying like he had never prayed before that it wasn't too late, that the cop didn't have his heart set on a shooting.

Jessica's whole body throbbed from her collision with the car but she reeled forward, getting herself between Martin and the cop. "It's all right," she gasped, "it's all right, it's all right."

"Step aside, miss, keep your hands up there, son," the officer's voice droned as he moved forward at a stalking pace, the gun unwavering.

Martin didn't move. He was terrified with the realization of how close he had come, as well as the fear that he wasn't safe yet, although god knew he wasn't doing anything and there wasn't any reason to shoot him, not now.

Jessica doubled over, her hands on her knees, fighting for breath. The officer ordered Martin to turn around and then to lower his hands behind his back. He didn't holster his gun until the handcuffs were on. "Are you all right, miss?" he asked.

Two more officers approached on foot and a third got out of a police car that Jessica noticed now for the first time. In fact, she realized, it was the police car she had run into.

"He's my mother's driver," Jessica said, in command of her voice now.

The officer who had almost fired his gun looked at her with listless disinterest. Another one, probably the one from the car, took custody of Martin and started to lead him away.

"Wait a minute, listen to me," Jessica protested.

"You'll have plenty of time to straighten it out, miss," the officer with the gun said. He was the only one who had done any talking.

"No," Jessica said firmly. "That officer pulled his car right in front of me. I could have gotten a concussion or broken a leg. If I'm hurt, it's that man's fault, not this man's. My name is Jessica Blaine and I am a spoiled rich bitch from a very influential family. So let's stop right here and listen."

The officer holding Martin's arm stopped walking and turned to face her, possibly intimidated, more likely just curious enough to want a better look at this spoiled rich bitch with one hell of a mouth on her.

"All right," Jessica said in the tone of a schoolteacher who has been waiting for the kids to settle into their seats. "I was in the hospital. It was drug-related. My mother came to pick me up and I ran away from her. Martin is her driver and she sent him to stop me so she could take me home."

She looked from the officer with the gun to the officer holding Martin and then to the other two. She read confusion on all their faces.

"I'm sure my mother is still in front of the hospital," she went on, pressing her advantage. "Why don't we go back there and she'll confirm what I told you?"

The four police officers communicated briefly through an exchange of uncertain looks. The one who had been threatened with a lawsuit for blocking her path with his car settled the issue by suggesting they check out her story like she said. He led the parade, marching Martin, still in handcuffs, in front of him.

All through the parking lot, and with greater frequency as they neared the front of the building, people stopped and stared. No one in Martin's family had ever been arrested. No one. Ever. He was practically crying from the shame of it by the time they reached Jessica's mother.

After Phyllis confirmed everything that Jessica had said, one of the officers called his colleagues aside for a whispered conference and then went inside, presumably to confirm the part about Jessica's hospitalization and release. He was gone almost half an hour, and Martin remained handcuffed the whole time. At least they let him stand with his back against the Blaines' car, so that the handcuffs weren't visible to strangers. Finally, the officer came back out.

"All right," he said, "cut him loose."

Phyllis actually apologized to them for causing so much trouble.

When they were gone Jessica said, "Do you have any idea how stupid that was? You could have gotten him killed," and Phyllis said, "I wasn't the one running away, dear."

Neither one of them had much experience dealing with reality.

Christ. The kid looked worse than death itself. His arm was in a cast that went all the way down and covered his whole hand. His face was all stitched up like a quilt and one of his eyes was completely covered with a bandage that wrapped around his head like a turban. There were big purple patches on his face, the kind that looked like they had been a lot bigger a week ago, when the borders of the bruises didn't smooth evenly into the clear skin of the rest of his face. It broke your heart to look at him. Such a good-looking kid.

He looked scared when Fiore walked into the room. Probably having nightmares about everything, Fiore thought. Even wide awake.

"How are you doing, Eddie?" Fiore asked, slipping off his topcoat as he walked over to the bed.

"You didn't say I couldn't see her, Mr. Fiore. I never woulda, I swear it, I wouldn't've even called her if you said it. Honest to god, Mr. Fiore," Eddie said, the words tumbling out with a desperate haste. It must have hurt him to talk. His voice was thick, his diction slurred, like someone talking when they're eating.

Fiore stood next to Eddie's bed. "Hey, it's me," he said. "What the fuck are you talking about, Eddie?"

"I figured, y'know, you said it's over. Okay, it's over. I just figured . . ."

Fiore realized that he was talking about the Blaine girl. And that he must have thought Fiore had ordered the beating. Over the Blaine girl. At least that was what came through the fear and the panic. "What happened to you?" Fiore asked.

"I'm telling you the truth," Eddie whined. "You said over, you never said I couldn't—"

"Never mind that," Fiore said sharply. "Just tell me what happened."

"I'm telling you the truth. I am," Eddie pleaded.

"I know you are, Eddie," Fiore said, keeping his voice low and even, no particular tone at all, offering just the plain reassurance of the words. "They told you this was about the Blaine girl, is that what you're telling me?"

Something changed in Eddie's face. Fiore could see it just in the look of the one eye that wasn't covered. Eddie knew that Mr. Fiore wasn't mad at him, and that was all he needed to know. "That's what they said, yeah," he said.

Fiore was fairly certain the boy was telling the truth. Which meant that Blaine was behind it, evening up the score for fucking with his daughter. Maybe that was all right, maybe it wasn't. Certainly he was entitled to something for what happened to the girl, a nice, quiet kid who all of a sudden is running all over the country getting laid. If he had come to Fiore and said, *Now that we've got everything worked out, I want that kid's head on a plate,* Fiore would have had to give serious thought to what needed doing, even though Eddie hadn't done anything he hadn't been asked to do.

But this was different. Because Blaine went out on his own and got someone to do a major number on someone who works for Chet Fiore. An attack on someone who works for Chet Fiore is an attack on Chet Fiore. There's no other way to look at it.

Fiore said, "Don't worry about anything, Eddie. You're going to be all right. I'll talk to the doctors. Whatever you need, you've got it."

He touched the boy's hand, the good hand, the one that wasn't all wrapped up, and then he left the room.

His brain was burning. He had to do something about Blaine. There are very few rules in life. Talking care of your own people is one of them.

He found a nurse and told her he wanted to see Eddie's doctor. The doctor, an old Jewish guy named Fishbein, said that Eddie's cheekbone was broken like crackers you drop on top of a bowl of soup. He said all the pieces were back together but it would take a long time for them to turn into anything like real bone. Fiore asked about scars, and the upshot was that a plastic surgeon would come around to talk to Eddie. Fiore intimated that he would be responsible for the expense, but he didn't leave a number where he could be reached.

When he walked through the revolving door at the hospital's front entrance, he saw the headlights of his car come on. Jimmy was already rolling forward to pick him up. By the time the car got there, Fiore had already realized that he was no more entitled to take action against Blaine on his own than Blaine was entitled to exact his revenge on Eddie Vincenzo. Because Blaine was Gaetano Falcone's banker, Mr. Falcone was owed the courtesy of an explanation.

Fiore didn't say a word on the long drive out to the Island. He didn't even tell Jimmy the purpose of the visit. "How is he?" Jimmy asked when Fiore got in the car.

"He'll be all right," Fiore answered.

That was the end of the conversation. Jimmy knew his boss well enough to know when his silences could be broken and when they couldn't.

"I think we've got a problem, Mr. Falcone," Fiore said when he was seated in Gaetano Falcone's brightly lit living room overlooking the Sound. "Somebody did a number on Eddie Vincenzo. I'm reasonably certain the banker's behind it. Blaine. I've got to do something about it but he's holding your money, so I wanted to clear it with you first."

"I've been wondering how long it was going to take you to get here," Falcone said.

"You know about Eddie?" Fiore asked. He could feel the room spinning away from him. He felt the way he imagined people feel when they sense the first tremors of an earthquake. Even if very little has been changed just yet, it won't be long before nothing is in the right place anymore. By far the biggest shift in the landscape was the fact that Blaine had a direct line to Mr. Falcone. Fiore needed time to sort all this out. "You know you could have come to me," he said.

"I could have," Falcone agreed, in a tone that seemed to end the possibility of taking the discussion further.

Fiore turned to go, but then he stopped and turned back. "They didn't have to break his hand, did they?"

"They did what they were supposed to do," Falcone answered, settling back in his chair. "Don't question my judgment, Charles. That's never a good idea."

21

Gus Benini lived in half of a little postwar two-family in the Rego Park section of Queens. His neighbors thought he was in real estate because that was what he told them when he moved in twenty-five years ago. His wife didn't know what he really did but she knew it wasn't real estate and she knew better than to ask. His daughter, who was twenty-two years old and had just graduated from Queens College, had a pretty good idea but kept it to herself. When she was in junior high some of the other kids started teasing her about her father being a gangster but she put a stop to it real fast. "You want your legs broken, just keep that up," she said.

All in all, she had no problem with her father being a gangster. He was home a lot, which she liked, because he never yelled at her and he said funny things all the time. They took two-week vacations in the car every summer, just like a normal family, driving around and seeing the country, Niagara Falls and the Corning Glass factory in upstate New York, the battlefield at Gettysburg, and some really beautiful caves in Virginia.

She had her own apartment and a job at a company in Queens that manufactured dental appliances, but she was home the morning two federal agents rang the doorbell while her father was still in the bathroom. She was home because her mother was sick with the flu and someone had to make her father's breakfast.

For years she had known that sooner or later this day would come. She gave a lot of thought to what she would do if she was home when it happened. She would plead for him, or she would tell them he wasn't home in a loud enough voice for him to hear and get out the back door. When the time came, she didn't do any of those things. She let them in.

They followed her through the tiny living room and into the tiny kitchen, where scrambled eggs sat in a skillet that had been taken off the fire and the toast had already popped up. She was a religious girl and her mouth moved in the most ardent prayer of her life, praying that her father wouldn't turn out to be anything disgusting, like a hit man.

Wally Schliester looked around. The range and the refrigerator were older than the girl. There was a dishwasher but that was old, too. He knew there was no truth to the saying that crime doesn't pay because it did. But it sure as hell didn't pay well for people like Gus Benini. He probably would have done better for himself driving a city bus.

Schliester thought the girl was taking them to Benini, but he obviously wasn't in the kitchen. "Where is Mr. Benini, miss?" he asked.

"He'll be right down," she said.

The two agents exchanged looks. It was possible but not likely that this was some kind of trick. The second agent, the one who hadn't spoken, took a step backward to the kitchen door, which had swung closed behind him. He inched it back so he'd be able to see anyone coming downstairs, trying to sneak out the front door while they were in back.

"He's in the bathroom, for Pete's sake," Benini's daughter said. "Do you have to go up there and drag him off the toilet?" Her voice dripped with contempt. She was a short girl, definitely on the heavy side, but with a pretty face she must have gotten from her mother.

"You're his daughter, miss?" Schliester asked.

"Do I have to answer your questions?"

"No, you don't, miss," Schliester said. "We're not arresting your father. We've just got to ask him some questions."

If she was grateful for this information, she didn't show it. She turned away and yanked the two pieces of toast out of the toaster and dabbed them with margarine from a little plastic tub. She was angry with herself for letting them know what she was thinking and worried that she hadn't done her father any good practically telling the cops that Gus Benini's own daughter simply assumed that he would be arrested. She slid the eggs out of the frying pan and onto a plate. Since they weren't arresting him, she hoped they'd let him eat his breakfast. He hardly ever ate. If he missed breakfast and then didn't have anything all day, that wasn't good for his stomach.

They heard a toilet flush upstairs, then footsteps. The second agent—his name was Matt Thompson—stepped to the side of the door so that he would be behind it when it opened and behind Benini when he came in. Not that Benini would do anything reckless with his daughter in the room, or even without her there for that matter. But it never hurt to be safe.

Normally, in an undercover operation, the undercover agent doesn't take part in arrests or interrogations. He doesn't want to blow his cover. But Schliester wanted to be here. He had to argue the point with Elaine Lester, who was all for leaving him out of this phase of the operation. She thought it was important to avoid tipping their hand as to the nature of the case against Benini. Schliester thought that was ridiculous and said so. "If you want him to roll over," he said, "then you've got to let him know how jammed up he is. He sees me, he knows he's been doing deals with a federal agent for three months. How do you think that's going to make him feel?"

They compromised by holding back Gogarty, who had posed as one of the shakedown victims. This gave them the best of both worlds, high cards showing and a high card in the hole.

As the door swung inward Benini was already saying, "Is it ready? I've got to meet some people in a little—"

He stopped himself in midsentence the second he saw Fred Linkletter standing in his own kitchen right next to the table.

Benini was wearing the same suit he had worn the night before. Come to think of it, he only seemed to have two suits.

"What are you doing here?" he asked, momentarily confused. "How did you know where I—"

For the second time in a row he didn't get to finish his sentence, this time because Schliester's hand was coming out of his breast pocket and Gus Benini knew what would be in it. He could see how the whole thing was going to play out.

Schliester flipped open a police-style shield case that had an ID with his picture on it and something about the U.S. Attorney's Office. "I'm agent Wally Schliester and this is agent Matt Thompson. We have some questions we'd like to ask you if you can come with us, Mr. Benini," he said.

Benini's daughter said, "Daddy, they're not arresting you."

Benini's mouth was open and he was looking at Schliester the way you might look at a man with two heads. "What did you say your name was? Schliester? Is that German or something?"

"Benini," Schliester said. "What's that? Italian?"

"Is that what this is about?" Benini demanded shrilly. "You think because I'm Italian you can just come in here with all this shit?" And then he looked at his daughter and said, "I'm sorry, honey. I got upset. I'm sorry."

He didn't use language like that in front of his daughter.

"That's all right, Daddy," she said.

"You're a rat, you know that, Linkletter," Benini said. "I stood up for you. You wanted more money, I stood up for you. Whose pocket do you think that came out of?"

"Sorry about that, Gus," Schliester said. "Do you mind just raising your hands above your head?"

Benini glanced to his daughter. This was a humiliating thing for her to see. But she nodded her head, more or less giving her approval, and then turned away, pretending she had something to tend to on the stove. Benini dutifully raised his hands. Schliester patted him down, just a few perfunctory touches. He tapped the man's armpits and then he ran his hands over the front of the suit, which wasn't a normal thing to do in a frisk. He cocked his head as though he had found something, reached into the outside breast pocket where he put his business card the night before. It was still there. His lucky day. They not only wired the guy, they were getting their wire back. He took out the card, looked at it, and then showed it to Benini.

"You need this?" he asked.

Benini looked at the thing and wanted to spit on it. *Frederick Linkletter. Exhibitor Relations.* He didn't remember taking it but he must have. Probably a while ago, he figured. When he first started coming around the office.

"Get it out of my face, weasel," he said.

"You did what you had to do, Gus, I did what I had to do," Schliester said as he pocketed the card. He didn't hold out any real hope that he could get this nervous little man who was being frisked by the police in front of his own daughter to see it that way, but he had to try. They were simply two professionals. There was no reason they had to hate each other. "What do you say we go?" he said.

"I thought you weren't arresting him," Benini's daughter protested.

"We're not."

"He's got to have his breakfast," she said. "It's important."

Schliester nodded. "Most important meal of the day," he said.

"Let's get this over with," Benini said.

"She fixed you a breakfast. She worries about you. Eat your breakfast, then we'll go."

Benini wasn't in the mood for eating. But it didn't strike him at the moment that he had much of a choice in the matter. As he sat down at the table and pulled the plate of eggs in front of him, Schliester said, "That's all right, miss. We ate already."

It wasn't that Chet Fiore smelled a rat, but he certainly smelled Mel Gottlieb. Sweat oozed out of the man. His clothing absorbed it, as did his skin, so that his entire person took on the consistency of gummed bread. It would have been better if Fiore could have met him outdoors, but that wasn't one of the options. Gottlieb simply showed up at the Elizabeth Street restaurant when it opened for business late in the morning and told the first waiter he encountered that he wanted to speak with Chet Fiore.

The waiter professed not to know what the fat man was talking about and seated him at a window table, where the morning sun poured in on him so that he came to glisten like softening butter. Half an hour later Jimmy Angelisi entered the restaurant. Gottlieb, whose table commanded a view of the door, saw his waiter conferring with an affable-looking and slightly balding gentleman in a light gray suit. He saw himself being pointed at. Then the gentleman in the gray suit walked to his table and sat down as naturally as if he were joining a friend for lunch. Gottlieb didn't think this was what Chet Fiore would look like and he was right.

"What's this about wanting to see Mr. Fiore?" Jimmy asked without any preamble. There were breadsticks in a basket and he helped himself.

Gottlieb had a plate of fried calamari in front of him. He had stopped eating when he saw that he was being talked about at the door but he was still holding a flabby length of breaded squid in his sausagelike fingers. "That's right," he said. "I've got to talk to him."

"And why would that be?"

Something apparently reminded Gottlieb that he was holding a piece of food in his right hand. He popped it into his mouth, licked his fingers clean, and dried them on a napkin. "I'm Mel Gottlieb," he said. "I work at the Javits Center."

The food rolled around in his mouth and then disappeared like a golf ball rimming the cup before falling in.

"You're gonna have to help me out a little on this one, mister," Jimmy said, but Gottlieb only shook his head.

"I wish that were possible," he said. "But I really can't talk to anyone except Mr. Fiore about this. He will want to talk to me, I can assure you of that. You'd be doing him a disservice if you didn't let that happen."

Jimmy figured the fat man was probably telling the truth. He reminded Jimmy of the fat guy in those Humphrey Bogart movies, maybe because he talked in the same fancy way. That probably meant he was on the level, because you don't try to con anyone talking like a movie. "Let's you and me take a little walk," Jimmy said, getting to his feet.

Gottlieb looked down at the plate of calamari as though it were a friend he was reluctant to leave. But he did the right thing, pushing himself up from the table and following Angelisi toward the back of the restaurant. Jimmy pushed open the door to the men's room and held it open, turning back to invite Gottlieb to go first. Their eyes met. Gottlieb had big brown cow eyes. Jimmy waited, holding the door until Gottlieb waddled past him.

"Okay, turn around, please," Jimmy said when they were alone in the tiny men's room, which had one urinal, one stall, and a sink. The place had the pink sweet smell of the disinfectant tablets they put in the urinals. And now it also had the smell of Mel Gottlieb, who dutifully turned his back to Angelisi. "Raise your arms," Jimmy said.

He performed a frisk that was as unpleasant as it was thorough. On a man with that many bulges, there were a lot of places to hide a piece and a lot of places to hide a wire. Jimmy wasn't taking chances. He probed Gottlieb's armpits and his groin and up and down his legs and across the vast expanse of his butt, like the ass end of a horse, or even two horses. The man was clean. "Awright," Jimmy conceded, "c'mon."

They went back out to the restaurant. When they got to Gottlieb's table, Jimmy said, "Sit down. And don't go anywhere I can't see you."

He walked away. Gottlieb would have had to turn around to see where he went, which he assumed he wasn't supposed to do. It seemed to him he had passed the test, so he settled in to wait until the next thing to happen happened. He needed the time to unwind anyway. That deal he made with the feds got the IRS off his back, but at what price? He was setting up a mobster. He, Mel Gottlieb, introduced a federal undercover agent to a member of an organized crime family. It was the most idiotic thing he had ever done in his life.

Or ever would, if he didn't do something to fix it before it became unfixable.

He had been thinking the same thing every night before he fell asleep and every morning as soon as he woke up for at least a month and a half. It was like thinking you have cancer and being afraid to go to the doctor to find out. Every day convinces you that the symptoms are getting worse, until finally it doesn't make sense to go because it's too late anyway. He woke up with his sheets soaking wet from dreams straight out of gangster movies.

He woke up one morning feeling like he was going to be sick, like his bladder was going to burst, like his eyes were going to roll back in his head and he was going to fall into a dead swoon on his bedroom floor the way girls used to do. If he didn't do something soon, he was as good as dead. He grabbed for the phone and started calling everyone he knew who might be even the least bit crooked. He didn't go into work. He spent the whole day on the phone. He talked to bookies, ticket scalpers, union bosses, and pimps. He wanted to know who he had to talk to to save himself.

A scalper by the name of Lionel was the first one to suggest that the West Side rackets, which would include hustles at the Javits Center, were probably operated one way or another by Chet Fiore. Who in turn worked for Gaetano Falcone.

That was the first time Gottlieb heard those names in connection with his problem. He got the shakes so bad he could hardly hang up the phone. He remembered Falcone's name from those gang wars a long time ago. He didn't remember the details, just that a lot of people got killed. Gaetano Falcone wouldn't have to think twice about killing the man who set up his man's man with a federal undercover agent.

That very morning Mel Gottlieb took the subway all the way down to Canal Street and walked over to Little Italy and found the restaurant on Elizabeth Street Lionel told him about. But he was afraid to go in. He was afraid if he went in he'd never come out.

This went on for a couple weeks. He didn't go *every* morning, but he told himself every morning he would go. And then he figured out some reason why tomorrow would be better. He never got closer to the inside of that restaurant than the sidewalk across the street.

And then, on this very morning, he went into the office and found that federal agents were packing up all of the undercover agent's things. They said he wouldn't be back.

The first thing Mel Gottlieb did was go to the bathroom. He had the worst diarrhea he'd ever had. He sat on the toilet with his head in his hands, crying and cursing himself for not having done something about this sooner. Now the investigation was over. Now the federal agents were going to do whatever they were going to do.

He went outside and grabbed a cab and had it take him to Elizabeth Street. Maybe the agents hadn't done anything yet. Maybe it wasn't too late to come across as a good guy who was trying to do the right thing, as these people said.

So now he was inside the restaurant waiting. The sunlight that had been assaulting him through the window gave up and moved across the street. It became cooler and more comfortable, but that didn't help. He felt like a turkey being looked at through the window in the oven door whenever people passing on the sidewalk looked at him.

The next thing he knew, the man in the gray suit was at his table again. This time he took him outside and down the street a few doors to a cluttered appliance store with refrigerators ranked along one wall, washing machines, dryers, and dishwashers packed so close together it was almost impossible to navigate the narrow aisles between them. A woman wearing a baby in a carrier strapped to her chest was browsing among the washing machines. The only employee seemed to be a salesman in shirtsleeves, who stood at the woman's shoulder, pointing out features of each of the machines. There was one other customer, a well-dressed man who seemed to be inspecting the refrigerators, pacing back and forth in front of them, his hands clasped behind his back.

And then the oddest thing happened. The salesman looked over to the man in the gray suit and the man in the gray suit nodded his head. The salesman took his customer's arm and Gottlieb heard him say, "Why don't we go outside and talk about our payment options?" In a moment they were gone, pulling the door closed behind them.

Mel Gottlieb knew for an absolute fact that he was about to be murdered. The well-dressed man among the refrigerators turned around. There was no gun in his hand, no silencer. "I'm Chet Fiore, Mr. Gottlieb," he said, offering his hand. "I believe you wanted to talk to me."

Gottlieb swallowed hard, making a sound like the last water sucked down a drain. "Here?" he gasped.

"You're here, I'm here," Fiore said. "Why don't you tell me what this is about?"

Gottlieb saw that the man in the gray suit was standing by the door, presumably to keep strangers from coming in. "I don't know if this concerns you, Mr. Fiore," Gottlieb began. "That's none of my business, so I'm not going to ask. I suggest that you hear me out, and when I'm finished I'll leave and you make up your mind what you do about this. If it's got anything to do with you, that is. And I'm not saying that it does."

He paused for a moment and wiped his sweaty face with a meaty hand. He wanted Fiore to give him some sign to continue, but he could read nothing at all in the man's face. Christ, it was chilling. But he was in this far already, so he kept going.

"As your associate may have told you," he resumed, "I work at the Javits Center. I'm the personnel director. I hire people. There was a man in exhibitor relations who would, on a regular basis, provide an associate of yours, if that's what he was, with contact information about our exhibitors. No one ever told me which names he gave him, which ones were contacted, what happened, but look, I'm not stupid. On the other hand, the less someone in my position knows, the better off he is. I don't draw conclusions. I'm just telling you what the arrangement was so you know that I know what I'm talking about."

So far so good. This was all coming out pretty much the way Gottlieb hoped it would. He would have liked it better if Fiore said something, but he didn't.

"In any case, back in the spring the employee I've alluded to in exhibitor relations resigned his position and relocated to another state. Very soon after that, I was contacted by some individuals associated with the United States Attorney's Office. District something, Southern I believe. I don't know if that matters, I wish I had been paying more attention to that part of it, but these people were very menacing. And very demanding. They wanted me to hire one of their agents to fill the vacancy in exhibitor relations. They didn't tell me why and I didn't ask. That's a principle with me. I don't like to know things I'm not supposed to know. The long and the short is that I agreed to assist them with this subterfuge because I didn't think it was my place to question the policies of the United States government."

"What kind of trouble were you in, Mr. Gottlieb?" Fiore asked. It was the first sign he gave that he had been listening at all.

Gottlieb knew that everything depended on this moment. If the guns with silencers were ever to come out, it would be now. He had to be honest. "IRS," he said.

No tic of Fiore's eye or wrinkle of Fiore's lip measured Gottlieb's answer or invited him to go on. Chet Fiore, quite obviously, was a man who powerfully combined two of the rarest virtues in common circulation, patience and will. Like an insect he would wait; like an insect he would strike.

Gottlieb could feel all this simply standing in the man's presence. He gathered the threads of his story around him and carefully selected the one he would follow. "Suffice it to say," he began again, "these agents threatened me about things that would happen to me if I ever told anyone about Linkletter's real identity. I did as I was told and kept silent, but I can't keep silent anymore, Mr. Fiore. That's why I've come to you."

He could feel the sweat dribbling under his collar and down his sides, like a faucet with a drip. Fiore was going to say, *Thank you for telling me, Mr. Gottlieb, you did the right thing.* Or he was going to say, *You set my man up with a federal agent, you cocksucker.* And the whole rest of Mel Gottlieb's life was going to depend on which one he said.

Actually, he said neither. "Why this morning, Mr. Gottlieb?" he asked. "Why not yesterday? Or tomorrow?"

"I just . . . it was eating at me," Gottlieb stammered, losing his composure completely. And then he closed his eyes and blurted out everything. "They came," he said. "Two agents I never saw before. They were in Linkletter's office this morning. They cleaned it out and took everything. They said he wouldn't be back."

Fiore nodded his understanding and made a small gesture with his head in the direction of the door. Gottlieb wasn't sure. Was he being told to leave? He had hoped he would be thanked but that didn't seem to be in the cards. He had no way to measure whether in Fiore's mind his confession canceled his guilt. He hesitated, and then he felt a hand on his arm and he was being guided to the door by the man who had brought him here. Desperate, Gottlieb turned back for one last plea for clemency. But Fiore wasn't there.

"Please, Mr. Fiore," he called out to the cluttered emptiness. "I'm trying to do the right thing, that's all. I'm just trying to do the right thing."

He felt the tepid air from the street wash over him. And the next thing he knew he was on the sidewalk.

The salesman who had been banished from the store hurried back inside, leaving the door open, inviting customers. The world went back to the way it was.

Mel Gottlieb stepped to the curb and carefully lowered all three hundred and fifty pounds of his unwieldy bulk to the sidewalk. He sat on the pavement, his feet in the gutter, while tears as big as raindrops cascaded down his full-moon face.

When they pulled off the highway at the exit between LaGuardia Airport and Shea Stadium, the thought hit Gus Benini that these guys weren't taking him to Manhattan, which is where the U.S. attorney has his offices. They must have had something else in mind.

They pulled up outside a sorry-looking motel with only three or four cars in front of the rooms. This was bad, Benini thought. People were always kidding him about being so nervous, but no one would be kidding him now because even a boa constrictor would be nervous with a bunch of cold-as-ice assholes dragging him out of his house just after breakfast and taking him god knows where. If they had been cops instead of feds he would have been scared, not just nervous, because cops would do anything they felt like doing. Feds didn't work like that. At least he couldn't remember hearing stories about feds working like that. But maybe they did. Maybe they were just better at keeping their own and other people's mouths shut.

If these guys were feds, that is. He was sorry all of a sudden that he didn't take a better look at that badge Linkletter flashed at him. What if this whole thing was some kind of setup for someone who had a score to settle with Chet Fiore or Gaetano Falcone? What if someone was planning to FedEx Mr. Fiore Gus Benini's dick?

They pulled up a long way from the motel office, right in front of a room at the end of the row. It was one of those motels like you see on highways, way out in nowhere, the kind he used to stop at with Lucy and Theresa on their trips. They would get a cot for the girl. He hadn't known there were motels like this in Queens.

Linkletter opened the door to the room. Inside there was a little table that was supposed to be next to the window with a lamp on it, except the lamp was on the floor and the table had been moved over into the middle of the room near the foot of the bed. The carpet, which was dirty, was clean in a little square where the table used to be. That's how Gus knew they moved it. He was pleased with himself for taking in all these details. It meant he wasn't missing a thing.

A lady was sitting at the table but she stood up when the door opened. She was very tall, on the skinny side, and her hands did something to her skirt, kind of smoothing it across her hips. She had the kind of body that was very popular with young people these days. Benini guessed she was around thirty, give or take a couple. He was glad to see her because the people he was *really* scared about didn't use ladies to do any of their dirty work.

There were two tape recorders on the table, a big one with reels and one of those little ones you can put in your pocket.

"Sit down, Mr. Benini," the lady said. "Don't trip over the cord."

Right, Benini thought. He'd fall on his face and chip a tooth and then he'd sue them. He'd be rich.

In a fucking dream.

"I'm Assistant U.S. Attorney Elaine Lester," she said. "You've already met agents Schliester and Thompson."

Benini stepped over the cord from the tape recorder and sat down like she told him to.

"Are you comfortable?" she asked.

"Am I comfortable? No, I'm not comfortable. Why would I be comfortable?"

"Well, you're going to be here a little while, Mr. Benini," she said. "Can we get you something? A cup of coffee or a soft drink?"

"You can tell me what the fuck this is about," he said. "You'll pardon my French."

Gus Benini never swore in front of ladies. But this was different.

"I think you already know what the fuck this is about," she said, showing off that she could say any word he could say. "We want to talk to you about the Javits Center."

"It's on Eleventh Avenue," Benini offered helpfully.

He felt a hand on his shoulder. Not a friendly hand. The fingers bit right through to the bone like they were trying to find out where the tendons and the muscles and the other stuff in there were all located. It hurt like a son of a bitch. Linkletter's voice said, "We know it's on Eleventh Avenue, Gus."

The lady said, "We know that you're operating a shakedown operation at the Javits Center, Mr. Benini. And you know we know it. Let's not play games."

"What are you asking me questions for if you know all the answers," Benini said. "It sounds like you're the ones playing games."

"We want your cooperation," Elaine Lester said.

She put something in her voice that made her sound like a lady who needed help getting her suitcase to the train. She had these two galoots standing over him and one of them was taking his bones apart, and she had the gall to come on like she was helpless. It was sickening, but maybe she didn't do it on purpose. There were some women that just sounded that way, every word that came out of their mouths.

"How about I work that out with my lawyer," he suggested. "I talk to him, you talk to him, that way there's no hard feelings."

The fingers moved a tendon aside to see what was underneath. Benini's eyes watered and he said, "And tell him to get his god-damned hands off me."

She ignored that part of it and said, "You don't want to call a lawyer, Mr. Benini."

"Yeah, I do."

The guy who hadn't said anything said, "Don't contradict her, pal," and the fingers bit even harder. So they were his fingers. That was kind of what Benini figured. Linkletter didn't have fingers like that. He didn't look like a particularly strong guy. This one, who wasn't very big either, probably worked out squeezing things in his spare time about a hundred times a day.

Benini said, "I can't even think with you doing that. I know my goddamned rights."

"Matt, please," she said in that same helpless-lady voice. But it worked. The fingers let go. In another minute blood would start circulating again.

She leaned across the table and crooked a finger, inviting Benini to lean close to her. He realized they hadn't turned on either of the tape recorders, so this was a part of their little party they didn't want recorded.

"Mr. Benini," the lady said so softly that there was something almost sexy about the way he had to stare at her lips just to make out what she was saying. "We have tapes of you conspiring with a federal agent to extort money from exhibitors at the Javits Center. We have every dollar you paid the agent for his services, and you know we've got these things because that federal agent is right here in this room with us. Are you with me so far, Mr. Benini?"

"I'm not with you, I'm not against you," he said.

"Fine. We also have statements from some of the people from whom you extorted money. Right now we believe we have six very good extortion cases and conspiracy to commit extortion. That

number could go up and it most certainly will not come down. If
you did get a lawyer he would look at the evidence and he would
tell you to take a plea, but the way it stands right now, the most we
would offer in return is a recommendation that the sentences run
concurrently. How old are you, Mr. Benini?"

He didn't answer. He knew that everything she said was true,
so he just concentrated on her lips to hear the rest of it.

"You'd certainly be under seventy when you got out, Mr.
Benini," she said. She smiled a little, so that those lips parted
around her teeth. Nice teeth, too. She was pretty, no two ways
about it. "I'll be honest with you," she went on, her voice even
softer, taking him into her confidence, "the way they let people out
of prison these days, you might even be as young as sixty. Sixty or
sixty-five."

Gus Benini was fifty-three years old. Sixty-five sounded like it
might as well be the rest of his life. He ran his tongue over his lips,
and she looked up, taking her eyes off him, and said, "Matt, I think
Mr. Benini wants that drink now. Coffee or something cold?"

Benini said, "Cold."

"Pepsi? Something like that?" she asked. "It's just a machine."

"Whatever they got," he said. "Pepsi, yeah, that's fine." He
heard the door open. "Diet Pepsi if they got it," he said.

The door closed and he knew that the guy with the fingers was
gone. He was convinced without even thinking about it that if he
turned around to look, Linkletter would hit him on the top of his
head, so he didn't do it.

Linkletter came around where Benini could see him and pulled
up a chair to the third side of the table between them. He sat down.

"I was at your house, Gus," he said. "I'll be honest with you."
Everyone was being honest with him this morning, Benini thought.
How often do you run into that? "It's not much of a house. I've got a
better place and I'm half your age on government pay."

Benini's face flushed red all the way to his ears. Schliester knew
it wasn't just anger. It was anger mixed in with shame, and he was
sorry he had to say what he just said. But there was an important
point to be made.

"I've got news for you, wiseass," Benini snapped. "I brought up three kids in that house, sent them all to college."

"Yeah, but what's that?" Linkletter said. "I mean, what, City College, right? How much was that? You see what I'm getting at? The people you work for don't take very good care of you. You make them money, you don't get to see a whole hell of a lot of it. You don't owe them shit."

Benini didn't say anything. He didn't like the direction this was taking.

"Was that true what you told me at the house?" Linkletter asked. "When I needed more money, it came out of your pocket?"

Again Benini didn't answer. Fucking A it came out of his pocket. That still galled him. And Linkletter just said, "Jesus, Gus. Isn't it about time you did yourself some good for a change?"

He got up and walked away from the table, as though he had said everything he had to say.

The door opened again and Fingers came back with a couple cans of diet Pepsi. "They didn't have glasses," he said. "Is the can okay?"

Gus popped the top and took a long drink. *Is the can okay? Was he comfortable?* for Christ's sake. They were falling all over themselves being nice to him. They must have thought he was stupid or something but he wasn't. It was a con and he knew it. They weren't going to buy Gus Benini with a kind word and a freaking can of soda.

On the other hand, he also knew that everything the Linkletter guy who really had a German name said was true. Gus Benini never got something for nothing. Never. Not once in his life. Which meant it was true that he didn't owe anyone shit.

"What Agent Schliester is trying to tell you, Mr. Benini," the lady said, "is that you don't matter to Chet Fiore."

"Who?" Benini deadpanned. But his heart wasn't in it.

"We'll get back to that in a minute," she said. "What I want you to know right now is that you don't matter to us either. We'll lock you up if you don't give us a choice but we don't need to do that and we really have no interest in doing it. We'd rather work things out. I'm sure you understand that, so let's get back to that other thing. You're not telling us you don't know a man named Chet Fiore, are you?"

"Doesn't ring a bell," Benini said.

She hit a button on the little tape recorder and the next thing Benini knew he was listening to himself telling Fiore that the kid at the Javits Center was getting nervous and Fiore telling him to shut it down and not to worry.

They played him a lot of tapes, and Linkletter even talked to him about his kids and the daughter he met at the house and where she went to college and what she was doing now. They ordered lunch, which was sandwiches Fingers brought back from a deli that must have been pretty close because he made it back in a couple minutes. Benini didn't really want anything but he asked for a sandwich because they offered and he didn't want to get into a whole discussion. He couldn't remember the last time he sat in one place so long, and if you had asked him this morning he would have said that it would drive him crazy, being stuck in one chair for hours. But for some reason it wasn't driving him crazy. He sat there and listened to what they had to say like he was in church or something.

The part that really got to him was when they explained, both of them, Linkletter and the lady, kind of taking turns, that if they went ahead with the Javits Center case against Fiore, they would have to play the tape from the restaurant when Fiore says to shut it down, and then Fiore would think that maybe Benini had been wearing a wire because he had the place checked all the time for bugs. But on the other hand, if they had other information about Fiore, stuff that didn't concern the Javits Center, then they could go in a different direction and maybe even leave the Javits Center out of it, so Fiore wouldn't ever have to hear this tape, would he?

That was when the sandwiches came. Gus had egg salad. He ate about half of it. "You had eggs for breakfast and you're having eggs for lunch," Linkletter said. "You're not worried about cholesterol?"

"You worry about cholesterol," Benini said. "I'm more worried about someone putting an ice pick in my neck."

They all laughed, even Benini, and then they got serious again because Linkletter said, "Gus, we want to make sure that doesn't happen."

The lady offered him some time to think it over and come back to them with things he could tell them about Chet Fiore where he wasn't involved, so it wouldn't come back to him.

He looked at the rest of the sandwich and he looked at her, and he started to talk. Which is when the second tape recorder was turned on.

One of the things he said, just in passing because he didn't know much about it, was that there was something about a banker and a new way to clean up money but he didn't know any of the names.

The lady said, "Well, let's move on to something you do know something about."

Which is when Linkletter got up from the table and went for a little walk around the room. He was pissed off at something, but Gus couldn't figure out what he had done to piss the guy off. Actually, it seemed more like he was pissed off at the lady, but what sense did that make?

None.

Besides, Gus had other things to worry about.

The mood in the car on the drive out to Queens was tense. Fiore didn't say a word and Jimmy didn't either. "Do you want me to come in?" Jimmy asked after he braked to a stop in front of Gus Benini's house.

He said it as though he expected trouble.

Fiore laughed it off. "Come on, Jimmy," he said. "I just want to talk to the guy, that's all."

Jimmy waited in the car, with the engine running.

Fiore rang the front door bell and let his eyes roam down the line of identical two-family houses set almost side to side. Each had a little ten-foot driveway that marked the end of the property and doubled as a passage to a little backyard the size of a dinner napkin.

The houses were set back about four feet from the sidewalk behind a tiny rectangle of lovingly tended grass. Window boxes of potted pansies and chrysanthemums hung from the front windows of each home. But it was those patches of grass that Fiore's eye kept coming back to as he stood with his back to the door, facing the street, waiting for someone to come to the door. He could understand a window box of flowers. It is what it is. But this four-foot-by-eight-foot patch of lawn shared by two families struck him as inexpressibly sad. It's a lie. Worse, it's a lie that doesn't even call to mind what the truth is. It was barely enough grass to be buried under.

He heard footsteps on the other side of the door and he heard the door open, and when he turned he was facing Benini's daughter. "Theresa," he said, "how are you doing?"

She said she was fine but her voice sounded tense and overwrought.

Fiore made it a point to know the families of the men who worked under him. During the holiday season they would have dinner together, two or three families at a time, with Fiore at the head of the table and his wife just to his left. His guests brought their wives and their children, if the children were old enough to sit still through a meal. It was always a big deal the first year a son or a daughter was old enough to come. Fiore started a couple weeks before Christmas, and by Christmas he had been host to all of his people. In organized crime circles this was a very unusual thing to do. In fact, it wasn't done at all. Gaetano Falcone himself had summoned Fiore out to the Island to question him about the practice. "A man doesn't mix family with his business," he said.

"With all due respect, Mr. Falcone," Fiore answered, "how do you trust a man if you don't know who he is?"

Very few of the wives knew in any explicit way what their husbands did. Fiore was introduced to the wives and the children simply as Mr. Fiore with no explanation as to the nature of the relationship. This might have been expected to produce some awkwardness but it never did.

"Is your father here?" he asked Theresa Benini. "I'd like to talk with him."

She shook her head and then said, "He's not here," as though the words were an afterthought.

"Do you know when he'll be back?"

She looked at him a moment, a careful look, and then she stepped backward, widening the door. He'd been on the stoop to this point while she held the door. Now he stepped in and she closed the door behind him. He could see that she would have been crying if she let herself.

"The police were here this morning. They took him," she said, keeping her voice low but still managing to convey all the ferocity she had kept bottled up to this point. "They said they weren't arresting him," she added, as though she didn't believe this part of it.

From the moment her father was taken away, she fought with herself hard over what she should do to help him, but couldn't come to a conclusion. Her uncertainty intensified when she saw who was at the door, but in the end she decided she had to ask Mr. Fiore for his help. He was the most powerful man her father knew. All he had to do was pick up a phone and her father would be home.

"The police?" he asked.

"I'm sorry, not the police, the government," she corrected.

"Federal agents?"

"Yes."

"Did they say what they wanted?"

He knew the answer. He wanted to know what she knew.

She shook her head. "Just that they wanted to talk to him and they weren't arresting him," she said.

From upstairs a voice, thin and pinched, called down, "Who is it, Theresa?"

"It's all right, Mom," the girl called back. "It's just someone for Daddy."

Apparently that answer was enough.

"Is your mother all right?" Fiore asked.

Benini's wife was always sick with one thing or another. Gus himself had given up trying to do anything about it a long time ago.

"Just the flu," Theresa said. "She's mostly over it."

Fiore put his two hands firmly on the girl's shoulders, squaring her away to him, and looked deep into her troubled eyes. They were dull eyes, as lifeless as stone. "Don't worry, Theresa," he said. "It's all right. I can take care of it."

She was sure this was true and she was grateful to him already just for telling her that and saying it the way he did. Now she knew she had done the right thing in telling him, even though her father wouldn't have approved.

Mr. Fiore told her to tell her father to come see him that night. She invited him to wait, offering coffee. "I have things to do," he said, and she didn't press the point.

In the car he told Jimmy to drive halfway down the block and park there. He wanted to talk to Benini before he went into the house. There was no danger of the feds driving him back. If he told them he wouldn't cooperate, they weren't about to provide him with free cab service, and if he told them he would, then they wouldn't risk being seen with him unnecessarily.

Fiore didn't have long to wait. In less than half an hour he saw Gus heading toward him, loping from the corner with his erratic, headlong gait, his body pitched forward as though he were tacking into a heavy wind. Fiore's car was on the opposite side of the street and Benini didn't see it until he was almost past it. Fiore got out, and the movement caught Benini's eye.

"Jeez," he said as he crossed the street, "what are you doing here?"

Fiore had never come to his house before. This should have alerted Benini. If he were a more intelligent man it would have. But the thought passed through his mind quickly and he just as quickly decided that Fiore couldn't possibly know about the feds yet.

"I was on my way out to the Island. There's a couple things I wanted to talk to you about," Fiore said offhandedly, his voice comfortable and relaxed. "Come on, get in, we'll talk. I've only got a few minutes."

He opened the door for Benini and then slid in after him.

"How you doing, Jimmy?" Benini asked.

"Yeah, and you?" Jimmy answered over his shoulder.

Benini shrugged and turned to Fiore. "I hope you weren't waiting long," he said. "You should have rung the bell. My girl's there, she would have given you something."

"I did," Fiore said.

There was a flicker of confusion in Benini's eyes. His upper lip did something funny. "You went in?" he asked.

"Yeah," Fiore said. "That was Theresa, right? I hope so. I called her Theresa."

Benini's tongue flicked in and out like a lizard's. "Right, Theresa," he said. "What did she tell you?"

Fiore saw Jimmy's eyes in the rearview mirror, watching. *What did she tell you?* It wasn't a question Gus Benini had any business asking.

"She said she didn't know where you went," Fiore said. "She said she didn't know when you'd be back."

Benini's whole face seemed to come instantly alive. "I've been having this prostate problem, you know," he said. "Just gotta pee all the time. I figured I'd better get it checked out."

"You were at the doctor's?"

"Yeah. I didn't tell her, I didn't want her getting worried, you know."

Jimmy Angelisi didn't need to be told what to do. He started the engine and put it in drive.

"And what did the doctor say?"

The Mercedes slid from the curb even before Benini answered.

"He says it's not cancer," he said.

But he knew they knew he was lying. He knew he had something worse than cancer now.

22

t was almost six o'clock when Chet Fiore showed up at the Layne Bentley reception desk. In a minute Jennifer came out to meet him. "I'm sorry," she said, "Mr. Blaine's gone for the day."

The man looked at her as though she had just insulted him, his eyes dark and hooded, so cold she could almost feel the temperature drop. If she didn't know better she would have had trouble convincing herself that this was the same man who had come to the office before. This one, she realized, was the Chet Fiore who got written up in the newspapers. There was no telling who the other one might have been.

She knew without his even telling her that her answer had been inadequate and she didn't want to wait to be told. "I'm sure I can reach him," she said. "I'll just be a minute."

There were half a dozen telephones next to the couches in the reception area. She made the call right there. Fiore came and stood over her. He wanted to know what she said and what Blaine said.

"Mr. Blaine, it's Jennifer. Mr. Fiore just came in. He wants to see you."

She waited. And then she covered the mouthpiece. "He's got concert tickets. He's on his way to Lincoln Center. He wants to know if you can meet him there," she said.

"Yeah," Fiore said. "That's fine."

He had Jimmy drop him off on Broadway across the street

from Lincoln Center. He told him not to wait. As he crossed the wide double avenue where Broadway and Columbus cross each other, he looked across at the three monstrous buildings with a displeasure that was more a function of his mood than anything else. They didn't look like they belonged in New York. They didn't look like anything else in the city. And if they had to put a fountain right in the middle of the whole thing, then they should have at least put a little grass around it, made a kind of park out of it. One of the buildings was all stone, one was all glass, and one was kind of a combination of the two.

He saw Blaine standing near the fountain. All in all, it wasn't a bad place to meet. Two men with time on their hands could count on being inconspicuous here, just two cultured music lovers who got there early.

Blaine saw him coming and started toward him. He spoke before Fiore had a chance to say anything. "Our friend in Oklahoma City passed away," he said.

It was hard to tell what point he was making. There was an edge in his voice, a sharpness. What? He didn't approve? Nobody asked him to.

Fiore pursed his lips and shrugged. "Those things happen," he said.

"I suppose," Jeffrey said. "Let's get something to drink."

He didn't wait for Fiore's response, but led the way toward a kiosk that would soon be dismantled as the weather turned cooler. Right now it was doing a lively business selling overpriced pastries, shrimp and avocado sandwiches, cocktails, and wine.

Fiore followed. He knew that Blaine understood what happened in Oklahoma. You don't get rich believing in coincidences and Blaine was pretty damn rich. For an upright solid citizen, Blaine had come a long way in a short time. No hysterics. No wailing of offended innocence or cries of outrage. *Our friend in Oklahoma City passed away.* He *supposed* that those things happened. He wasn't crying about it and he wasn't going to cry about it.

They were standing on line behind an elderly gentleman in a suit that hung so loosely on him one could chart the progress of terminal illness in its folds. The man ordered by pointing and then thanked the girl who served him in a croaking voice so faint she couldn't possibly have heard him. Fiore and Jeffrey helped themselves to plastic glasses of white wine already filled and marshaled on the countertop, the empty bottle next to them so that those who cared could inspect the label. Fiore slapped a twenty on the counter before Blaine had a chance to. He didn't wait for change. As they turned to walk off toward the gaudy murals of the opera house, Fiore said, "I watched my old man shrink like that. There's got to be a better way."

Jeffrey resisted the impulse to point out that Fiore apparently had the better way at his fingertips. *Euthanasia* means "good death" but leaves open the question of whose good is being served. Sometimes it's the good of the person dying, sometimes, as in Bolling's case, the good of others.

They walked around the side of the concert hall, where there was less traffic. Suddenly Fiore's hand was on Jeffrey's shoulder and the force of the man's grip pulled him around with sudden and unexpected violence. Even before he had a chance to frame an objection, Fiore's face was inches from his own and his left hand was under Jeffrey's throat. The rage had come from nowhere, turned on by the simple flick of a switch. Or maybe it was the other way. Maybe it had been there all along, covered over with smiles and pleasantries the way snow covers the contours of the land. Either way, there was something terrifying about a man who could hide or summon such ferocity with such impulsive haste.

"You're an important man, Blaine," Fiore said. "If you fuck with me or any of my people, you'll be a sorry man. I'm the one who made you important. Do you understand that?"

From the moment Gaetano Falcone assured him that his problem with Eddie Vincenzo was taken care of, Jeffrey had known this moment was coming. "Your friend Eddie was still seeing my daughter," he said. "That wasn't our deal."

The grip on his throat tightened, the pain so sharp and precise he could feel each of the man's fingers. People were passing behind them in greater number now. Not one of them stopped or slowed or turned his head to where one man was strangling another two feet from the side entrance to Avery Fisher Hall.

"I don't care what he was doing," Fiore hissed. "If you've got a problem, you come to me. You tell me about it and I take care of it. Do you understand that?"

"Yes," Jeffrey gasped.

"You don't go to Falcone. You come to me. Is that clear?"

"Yes."

Fiore released his grip and Jeffrey found himself taking in great gulps of air. Fiore took a step back and let his face relax into a smile, the same smile he was wearing when he walked onto the plaza. "The only reason you're still alive," he said, "is because I'm thinking maybe you didn't know the rules. I know that's not true but I'm giving you the benefit of the doubt. What time does your concert start?"

"Seven-thirty," Jeffrey said. They were just two normal men again.

"Isn't that your wife?" Fiore said as they walked back toward the fountain. He pointed across the plaza to where Phyllis was hurrying toward them.

Jeffrey and Phyllis exchanged meaningless kisses. "I was so afraid you'd be late," she said. "This is a pleasure, Mr. Fiore. Are you joining us?"

Jeffrey was surprised that she remembered his name and even more surprised by the invitation. She had done everything she could to put the aftermath of Jessica's party out of her mind.

"I'm afraid I don't know much about music," Fiore said.

"Then why are you here?"

"Mr. Fiore is a client these days," Jeffrey said.

Her eyes hadn't left Fiore. "Really," she said. "I hope my husband is making you lots of money."

"He tells me it's a good time to invest," Fiore answered noncommittally.

"Always," she said. "When the market's up, when the market's down. Jeffrey believes in investing. I'm sure there are plenty of tickets available. Do join us."

Fiore shocked Jeffrey by accepting the invitation. They had no trouble buying an extra ticket at the box office. In fact, tickets had been turned in for all four of the other seats in the Blaines' keyboard-side first-tier box.

The orchestra played Ives's Second Symphony. He wrote it, according to the program notes, in 1902, when he was twenty-eight years old and still had hopes of hearing his music played. By the time of its premier forty-nine years later, he was too old to attend and listened at home on the radio.

"That's kind of sad," Fiore said when Phyllis relayed the facts to him.

The music seemed strange to him, odd and awkward, as though it was stumbling from place to place. There were moments, though, when it sounded familiar, and he settled lower into his seat and let the clamor of it invade his senses. When he glanced to the side, Phyllis Blaine felt his eyes on her and looked over at him, her gaze as steady as if they were in the middle of a conversation. He could see Blaine sitting stiffly on the other side of his wife and at the moment he hated the man.

The music turned suddenly loud, like a child demanding attention, and his eyes went back to the stage, where the conductor was gesticulating wildly for the benefit of a hundred musicians who sawed away on their instruments with such ferocity that they didn't have time to pay him any attention. Phyllis's hand moved until it rested on his, on the seat arm between them. He looked over again but she had turned her face back to the music. The corners of her mouth moved slightly in the faintest gesture of a smile.

Now the music was a march instead of a dance. Fiore was, it had been said, the most powerful man in New York, and he knew for a certainty that it was almost true. Only a powerful man would have one of his best men killed because the man lied to him. Fiore hadn't been given a choice about it. If there had been a choice at all he wouldn't have done it. So that was the funny thing about power. It didn't free you up to do whatever you wanted. It cut down on your options. It issued commands. It told you what to do and you had to do it.

As the music slowed and softened, like a clock running down, he remembered a time when he was a kid, maybe seventeen or eighteen years old, and he and Jimmy and two other kids got into a fight with some black kids waiting for the 6 train in the 125th Street station. It was a stupid fight, somebody taking exception to the way somebody looked at him. There were words, and then they were punching each other and wrestling around, which was okay for a while until one of the black kids pulled out a box cutter and cut a friend of Fiore's named Albert, whom they all called Angel, right across the biceps. Nowadays he was Albert again, and he worked for Con Ed, but that night he was Angel and he kept fighting with blood running down his arm and all over the platform. It was summer and he was only wearing a shirt or he would have had a little protection. This was at a time in Fiore's life when he carried a gun. So did Jimmy. Angel and the other kid didn't or they would have been wearing coats to cover them. Fiore kept his piece in his pocket, even after the box cutter came out, because even at that age he knew that if you capped a colored kid on 125th Street it was game over. In a white neighborhood it would have been a different story. But Jimmy, who didn't think it through like that because he couldn't fight and think at the same time and didn't know anyone who could, except of course for Charlie (which is what they called Fiore in those days), came out with his gun and yelled, *Back off, nigger!* The kid with the box cutter looked at him with a kind of wild-eyed, crazy fear, like someone who has just seen Jesus, and Angel, who still had one good arm, clocked him with a straight overhand right that sent him crashing backward and upside down off the platform and onto the track. For a minute they all could have been pictures of themselves. No one moved, as though, if they held their positions like that, something would tell them what came next. There was something actually funny about the way that kid flew off that platform, with the soles of his Felony Flyers facing out. And then one of the colored kids with him said *Jesus fucking shit* because a train was coming down the tracks and they were standing right at the north end of the platform, so it would still have a pretty good head of steam when it got close enough for the motorman to see the kid on the track. They all rushed forward, to the edge of the platform, and looked down. The kid was lying on his back, with the box cutter still in his hand and his head twisted funny, kind of over on his shoulder and turned around to the side, and his legs were bent funny, too, one leg over the other, the one underneath bent in the middle in a way no leg was supposed to bend. *Jesus, he looks like Theismann*, Angel said, because that was exactly the way Joe Theismann's leg looked when Lawrence Taylor snapped it for him in the Meadowlands. Except that Joe Theismann's head wasn't busted open, which this kid's might have been, and his neck wasn't broken, which this kid's probably was, and there was no subway train headed for Theismann as he lay there on the twenty-three-yard line. And then one of the black kids, the one Fiore had been fighting, a gangly skinny kid with long dangling arms, jumped down onto the track with the subway coming closer and shouted something but none of his friends moved. He crouched down over his friend and said something to him and his hands fluttered over the kid, big, long-fingered hands, fluttering like a bird that can't take off for some reason or other, as though he didn't know how to touch him or where. The next thing any of them knew, he was running up the track, straight toward the one-eyed headlight of the train, screaming *Stop, stop!* with those long arms waving like windmills. It was the bravest thing Fiore had ever seen anyone do, black skin and black clothes running right at a subway train coming toward him out of the darkness, but it made sense because at least he stood a chance of flagging the train in time if he ran toward it.

For some reason the music sounded like something he had heard a thousand times even though he knew he had never heard it before, and Phyllis Blaine's hand still rested on the back of his, and he couldn't figure out why he was thinking about Gus and why he was thinking about that thing in the train station that he didn't even know he remembered anymore, except that here it was, everything as clear as it must have been the next morning. He remembered that when the kid started running, he hopped down onto the track himself even though he had no idea what possessed him to do a thing like that. *Put that fucking thing away*, he said to Jimmy, and then he was down on the track and the other kid, Angel's friend, was down there with him, and they were trying to see how you could pick up this kid and get him up on the platform without him falling apart in their hands. There was a lot of blood under his head and it didn't look like they should be moving him. Except of course for the train. He remembered looking up at the track and that headlight and being more scared than he had ever been in his life. Still, there he was, kneeling down on the track with a train coming and blood all over his hands from the colored kid's head, and then he heard the shriek of the train's brakes, really a shriek, exactly like someone screaming. Fiore said, *I'll get his legs*, and when he touched the kid, the leg flopped around like it was just a stick and the kid groaned, so at least he was alive. And then Fiore said, *Hold it, hold it*, because the shrieking was dying down. And then it stopped, which meant the train was stopped. So he said, *Let's get the fuck out of here*, and they pulled themselves back up on the platform and ran out of the station, Fiore and Jimmy and Angel, with the blood still running down his arm from where the box cutter got him, and Angel's friend. They never found out what happened to the kid on the tracks, whether he died or not.

And then Fiore realized why he was thinking about all this now and what the connection was. The connection was fear. Because he was afraid now, and he couldn't remember ever having been afraid of anything since that night on the train tracks.

But this Blaine business was different. Fiore had dealt with dangerous men his whole life, and this guy was just a banker. He shouldn't have been afraid.

But he was.

The music came at him in a roar of complicated sound.

Gabriel Enriquez studied the files on the flight out to Oklahoma City, familiarizing himself with the details of Bolling's investments. He was met at the terminal by a Mexican holding a hand-lettered cardboard sign that said LAYNE BENTLEY. The Mexican wasn't pleased that the banker they sent was Hispanic, and so young. He was a wise man in a simple way and he grasped at once the signification of the choice. Gabriel only made matters worse by getting into the front seat of the car with an offensive disregard for social distinctions. One was a handyman and the other was a banker. Differences mattered.

They drove in silence until the city rose up ahead of them, flanking the highway on both sides.

"This is a larger city than I believed it would be," Gabriel said in Spanish.

Miguel's eyes darted across to his passenger but he didn't turn his head. The accent, he knew at once, was not Puerto Rican but he didn't know how to locate it. There was a stilted singsong to it that made the words sound effeminate to his ears. "Yes," he answered in Spanish. "A big city. You are not Puerto Rican. *Cubano*, perhaps?"

"My parents, yes. Cuban."

"But you are American?"

"Yes."

He had known Cubans in Mexico and found them to be earnest and serious people, but the American Cubans were earnest without seriousness, filled with an exaggerated self-importance. His own children called themselves Mexican, although they, too, were born in the United States of America. This one called himself American.

The silence returned to the car while Miguel thought carefully about what he would say. Ten miles passed in this fashion and the city was now behind them. "Señor Bolling was a fine man," he said at last. "Even now that he is gone, his memory is owed much respect."

"Yes, I understand that," Gabriel said.

Miguel said, "And the señora is very young. Do you understand that also?"

"No," Gabriel said, "I wasn't aware of that. But I understand what you are saying."

When *the señora*, as the driver insisted on calling her, came in to meet her guest in the large drawing room, as cool and dark as a cave, she, too, seemed surprised to see that they had sent a young *latino*.

She hung back in the doorway a moment as Gabriel Enriquez came forward to greet her. The draperies in the room were all drawn, letting in only a soft, earth-colored light. Was darkness, he wondered, a sign of mourning? It seemed to him he had read something about that once. Or was it merely that she throve in shadow, like an orchid?

When she moved forward, her dress billowed about her like a cloud, gentle and formless, a lightning-lit cloud of red and gold peonies on a pastel background. Just from the tautness of her arms, he sensed the firmness of her body.

He introduced himself. "Mr. Blaine asked me to come see you to discuss some of your late husband's investments," he said.

"I know why you're here, Mr. Enriquez," she snapped in a tone of petulant impatience.

Of course she knew. It had been arranged; she sent the car for him. His words must have sounded condescending, he was afraid, as though he took her for some vacant plaything. He had meant no condescension but he didn't know how to fix it.

She offered to show him to his room, and when they got there he found his suitcase, which the driver had taken from him, already on the bed. He took a moment to examine the room and his eyes fell almost at once on a pair of paintings that hung side by side on an otherwise unadorned wall. They were done in oils, he saw when he moved to them for a closer inspection, but the paint was applied so finely, the muted colors washed in with such subdued delicacy, that he had taken them at first for watercolors. The figures, the buildings, the landscape beyond the village were all suggested in the gently curving geometry of the shapes. There were no straight lines and there was no modeling, as though each person and each object somehow shared its identity with the objects before it and behind it and with the spaces between. There was no distortion, no subjectivity, no point of view.

"Yours?" he asked, turning to look at Señora Bolling over his shoulder. The signature at the corner of each painting was a simple lower-case *r*.

"Yes," she said. "The village where I was born."

"You must have loved it," he said.

She looked at him a moment and then turned away without answering, as though he offered her a challenge she didn't care to accept. She stopped with her hand on the open door and suggested a swim and lunch before they got down to business. He would find bathing suits in the dresser, she told him. The pool was right outside his window. He would have no trouble finding it. "Your hips are so narrow," she said, "I hope you'll find one that fits. My husband's friends," she added, then hesitated before finishing the sentence, "were heavier men."

And then she was gone, having given him, just in those last words, a glimpse into the loneliness of her life.

She was in the water when he got there, swimming strongly. He watched her, spellbound by the power and beauty of the most perfect body he had ever seen. In the only suit he found that wouldn't have fallen off his body, the blatancy of her beauty read out with embarrassing clarity.

He plunged into the water and easily crossed half the length of the pool before he broke to the surface near the lane where she was swimming. She stopped when he reached her, the two of them treading water. She was breathing heavily from the exertion, her breasts rising and falling in her black suit just below the splintered surface of the water. She invited him to join her for a few laps, and he set off at once. He was a powerful swimmer, strong in the chest and shoulders, but she caught him in the turn and he let her set the pace from that point. He sensed that she was taking it easy on him and would have had no trouble outdistancing him if she chose to. He felt her presence in the water beside him.

Before they had finished the first full lap, the rhythm of his arms and legs, the flow of the water along his body took over and the swimming began to feel effortless, as though the pool were a river carrying him with it, his mind maintaining the contact with her simply as a matter of will and acquiescence. By the second lap he was conscious of feeling utterly free of his body, borne along by an energy in his arms and legs that seemed limitless. He lost track of time and place, lost count of the laps, as they crossed the length of the pool again and again.

And then she stopped, resting her arms on the lip of the pool, and he stopped beside her, neither of them for a moment capable of speech. She threw her wet hair back from her face with a toss of her head and climbed out of the pool. She led him to a pair of chaises set side by side, and they stretched out next to each other. For a moment the silence was broken only by the sound of their own breathing and the lapping of the water in the pool, still stirred by the echoes of their passage through it.

He heard footsteps and opened his eyes. A short, square-faced Mexican woman stood over him, transferring laden plates and full glasses from a wide wooden tray to a table that stood between them. She said nothing and padded off when she was finished.

"You swim well," Rachel said, breaking the silence.

They talked pleasantly while they ate, about his childhood in a Cuban community in Florida and hers in Mexico. When they had finished eating, he asked her if she wanted to talk about her investment accounts.

"I don't think Mr. Blaine understands how little I care about these things," she said.

"Then why am I here?"

"It was Mr. Blaine's idea."

"And you didn't want to say no to him?"

"Perhaps that's it, yes," she answered enigmatically.

She reached a hand over, lightly touching his chest with the tips of her fingers. "You didn't happen to notice the cut-glass bowl in the bathroom?" she asked.

"With the silver spoon next to it?" he said. "Yes. I noticed it."

He hadn't done any cocaine in more than three years. That stuff cost him his job at First Boston, and he swore at the time that he would never go back to it. Now he wasn't sure what he would say if she offered it.

"My husband kept all the guest rooms well supplied," she said. "I've lost my taste for it. Because of my husband, you understand. Because of the way he died."

Gabriel knew nothing of the circumstances surrounding Bolling's death but it seemed to him that she wanted to talk about it, so he said nothing, letting his watchful silence open the way for her to go on.

Her fingertips drew small circles on his chest and then walked slowly down his body, stopping when they reached his belly. The delicacy of her touch, so openly provocative, sent a shock wave of excitement through his body. A simple seduction would have been easier for him to understand, even being seduced by a young woman so recently widowed. But not while she was talking about her deceased husband.

He felt in an instant almost shamefully young and guiltily naive, as though he should have understood what she wanted from him now, should have known how to reconcile her words and her fingertips. He felt stupid. Everyone knew that life was full of contradictions. Why was he so confused by them?

"You don't know how he died?" she asked.

"No."

Her hand stopped moving on his body. "Toward the end of his life my husband got involved in some sort of illegal investment scheme," she said.

She felt a sudden knotting in the sheath of his muscle under her touch. *Well,* she thought, *Mr. Gabriel Enriquez knows more than he is letting on. I have frightened him.*

"They warned him they could kill him if he betrayed them in any way," she went on, as though she were telling a story. "I don't know what happened, except that they did what they said they would do."

Of course Gabriel knew what the scheme was. He was the one who made it work. He felt the sudden coldness of sweat drying on his body. Images of Jeffrey Blaine's handwritten notes literally flashed in his mind like so many pages spasmodically illuminated by lightning. At first the transactions always involved the Bolling accounts. After a week or so, other accounts came into play, with Bolling's name soon vanishing from the records. *What you're saying can't be true,* he wanted to protest. *Your husband's death had nothing to do with this scheme you're talking about. He was hardly involved at all.* But even before any of this could be spoken aloud, he understood what happened, what must have happened, what had to have happened. Bolling hadn't betrayed anyone. That wasn't why he was dead. He was dead because his participation in the scheme had become unnecessary.

Her fingers moved again, prowling to the top of his suit. And now her hand plunged under it, gripping his cock in a tight fist. "You were so hard," she said, "so beautiful and hard. I hope I haven't ruined it."

He could feel his penis throbbing back to life, in spite of the warnings that screamed in his brain like metal shrieking against metal.

She leaned across the space between them. Her lips were at his ear. "You're the bribe they're offering me," she whispered, her breath against his ear as thrilling, almost, as her hand. "You're what they're paying me for my silence."

Her fingers caressed the head of his penis, stroked the shaft. She slid from her own chaise, crouching on the patio tiles beside him. She raised the waistband of his suit and laid her head on his belly, watching the effect she was having on him. Her long hair, still wet, spread over his body, exciting him in ways that felt surprisingly new.

She let go of him and rose to her feet, her bathing suit sliding down her body as if she were a snake slipping from its skin. His eyes went to hers, then down her body, past those perfect breasts, to the thick, dark tangle of her pubic hair, so dark and dense it hid everything. He lunged for her, plunging his face into the thicket, pulling her over on top of him, her legs wreathing his neck.

He could feel the lightest touch of her lips on the tip of his cock, while his own tongue prowled inside her and his head swam dizzily with the complex fragrances of her body.

He wanted her to stop, to wait, to let him have her first. She seemed to read his mind. He heard her moan softly as her hips writhed in response to the relentless prowling of his tongue, and he felt only the light, slick movement of his cock against her unparted lips.

And then she moaned harder, her hips thrashing and churning, and all he knew and tasted and felt was the wonderful wetness of her cunt sliding across his lips, his chin, his nose. She pressed hard, her lips to his, and he plunged his tongue into her one last time and she stopped moving entirely and lay still.

Slowly, like a sunrise, she rolled off him, crouching again by his side. She took him deep into her mouth, her hand wrapped tightly around him, working him with her tongue, her lips, and her hand all at the same time. He looked down and saw her head rising and falling, saw himself throbbing into her and out, and he fought to hold the moment as long as possible, to resist letting it end.

He felt the bite of her teeth around him, far down his cock, like a tickle at first, thrilling and then sharper. A second later he felt pain and he felt her movement stop and he felt only the pain, sharper and sharper. He called out "Hey!" as though there had been some misunderstanding, as though she were confused about the distinction between what thrilled and what hurt, but he knew it wasn't that, knew it already. He grabbed at her hair, wrapping his fingers in it tightly, trying to pull her back as the grip of her teeth tightened and tightened until he felt something break and her mouth filled with blood and still he couldn't stop her, the pain unbearable now, and he thought in panic that even if he ripped handfuls of her hair from her head she would still be there like the severed head of a leech, gnawing.

He could feel his blood spilling from her mouth onto his thighs and balls, and he thought *god no don't let her do that please* and he knew only because of the clarity of the pain that she hadn't bitten it off yet.

She stopped. And stood up. And spat the blood from her mouth, but her lips were still colored with it.

"Miguel will get you to a doctor," she said. "Make sure you tell Mr. Blaine what happened."

He stayed in a hospital that night, and well into the next day, and then he caught the last flight back to New York. He took the rest of the week off, phoning in to say he was ill. But no, he never told Blaine what happened. He never told anyone.

23

When **Gus Benini** didn't get in touch with Schliester for two days, Schliester figured it was time to get in touch with Gus. He drove out to the house, where Benini's daughter Theresa opened the door. She started screaming the moment she saw who was there, her words almost unintelligible. She demanded to know what they did to her father, where he was, what they wanted, all of this tumbling out in unformed fragments of hysteria. "You bastards, you bastards, you bastards!" she screamed over and over.

She began to pound on Schliester with her fists, as though he were a door that wouldn't open.

Schliester caught her hands and Matt Thompson, who was accompanying him again, took her firmly by the shoulders. They managed to get her inside and Schliester closed the door with his foot. She was still flailing with her hands, even though Schliester held her wrists, so that her forearms flew about like convulsed marionettes. "Listen to me, listen to me, listen to me," he kept repeating until finally she subsided enough for him to take a chance on letting her hands go. When he released her hands, they remained trembling in the air. Thompson let go of her as well.

Schliester knew he was good at calming things. It was a gift he had. Once, in St. Louis, he talked a man who had cut his own child into giving up the knife. It was his proudest moment as a cop, even though all his partner said afterward was, "Next time you might want to consider capping the guy."

The girl's whole body trembled now, but she made no attempt to renew the assault.

"All right now, listen to me," Schliester said. "This is important. We didn't do anything to your father. We talked to him and then he left. Are you telling me he hasn't been home since then?"

She nodded her head, her lips so tight she seemed almost to have no lips. There were no tears, but he could tell that she was crying.

"He hasn't called? He hasn't been in touch?"

She shook her head.

From upstairs, a voice called, "What's the matter, Theresa? What's going on down there?"

"It's all right, Mama, it's nothing. Go back to bed," Theresa called back, finding a calmness somewhere that she managed to put into her voice for her mother's sake.

Benini was nothing more than a cheap little gangster, Schliester thought. Not a bad guy, just a little on the sleazy side. How did people like that end up with kids like this?

A frail-looking woman in a faded bathrobe started down the stairs, her left hand gripping the banister. Her skin was the color of paper. "I heard screaming," she said.

Theresa started up the stairs and helped her mother down. "Who are these men?" Mrs. Benini asked her daughter as the two of them picked their way to the foot of the stairs.

"They're policemen, Mama," Theresa said.

"Did something happen to your father?"

"No, Mama."

Schliester took Mrs. Benini's arm, which felt as lifeless as a stick, and, with Theresa's help, escorted her to a couch in the living room. There was an electric fireplace with fake logs.

He explained as carefully as he could that her husband had been brought in for questioning about some illegal activities but that he wasn't in trouble because he agreed to cooperate. "Sometimes when a man does that, he has second thoughts," he said. "He may have gone off by himself to think it over for a few days. I'm sure he'll be in touch with you."

Both women nodded as though he had said something eminently sensible.

"Do you understand what I just told you?" he said, looking from mother to daughter. "He's not in trouble. But it's important that he get in touch with me."

He handed the girl a card.

"Please," he said. "Make sure he calls me. I can help him. Nobody else can."

Both women nodded again.

When Schliester got back to the office, he sat down with Elaine and Gogarty to analyze the situation. They all figured Benini was scared and he was running. If they could bring him in, calm him down, promise him protection, they could still save six months of work that would go down the crapper otherwise. Schliester filled out the paperwork and put it out on the air.

At about the time he was doing this, the doorbell at the Benini house rang again. Mrs. Benini was still on the couch, covered with a blanket now.

Standing on the stoop, New York City detective Raul Alvarez waited for someone to answer the door. All he knew was that a body had washed up on the shore at Jones Beach like a piece of driftwood. The body was naked and no clothes were found anywhere near the site, so there was no telling where he had gone into the water, although it might have been possible, with tide tables and a good guess as to the time of death, to figure it out. The body was identified by fingerprints, which is the only known benefit of having a criminal record. Otherwise, the family would have had to live with the uncertainty of not knowing.

The detective didn't say any of this. What he said, when a girl opened the door, was, "My name is Detective Raul Alvarez. I'd like to speak with the wife of Gus Benini."

Theresa already knew what he was going to tell her. Her stomach clenched like a fist. "She's lying down," she said. "I'm his daughter."

"There seems to have been an accident, miss," the detective

said. "We'll need you to come with us to make an identification."

Theresa nodded numbly and went back into the house. All she told her mother was that she had to go out. She didn't want to say more just in case it wasn't true.

The answer came back almost before Schliester put the question out on the air. Detective Caz Armintella of the NYPD's Organized Crime Control unit called the federal task force office. "What's this about you guys wanting Benini?" he asked.

It was Gogarty who took his call. "Right. We want him," he said.

There was a brief silence while Armintella sized up the wiseassed fed on the other end of the line. Then he said, "Yeah, okay, no problem. You want him, you can have him. Meet me at the Brooklyn morgue in half an hour."

Gogarty said, "What's he doing at the morgue?"

"He's been inducted into the next world," Armintella said. "He's taking his physical."

Schliester could hear only one end of the conversation, but that end contained the word *morgue*. "Gus?" he asked when Gogarty hung up the phone.

"Yeah, Gus," Gogarty confirmed.

Forty-five minutes later Gogarty and Schliester walked through the door at the basement drop-off entrance of the King's County Morgue. The air felt like it hadn't been changed in weeks. Armintella was waiting for them.

"I hope we're not too late," Gogarty said. "He's still dead, isn't he?"

Armintella smiled. He was a big guy, heavier than he should have been, but he looked like he knew how to carry it. If you were choosing up sides for a brawl, you'd pick him in a minute. When he asked why the feds were looking for Benini, Schliester answered him before Gogarty could get in the way. "We had him on a shake-down thing," he said. "We brought him in and we gave him the usual choices. He went home to think it over."

"Let me guess. He could go to jail or he could help you out," Armintella said.

"That's right."

"Or he could take all his clothes off and go for a swim in the fucking ocean."

Schliester bristled at the cheap shot. He was being blamed for the man's death.

"Next question," Armintella said. "What kind of cooperation were you looking for?"

"Full and sincere."

"It wouldn't have concerned Chet Fiore by any chance, would it?"

"I don't know what he was going to say," Schliester said. "He never got around to saying it."

Now it was Armintella's turn to take offense. He took a step forward, his belly preceding him. "I've got a homicide here," he said, "so let's not play games."

And then a voice behind him said, "Excuse me but I'm not sure that you do."

The new arrival was a small and dainty-looking man in lab whites. He had no chin and a big nose, and he introduced himself as Dr. Grimm, which wasn't a bad name for a man in his line of work. "The man drowned," he said. "Water in the lungs. No question about that. Of course that leaves open the possibility of another party or parties drowning him or helping him drown. Evidence? No. No evidence whatsoever. What was I looking for? Abrasions, contusions, anything that might suggest a force applied to hold him under the water. Neck, body, arms, face. Other possibilities? Of course. He could have been rendered unconscious, chemically or by means of a blow. Chemically? No. There was nothing in his blood but blood. That leaves a blow. No sign of one. The evidence would have been subtle, mind you. When death eventuates shortly after an injury, there is very little bruising. A lot of pathologists, even good pathologists, could miss the signs."

"But not you?" Gogarty prompted.

Dr. Grimm smiled. "Ask around," he said smugly. "I'm thorough. I'm listing this as an accidental drowning or a suicide, depending on the life circumstances of the decedent. You don't have a homicide."

"These gentlemen will fill you in on the life circumstances," Armintella said, already in motion toward the door. Whether the doctor was right about there being no homicide was beside the point, because once he filed his report there was certainly going to be no homicide *case*. It's hard enough to prove murder under the best of circumstances, impossible when the medical examiner says there hasn't been one.

Gogarty waited until the door closed behind the organized crime detective. Then he said, "The decedent was under investigation. We invited him to cooperate against certain underworld figures and he was thinking it over."

Grimm nodded, the nod of a man who now knows what to put in the few remaining blanks on his form. He turned to go but Schliester said, "Don't put anything down yet. I'd like another talk with his family."

"His daughter's upstairs," Grimm said. He gave directions to the viewing room.

The corridor smelled like formaldehyde, if that's what formaldehyde smelled like. If death was a business and it had a head office, this was it.

Gogarty tagged along next to his partner. "Whatever you're thinking, *boychik*," he said, "don't bother thinking it. When the white parrot says case closed, that means case closed. You can't open it with pliers."

Gogarty was right. Grimm *did* look like a parrot.

"I don't care about opening the goddamned case," Schliester said.

"What do you care about?"

"I just want to know, that's all," Schliester snapped. "I knew the guy, I worked him, I want to know. Is that so hard to understand?"

It wasn't. Gogarty didn't work that way himself. But he understood.

Viewing rooms at city morgues weren't what they used to be. When a body is to be identified, they roll open the drawer of the refrigerated cabinet where it's stored and point two television cameras at it, one low, mounted to the side, the other set in the ceiling. The bereaved wait in a little windowless room until an attendant comes in and turns on the TV. In Theresa Benini's case it had been a long wait. She was alone in a big waiting room for over an hour before a dark-skinned Indian man came to get her. He was carrying a clipboard. He took her to the little room without windows. "You sit down, please, miss," he said in that pretty accent they have. Theresa always liked that accent. She sat down in one of three chairs lined up in front of the television mounted on the wall and he turned on the set. She took a breath and held it while she waited for the picture to come on.

Two pictures came on actually, split screen, next to each other. Front and side, like those police pictures. As though he had already been arrested and convicted and sentenced and even executed. She broke down and cried when she saw him, cried as though she had never let herself cry before, not over a broken toy or a broken date or a ruined love affair. All these things had happened in her life and the crying for them didn't count anymore.

The Indian man let her cry for a long time and then he was standing in front of her holding a paper cup of water in his hand. She took it and drank it down, and it was then that she noticed that the television was off now. It was like her father had been taken away from her one more time.

"Please," the Indian man said in that lovely singsong voice, "it is required that you sign this."

He handed her the clipboard and a pen. The blanks on the form had been filled out by hand with her name and her address and other information of that nature, which she vaguely remembered giving them when she first got there. There was also information about her father, which she was sure she hadn't given them. She didn't read all the words but she knew what they meant. She signed where he showed her to sign and handed the clipboard back. "Can you turn it on again?" she asked.

"No, miss," he said, "that is not possible."

There was a little light down in the mortuary that went on

when the TV set was turned on and off when it was turned off so that they would know when the viewing was over and they could put the body away.

He told her she could stay a little while if she liked and even offered to stay with her.

"No, you don't have to do that," she said.

He brought her another drink of water and left.

She stared at the blank screen for a few minutes and then stared at nothing, really. She realized she hadn't asked anyone how he died and now she was sorry. Her pocketbook was on the floor between her feet and she bent over to pick it up and then stood up just as the door opened and the government agent who said he was the only one who could help her father came in.

"I'm sorry, Miss Benini," he said. "I really am."

She tried not to look at him as she walked to the door and he stepped aside to let her pass. She had no intention of saying a word to him or listening to a word he said. He said he could help her father and *this* was how he helped.

As she stepped through the door he said, "The coroner is saying it was suicide."

She stopped walking as abruptly as if a bolt of lightning had come down from the sky and struck the earth at her feet. She felt like she was going to be sick. "No," she said without turning to face him. "Daddy wouldn't do that."

That was what Schliester thought, too. Fiore could have had the man killed without leaving anything for Dr. Thorough to find. Schliester had no doubt of that. What he couldn't understand was how Fiore found out so quickly that Benini had been taken in for questioning.

"You have to help me, then, miss," he said. "We're trying to figure out if there's any way Chet Fiore might have known that your father was under investigation."

He was just fishing, but he wanted Fiore for this murder more than he had ever wanted anything in his life.

The girl gasped and looked so much like she was going to pass out that Schliester put out a hand to steady her. "Oh my god," she cried, "I did it. He came to the house. I told him Daddy went with you. Oh my god oh my god oh my god."

There was nothing more for either of them to say, the cop and the orphaned child of a petty gangster. Both of them were thinking the same thing in different ways. Gus Benini was a harmless little man, and yet it took four people to kill him. There was Chet Fiore, who gave the order. And there was someone else, who actually did the deed.

And there was Wally Schliester, who was trying to tell himself he was only doing his job.

And finally there was Theresa Benini. Who set it up, too, even though she was only trying to help.

Georgie Vallo drove all the way out to New Haven in his brother-in-law's car. Eddie had given him good directions—amazing considering the shape he was in—so he found the dorm without any trouble. Which was a good thing, because he didn't like talking to the kind of people he would have had to talk to on the Yale campus if he was going to ask directions. They pissed him off. They thought they knew everything just because they had money and went to an expensive college.

When he knocked on the door he was thinking that he wasn't even sure he remembered what Eddie's girl looked like, but he knew when a girl opened the door that this wasn't her. She was tall, maybe an inch taller than he was, a couple inches taller than Eddie. Who would never go out with a girl that tall. He was touchy on the subject.

Georgie, though, wouldn't have half minded. He took a minute to take her in from top to bottom, especially the bottom, and then he said, "I'm looking for Jessica Blaine."

She said, "Jessica's not in school anymore. She's home in New York."

Oh fuck, Georgie thought, but he thought it out loud.

"I'm sorry," the tall girl said. "I've got her number if you want to call her. You're a friend of Eddie's, aren't you?"

She stepped back from the door to let him in. Maybe the drive out wasn't going to be a waste after all.

He looked around and was surprised to see he was standing in a totally nothing little room. Georgie had an apartment of his own, which may not have been much but it had a forty-eight-inch TV and a couch you could lie all the way down on. It made this place look like a shithole. So it was at least slightly possible that, Yale or no Yale, under the right circumstances this girl would be impressed.

She found the number in a little book and handed it to him.

"Do I have to dial anything, like for an outside line?" he asked.

She was standing right next to him, her shoulder practically touching his shoulder. "It's just a regular phone," she said.

He dialed the number and a girl's voice answered. She sounded very young. "Jessica?" he asked. Then he said, "Jessica Blaine?" (The girl smiled, like there was something funny about that.) "Listen," he said, "this is Georgie Vallo. Eddie's friend, right. He asked me to call you. He's in the hospital."

He listened a minute and then he said, "Well, he had a problem. He wants to see you. It's Montefiore, do you know where that is?"

She couldn't have said very much because he said almost right away, "I was supposed to give you a ride, see, but I'm up in New Haven. He figured that's where you were going to be." Then he said, "Great, yeah, great," and hung up the phone.

The tall girl said, "You drove all the way out here to take her to see your friend in the hospital?"

"That's right," he said.

"You're a very good friend," she said.

That's when Georgie Vallo knew he was going to get laid.

Schliester didn't say a word on the drive back from Brooklyn. He let Gogarty do all the talking while his own mind turned sickening somersaults. He couldn't get his mind off Benini's daughter and some of the things she said. *He's got to have his breakfast*, she said. *It's important.* That was the first time. The second time she screamed. And the third time, just a couple minutes ago, she said, *Daddy wouldn't do that.*

Which was exactly right. Daddy wouldn't. Chet Fiore would. Chet Fiore would throw a harmless little man into Long Island Sound. With Wally Schliester's help, thank you very much.

When they got back to the office, Schliester told Gogarty he wanted to walk around and think a little. Or not think, if at all possible. Not think would be better.

He bought himself a coffee at a lunch cart at the foot of one of the piers and walked out to the end. He could hear the water lapping under his feet and he tried to put everything except the sound of it out of his mind. The East River was a river but it didn't flow like one and didn't sound like one. It sounded more like a beach. It smelled like one, too. Salt water, when the tide was up and the river ran backward. In St. Louis you could stand at the water's edge for a million years and you would never once see the Mississippi run backward. In this fucked-up city it happened twice a day.

He came to the house. He could hear the girl's voice again in his ears. *I told him Daddy went with you.*

He cocked his head as though he had just heard his name being called. He narrowed his eyes as he looked out over the water and played her words back a second time. *He came to the house.* Why did Chet Fiore come to Gus Benini's house? It wasn't a social call. He knew something was up before he got there. How could he have known? How could he possibly have known?

Something was wrong here and Schliester didn't know what it was. He went back to the beginning, going over everything he knew about the case, from that night in February when he and Gogarty tailed Fiore to a birthday party for a banker's kid. Dennis Franciscan blew a gasket because of that fucked-up chase through Prospect Park in a civilian car that had to be towed out of the snow. Okay, that made sense. Franciscan liked things neat and there was nothing neat about that night. The next morning, though, Elaine Lester was all over the two of them. She wanted the case. And when Franciscan got caught wagging his dick at an inappropriate moment, she came back at them again. She was interested in the banker. She said making a case on the banker was going to get her an office with windows.

All of a sudden he heard Gus's voice in his mind. *Something about a banker.* Was that the way he put it?

Schliester dumped his coffee cup into a trash can and ran back to the office. He yanked open the file cabinet and found the tape of their interview with Benini. He listened with earphones because he didn't want Gogarty hearing what he was listening to. Gogarty asked and he waved him away.

He sped the tape forward. He knew about where it was, an hour into it, maybe a little less. He wanted the exact words. He jockeyed back and forth until he found the spot. *I don't know,* Gus was saying. *I keep hearing something about a banker, something about cleaning up the money, something something, I don't know what it is. It's just something I hear, but that's all I can tell you, that's all I know.*

And then Elaine's voice on the tape: *Well, let's move on to something you do know something about.*

Let's move on? Was she fucking kidding? *What banker? Who do you hear this from, Gus? If you heard that much, you heard more.* These were the things that should have been said. She should have made him say more, and if it turned out he really didn't know any more, she should have given him some homework before they sent him home. *Find out about this banker and get back to us.*

How the fuck does a person who knew eight months ago that linking Chet Fiore to a banker would get her an office with windows suddenly lose interest? *Let's move on.* Where exactly were they moving on to?

He hit the stop button and rewound the tape, impatient as the reels spun. Gogarty had gone back to his desk but now he came over again and asked him what he'd found. Schliester didn't answer. When the end of the tape slapped off the reel, he stopped the machine, returned the tape to the file cabinet, and walked into Elaine's office without knocking on the door.

She was reading something and writing notes, and she held up a hand without looking up. He waited while she finished what she was writing and capped her pen—she always used a fountain pen—

and then she looked up at him but didn't say anything. Waiting for him to say something. First he waited, now she was waiting. It was a hell of a note.

Their first night together at his apartment had also been their last. He didn't know why. The next time he asked her to meet him for a drink, she asked him if they couldn't talk in the office. He tried another time and she said the same thing. She didn't explain, and Schliester wasn't going to ask. He didn't need diagrams.

He couldn't think how he was going to say what he wanted to say but he gave it a try. "Let me ask you something," he said. "How come you weren't interested when Benini said something about a banker?"

It was best this way. Just ask it straight out.

She was on her feet now. "Is that what this is about?" she demanded angrily.

"Yeah," he said. "It's a legitimate question."

"I *am* interested," she said. "Very interested. Of course I'm interested. You didn't want me to tell Benini that, did you?"

He wanted to make sure he was getting this right. "You were going to follow up on it?" he asked.

"I *am* going to follow up on it," she said.

"No, you're not," he said. "Benini's dead."

She seemed genuinely surprised. "What are you talking about?"

"He's in the Brooklyn morgue. They fished him out of the water this morning. Too bad we didn't ask him about the banker when we had the chance."

She took a step toward him. "What the hell are you getting at?" she demanded angrily.

"Nothing," he said. "Nothing at all."

On the long subway ride to the Bronx, Jessica wished she had asked Georgie Vallo why Eddie was in the hospital. But the call was so quick she didn't even get a chance to think.

The hospital was a depressing fortress in red brick, the perfect match for Jessica's mood by the time she got there. *Objective correlative.* Professor Hairston, who taught Jessica's freshman English course, was absolutely obsessed with the phrase. As though it explained everything. Poetry was full of objective correlatives for the emotions it was trying to convey. Stories were full of them, novels were full of them. Well, life had objective correlatives of its own, she thought, and this place was sure as hell one of them. For that matter, while she was on the subject, how about the name? Montefiore. Mountain of Fiore. Whatever that meant. Very symbolic, the way it tied everything together.

The lady in the lobby directed her to a ward on the fourth floor. It was like a scene from *The English Patient*, she thought, and then realized, while she was still standing in the doorway, that she had never visited anyone in a hospital who wasn't in a private room.

There were eight beds along each wall, all of them occupied. At first she thought she had been sent to the wrong place, because all she could see was old men. She hesitated a moment and then walked into the ward, tentative and unsure. She felt the eyes of the men on her, as intrusive as hands on her body, feeling her up. An old man, skinny as a scarecrow, licked his lips and put his hands under the covers, playing with himself.

And then she saw Eddie. Or was it Eddie? She thought she saw his eyes on her, from the corner bed, and she hurried forward. The room smelled of sickness, a close, fetid smell of bodies and urine and dressings on wounds. She stopped short, still half a dozen feet from the foot of his bed.

It was Eddie, and it wasn't. His face, the part of it she could see, was livid purple, and the other side of it, even his eye on that side, was covered with bandages held in place by strips of tape that ran across his forehead and under his chin. His lips were swollen, cracked, and oddly slack, as though the muscles that made them work had ceased functioning, so that his face looked like something drawn on a balloon that was losing its air.

He said something, but his voice was so thick and slurred that she couldn't make out the words.

"Eddie, what happened?" she asked as she stepped closer.

"D'ya like?" he asked, croaking the words at her.

She was sure that was what he said, but it didn't make sense. He gestured with a wave of crooked fingers, and it was only then that she noticed that his right hand was completely encased in a heavy cast that extended up past his wrist. She stepped to the side of the bed and bent to him, so she could hear what he had to say. His one eye moved over her face, from her lips to her eyes to her hair, back to her eyes again, as though he had to process her piece by piece.

"What is it, Eddie?" she asked, because he didn't say anything.

"Hand. All broke," he said. "All of it."

"Oh god, Eddie," she said. There were tears in her eyes. He saw them and made a weak and crooked attempt at a smile.

"Comes off, y'know," he mumbled. "Skin. Skin comes right off. Bet y'didn't know that."

The fingers on his good hand waved in front of his face.

She felt sick to her stomach and tried not to think about what he was telling her. "Don't talk about that, Eddie," she whispered. "Don't think about that."

"Yeah," he said. "How 'bout kiss? Gimme kiss."

"C'mon, Eddie," she pleaded, desperation in her voice now. In her mind she could see under the bandages, the raw meat of his body, pulsing red and sticky with blood. She fought off another wave of nausea, fought with herself to keep from looking away.

She saw his hand move, and could have reacted if she had her wits about her. Gripped by a paralyzing passivity, she let his hand catch her, clutching the front of her shirt above her breasts. And then his hand went tight and he jerked her toward him, pulling hard, pulling her face to his, almost costing her her balance. She had to slap a hand down on the bed—not the bed, his shoulder—to keep from falling over onto him and he made an awful sound from the pain, not a scream, not a groan, more like the calls she sometimes heard at night in Bedford Falls when an owl caught some little animal that shrilled its distress before it died.

She tried to move her hand off his shoulder but he wouldn't let go of her, even though the pain must have been terrible. His right arm came up, the one with the damaged hand, and he flung it around behind her, his forearm at the back of her neck, and pulled her down until their lips touched. His lips felt soft and gummy. She heard a strange, cackling laugh that couldn't have come from Eddie, and she felt a hand on her butt, under her skirt, which had ridden up as she fell forward. She felt rough fingers on her panties, at the tops of her thighs, probing the fabric, pushing it aside, prying into the crack of her butt.

She was fighting desperately now, flailing to get free of Eddie and free of the groping stranger in the next bed. She managed to turn sideways and the hand caught her skirt, but at least it wasn't touching her skin anymore. She pulled back from Eddie just at the moment he released her, and she lost her balance and fell to the floor between the two beds. She heard the sound of footsteps hurrying toward her and a man's voice called out, "All right, leave her alone, leave her alone."

A black orderly ran toward her, down the line of beds.

Even with help coming, the man in the next bed grabbed for her again. He was a fat old man and he leered at her idiotically, grinning like a child who has done something naughty but adorable.

"Are you all right? What's going on here?" the orderly demanded, striking an authoritative pose.

Jessica pointed a finger at the old man.

"You're giving this girl trouble, Howard?" the orderly said. "We've had enough out of you."

He kicked at the wheels of the bed, releasing the brakes. Before Jessica even understood what he was about to do, he was wheeling the bed into the aisle. The old man didn't change his expression, the grin plastered on his face like a mask. "Sorry about this, miss," the orderly said, and in a moment the bed was rolling rapidly away.

"You don't have to do that," Jessica called helplessly after him.

She had a vague sense that it was somehow her fault, that the old man couldn't help what he did, that he was being banished over something that was really, now that it was over, nothing.

"Worth it?" Eddie said, and she turned back to him, as though for a moment she had almost forgotten he was there. She didn't understand, except that it felt as though she were caught in the middle of a nightmare.

"Where are they taking him?" she asked. "They don't have to do that."

"Not him! Me!" Eddie shouted, his voice suddenly sharp and clear, like the barking of a dog. "You think you're worth it? You think you're worth this?"

His good hand formed a claw in front of his anguished face, as though he were going to scratch the bandages off to show her.

"What are you talking about?" she pleaded, confused.

"Your old man sent the guys who did this," he said. "Protecting his little girl."

Somewhere in the deepest recesses of her mind she had known he was going to say that. She wanted not to believe him, and made herself not believe him. But at the same time she knew it was true.

"Cheek's all busted and the skin came off," he said. "Kicked me. Kicked me till the skin came off. Hoping I'd just pass out. Couldn't. Couldn't. Standing on my hand. Heard the bones break."

"Oh god, Eddie," she moaned. Her hand went toward his face, to touch him and offer comfort, but it stopped short and hung in the air.

"Just a warning, kid, he says. Man wants you to leave his daughter alone. That's what he said. *Next time there won't be nothing left."*

24

Tailing someone in New York City is the easiest thing in the world. In the daytime anyway, when there's traffic. In a snowstorm at night it's a different story, and neither Schliester nor Gogarty could quite manage to forget the nightmare of the last time they tried following Chet Fiore. But take away the snow and add a million and a half cars, and all of a sudden it's impossible for anyone to twig to the fact that someone is shadowing his every turn.

On the other hand, Schliester wouldn't have half minded letting Fiore know he had company. As he and Gogarty sat at a sidewalk table in front of a coffeehouse on Elizabeth Street across the street and one door down from Seppi's, Fiore's restaurant hangout, they debated the point over cappuccinos. "I want him to see us," Schliester said. "Everyfuckingwhere he goes. I want him to see my face in the mirror when he shaves in the morning."

Gogarty shook his head. "You just want to drive him crazy. Exactly what good does that do us?"

"It does *me* good," Schliester said.

Gogarty took a loud, slurping sip of his cappuccino and licked the foam off his lips. "Before there was a Starbucks on every corner," he said, "before there was one in every city, before there was even one Starbucks in Seattle, which I believe is where they all come from, these people right here are the people who invented this shit. Which beats whiskey, if you ask me, and that's coming from an Irishman."

"Great," Schliester said. He was in a foul mood. "Let's hear it for the wonderful folks who gave us cappuccino and organized crime."

"Don't knock organized crime, *boychik*," Gogarty said. "Where would we be without it?"

Schliester took a taste of the cappuccino. As far as he was concerned it was just coffee. "Come on," he said, "we can jerk ourselves off watching him drive around all day or we can get in his face. Which is it going to be?"

"Let me ask you a not unrelated question. Are you shtupping Miss Lester?"

"How the fuck is that related to anything?"

"That's a yes?"

"How the fuck is that related?" Schliester repeated.

"All right, I'll answer yours but you've got to promise to answer mine," Gogarty said. "It's related in the context that if we were to do anything so incredibly stupid as to purposely botch a surveillance, it would help to know that at least one of us enjoyed a good relationship with the small-breasted but long-legged lady we both work for."

"What in hell would give you a ridiculous idea like that?" Schliester asked, putting the appropriate indignation in his voice. The fact of the matter was he did *not* have a special relationship with Elaine Lester. Not anymore, not by a long shot.

"I'm a trained investigator, *boychik*," Gogarty said.

"You followed us?" Schliester asked. Now the indignation was genuine.

It was answered with a bray of triumphant laughter. "Fell into the trap, *boychik*," Gogarty brayed. "Gogarty always gets his man."

But he didn't have time to enjoy the moment. Chet Fiore and Jimmy Angelisi came out of Seppi's and turned right, walking away from the two agents on the opposite side of the street. "Settle up," Gogarty said. "I'll get the car."

He got to his feet, drained the last of his cappuccino, and hurried off while Schliester attempted to engage the attention of their waiter. Somehow Gogarty always managed to disappear just before it was time to pay the check.

Schliester turned one way and the other. Fiore and his man were almost a block away in one direction and Gogarty was just reaching the car in the other. He must have run. Inside the coffee-house, the waiter stood at the bar with his back to the door, deep in intimate conversation with the girl who worked the coffee machines. Schliester reached into his pocket for his money, peeled off a ten, and dropped it on the table. Without a receipt, this was going to be out of his pocket.

The thought passed through his mind as he stepped onto the sidewalk that Chet Fiore didn't sweat the change from a ten dollar bill and had probably never gotten a receipt for anything in his life. That difference about summed it all up.

Gogarty was already rolling toward him. He stepped around the wooden railing that separated the outdoor tables from the side-walk and hurried into the street to get in on the passenger side. A shrill voice called after him, "Hey, mister, the check."

All of a sudden this kid was a waiter again.

"I left a ten on the table," Schliester said.

"The bill's twelve," the waiter said, holding up the ten like it was State's Exhibit 1.

"Twelve dollars? For coffee?"

"Cappuccino," the kid corrected.

"I don't care what it is. Twelve dollars for two cups of coffee— you've got to be kidding."

"Four," the kid said.

Right. They had refills.

The kid said, "Twelve forty-eight with the tax."

Schliester stepped back to the railing, pulling a five out of his pocket. He held it out and then jerked it back when the kid reached for it. "The check," he said.

He stuck the check in his pocket and handed over the five. Then he got in the car.

Up ahead, Fiore's Mercedes was pulling away from the curb. It turned onto Mulberry.

"I got him. Piece of cake," Gogarty said. "You were gonna stiff the guy?"

"I wasn't gonna stiff the guy. Can you believe a couple cups of coffee is twelve forty-eight with the tax?"

Gogarty didn't know whether he believed it or not. "For the record, I wasn't following either you or Ms. Lester," he said. "There's a kind of leering way a man looks at a woman when he's wondering what goodies she's got in her skirt and there's a way he looks at her when he knows the answer. You had the latter look."

"It's over," Schliester said. "It was one night. I didn't pass the test."

The Mercedes headed straight uptown on Lafayette, then on Park. In the Forties, just above Grand Central, Fiore told Jimmy to turn right.

A couple blocks later he said, "There she is, pull in here."

Jimmy eased the car to the curb behind a Volvo station wagon with its warning lights flashing. A woman stood by the Volvo. She was just a couple inches over five feet tall, definitely on the plump side, definitely on the wrong side of fifty. Her hair looked like it wouldn't move in a stiff wind. She was wearing a Chanel suit, nothing cheap about it. She had large, heavy breasts that she was obviously proud of. Her name was Emily Rudin and she was generally regarded as the most important real estate broker on the East Side of Manhattan.

She took the hand Fiore offered with chubby, perfectly manicured fingers that could have been a display rack from Tiffany's. She wore rings on every finger, two or three of them, up to the first knuckle. He apologized for keeping her waiting and she said it was no problem. She took a key ring with a dozen keys from her pocketbook but he stopped her, explaining that they were waiting for someone else to join them.

"Of course," Ms. Rudin chirped. "I should have known a handsome man like you wouldn't be looking for a house by himself."

They were standing in front of a four-story town house in the East Forties, a few blocks from the United Nations. There were crescent-moon cornices over the front door and some of the first-floor windows and triangular cornices over the windows above. The combination struck Fiore as curiously mismatched.

"There's quite a story behind it," Emily Rudin said. "It was built by one of the Astors. Not John Jacob, I don't think, but I'm not quite sure. I have it in the car if you'd like."

She took a step toward her Volvo but he held out a hand to stop her. "That's all right," he said. "One Astor is pretty much as good as another."

She laughed, a curious, tinkling laugh, like glassware rattling. She knew that he was a gangster and had been expecting a snarling creature out of an Edward G. Robinson movie even though her secretary had warned her that this particular gangster was famously handsome.

"Well," she said, gathering her momentum for a fresh start, "whichever Astor it was, he built the house for his daughter. She had a great deal to do with the design, a very artistic young lady. She was supposed to move in with her husband as soon as they got back from their honeymoon, but she ran off to Europe with some painter or poet, I'm not sure which, a week before her wedding. Her father gave the house to the young man."

"The painter?"

"Oh my, no," she gasped, with almost a giggle. "That would have been incredibly romantic, wouldn't it? He gave it to the young man she rejected. But he never found anyone to live here with him and sold it the moment old man Astor died. Students of these things say that some of the paradoxical features of the house—I noticed you looking at the windows—reflect the divided nature of the girl's soul. That's a lovely notion, isn't it?"

He wouldn't have called it lovely, or a notion for that matter, but yes, there was something kind of sad and touching in the story. "What happened to her?" he asked.

"What happened to whom?" a woman's voice asked.

They turned as Phyllis Blaine approached them. She leaned in to plant a kiss on the cheek of Ms. Rudin, whom she called Emily, and then favored Fiore with the same greeting.

"What a surprise," Emily Rudin said with that little glassware laugh. "Mr. Fiore didn't tell me it was you we were waiting for. I assumed it was a lady friend."

They all laughed at that.

"I'm here strictly in my capacity as expert," Phyllis said. "What were you two talking about?"

"The Astor girl," Emily said, sorting through the keys as they moved to the front door. "I don't imagine he wants me to go through the story again. Perhaps he can fill you in later."

"You didn't tell me what happened to her," Fiore reminded her as she opened the front door, pushing it back and standing aside.

"Oh, I'm sure I don't know," Emily Rudin said. "The literature on the house doesn't go into that. She was out of the picture, you see."

They found themselves in an immense entry hall. The brilliant whiteness of the freshly painted walls made it feel even more vast. An enormous staircase, like something out of *Gone With the Wind*, rose up to the second floor. "It will make quite an impression when it's decorated," Emily Rudin said.

Phyllis raised an eyebrow. "A bit monstrous," she said. "You're definitely going to have to do something about these walls."

Fiore didn't think it was monstrous at all. He could picture himself in this hall already. There would be a couple tables, with a vase or something like that on them. And a big grandfather clock. He could see himself opening the door for his guests.

Then it struck him that people who live in houses like this don't open the door for their guests themselves, but he wasn't ready to deal with that part of it yet. If he wanted to open the door himself, there was no law against it.

Emily Rudin led them through a series of downstairs rooms until they came to a wood-paneled study. It reminded Fiore of the Partners Room at Layne Bentley. He looked at Phyllis to see if she was as impressed as he was, but he couldn't tell. "What's upstairs?" he asked Ms. Rudin.

"The living quarters."

"The bedrooms?"

"That's right," she said.

Fiore nodded. "I'd like to talk with Mrs. Blaine," he said. "You couldn't leave us here with a key, could you?"

No one had ever asked her that before. It seemed odd. But there was nothing they could take. Even if he was a gangster, he wasn't a petty thief. "I don't see why not," Emily said, reaching into her suit jacket for the key.

"We'll drop it by your office," Phyllis promised. Then they walked Ms. Rudin to the front door, where they waited in the doorway like a married couple seeing off the guests. When she got into her car, Fiore closed the door and gestured with a sweep of his hand toward the staircase. "The living quarters, madame," he said.

"By all means, sir," she answered.

He followed her up the stairs. They paused at the top for a look at the entrance hall from this vantage point. The excess of it made her uncomfortable. "Could you really live in a place like this?" she asked.

He smiled, a very open and boyish smile. He had smiled like that when she walked into the room that morning he came to the house in Bedford Hills. As though he had been waiting for her.

There are men who make women feel that way. It seemed to Phyllis that years ago, before Jessica was born, Jeffrey had been one of them.

"Sure, I could live here," he said. "Your husband tells me I've got too much disposable income, I've got to dispose of some of it."

They both laughed. Not about the money. About his mentioning Jeffrey. If he was testing to see whether it made her uncomfortable, it didn't.

He followed her through the door to the first bedroom they came to. It had a fireplace with a stonework facing and a slate mantel. Phyllis walked over to it and Fiore came up behind her. He put his hand on her shoulder, and her back straightened almost convulsively, as though a powerful current had just run the length of her body. She leaned back slightly, into him, her spine pressing against him.

He pushed the hair from the back of her neck and let his lips touch there lightly. He could feel the pressure of her body against him. And then she turned and buried her lips in his, her hands pulling at her skirt until it rose above her hips.

He fucked her against the wall until she came, and then he fucked her again on the floor.

Schliester and Gogarty were watching from the roof of a convenient building. When they saw the real estate lady driving off, they more or less guessed what was going to happen, so Schliester raced to the car for their surveillance camera while Gogarty used his badge to secure entry to the four-story building across the street. They got to the roof in time to get some damn good pictures of Fiore and his lady friend in the upstairs bedroom. Then, when Fiore and the lady left the bedroom, the two federal agents ran back down the stairs, getting to the foyer in time to see the two subjects of their surveillance coming out of the town house. Fiore's car was waiting only a dozen yards away, with the motor running and Jimmy Angelisi behind the wheel, but Fiore didn't head toward it. Instead, he walked the lady up the street.

"That's not one of his usual babes," Schliester whispered. "I'd love to know who the hell she is."

Fiore walked the lady around the corner and up Second Avenue. A car was waiting under a NO STANDING sign just up from a bus stop, a black driver behind the wheel. Fiore shook the woman's hand.

"Married lady," Schliester said.

When a guy fucks a woman and then shakes her hand when they get to her car, it usually means the driver works for her husband.

Gogarty was radioing in the plates when Schliester charged ahead, straight toward the couple. His badge was out.

"Federal agent, ma'am," he said. "Your car's parked in a no-standing zone."

"She's just going," Fiore said. He noticed that the agent didn't give his name, which he's supposed to do whenever he identifies himself. It wasn't hard to figure that this was probably the guy who had been dogging him since last winter—probably the same one who got Gus in trouble.

Schliester said, "I wasn't talking to you, sir. Can I see some identification, ma'am?"

Gogarty, still on the radio, was enjoying his partner's performance.

Phyllis had her feet planted well apart. "What is going on here?" she demanded. "What exactly is this about?"

Schliester smiled. "I told you, ma'am. Your vehicle is parked in a no-standing zone."

"And you're a federal agent? Since when do federal agents enforce traffic regulations?"

"I can call a police officer if you'd like, ma'am."

"I didn't see your identification," Phyllis said.

"And I haven't seen yours, ma'am."

Gogarty lowered the radio from his ear. "This vehicle's registered to a Jeffrey Blaine," he said. "Would you be Mrs. Blaine?"

Schliester's entire conception of what was happening changed in an instant. Jeffrey Blaine's wife? What the fuck?

The lady said, "That's right," in answer to Gogarty's question. And Schliester said, "Fine. Why don't you run along home. And you, fuckface, you stay right here. We have something to talk about."

Phyllis didn't move.

Fiore said, "I don't have anything to talk about with you."

Schliester mimed disappointment. "That's too bad," he said. "I was hoping you'd be kind enough to deliver a message for me."

Fiore bit. "What's the message?" he asked.

"I wanted you to give my regards to Gus."

Something in Fiore's mind exploded. Any man who could make jokes about a dead man was lower than vermin.

He lunged at the agent, grabbing him by the lapels and knocking him back against the car, his face right in Schliester's face. The bastard was actually smiling at him.

"Gee," Schliester said, "you knew Gus passed away. How did you find out?"

Fiore hit him with a short chopping right that caught him square on the left cheek. Bone against bone, it broke the skin and sent a gush of blood running down Schliester's face. If anyone were keeping score, it would go in the books as a one-round TKO. Before either man could take it further, Gogarty was between them. Jimmy Angelisi, who had followed the agents around the corner just to make sure there was no trouble, wrapped his arms around Fiore's shoulders. No one had even seen him come up. "Leave him alone, leave him alone," he was saying. "Leave him alone, boss, he ain't worth it."

The driver got out of Mrs. Blaine's car and looked like he knew he was supposed to do something only he didn't know what.

Phyllis's hands were over her eyes. She was terrified. A disastrous scandal seemed inevitable. They already knew her name.

Fiore tried to pull away from Jimmy, who wouldn't let go. A steady flow of blood ran down Schliester's cheek and dripped onto his shirt. He shook his head once, sending a shower of sticky droplets all around, and thrust a hand over Gogarty's shoulder straight at Fiore. "I am going to get you, asshole. Take another shot. Go ahead. Take another."

Fiore was shouting, too, shouting at Jimmy to let go of him, shouting at Gogarty to get out of the way, shouting obscenities at Schliester. And Gogarty, his massive body like a moving wall between them, kept saying, "That's it, that's it, it's over. Both of you, it's over."

With Jimmy hanging on to Fiore and Gogarty blocking Schliester, things finally quieted down enough for Schliester to take a step backward and straighten his shoulders. "You had your shot, baby," he taunted. "Now it's my turn. Me and Gus." He turned to Phyllis and said, "I'd get home if I were you, Mrs. Blaine. Your boyfriend sometimes finds it necessary to have people killed."

"You dropped out of school?" Grace Tunney gasped. "I can't be*lieve* it!"

Grace always seemed younger than everyone else in Jessica's circle, but a few months of college had done remarkable things for her. Her hair was shorter and she seemed to have lost a few pounds. She didn't look like a baby anymore.

"Believe it," Jessica said. "It's a long story."

They were standing in front of the main administration building at Vassar, a stately old nineteenth-century structure that had been enlarged over the years with modern additions that seemed to poke out from behind the original facade like a kid trying to hide behind something too small to hide him.

Grace said, "I still haven't heard the true and official story of your heavy vanish over the summer. C'mon, let's get something to eat."

Jessica followed her into the administration building, down a corridor lined with an exhibit of lithographs, and into an expansive cafeteria that looked like an oversized fast-food restaurant. Animated discussions were being carried on at virtually all the tables. Hands were flying everywhere as long-haired young men and short-haired young women gesticulated with forks and half-eaten sandwiches. Jessica looked at them and missed being in school. She knew perfectly well that it was all her own fault. The choices had been hers. But none of the choices were the ones she thought she was making, and so she was filled with an anger that far overrode the regret.

Grace selected a not especially interesting-looking salad from the cooler and a plastic pint of apple cider.

"Let's eat outside," Jessica said. Through a window she could see a patio filled with unused tables.

"It's not exactly *summer* out there," Grace protested, but she did what Jessica wanted. For as long as she could remember, all the girls always did what Jessica wanted, and she was annoyed with herself for letting the pattern perpetuate itself here.

"Did you really run off with Eddie?" she asked as soon as they were seated.

"Yeah," Jessica said in an offhand tone that suggested she didn't want to talk about it. "Let me ask you something."

"Where did you go?"

"Around. It doesn't matter," Jessica said. "Do you remember, when we got to the party, there were reporters outside?"

"What do you mean, *around*?"

"All right, we went to New Orleans. I don't want to talk about that. Do you remember the reporters?"

Grace looked disappointed. "Yes, I remember them," she said sullenly.

"And there was one of them, a lady, you said you knew her."

"Are you kidding? What's this *about*?" Grace protested.

"It's not *about* anything. I want to know her name."

Grace put down her fork and put the plastic cover back on the remains of her salad. "Her name is Sharon Lamm," she said. "She does business stuff for *Newsday*. She was very nice to Daddy when he had that problem."

Grace's father had been indicted for insider trading.

"Thanks so much, Grace. We're really going to have to talk, I can't now," Jessica said. She stood up, said "Thanks" again, and turned to go.

Grace watched her a moment, baffled. Then she got up and hurried after her. "What's wrong, Jess?" she asked.

"Nothing. I've got to get going, that's all."

"Get real, please. We haven't seen each other since graduation, you drive all the way up here, ask one question, and go. That doesn't strike you as odd?"

"Actually," Jessica said, "we saw each other at Amy's funeral."

Sharon Lamm listened without interrupting for almost twenty minutes. Then she leaned back and looked across at the pretty and eerily calm young lady sitting at the opposite side of the desk, her legs crossed, her hands resting like a kitten on her lap. "Why are you telling me this?" Sharon asked.

She had been taking notes on the little steno pad she always used for interviews, copying down whole sentences in her self-invented shorthand. She never used a tape recorder for interviews because it made her feel like a television reporter, just sticking the technology in someone's face and letting the journalism happen.

Writing the words down, choosing what to summarize, what to ignore, what to transcribe verbatim made her feel as though she were already shaping the story. She believed in stories more than she believed in facts.

A hundred questions raced through her mind while she was listening, but none of them was worth asking until she had an answer to this one. *Why was this girl telling her all the things she was telling her?*

Jessica had known she would be asked this question because it was the first question she asked herself. On the ride down from Poughkeepsie, flanked by the throbbing colors of the autumn forest that spread out on both sides of the parkway, surrounded by carpets of orange flame, carpets of yellow flame, blankets of rich russet, she felt almost as though she were in danger of being swallowed up by the death of all these things dying back around her. Here and there, young deer, two or three together, browsed listlessly by the side of the road, showing no sign of that intent alertness that always made the deer she saw in the Bedford Hills yard seem so achingly fragile.

How many different forms, she wondered, could the same thought take in one person's mind? It had taken a hundred different forms since this morning, when Martin came into the kitchen where she was having breakfast and said, "I don't know what to do, miss, I don't know whether to tell your daddy or what." And then he told her that he took her mama downtown yesterday and waited for her and she came back with a man and the police showed up and made a big scene, and one of them said something about the man killing someone. Martin didn't tell her who the man was because he didn't know, but Jessica didn't need to be told. She knew it was Chet Fiore, her father's gangster associate, and she figured the police were there because they were following her father's car. She wasn't sure how much trouble her father was in, but it sounded serious.

That was when she decided to go see Grace, who knew a reporter who helped her father when he had *that problem.* For weeks she had hated her father but now she was sure she loved him and that he needed saving. If she had been older, she might have known herself well enough to distrust her better instincts, but for all the growing up she had done in the past eight months, she was still a child. She still believed in the stories that had been read to her as a child, simple stories about innocent creatures touching one another with tender acts of kindness. Jessica liked to imagine that the world was really like that even though she knew better. Above all, she thought that she was like that. It meant nothing to her that saving her father and destroying him took exactly the same form, and that only a few hours before, relatively speaking, she had walked out of Montefiore Hospital hating her father with a fierce and piercing hatred. That was when she first thought about telling someone he was involved with a gangster. She wanted to pay him back for everything that had happened to her. She didn't do it, though. Until she decided she had to do something to save him.

"I think my father's in trouble," she said in answer to Sharon Lamm's question. Both her feet rested on the floor, her knees touching, her feet splayed apart, like a little girl waiting to be asked to dance. "Grace said you helped her father."

Well, Sharon Lamm thought, she had her answer. But she wasn't sure she believed it. Oh yes, she believed the facts she had been told. But not the story that shaped them in this girl's mind.

It was after eight o'clock when Elaine Lester got home and found Jeffrey in the living room, his bare feet up on the coffee table, his ankles crossed, his fountain pen in hand, a stack of reports in his lap. He had taken off his suit and was wearing the robe she had given him. A symphony by Vaughan Williams was playing on the stereo. It was one of his gifts to her.

"Am I that late?" she asked.

She looked tired. There was a tightness at the corners of her lips, a slackness at the corners of her eyes. He had thought of ordering in dinner, and it would have been here already, and now he was sorry he hadn't done it.

They kissed just inside the door and then she stepped out of her shoes and handed him the brown paper bag she was carrying. "Open one of these," she said.

He felt two wine bottles in the bag. He pushed through the door into the kitchen and took the bottles from the bag. There was an American Cabernet and an Italian Chianti. It was like her to buy two bottles of red, leaving him a choice only after her choice was made. He decided on the Cabernet. The thought struck him that when he and Phyllis had their first apartment there were three different wine racks in the kitchen, all of them always well stocked.

Christ, he thought with a wry, self-mocking laugh, *in another minute I'll be quoting "The Gift of the Magi."* It wasn't true that he had been happier when he first came to New York, single and nearly broke. It really wasn't. It wasn't true that life was simpler then, carrying home a wine bottle with a sense of something like triumph, opening it with a sense of something like ceremony. The plain simple honest bedrock fact of the matter was that he had never, as far as he could remember, found life simple or enjoyed it simply.

Until now.

Elaine joined him in the kitchen. She had changed into jeans and a T-shirt, and she looked fresh, and younger. But it took him only a moment to see that the careworn look he noticed when she came in was still there, underneath the brightness.

"Hard day?" he asked, handing her one of the wine glasses he had just filled.

"Let's see what we can find to eat," she said, "and then we've got to talk."

Got to talk was different from *talk.* It sounded a warning bell in the back of Jeffrey's brain.

They found the remnants of a salad in the refrigerator. And some chicken in a peanut sauce from a Thai restaurant. There was some nice bread, and some Brie, which needed just to sit out a little while to soften. They ate the chicken with their fingers straight from the container and then moved to the living room with the wine, the bread, and the cheese. Jeffrey sat down but Elaine walked about restlessly, adjusting the positions of small objects on the coffee table and the lamp table next to the couch. She stood in front of him a moment, as though she couldn't make up her mind where to alight.

"I don't know if anyone's ever mentioned this to you," he said, "but when a man knows a woman isn't wearing anything under her jeans, it's almost impossible for him to look at her without thinking about that."

"Is that so?"

"Mm-hmm. It's exactly the same as when you know that the guy sitting next to you on the plane has a bomb in his briefcase. Even if you can't see it, you can't think about anything else."

She laughed, but not with her eyes, which studied his face for what seemed a long time. She knew how astute he was, that he never missed anything. She had seen the flicker, the momentary tightening of his lips when she said *We've got to talk*, and she was certain she understood the purpose of his playfulness now. She felt for a moment an almost overwhelming tenderness for him, as though, just possibly, he was a far more fragile man than she had ever allowed for in her thoughts.

"Jeffrey," she said, "two of my men followed Chet Fiore today. He met your wife."

He tipped his head back, resting it against the back of the couch, and closed his eyes. He didn't want to be talking to Elaine about Phyllis. He said nothing, waiting for her to tell him the rest.

"They went to an empty town house on the East Side," Elaine went on. "They made love."

They did, did they? Jeffrey thought. *Empty* made it possible for him to see it all, exactly as it happened, as though he were in the room with them, invisible. Bare walls and a bare floor. They wouldn't have even gotten naked. Once, the winter before he and Phyllis announced their engagement, he took her to Massachusetts to introduce her to his parents. In the evening, after his parents were in bed, he made love to her in the den and she didn't even get undressed for it, didn't even take off her panties. She guided him into her and he came almost as soon as the head of his penis touched the wetness of her flesh. It was the silk above all that excited him, because it meant that all of a sudden there was no distinction between dressed and undressed and because in that moment he believed, with the clarity young men enjoy when they are in love, that for the rest of their lives together she would always be naked for him under her clothing.

Well, he thought with bitter and wry detachment, *it hadn't quite worked out that way, had it?*

He got to his feet and walked away, moving to a window.

"I thought you should know," Elaine said.

He turned to face her, and for a moment she was confused. "You knew already?" she asked.

"No," he said.

Now she was even more confused. He could see it in her eyes. He moved to her.

"I'm sorry," he said. "I'm supposed to be outraged, aren't I? I hope I'm not disappointing you but I can't quite manage outrage."

She smiled, a pleasant, comfortable, even triumphant smile. There are few things more gratifying than learning that your lover's wife has a lover, and one of them is learning that he doesn't care.

For the first time she had the courage to ask the question that had been hanging over their relationship from the moment she spoke to him in the fiction section of Barnes & Noble. For the first time she was confident she knew what the answer would be.

"Jeffrey," she said, "what's going on between you and Chet Fiore?"

"Other than his sexual relations with my wife?" he asked.

She felt happy, joyful, exultant. All this while she and Schliester and Gogarty kept talking about Fiore and the banker. They had never once considered the possibility that it was Fiore and the banker's wife.

"Yes," she said. "Other than his sexual relations with your wife."

"Do you want me to tell you even if it's something you don't want to know?"

"No," she said, feeling suddenly hollow and empty.

Why hadn't he said, *There is none. Fiore and my wife—that's the only connection?*

Why hadn't she said *Yes?*

Part Six

25

The voice at the other end of the line was almost incoherent. "Where are you?" Fiore asked. "I'll be right over."

"Where am I . . . , where I am . . . , doesn't matter, that's no good," Noel Garver mumbled.

The man was clearly drunk.

"All right, look," Fiore said, "take a couple hours. Do you know the Hudson Diner?"

"On Twelfth?"

The Hudson Diner was on Twelfth Avenue in the Twenties.

"That's right. Get yourself a cup of coffee. Don't have anything else to drink," Fiore lectured. "I'll meet you there at nine o'clock. Tell me what I just said."

"Nothing to drink," Garver parroted. "And coffee."

"And where am I meeting you?"

"Can't be here. That's no good."

"The Hudson Diner," Fiore repeated patiently. "On Twelfth Avenue. At nine o'clock. Have you got that?"

"Right, right."

"Now tell me."

Garver repeated the information in the irritated tone of a man who was being greatly put-upon. Fiore pegged the odds at slightly better than even that Garver would be there.

In cold weather the Hudson Diner does a brisk business with

the net-stockinged crowd of West Side whores. The window booths, especially the ones facing the parking lot, are popular with drug dealers. The decor is pure art deco, chromed like a fifties Buick. According to legend, it was here that left-wing journalists, left-wing novelists, and left-wing dramatists rubbed shoulders with cabbies and truckers. But that was a long time ago.

Garver was already sitting at a corner booth far from the door when Fiore arrived with Jimmy Angelisi at his shoulder. A young man, no more than twenty-five years old, with short, neatly trimmed hair, sat next to Garver in a charcoal gray sweater. Fiore wasn't pleased at the addition of a stranger to the party, but at least they had coffee cups in front of them.

"I was just telling Wayne a little bit about this place," Garver said, dispensing with introductions. "It has rather an illustrious literary history."

Even at the best of times, Fiore wouldn't have been inclined to waste time on the folklore of a diner. Garver's message said that he had urgent information to communicate and Fiore would have preferred a sense of urgency. "Never mind that," he said. "If we've got business to talk about, it's going to have to be just us."

"Wayne is my secretary and assistant, practically a partner," Garver said. "I have no secrets from Wayne."

He smiled a lopsided smile that was probably meant to be seductive. His eyes were filled with the chronic sadness of an aging queen, but at least he didn't sound drunk anymore.

"Maybe you don't have secrets from him," Fiore said. "I do."

"Strictly speaking, that's not true," Garver said, smirking as though he had just made a joke. "Not as far as this business is concerned anyway. Wayne knows everything about it I do. If you can keep a secret," he added, leaning so far across the table that he had to put his hand on his tie to keep it from dangling in his coffee cup, "that little story I wrote that never got published—you remember that one, don't you? That was Wayne's work."

His breath smelled like some kind of flowers, whatever it was drunks used to hide the fact they were drunks. When he had made his point, he sat up straight, smiled again, and tried to put everything he had just said in its proper context by adding, "From time to time Wayne writes under my byline."

There was no point, Fiore realized, in making an issue of the young man's presence. Garver probably couldn't even take a leak without this kid's hand on his cock.

"And besides," Garver grinned, "it was Wayne who took the call."

"What call is that?"

"From Sharon Lamm," Wayne said.

The name meant nothing to Fiore.

Garver laid his long-fingered hand on the back of Wayne's hand. "You've answered the gentleman's question," he said sweetly, "but you haven't given him the information he needs. If you'll permit me."

The young man looked down at the table. It was easy to imagine that these little tutorial sessions went on all the time, all wisdom and graciousness on Garver's part, all humility and mortification on Wayne's.

Without removing his hand from Wayne's, Garver took Fiore back to the night of Jessica Blaine's birthday party. Fiore hadn't known that Garver had taken the liberty of inviting Sharon Lamm, from *Newsday*, to join him inside the restaurant. Someone on Stasny's staff removed her from the premises before Fiore arrived, but she had seen enough for a story and would have filed one if she had been able to find anyone to corroborate what she saw with her own eyes and heard with her own ears. Instead, the mothers of all three of the girls involved assured her that she must have been misinformed, that their daughters had all returned home safely, and she knew she would have gotten the same answers if she called the fathers.

"By that point," Garver purred, listing sideways so that his head was practically on Wayne's shoulder, "the dear incompetent woman was so stressed out she actually called me to see if I was having better luck with the story. I told her that I wasn't and that it was just as well. Or words to that effect."

A waitress approached the table, but Fiore waved her away with an impatient gesture. Garver went on to say that Sharon Lamm continued to work on the story for a while but came up empty. "Pathetic," he concluded. "The woman has absolutely no journalistic competence whatever. At least *I* had a good reason for killing the story."

He laughed a quick laugh, like coins jingling onto a table.

"Is there a point to this story?" Fiore asked.

"Every story has its preface, young man, its preamble—its back story, as they call it," Garver said. "Now the narrative moves into the present tense. This evening the intrepid Ms. Lamm called me, the first time she's called in months. I was a bit under the weather, as you may have noticed when we spoke earlier. Wayne took the call."

Wayne was ready for his cue. "One of the girls from the party appears to have killed herself over the summer." He produced a small memo book from somewhere under the table and flipped it open. "Laidlaw," he said. "Apparently she was the one who screamed."

"She killed herself, nobody killed her," Fiore said testily. "What's the point?"

The fate of the girls didn't interest him. There must have been something wrong with her from before. A healthy girl doesn't kill herself because someone fucked her at a birthday party.

"The reason Ms. Lamm called," Wayne went on, "was to tell me—well, to tell Mr. Garver—that one of the other girls has come forward. The girl told her everything."

Noel Garver added, "Including the fact that you were there."

Fiore did a quick calculation. He didn't see how the story could hurt him at this point. No one would confirm it anyway, and even if they did, it had no significance.

"According to this girl," Wayne continued, "the whole thing had something to do with banking arrangements between you and Mr. Blaine."

Fiore's hand flashed across the table, snatching the memo book from the young man's hand. He looked down at the notes written there and then ripped the page from the book. A few other pages had notes as well, and he tore them from the book. He crumpled them in his fist and handed back the empty book. "All right," he said, "from memory now. What else did she tell you?"

The Blaine girl, he was thinking. It had to be. None of the other girls could have put it together. She couldn't either, unless somebody told her. Who. Eddie? Impossible. He didn't know anything. Then Blaine. But why? Did he want out? Was he ready to burn his bridges, with himself on them? It didn't seem likely.

Wayne looked lost without his memo book. He stammered for a moment. "That was the facts," he said at last. "I mean, that was all the information she gave me. She said she was going to look into it."

Fiore had one more question. "Why did she call you?" he asked, addressing Garver.

"Just to let me know she had broken the story," Garver said. "So I wouldn't think her such a pathetic little twit."

The phone call scared her witless, which she assumed is what it was intended to do. A man's voice she didn't recognize told her that someone would be wanting to talk to her about the story she was working on. "I'm working on a lot of stories. Who is this?" she said, and the man's voice said, "Never mind that. We'll be in touch."

Sharon Lamm had never gotten a call like that in her life. The vagueness of it was in a way more threatening than a threat would have been. She thought at first that the story was going to be about teenage sex and a cover-up of teenage sex, but as Jessica talked to her she realized that it went way beyond that. It was the story of a connection between Wall Street and Mott Street. She had already put it that way in a lead paragraph that kept forming in the back of her mind. A link between investment banking and organized crime was without a doubt the biggest story she had ever found or would ever find.

Which is when the phone rang. The call not only frightened

her, it made her feel stupid. Obviously, if you're going to do a story exposing organized crime, you have to expect a call like that. Sharon hadn't even considered the possibility. Her hand was shaking when she hung up the phone. She put cold water on her face in the ladies' room and then reapplied her makeup, gathered her coat and purse, and hurried for the elevator. She wanted to be out of the office before the promise in the phone call was fulfilled.

She knew when she saw a man getting out of a car and heading toward her that she hadn't made it in time.

"Sharon Lamm?" he asked.

"That's right."

Jimmy Angelisi knew that. She wrote columns and her picture was on them. She actually looked better in person. "I told you someone would be in touch," Jimmy said. "Please get in the car."

She glanced toward the car at the curb, half expecting to see a big, ugly Lincoln. It was a Mercedes instead. She could see there was a man in the back seat. "What is this about?" she asked.

"Just get in the car, please," he said.

Jimmy Angelisi was not a frightening man. He had a round face and a soft body. His hair was thinning, and he seemed almost to be smiling, although not quite. But that didn't make the moment any less frightening, and she knew she couldn't refuse him. Even at this hour, there were at least half a dozen strangers walking briskly along Park Avenue with that dark and hooded New York purposefulness. The problem was that if she saw them, then he saw them, too, and obviously they played no role in his calculations. Which told her what she knew already. She would be taking a big chance if she thought she could count on strangers.

"Really, this isn't the way to do this sort of thing," she said, putting as much indignation into her voice as she thought she could afford under the circumstances.

She stepped across the sidewalk to the car so quickly and unexpectedly that she had to wait there a moment until Jimmy Angelisi hurried up behind her and opened the door. She certainly wasn't going to open it for herself.

She had never seen a picture of Chet Fiore that she could

recall, but he was always described as dashingly, darkly handsome, or words to that effect. The man beside her in the back seat of the Mercedes certainly fit the bill.

"I'm glad we're going to have this chance to talk, Miss Lamm," he said, his voice smooth and pleasant, as though she had just joined him at his table for a perfectly normal business lunch at the latest *in* restaurant. It would be a rather nice lunch, too. His suit suggested carefully developed tastes.

The other man hurried around and got in behind the wheel. She heard the door locks click down a second after he closed the door. The car slid smoothly from the curb.

"Don't be so polite," she said. "You didn't exactly give me much of a choice."

"Oh," he said, "I think there are always choices."

She could see his smile as they passed under a streetlight. It seemed a surprisingly benevolent smile, with no malice, no trace of the sneer she had expected to see there.

"That's probably true," she said, "but I imagine some of them are not very pleasant."

"Admittedly. But if that weren't the case, how would we ever make any decisions? My name is Chet Fiore. I assume you know what I want to talk to you about."

"You're going to have to tell me," she said.

Fiore let a few blocks pass before answering her question.

"Jeffrey Blaine," he said.

"What about him?"

His eyes darkened and he turned to look her full in the face. "Don't play games with me, Miss Lamm," he said. "I'm not someone you can do that with."

She felt a chill run down her back, as though a window had just opened. She felt her jaw trembling.

"Yes, you're right," she said, choosing her words carefully, afraid of making a mistake. "I have some information about Mr. Blaine."

For a moment he considered probing to find out how much she knew, but it was better, he decided, to let her think it didn't matter. So he said simply, "Miss Lamm, you know that information like that is worthless without corroboration. And if you start looking for corroboration, you're going to get a lot of people upset."

"Are you threatening me, Mr. Fiore?" she asked bravely, even though she didn't feel in the least brave.

"I am definitely threatening you," he said. "I don't know if you've had time to think about this yet, Miss Lamm, but you'll have plenty of time when you get home. After you've closed all your windows and locked all your doors, you're going to start to wonder how the hell I knew you had this story just a few hours after you got it. And you're not going to come up with the right answer. Do you understand what I'm saying? If you pursue this story in any way, if you start asking questions, I'm going to know about it as quickly as I found out about this. Just so there are no mistakes about it, I want you to know right now that if any of the information you have or think you have compromises my interests in any way, it's not going to be published. You can accept that as a fact."

And then he said, "Tell the driver where you want him to drop you, Miss Lamm."

Fiore figured that Georgie Vallo might know the Blaine girl's personal number, so he had Jimmy send for the kid. There was no telling what might come unglued as long as this girl was running around out of control, shooting her mouth off about things she didn't understand or even, really, know. He tried to get a grasp on how her mind worked, what she thought she was doing, but there was no way he could make any sense of it.

Jimmy made a few calls and reported back that Georgie Vallo would be there in a few minutes. A few minutes turned out to be almost half an hour.

Georgie Vallo had that funny, loping walk that kids nowadays picked up from the black kids they saw on TV, their feet flat and wide apart, rolling a little from side to side, an insolent kind of walk, without purpose. Georgie always came in like that, and then he stopped just inside the door and looked around like he was counting the house. Fiore was always at the same table, toward the back, so he didn't have to look around, but he did.

"You wanted to see me, Mr. Fiore?"

"Do you have a number for the Blaine girl?" Fiore asked.

"I think so. I'd have to check at home," Georgie said.

"Check at home," Fiore said. "Call her. Tell her I want to see her. Now. Here. As soon as she can make it."

Georgie nodded his head but didn't move. He was like a car. First you had to start him and then you had to put him in gear. "If she doesn't answer, don't go leaving any messages on any machines," Fiore said. "Now get going."

Jessica was in bed when she got the call, lonely, unhappy, and unable to sleep. Her first thought when she heard Georgie's voice was that it was another message from Eddie. But Georgie said exactly what Fiore told him to say and then hung when she said she'd come.

She was dressed in a minute, except for her shoes, which she carried in her hand as she made her way down the bedroom corridor. She could see from the light under her mother's bedroom door that she was still up, so it was a good thing she was being careful about making noise. She put on her shoes out in the hall. All that remained was to make it down in the elevator and out onto the street without running into her father on his way in.

Out on Fifth, she walked quickly down to Eighty-ninth and broke into a run after she turned the corner. The light was against her when she got to Madison but there was nothing coming up the avenue so she sprinted across, then steadied her pace to a rapid walk. She alternated walking a block, running a block, until she was all the way over to Third Avenue and all the way down to Eighty-fifth. A coffee shop was open. Everything else was closed. It wasn't hard to find someone who had what she wanted. She was going to the most important meeting of her life. She had to be calm. She had to be on the highest possible plane.

Her feet felt like they were flying half a foot above the pavement when she grabbed a taxi and settled into the back seat. She closed her eyes and could still see through her lids the pulsing alternation of light and darkness as the cab cruised steadily down the avenue, timing itself to make all the lights. She felt rather than saw the streetlights sailing by over her head like leaves on a stream. Dead leaves. Autumn leaves. She was completely in control of herself, completely in control of everything that was about to happen.

When the cab stopped on Canal Street she opened her eyes and looked around. She felt like a little kid waking up in the back seat when the car pulls into the driveway. In a second the cabbie would ask if she wanted to walk or wanted him to carry her inside. The cabbie was a bearded Russian. She laughed at the thought, paid him with a twenty, and got out without waiting for change. On the sidewalk she looked around to get her bearings. She felt as though she had been dropped off in a strange city. It was a nice feeling. Like a dream.

She and her friends never went to Little Italy, or even Chinatown, for that matter. That was something from her father's generation. The tacky neon signs in every storefront looked like something from the distant past when neon was the latest thing. *Oh please*, she thought, laughing to herself. When Mr. Fiore showed up at her birthday party, with that gorgeous suit and that luscious shiny black hair, taking command like a general, she thought he was one of the most handsome men she had ever seen. Now it turned out that the world of this glamorous gangster was a grubby Italian restaurant with a gaudy neon sign.

Good. That made everything she was going to say easier. It was her turn to be in command. She was capable of anything she wanted to do.

She saw Mr. Fiore at the corner table as soon as she walked in. It was late and most of the tables were empty, and the few people at the few occupied tables looked like they came here every night. Except for Mr. Fiore, everyone in the place looked old.

A pot-bellied Italian guy in an apron came toward her, peeling off the apron as he walked. "You're looking for someone?" he asked.

She had already started toward the back, but she stopped. "Mr. Fiore," she said.

Mr. Fiore was on his feet, coming around from behind the table. The guy saw that, and so he said, "Yeah, okay."

Mr. Fiore was smiling. She thought he was going to kiss her, but he didn't. He put a hand on her arm and said, "Come on, we've got a lot to talk about."

He led her to the table and then right past it. They went into the kitchen, where three young men were sitting on the counter, their legs dangling above the floor, smoking cigarettes. A fourth guy, the only one working, was cleaning up. At the back of the kitchen was a door with frosted glass on it and the word OFFICE actually stenciled across the glass. Like people wouldn't know it was an office without that. That's where they went.

"I can get you some food if you want," Mr. Fiore said. "Everything's good here."

I bet, Jessica thought.

The room looked more like a storeroom than an office. There was a desk, but there were also shelves stacked with canned goods and crates of vegetables on the floor. There was a lamp on the desk, which was lit, and a globe light dangling from a post in the middle of the ceiling, which wasn't. There wasn't anywhere for more than one person to sit. For the first time since she got Georgie's phone call, Jessica felt uncomfortable, and even more uncomfortable when Mr. Fiore closed the door. She heard the click as he turned the bolt, and that was when it hit her that he had said, *We've got a lot to talk about.* Until that moment she thought she was the one who had things to talk about.

"Nice place," she said, wrinkling her face. She wanted to sound cool and superior, like a tough lady in an old movie. Her heart was pounding and her mouth was dry. She wasn't sure if she was dizzy or not.

He moved closer to her and said, "Do you want to tell me what it is you've been doing?"

"Well, I'm not in school," she said. "I guess I'm not doing very much."

"That's not what I'm talking about."

She didn't say anything. The desk lamp was behind him, so

that his face was all in shadow. He didn't look at all like the man who showed up at her birthday party and she couldn't remember why she thought he was so good-looking. His head looked big and flat, like a carnival mask, and even more like a mask because his eyes seemed to glow from somewhere inside.

He said, "You've been talking to reporters."

It had never dawned on her that the reporter she talked to might be working for Mr. Fiore. She felt stupid for not even considering the possibility. Well, she thought, if he knows, then he knows. That didn't scare her. In fact, it helped. Because if he was as powerful as all that, then he didn't really need her father.

She managed a smile and tipped her head to the side. "Yes," she said. "About my father."

"What about your father?"

"That you used me to get him to do something for you."

"I did that?" he asked, in an almost quizzical tone.

She was a lovely girl, tough and defiant. Blaine, he figured, had his hands full with this one.

"Yes," she said. "You did that."

"I've never even talked to you. How did I use you?"

"Eddie."

"And you figured all this out?"

"He told me."

"Eddie?"

"My father."

"What else did your father tell you?"

"That was the important part," she said. "I don't want my father working for you."

She reached out and with just one finger touched his shirt just inside the lapels of his jacket. "Eddie was in love with me, you know," she said, her voice very low. "Did he tell you about that?"

Fiore said nothing. Her finger traced a line down his chest.

"Did he tell you I was worth getting beaten up for?" she asked. "He got beat up, you know. Over me."

The fingers of her other hand toyed absently with the top button of her shirt, provocative and playful at the same time, as though she didn't understand what she was doing. But she understood. She understood perfectly. He could see that in her eyes. "We spent the whole summer together, you know. He couldn't get enough of me," she purred. "That was your idea, wasn't it? You paid him to seduce me, right? *Get together with that girl, take her wherever you want.* I was the best thing that ever happened to him, Mr. Fiore. I fucked him silly. You shouldn't send other people to do your work for you."

She leaned forward, her lips close to his ear. He could feel the touch of her breasts against his arm, the pressure of them. The thought passed through his mind that he had fucked this girl's mother in hotel rooms and on the floor of an empty mansion, and that the mother didn't have tits like this and wouldn't have known how to use them if she did, grinding grimly with her hips, passionless, rubbing at him the way people rub at the silver coating on lottery tickets, eager and heartless, checking for a jackpot.

This girl was the jackpot and she knew it. He could feel the excitement of her. He toyed with the idea of telling her he was balling her mother, just to see what she would do. There'd be no horror, no screaming. She'd laugh and say, *You send Eddie to fuck me and you fuck my mother, and you're supposed to be a smart man?*

He stepped back from her, and her hands fell to her side. She had a funny, puzzled look on her face.

"Are you trying to bribe me, Jessica?" he said.

There wasn't the same certainty in her voice anymore when she said, "That's exactly what I'm doing."

"Why?"

"You don't need my father," she said. "You could have any banker you want."

"You'd do that for him?"

"I like to fuck, Mr. Fiore," she said. "I love to fuck. It's no big sacrifice."

It was her last try, and there was an edge of desperation in her voice just under the bravado.

"Get out of here," he said. "You're just a kid."

He turned and walked out the door, leaving it open behind him.

Tears welled in her eyes as she stared after him. There was nothing, nothing in the whole world, nothing that would ever happen to her as long as she lived, more humiliating than this.

She walked to the door and leaned her head against the frame. She knew she couldn't possibly walk out through that restaurant, past him sitting at that table again. He'd point her out to the fat guy in the apron and they'd have a laugh about her. *Little cunt wanted to fuck me*, he'd say. The fat guy would say, *Hey, I'll take a shot if you don't want her*, and they'd laugh some more.

She closed the door and leaned back against it, put her head back and closed her eyes, but her eyelids didn't hold the tears the way she thought they would.

Wally Schliester's head hurt. His eyes hurt. Even his hair hurt. He couldn't remember waking up so sick in his life, and he wasn't even sure he *was* waking up because maybe he hadn't been asleep. A little while ago it was dark outside his window and now it was kind of light, this sort of milky color in the sky, more like, say, something on a blackboard you try to rub out with your hand and it just turns into a smudge that gets bigger and bigger the more you rub it.

What, he wondered, did it say on the blackboard?

No, no, that wasn't the question, there was no blackboard, blackboards had nothing to do with it. He was standing at the window in his apartment holding the neck of a whiskey bottle. *Get a hold of yourself*, he told himself, and something about that turn of phrase made him chuckle.

Christ, when was the last time he got drunk like this? In St. Louis for sure. In St. Louis he drank a fair bit, with his friends on the weekends, because it was what you did when you were hanging out with your friends. *Getting blotto*, they called it, a stupid phrase that sounded like something left over from World War II, sailors on shore leave, guys home for the last time before shipping out to the Pacific or whatever. Nobody said that anymore, and he doubted that anybody even said it during his own lifetime, that's how old-fashioned it was. But that's what they said in St. Louis, Wally and Arnie and Ben and Gil. *Let's get blotto,* one of them would say, and there was never an objection or even an alternative suggestion.

He stopped doing that shit years ago. All of them did. They just grew out of it. They settled down, they got married. Schliester moved away. They all led civilized lives now, and if they drank too much once in a while, it was at a party or something like that.

Until last night.

It all started with the look on Elaine Lester's face when they told her about Fiore and the well-dressed blonde, Gogarty piling on the details, trying to get her to blush, or just say anything one way or the other. She didn't bite. She listened patiently. *Do I need all this detail?* she asked, when it was beginning to seem like Gogarty couldn't possibly go on any longer unless he started drawing pictures, and so Schliester decided to put a stop to it and get them back on track. He told her the lady in question was married to a prominent banker, and in just that second he saw the oddest look on her face, as though she knew already, or at least knew something they didn't know, a look that wasn't part of this conversation in the office at all, but he didn't know what it could be connected to. It sent a shiver down his back. And then, when Gogarty told her it was Phyllis Blaine, she said, *Yeah, okay,* and that was all.

But it wasn't all.

He went out to eat with Gogarty and couldn't get that look on Elaine's face out of his mind. By the time he got home, it was mixed up somehow with the fact that she dropped him after one night, which wasn't a bad night at all, and the fact that he didn't know why. He hadn't gotten involved with anyone since he came to New York. A casual lay here, at most balling the same chick for a couple of weeks steady if she was reasonably bright and good-looking and didn't make his life needlessly complicated. But Elaine Lester was different, and so even before the night he took her to his place he had let himself fall in love with what it felt like to sit in a bar talking cop talk with her at three o'clock in the morning.

Silly, right? Not even silly. Stupid. But there you were. Like a junior high school jerk, he couldn't even bring himself to ask her to come home with him. She brought it up. *Are you trying to seduce me?* That was what she said. So they went to his place and after that he had no trouble asking her to come back. And she had no trouble shooting him down like one of those milk bottles you knock over with a lopsided ball. Twice. And after that he spent more time thinking about what went wrong than he had spent in the relation-ship itself, which lasted only a few hours.

Let's move on to something else, she told Gus Benini. Oh sure, after Gus was dead she had an explanation. But that was after Gus was dead. And then that look on her face when Gogarty told her the rich lady fucking Chet Fiore without window shades was Phyllis Blaine. Just for a second, but it was there. That look wasn't something he made up. It kept driving him crazy all through din-ner and it was still driving him crazy when he got home. It was something in her eyes, *click*, and it was gone, like a bulb winking out and then coming back on.

So he put his clothes back on and went out again, and when he got back this time it was three o'clock in the morning and he had a whole new set of things to drive himself crazy with. Because what he had done while he was out was spy on a woman he used to think he was in love with. He tried to tell himself it was part of his job, it was nothing personal, but even a whole whiskey bottle couldn't make him believe that.

When he saw a guy leave her apartment he knew perfectly well that this was Jeffrey Blaine even though he had never seen Jeffrey Blaine in his life. *Nice to meet you, Mr. Blaine,* Schliester thought bitterly. *Why couldn't you just stay the fuck out of my life?*

The whole thing was disgusting, and Wally Schliester knew enough, even drunk, to put himself at the top of the list of the things that disgusted him.

26

Phyllis padded into the kitchen and turned on the cappuccino machine. Jeffrey was still in bed. He hadn't come home until hours after she went to bed. We're a fine pair, she thought, Jeffrey and whoever the other woman happened to be, herself and Charles. Not that you could equate one with the other. Her own affair was more or less in the nature of an experiment. It wasn't so much the sex as the cheating that interested her. She wanted to know what it felt like to be Jeffrey.

She measured out the coffee, tamped it down, and levered it into the machine. The steam made a sharp hissing sound as it forced its way through the coffee, and then a different sound when she steamed the milk. The sounds were an important part of the ritual.

She wrote a note for the cook, who should have been in already, and headed back for the bathroom, taking her coffee with her. She stopped as she passed Jessica's room because the door was closed and Jessica always slept with the door open. She couldn't imagine Jessica up this early, but apparently she was.

She knocked and waited, then knocked again more emphatically. When there was still no mumble of response from the other side, she eased the door back.

Jessica wasn't there.

Phyllis felt suddenly, queasily sick. Already she could see in her mind a complete reprise of last summer's melodrama. She ran back to her room, calling Jeffrey's name even before she came through the door.

He wasn't in bed. She heard the shower running.

"Jessica's gone," she said, bursting through the door into the bathroom.

"What do you mean, gone?" he asked. He swung open the glass door of the shower and stepped out, half shaven, his face still wearing a thin, slick layer of lather in the places he hadn't reached yet. He began toweling himself off.

"Her door was closed. She never sleeps with the door closed. I knocked and there was no answer, so I went in. She's not there, Jeffrey. She's gone."

"Did you check the rest of the apartment?" he asked as he pulled on a robe.

She felt like an idiot. She turned and ran out of the bathroom to check.

When Jeffrey came out of the bathroom, Carlos, alarmed by Phyllis's shouts, was standing in the corridor in his shirtsleeves as though someone expected him to direct traffic.

"Carlos, have you seen Jessica?" Jeffrey asked.

"No, sir, I just came out. I heard Mrs. Blaine and—"

"That's all right, Carlos," Jeffrey said without slowing down. His hair was dripping wet. His wet feet left a trail of footprints on the floor. He rushed into Jessica's room. A moment later Phyllis was standing behind him.

"I checked everywhere. She's not here," she said. "If she ran off with that boy again . . ." She left the sentence unfinished.

"She didn't," Jeffrey said without explaining how he knew.

"Then where is she?" Phyllis demanded sharply.

Jeffrey looked at her levelly. "I'll try to find out," he said, and walked away, offering no elaboration.

She followed, her voice flung at the back of his head. "Maybe we shouldn't have taken her out of school," she said. "At least she would have had something to do with her life. I mean, what was she doing here? How was that helping her, putting her under house arrest?"

He walked into the bedroom, threw off his robe, and started to get dressed.

For the first time in her life she felt uncomfortable with his nakedness. She walked to the window and looked out so that she wouldn't have to look at him.

"Obviously she wasn't under arrest or she'd be here, wouldn't she?" he said.

"That's hardly the point," Phyllis shot back, turning back to him, and then turning away again. "Maybe we didn't do enough. Maybe we should have put her in a drug program. We said we would. Why didn't we?"

He was putting on the brown suit she hated. She almost said something but stopped herself, and then cursed herself for even thinking about what damn suit he wore. It made him look like he was trying to pretend he was twenty-five years old, but what business was it of hers what he looked like?

He studied the selection of ties in front of him. She knew exactly which one he'd wear. The gold paisley. He always wore that tie with that suit. Why was he fumbling around as though he didn't know that? She watched for a moment with growing impatience, infuriated by the charade. And then she stepped up behind him, reached over his shoulder, and grabbed the paisley tie from the rack and held it out to him. "For god's sake, Jeffrey," she said.

He took the tie out of her hand and draped it around his neck. Something in her gesture, in the way she handed him the tie, with its claim of implicit control, as though she knew him better than he knew himself, infuriated him and made it easy for him to say something he had known he would have to say someday but hadn't planned to say now. She knew what tie to hand him but she didn't know him at all. She thought of him as a mild, bland, docile man, undoubtedly of considerable intelligence, undoubtedly with considerable integrity. But all that was changed now and it wouldn't ever be changing back. He was going to be what he had to be, and there was no way Phyllis could be a part of that.

"After I find Jessica," he said, "I'll be staying in a hotel for a while. Until I find a place."

Phyllis wanted to scream. The man was trying to drive her mad. Her daughter was missing and he was telling her *this*? She looked at him in stunned disbelief, her eyes wide, her mouth embarrassingly, unbecomingly open. In that instant she looked like an old woman, looked exactly like Jeffrey imagined she would look in thirty years. He had no intention of being there to see it.

Wally Schliester walked around in circles, trying to remember everything he knew about what it meant to be a cop. The sun was still low over the East River, playing a game as it dodged among the buildings on the Brooklyn side, then poking out a little higher up, a little farther to the right. The river hid a hundred tiny little suns.

When he thought he had gotten himself ready he went into the office. Such a crappy little office, he thought, although the location was certainly nice. He liked being by the water. He used to like the office, too, for that matter. He just couldn't get himself in that frame of mind anymore.

The bottom of the coffeepot looked downright geological, so he ran some water in to rinse it out the best he could. No one ever covered the coffee can, so the coffee had no taste to it except an oily bitterness, but at least it was an oily bitterness with some caffeine in it. His head still hurt from last night, and he needed something to help him focus.

He thought about Humphrey Bogart sending up Mary Astor at the end of *The Maltese Falcon*. Something something something because everything in my life, or something like that. But that was middle-of-the-night thinking, fine for four A.M. In the morning sunlight it was better to assume it wasn't going to come down to anything like that. Elaine was mixed up with Jeffrey Blaine but maybe she could get herself unmixed if he gave her a good reason to.

On his desk was a transcript of Gus Benini's debriefing in the motel. Someone had a great sense of timing. He always wondered who the hell typed all this stuff out. The tapes went away every night and they came back a week or so later as paper. Page after page of them. It was like Hemingway coming out with novels after he was dead. Half an inch thick. The collected works of Gus Benini. What a goddamned pitiful waste. A waste of six months on Schliester's part, a waste of a whole damn life on Gus's.

He leaned back in the chair with his arms behind his head and tried to take stock. Every goddamned fact was contradicted by another goddamned fact somewhere else. Fiore goes to the banker's kid's birthday party. *Looks like we're on to something.* Fiore porks the banker's wife. *Guess we're not.* Gus Benini sets up shakedowns for Fiore, reports to the boss when there's trouble. *That's good.* Gus is dead. *That's bad.* Which brings us to last night, when we learn that the banker himself is shacked up with the assistant U.S. attorney in charge of the case. Which means? Which means?

Schliester didn't know what it meant. If Fiore isn't tied up with the banker, then what's the problem if Elaine Lester is? None. No problem.

Once he put it that way, Wally Schliester felt as though a tremendous weight had been lifted from his shoulders. Because if the banker was clean, then Elaine was also—

"No, no, no," he said out loud. "Fuck! Fuck the whole fucking thing!"

The chair skittered backward as he sprang to his feet, and for a full minute he paced around the room like a man in a hurry to get somewhere, raking his hand through his sand-colored hair. Look at it from the banker's point of view, not Elaine's. He's in the sack with her. What were the odds of that in a city of eight point something million people? Put it another way. What is this guy after? Her body? Please. A nice ass and a receptive pussy sometimes make a man stupid. Off the top of his head, Schliester couldn't come up with a single instance where they made him smart, and there was definitely something smart about sharing a pillow with the head that heads an investigation into a man you're in business with.

Any other way there were just too many coincidences.

He struck the side of his fist against the windowpane, alarming the seagulls outside, and cursed under his breath.

"What's the matter?" Elaine's voice asked from behind him.

He whirled around with a funny look on his face, like a man who has just been caught playing with himself. "No, nothing," he said quickly. "I mean, just silly stuff. Nothing."

She was wearing a light green suit. There was a name for that shade of green but Schliester didn't know what it was. Her blouse was more or less ivory. "Nothing?" she said. "You're sure?"

"No, I'm not sure," he said. "When did you figure out that Blaine wasn't tied in with Fiore?"

"Oh, please, Wally," she sighed, "let's not go over this again."

"That was yesterday. This is a different question."

"Ask it again."

There was more defiance in her voice than he expected. The lady had balls, that was for sure.

"When did you figure out that Blaine was clean?"

"Who says I figured that out?"

He didn't say anything. He just waited. He could feel his anger rising up, and even before the next words formed in his mind, he knew that he was about to say the one thing he had been hoping not to have to say. He didn't want to be Humphrey Bogart any more than he had wanted to be the man who put Theresa Benini's father in the water. He had come a long way from that day in St. Louis when he disarmed a knife-wielding psychotic without using his gun. He remembered what that felt like when it was over, and it didn't matter that the guy didn't deserve the break he got. Who ever does? Being a cop is like being a doctor. *First do no harm.* Except there was already one man dead because Wally Schliester said *Let's reel him in,* and now he was about to wreck another life. He wanted to stop but couldn't make himself.

"He was at your place last night," he said. "What do you think he wants, Elaine? A little comfort for a bad marriage? Or a little protection?"

"You bastard," she snarled, "you goddamned cocksucking little prick. What gives you the right to spy on me?"

"Just tell me why Fiore went to Gus's house. He wouldn't have gone there if he didn't already know we questioned Gus. How did he know that, Elaine?"

"My god," she said, not angry now, horrified. "Are you suggesting—"

"I'm not suggesting, I'm asking."

Her hand flashed out and she slapped him hard across the face, with more force than he would have thought a slap could carry. He didn't even try to stop her. He had it coming.

"That's not an answer," he said.

"It's an answer, it's an answer," she screamed.

"Did you tell Blaine we had Gus?"

She slapped him again.

"Did you tell him to warn his partner?"

She stopped herself this time, and then she looked at him hard for what felt like a long time. He refused to look away.

"It's too bad about us, Wally," she said. "But it never would have worked out."

And then she walked out of the room.

If Jessica was mixed up with drugs again, the only person who could help Jeffrey find her was Chet Fiore. He had people who knew their way around that world. They could rifle through it like a magician running through a deck of cards. They probably even had cops on their payroll they could turn to. He didn't like asking Fiore for favors but he didn't intend to ask as a favor. Fiore was in his debt where Jessica was concerned. His vicious games put her in that world, and now Jeffrey was going to demand that he use whatever powers he had to get her out. As simple as that. No threat had to be made. Fiore knew what the threat was.

He had Martin drive him to Stasny's, where he pulled up in front of the service entrance. He told Martin to wait and rang the bell. The same insolent young man opened the door who had opened it the last time Jeffrey had come here because his daughter vanished. Again, Jeffrey followed him down a maze of corridors to the kitchen. This time Stasny made no pretense of not knowing how to get in touch with Fiore. He invited Jeffrey into the office and made a telephone call, speaking in the coded language Jeffrey had come to expect in all of Fiore's dealings. He used no names, not his own, not Fiore's, and said almost nothing. While he was making the call, Jeffrey dialed Jessica's number on his cell phone and waited for her machine to pick up. "Jess, it's Dad," he said. "Call me on my cell phone as soon as you get in. Love you lots."

Just that. If Jessica came home on her own, Jeffrey knew that Phyllis wouldn't bother to let him know.

Stasny suggested he'd be more comfortable waiting in the dining room. A waiter who took the trouble to put on a jacket brought him coffee and a sweet roll without his asking for either. Jeffrey drank the coffee. Ten minutes passed, then twenty. Another waiter, coatless, shirtless, came into the room and went about setting the tables. Then Stasny appeared, flanked by two young men. One of them looked familiar. "Could you come with us, Mr. Blaine?" he said.

Stasny led the three of them to the front door, unlocking it to let them out. As soon as the door opened, Martin got out of the car to see what was wanted of him. "You can send him home, Mr. Blaine," the young man said. "We have a car."

It suddenly dawned on Jeffrey that this was either the guy who raped Amy or the one he found with Renée. He couldn't be sure which but it didn't matter. The fact that he was Eddie Vincenzo's friend hit him like a jolt of electricity. He had assumed Eddie was out of the picture.

"Where is Jessica?" he asked sharply, throwing the boy into momentary confusion.

"I don't know nothing about that," Georgie Vallo said. "Just get in the car, okay."

The other boy, who was in fact Richie Demarest, Renée Goldschmidt's date at Jessica's party, stepped in front of Martin and said, "There's no problem here. Why don't you get back in your car?"

Martin wasn't about to take this punk's word for it. Or even Jeffrey's when Jeffrey said, "It's all right, Martin." He knew Mr. Blaine would have to say that even if it wasn't all right. So he held his ground, waiting to see what came next. This job was weird, he thought. And Mr. Blaine was into some very complicated shit.

Mr. Blaine didn't look like a man who was being kidnapped, which was the first thought that had run through Martin's mind when he saw them all coming out of the restaurant like that. In fact, Mr. Blaine actually took a step toward the punk, who took a step backward so that Mr. Blaine's face wasn't right in his.

"I want to know where my daughter is, I want to know that she's all right, and I want to know it now," Mr. Blaine said.

Georgie Vallo said, "I'm telling you the truth, Mr. Blaine. Nobody said nothing to me about Jess. They just said pick you up."

"And you did that. Now tell me where we're going and I'll follow you," Jeffrey suggested.

"I can't do that, Mr. Blaine," Georgie Vallo said.

The punk sounded nervous. He was supposed to be the tough guy and he was letting Mr. Blaine push him around. He was going to look like a great big asshole when the guy he was supposed to pick up showed up in a different car.

"You're going to do it," Mr. Blaine said. "Now tell me where we're going."

Georgie Vallo's eyes blinked as though he were sending signals. "You'll follow me?" he asked uncertainly.

"Practically in your tailpipe," Jeffrey said.

"No funny stuff?" Georgie asked. He just wanted a little reassurance.

Jeffrey turned to Martin. "We're following them," he said, starting back to his car. "No funny stuff."

Georgie and Richie Demarest hurried toward a blue Dodge parked a few cars down. Martin waited until they pulled out from the curb and then eased into the traffic right behind them. He looked in the mirror at Mr. Blaine. This was a banker who managed to twist a punk's head into knots without ever raising his voice or his hand. There was a trick to it, and he wondered whether, if he drove for Mr. Blaine long enough, he would ever learn it.

He followed the Dodge all the way down to Delancey Street, where it turned east, heading for the Williamsburg Bridge. When it got off at the first exit ramp on the Brooklyn side, Martin threw a glance back over his shoulder as though he wanted Jeffrey to confirm that they were doing the right thing. He didn't like the feel of this.

A few minutes later they were driving along the East River through a district of run-down one- and two-story industrial buildings. At least half of them looked abandoned and the ones that were still in operation didn't look much better. Martin checked the dashboard clock. It was still only a couple of minutes past eight. Which was an awful time of day to get stuffed into sacks like a litter of kittens and thrown into the river. Just the other day a crazy black man in the middle of Manhattan in the middle of the day picked up a brick and bashed some white girl's head in, so there were enough ways to get hurt in this city without going out of your way to find them. He wished he could just slam the brakes, jam it into reverse, wheel into a backward turn, and gun it out of there. They'd be half a mile away by the time the Dodge got itself turned around.

"He's turning in here, Martin," Mr. Blaine said.

Martin hoped he'd hear him say, *Keep going*, but he knew he wouldn't.

The Dodge cut in through a conveniently open gate in a chain-link fence on the river side of the road. Martin followed and they found themselves in a parking lot big enough for about thirty cars. The pavement was breaking apart and there didn't seem to be any lights on in the building. But the windows weren't broken, so it probably wasn't abandoned. A sign that should have been hanging over the front door lay on the ground, partly obscured by trash bins and discarded lumber. Jeffrey could make out the words SHEET METAL but nothing else. Martin noticed it, too, but didn't much care what it said.

The Dodge drifted around the lot and disappeared behind the side of the building, heading toward the back. "Go ahead," Jeffrey said.

"You sure?" Martin asked. It was as close as he would come to questioning his employer's orders.

Jeffrey was sure.

Martin sighed and pulled around to the back of the building.

There were two cars parked there, and one of them was Chet Fiore's Mercedes. This was going to be the showdown everything had been building toward, and now it occurred to Jeffrey for the first time that he might not be a match for Fiore. The man knew violence inside out. It had seemed such a simple matter to will oneself into being someone one had never been, like shedding a skin that no longer fit. But maybe it wasn't simple at all.

He glanced at the building and saw something move in the window. Georgie Vallo and the other boy were standing only a foot or so away, hovering near him like jittery jailers, ready to escort him in. "Come on," Georgie said, reaching for his arm.

Jeffrey pulled away from the young man's touch as he stepped through a warped steel door, leaving Martin waiting in the parking lot.

Chet Fiore was waiting just inside the door.

"Where's my daughter?" Jeffrey asked, before Fiore could say anything.

Vallo and the other kid stepped in behind Jeffrey, one of them swinging the door closed. It made a heavy, rasping sound.

"Your daughter's fine," Fiore said. "There's nothing to worry about."

"Just tell me where the hell she is, you son of a bitch," Jeffrey shouted, lunging at Fiore. It was the second time he made a move for Fiore, and for the second time he was grabbed from behind. There was a forearm across his throat, and his right arm was wrenched back violently until it felt like it was going to dislocate from the socket.

"All right, ease up," Fiore said.

The pressure on Jeffrey's arm and shoulder eased back but the forearm was still around his throat.

"We'll talk about your kid," Fiore said, "but first we're going to talk about you. I send these geniuses to bring you here and you show up in your own car. I'll bet you think that's cute, running a number on a couple kids like that. Makes you smart, right?"

432 · **Philip Rosenberg**

Jeffrey waited.

"I asked you a question," Fiore said.

"No, it doesn't make me smart," Jeffrey said.

He felt the pain in his shoulder again as his arm was pulled all the way back.

"All right, it makes me smart," he snapped. "I don't know what the answers are. Why don't you just tell me?"

"We'll get there," Fiore said. "If you don't know what the answers are, how come you act like you do?"

"I know my business," Jeffrey managed to say. It wasn't easy to talk because of the pain, but he knew that if he remained silent the pain would only get worse. "That's all I know. Is that what you want me to say?"

"I don't doubt that you know your business, Jeffrey. You don't know mine and you don't want to try to," Fiore said, stepping closer.

"I wouldn't," Jeffrey said.

Fiore reached out and grabbed Jeffrey's face, his fingers biting into the flesh just over the jaw. He had small but powerful hands capable of exerting immense pressure.

"You wouldn't try, you little cocksucker? Is that right?"

Jeffrey's jaw felt like it was going to split like a walnut.

"I've been straight with you, Jeffrey," Fiore went on, his eyes slitted with rage. "Your kid came back at the end of the summer like I said she would. If she started seeing Eddie again, that's not my problem. I didn't bring her up, you did."

"I didn't get her on drugs."

His arm wrenched so far back he heard something crackling in his shoulder. He gasped from the pain.

"Sorry about that," Fiore said. "Sometimes Georgie can't help himself. He's a friend of Eddie's. You put his friend in the hospital. Let him go, Georgie."

Jeffrey shifted his shoulders as he was released. All he could do was hope that nothing was broken.

"That's old business," Fiore said. "Now we get to new business. Let's talk about your little girl."

"Where is she?" Jeffrey demanded.

"You listen, I talk," Fiore said. "I had a problem with you and now I've got a problem with her. Little Jessica went to a reporter last night and told her all about everything. Including the fact that you're working for me."

Jeffrey was stunned. How could she do that? All the lawyers in the world wouldn't be able to keep him out of prison once he was publicly exposed. Having an intimate friend in the prosecutor's office helped only as long as the story stayed in the office. Once it got out, Fiore himself would have an easier time making a deal than he would, because one gangster more or less wasn't going to make much of a difference, but an investment banker who opened a money laundry on Wall Street would be turned into a front-page, lead-story example.

Jeffrey had planned for everything. Except betrayal by his own daughter. *Why?* he thought. *Why would she do that?* "Where is she?" he asked, in a level voice that betrayed nothing of what he was thinking.

Fiore noticed the calmness in him, noticed that he hadn't asked a single question about a newspaper story with the potential to destroy him.

"She came to see me last night," Fiore said. "She offered herself to buy your freedom."

"My freedom?"

"From me," Fiore said. "Lovely girl. And a very tempting offer. What do you think? Is she a better fuck than her mother or not?"

Blaine's calmness unsettled him, but now that calmness was gone. *Let's see what he's got,* Fiore thought as Jeffrey exploded toward him.

His left arm deflected the punch and he countered with a hard right straight into Jeffrey's gut that doubled him over. "Stay back, he's mine," Fiore barked to his two henchmen as he unleashed another blow, an uppercut, that followed the first almost in the same instant, straightening Jeffrey up.

Jeffrey could feel the scorching bitterness of vomit rising in his throat. He was a grown man who had never been in a fight in his life, but he was ready for this one. He liked the taste of his own blood in his mouth and welcomed the pain as he righted himself and charged back at Fiore.

A right hand that he saw coming but couldn't stop caught him square on the cheekbone with a sound like an explosion going off in his head. He reeled sideways, his vision blurred, but still clear enough to let him see Fiore stalking after him, his fist cocked, patient.

Jeffrey took a few steps to the side, like a boxer circling away from trouble. His hands were low by his side, until he remembered to bring them up. But he felt awkward like that. He didn't know the first thing about fighting and wasn't going to fool anyone pretending he did. He dropped low and dove forward, driving his shoulder into Fiore's knees, taking him to the floor.

Fiore rolled over and tried to scramble to his feet but Jeffrey wasn't about to let that happen. He drove his elbow into the small of Fiore's back, smashing him back to the floor, forcing the breath out of his body in a sudden rush. For an instant Jeffrey felt the immense satisfaction of delivering pain, so new to him and so surprising.

Not that Fiore was giving him time to savor the moment. He rolled onto his back and kicked out with both legs, straight into Jeffrey's chest. There was a sound that might have been a rib cracking. Jeffrey tried to spin away, to buy himself a little room, but he felt Fiore come down on his back, felt the floor against his face. And then Fiore was sitting astride him, his fingers twisted in Jeffrey's hair, and he yanked hard, pulling his head back for a chopping blow with his fist.

Apparently Fiore thought that would do the trick. With Jeffrey on the floor, facedown in a puddle of his own blood, Fiore got slowly to his feet, flexed the bruised knuckles on his right hand, and turned away, perfectly satisfied to leave Jeffrey lying there.

But Jeffrey wasn't finished. The moment he saw Fiore's back, he lunged after him and caught his shoulder with his left hand. He had big, strong hands. He rowed at Yale his freshman and sophomore years, and even now his grip was powerful enough to drag a man over backward. They fell across each other, both of them erupting at once in a barrage of kicks and punches, knees and elbows that finally mixed some of Fiore's blood with Jeffrey's.

Standing over them, Georgie Vallo and Richie Demarest exchanged looks. Georgie licked nervously at his lips, worried. They hadn't expected the banker to put up this much of a fight. But the two men were rolling on the floor, digging fists and knees into each other, groaning from pain and exertion. Richie took a step forward but Georgie put a hand out to stop him.

The room, which at one time must have been an office of sorts, was almost devoid of furniture, just the stuff too ruined to sell off or take. A steel desk and a couple of splay-legged chairs stood to the side, pushed back against the wall. Jeffrey rolled up against one of the chairs, which came apart with the impact, the seat falling onto him, the metal legs clattering to the floor next to him. He grabbed one of the legs as Fiore came after him and swung it in a slashing forehand that caught Fiore across the chest, the unfinished end ripping through his shirt and drawing a bright bloody line where it shredded the fabric.

He lurched backward and then came right back at Jeffrey. He kicked hard as the chair leg swung toward him again, catching him across the thigh, ripping through his pants. But he got a good piece of Jeffrey's forearm with his kick and the chair leg clattered to the floor, skittering away. Fiore went for it, and Jeffrey grabbed for another, which turned out to be still attached to the bottom of the seat. He twisted at the seat, levering the joint until it separated.

Fiore caught him across the shoulders as he turned. Jeffrey staggered but kept his feet. Now the two of them dueled across the room, slashing at each other with their awkward swords. Fiore, quicker and more agile, caught Jeffrey repeatedly across the upper arm, gouging his skin with the jagged edges of metal. But Jeffrey managed to keep his attack going, and for a moment he actually believed he was holding his own and could come out on top if he could only manage to get in the one good shot that would settle it. That would still leave the two punks to deal with but he'd worry about them later.

He tried to duck under a forehand slash and didn't quite make it. The metal tube caught him across the side of the head and for a moment, as he was falling, he may have even blacked out. He had a vivid sensation of flying through space, and then he was on the floor with only a vague awareness of where he was and what he was supposed to do. He couldn't be quite sure if he was still holding his precious chair leg, and by the time he realized he was, it was already too late.

Fiore's foot came down on his wrist and the chair leg fell from Jeffrey's grasp. Quickly, Fiore kicked it away and then for good measure added one more kick to the rib cage that sent an electric charge of pain through every part of Jeffrey's body. While he was fighting, the pain hadn't been important, but it seemed to be all that mattered now.

There was no doubt in Chet Fiore's mind that Jeffrey would stay down this time. He stood over him, breathing hard, his body more or less hunched together, vivid streaks of blood showing through his tattered clothing. He took a moment to let his breathing settle back to something more like normal and then flung the metal rod away.

"You want your kid, she's in back there," he said, gesturing toward a door leading into the interior of the building. Then he turned and walked toward the door Jeffrey had come in. Vallo and Demarest followed him.

As Jeffrey watched them go, he suddenly realized that it hadn't been necessary for him to beat Fiore. All he had to do was go the distance, keep Fiore from beating him. And he had done that. He was still alive.

In that moment he was certain he could see how the rest of the story was going to play itself out.

As he came out into the sunlight, Fiore saw the two federal agents who made a scene in front of Blaine's wife. He walked toward them, at a measured pace, with Georgie Vallo and Richie Demarest falling in step behind him. The younger agent, the one he hit in the face, the one who kept talking about Gus, took a step toward him. Fiore stopped walking.

"You want a piece, you son of a bitch," he called out, "come and get it."

The agent held his ground. He didn't answer, didn't move. The older one wasn't even looking at Fiore. He was looking at his partner.

"This is the only chance you're going to get, asshole," Fiore said.

Wally Schliester grinned at him. He shook his head. "No interest in you, pal. Not now anyway."

"Then get out of my way."

He moved toward the passenger door of his car.

Schliester opened it for him. "I thought you'd want to know," he said. "Gus Benini didn't tell us a thing. You killed him for nothing."

Awkward, turned the wrong way, his feet in the wrong place, Fiore lunged for Schliester but never got there. Georgie Vallo grabbed him before he could do anything. "You don't wanna do that, Mr. Fiore," he said.

Fiore tried to shake him off but it was no good. Besides, the kid was right. The damned agent was trying to provoke him, and he fell right into the trap. He should have had the sense to walk away, and now he was standing in the slanted light of the morning with a jerk of a kid holding on to him as though he wasn't Chet Fiore. He thought about Gus in the water and the hand on his head until the bubbles stopped, and then the way he floated with his face down and his ass up, like an empty thing floating away, and he felt a tightness in his chest and in his throat, as though the same dark cold water that closed in over Gus was closing in over him.

He shook himself free of Georgie Vallo's grasp and slid into the front seat of the car.

Schliester slammed the car door. He watched as Georgie Vallo hurried around and got in behind the wheel while the other kid ran to the Dodge. He watched the two cars disappear around the side of the building, the Dodge leading the way. When they were gone, he turned to his partner.

"Let's see what we've got," he said.

• • •

Jeffrey didn't even wait for his head to clear. He reached for the window sill above him and pulled himself to his feet. It felt as though he were lifting an immense weight, and his head, which was throbbing even before he tried to get up, felt as though it was going to explode. He was afraid he was going to black out again but his balance held. He stood there leaning against the grimy sill until he was certain he wouldn't fall. He didn't even have time to figure out what else hurt. The pain in his head was what was making it difficult to move, so he focused on overcoming that.

As he started to pick his way to the door on the opposite side of the room, he heard footsteps outside moving to the door. If Fiore or one of his men was coming back to finish him off, there was nothing he could do about it, so he didn't even turn. He kept going toward the door on the far wall because Jessica was somewhere on the other side of it.

And then he heard Martin's voice. "Oh, holy Jesus," it said.

Jeffrey stopped moving and turned his head, the way an owl turns, his body still. "Come on," he said, and saw the blood drip from his mouth with the words. "She's here somewhere."

Martin said, "I'll find her, Mr. Blaine. You sit down."

Jeffrey lurched toward the door, getting there just ahead of Martin.

"There's two police outside, Mr. Blaine," Martin said.

All Jeffrey cared about right now was finding Jessica. He pulled the door open and stepped into a workspace of some sort, with partitions and odd fragments of wall dividing it into a bizarre maze. A few scarred tables and benches were all the furnishings that remained. The light was very dim, only what came through a few greasy windows on the far wall, so Jeffrey and Martin had to stop and look carefully because Jessica might be anywhere, behind any of the walls, behind any of the worktables, under stray lengths of timber lying about. If she was tied up, or unconscious, they could walk right past her without seeing her.

Jeffrey called her name but there was no response. He and Martin circled around, moving behind tables, to make sure she wasn't on the floor somewhere. His fear for her grew into heavy, suffocating dread.

He rushed to a door on the other side of the workroom, moving quickly, ignoring the pain that shot through his body with each step, and found himself in a corridor with doors to either side, maybe four of them, and one more at the end that opened to the outside. He stumbled to the first and threw it open. The windows were boarded over or bricked over—he couldn't see well enough to tell which. Only the feeble light from behind him seeped into the room, making a small dent in the darkness. He felt the wall by the door for a light switch and found one but nothing happened when he flipped it. He started into the room, saying Jessica's name over and over, a kind of soft and prayerful mantra. "Are you there, Jess? Jess? It's Daddy. Are you in here, Jess? Jess?"

"Mr. Blaine! She's here!" Martin called from another room.

Jeffrey staggered back out to the corridor, grabbing the door frame to keep from falling. The walls seemed to be spinning around him, but he kept his feet moving, across the corridor and into the darkened room.

Martin knelt at the far side of the room. Jessica was lying on the floor, curled into a fetal position, covered with a sheet or a blanket of some sort. For a wrenchingly anguished moment, he was afraid she was dead. And then he heard her voice, softly, as though it were coming from a long distance away. "Daddy," she said, not quite a question, not quite a plea.

Martin stepped back, making room for Jeffrey.

"Are you okay, baby?" Jeffrey asked, moving into Martin's place beside her, kneeling on the floor, touching her face.

"Can I go home?" she said.

She sounded like his little girl used to sound when she fell asleep in the car and had to be carried into the house.

"Right away," he said. "Can you get up?"

She laughed, a drunken little-girl giggle. "Daddy, I don't know where my clothes are," she said.

His stomach churned with a wave of nausea, as though he had been hit again.

"Can you stand up? Can you walk?" he asked.

"I'm okay, Daddy," she said bravely. "Really, I am."

He sent Martin out to the car to get a flashlight and then he helped Jessica to her feet. She stood unsteadily. He picked up the blanket and wrapped it around her nakedness. She smelled of whiskey.

"Come on," he said. "We'll get out of here. Martin will come back with a light. He'll find your clothes. Do you think they're here?"

"I don't know. I'm not wearing them." She giggled again.

He put his arm around her. He could feel the warmth of her body through the thin blanket.

When she spoke again, she sounded less drunk, more in control of herself. "I thought you were in some kind of trouble," she said. "Because of me. I wanted to get you out of it."

"Is that why you went to the newspaper?" he asked.

"I guess it didn't work. He knew I went there right away. He called me. I went down to this restaurant."

"You don't have to tell me if you don't want," Jeffrey said.

Fiore had come back to the kitchen office when she didn't come out. She had found a case of liquor on a storage shelf and was drunk by then. This time when she offered herself, he didn't say no. Then, afterward, he had someone carry her out to the car. That must have been when her clothes got lost. She didn't remember being taken outside and so she figured she must have passed out.

She didn't tell her father any of this.

She let herself lean on his shoulder, taking short, mincing steps, still unsteady but managing better with each step. They made their way back to the room where Jeffrey fought with Fiore. A flashlight beam caught Jessica full in the face and she turned away, shielding her eyes.

A voice Jeffrey didn't recognize said, "Is she okay?"

"Get that light off her," Jeffrey snapped. "Where's my driver?"

He couldn't see the man behind the light beam.

The beam lowered, shining at their feet. "Is she all right?" the voice repeated. "Does she need an ambulance?"

"No."

"What about you?"

"Her clothes are missing," Jeffrey said. "If you want to be useful, see if you can find them."

"I'm not interested in being useful, Mr. Blaine," the man said.

Jeffrey tightened his grip on his daughter's shoulder and they resumed walking. When they reached Schliester, who was standing in the doorway holding the flashlight, Jeffrey said, "Please get out of the way."

Schliester didn't move. "I know what you've been doing, Blaine," he said. He looked at Jeffrey steadily for what felt like a long time.

"If you've got a case, make it," Jeffrey answered, keeping his voice level and toneless, as though he were simply giving directions. "Otherwise, go fuck yourself."

The federal agent was younger than Jeffrey imagined he would be. There was something about his coloring, his hair, the easy regularity of his features, that reminded Jeffrey of himself at another time. Then the man stepped to the side and seemed to vanish into the gloom of the building.

Outside, Jessica said, "Jesus, Daddy" when she saw her father's battered face and bloody arms and chest in the daylight. She cried. Jeffrey walked her to the car, while another officer, a heavy, dour man, watched without moving. The motor was running and Martin came out from behind the wheel to help them in, first Jessica, then Jeffrey. The blanket she was wrapped in turned out, in daylight, to be a checkered tablecloth.

They had driven almost a mile before either of them said anything. "Are you going to be all right?" Jeffrey asked.

"You mean for someone so fucked up? Maybe. I don't know, Daddy. I really don't."

27

Schliester and Gogarty were back in the office by noon. Gogarty typed out an application for a warrant to examine Jeffrey Blaine's business records. Schliester wrote the supporting affidavit. It was only two pages long, which was rather skimpy as those things went. There was the fact that a known member of organized crime was seen attending one of Mr. Blaine's social functions. There was the fact that a reliable informant, now deceased, had referred on tape to a new banking arrangement being used by the organized crime family for which he worked. There was a reference to a "meeting" between Mr. Blaine and an organized crime figure at a warehouse in Brooklyn. There wasn't a whole lot more.

Elaine read the search warrant application and the affidavit. When she was finished, she dropped them on her desk and looked up at Schliester and Gogarty, who sat next to each other on the other side of the desk. "This is perjurious and misleading. I'm not going to endorse it," she said flatly.

"Every word in it is true and you know it," Schliester said.

Gogarty kept his mouth shut. He had the best seats in the house and he wanted to see how this was going to play out.

"You're leaving out material facts," she said. "You're leaving out the fact that Fiore had an affair with Blaine's wife. Which the two of you witnessed and photographed. You're leaving out the fact that Fiore kidnapped and traduced Blaine's daughter, after which the two of them went after each other with metal pipes. I don't think it's accurate to call that a meeting. Put those facts in and see if a court will believe that Chet Fiore and Jeffrey Blaine are bosom buddies and business partners."

Schliester was on his feet. "Oh, Christ, Elaine, you know what happened as well as I do. Fiore was using the kid to make Blaine jump through financial hoops."

"Show me some evidence."

"How else can you explain—"

She cut him off sharply. "*How else* is not evidence. Do you have any?"

He glared at her but didn't answer.

"Do you have any evidence?" she repeated.

Schliester snatched the pages off her desk and headed for the door. Gogarty got up to follow him.

"Just so we're clear on this," Elaine said before they could get out the door, "I am explicitly notifying both of you that you are not, repeat not, authorized to go tramping in and out of the life of one of the city's more respectable citizens just because his wife can't keep her panties on. Are we clear on that?"

"Let's find a judge," Schliester suggested when he and Gogarty found themselves downstairs and out on the sidewalk.

Sometimes it worked. Some judges didn't ask too many questions. They would sign a warrant on the skimpiest of evidence, even without a prosecutor's endorsement. Even though Elaine had ordered them to discontinue their investigation, she didn't have the authority to keep them from executing a duly authorized warrant. It was worth a try, Schliester thought.

"It's not going to happen, *boychik*," Gogarty said. "Haven't you learned anything yet?"

Yes, Schliester thought, he had learned plenty.

The only thing he hadn't learned was how to walk away. He couldn't say that to Gogarty, because Gogarty would laugh at him. And why shouldn't he laugh? It sounded ridiculous.

I am not giving up. I am not walking away. I owe it to myself.

That was the kind of thing you couldn't say out loud.

• • •

Jeffrey used the service elevator to bring Jessica home, still wrapped in nothing but a tablecloth. Phyllis gasped when she saw them. She threw her arms around her daughter. "Are you all right, baby?" she asked with an urgency that was near hysteria.

Jeffrey had barely stepped through the door, and now he stepped back out. His clothes were shredded and his face was a mess. Although the cuts on his arms and chest had stopped bleeding, he was covered with bloody stripes.

"Oh, for god's sake, Jeffrey," Phyllis said, her voice dripping exasperation. Walking away in his condition struck her as a hostile and melodramatic gesture.

Downstairs, he gave Martin Elaine Lester's address in Chelsea. He fell asleep in the back seat on the way down but woke when the car stopped. Martin opened the door for him and helped him out. "Let me help you inside, sir," he offered.

He had never taken Mr. Blaine to this address before.

"I'll be fine, Martin. I won't be needing you," Jeffrey said.

He let himself in with his key. He thought he'd take a bath, get himself cleaned up, and take stock of his injuries before Elaine got home, but after he peeled off his tattered clothes, he lay down on the bed to rest for a minute and fell asleep again.

The next thing he knew, Elaine was standing over the bed. "Oh my god, Jeffrey," she said.

His eyes opened. It was still light outside and he managed a wan smile.

"Don't tell me," she said. "It's not as bad as it looks."

"Actually," he said, "I think it's worse."

Schliester had told her that Blaine was badly beaten. She called her apartment a few times, hoping he had gone there, hoping he'd pick up the phone, but got only her answering machine. But she was too worried to work, so she came home early. If Wally Schliester had the gall to follow her again, there was nothing she could do about it.

While the tub was filling, she sterilized Jeffrey's wounds with cotton and alcohol. He winced when she touched the cuts on his chest but she had to get them clean. They both agreed that he might have some cracked ribs and that there wasn't much one could do about a cracked rib except wait for it to heal.

She helped him into the bath and left him there while she went to get him a tall Bushmill's on ice. He didn't seem to want to talk and she didn't want to press him. She asked if she should stay. "Come back in a little while," he answered.

She changed her clothes and threw out the bloody cotton swabs. Then she changed the sheets. What she really wanted, she told herself with a wry, self-mocking smile, was a nice simple relationship with a nice simple man. Simple, in the sense that Sunday morning in bed with the *Times* is simple. Comfortable without being boring. Jeffrey Blaine wasn't simple and he wasn't comfortable. He was married, he was very possibly a criminal, and everything about him was dangerous. Even in bed, he was always in control of himself, and that frightened her, because it meant that she wasn't in control. Even though she was the one who initiated their relationship, that didn't change her marrow-deep sense that he was controlling it. And controlling her. How was that possible? Even if she hadn't known where it was going to lead when she followed him into that bookstore so many months ago, she certainly knew by the time he walked into her apartment the first time.

But knowing didn't count for much. She wanted this man. More, she wanted the recklessness of the relationship, and that frightened her about herself as much as she was frightened about Jeffrey and about his being here now and about the beating he had taken.

When she thought he had been in the bath long enough, she helped him out of the tub and into bed. She pulled the blinds and came back to sit by him. Even his hands were bruised and scraped, as though he had been digging in the earth with his bare hands. Her father's hands used to get like that.

"Jeffrey, I lied to you," she said, when it felt to her that she had been silent long enough.

He didn't ask any questions. He waited for her to go on.

"I didn't meet you by accident at Barnes & Noble," she said. "I was following you."

"Was there a reason for that?"

"Your name came up in a report. Some agents following Chet Fiore."

Now it was her turn to wait. She wanted him to say something.

He turned his head to the side, looking toward the light playing in the cracks in the blinds.

"Jeffrey," she pleaded, "say something."

He turned back to her, and she had never seen his eyes burn like they were burning now. "What do you want me to say?" he asked sharply. "You told me once you didn't want to know what I was doing. What makes you think I want to know about the games you're playing with me?"

"I just want to be honest with you, Jeffrey."

"Really? Then let's both be honest. I launder money for the mob. Does that make it easier for you?"

He reached for her hand and she pulled it back, as though she were afraid. He caught her wrist. His grip was powerful.

"Let's not get shy all of a sudden," he said. "You're the double agent here."

"I am not a double agent."

"What do you call it, then?"

"I've got a job, Jeffrey," she said.

"And you're going to do it?"

She looked at him a long time and said nothing.

"Are you still on the case?" he asked. "Is this part of your investigation?"

"No," she said, confused. "I mean, yes, I am. But no, this isn't part of it."

He let go of her wrist.

"Are you afraid of me?" he asked.

"No," she said. And then, "Yes."

He smiled. "Shouldn't I be the one who's afraid?"

She took a long breath and closed her eyes. He could see the tears she hadn't quite managed to hold back. Then she stood up and walked to the window. It had started to rain, and she could hear the drops against the pane. She parted the blinds enough to look through.

"No," she said at last. "You don't have to be afraid."

The street below glistened in the light of the street lamps.

Her back was to him and she didn't see his smile. When she turned to face him he said, "I've left my wife."

When he was young, Jeffrey loved driving the car. His father always had enormous Pontiacs. He bought them used because that was all he could afford, either a cheap car new or a big car used. Jeffrey learned to drive in those Pontiacs. In the hills outside town, no road was straight for more than a hundred yards. Now hired drivers did all his driving, Martin and half a dozen men before him. Except in the country, where he usually gave the driver the weekend off. But where did he ever go in the country? To the market and back.

Martin stayed with Phyllis but Jeffrey kept the Jag. It sat in the garage most of the time. Now it felt good to be behind the wheel, and he kept the needle at a steady seventy-five, his mind as clear as the road in front of him. The city faded down to nothingness as he ate up the miles in enormous gulps, big ungainly projects giving way to suburbs, suburbs to villages, villages to open fields. He veered off the highway at the Orient Point exit and followed the route he had taken before to the stone wall and the gate that guarded the entrance to Gaetano Falcone's wooded estate. He was just on time; Sal the Younger swung the gate open for him.

He drove slowly down the pine-flanked trail until the house came into view. He surprised himself by how calm he felt.

Fiore's Mercedes was parked in front of the house. Fine. Fiore was there first. It would have been presumptuous of Jeffrey to get there ahead of him.

Jeffrey pulled up behind the Mercedes. Fiore's driver was waiting behind the wheel, his head tipped back, his eyes closed. As

Jeffrey started up the walk to the front door, he amused himself remembering how he had been shadowed every step of the way on his first visit, as though he might steal the flower beds if left unguarded for a single moment. This time there was no one in sight.

Sal the Elder opened the front door for him. "This way," was all he said.

Jeffrey followed him into a wainscoted den with heavy French doors that opened onto a patio overlooking the ocean. A fire burned in the fireplace even though the day was mild. Falcone and Fiore were both on their feet. Jeffrey shook hands with both of them. The old man, he noticed, appeared to have aged a great deal since their first meeting. His stocky body hadn't changed, but the care with which he executed all his movements made him seem somehow frail. There was a bowl of fruit and a plate of assorted cheeses on the coffee table in front of the sofa.

Falcone motioned Jeffrey to a chair, then sat in the middle of the sofa, his stubby legs stretched out before him, his hands folded on his ample belly. "In the years since we consolidated the structure of our business," he began, "there is nothing we have undertaken as important as our banking arrangement. Nothing."

Jeffrey smiled at the euphemism. *Consolidation* obviously referred to the legendary bloodbath that brought Gaetano Falcone to power.

"This new arrangement opens a whole new world for us," the old man continued. "It was a brilliant scheme, Charles, and brilliantly executed."

Fiore leaned forward in his seat and helped himself to a wedge of Gouda so that he wouldn't appear to be basking in the praise. He nodded an acknowledgment.

"And my congratulations to you, Mr. Blaine," Falcone said, turning his heavy head. "Many people have tried to solve this riddle. You've succeeded where they all failed."

"That's very kind of you, sir," Jeffrey said.

Although nothing changed in Falcone's demeanor, he made it clear at once, in the pitch and tone of his voice, that the pleasantries were over. "I called you here because I want to know what's wrong and how you're going to fix it," he said.

A month ago Jeffrey cut the amount of money he processed through the funds by more than half, and since then he had kept it at that low level, waiting for the old man to notice. Fiore noticed right away and asked about it, but Jeffrey put him off with evasions.

"I've asked Mr. Blaine about this," Fiore said. "He said it's just a drop in the market. He can explain that to you."

"That's true, the market is down," Jeffrey said, "but that has nothing to do with the drop in receipts. The whole point of this system, sir, is that it's impervious to market forces."

"Wait a minute," Fiore said, jumping in with both feet, but Jeffrey cut him off before he could say more.

"I'm sorry I misled you," he said to Fiore with a cold and gracious smile, before turning back to Falcone. "I told him it was the market because that seemed the best thing to say under the circumstances."

Falcone bristled. "You misled him?" he asked pointedly. "Mr. Fiore speaks with my voice, Mr. Blaine."

"I'm aware of that, sir."

"Explain yourself," Falcone said. He wasn't leaning back anymore. His hands rested by his thighs, his thick fingers sinking into the soft cushions.

"I'm just being cautious, Mr. Falcone," Jeffrey said. "There's too much at stake here."

Falcone pushed himself heavily to his feet, which made it necessary for both Jeffrey and Fiore to stand.

"You have a problem with Mr. Fiore, is this what you're telling me?" Falcone demanded.

"I'm telling you," Jeffrey said levelly, "that I'm concerned about security."

Falcone aimed a warning finger straight at Jeffrey's face. "If this is about your daughter and her problems with Mr. Fiore—"

"My daughter has nothing to do with this," Jeffrey said, brazen enough to interrupt Gaetano Falcone as he was speaking.

"Because I did what I could for your daughter. If you still distrust Mr. Fiore—"

"I just told you. This has nothing to do with my daughter," Jeffrey shot back, interrupting again.

For a moment all of Jeffrey's calculations hung in the balance as Falcone's small, dark eyes studied him carefully. Jeffrey knew that any complaint about Fiore's mistreatment of Jessica would backfire. He had come to Falcone for help before; if he was still having problems with her, they were his own responsibility. Even with Falcone's elaborate and overdeveloped sense of family and honor, family and honor counted for only so much. Greed and self-preservation were the springs that made the clock tick. And so he hesitated a moment, letting the old man think whatever he wanted to think. Then he said, "We have a security problem, Mr. Falcone. The United States Attorney's Office is looking at us."

Fiore actually stepped between them. "They've got nothing," he said. "They look and they go away."

"You were aware of this?" Falcone asked.

"Of course I was," Fiore said. "This isn't something that ought to be discussed now, Mr. Falcone. These are internal matters. They're not Mr. Blaine's concern."

Blaine, he was saying, may be our banker, but that doesn't entitle him to know about our business.

"You'll pardon me, Mr. Falcone, but I am concerned," Jeffrey countered. "I'm the most vulnerable person here. I don't want to take chances."

"And I'm telling you the U.S. attorney has nothing," Fiore answered tersely. He turned back to Falcone to explain. "They put an undercover in one of our midtown operations and they brought one of my people in for questioning. That's all been taken care of."

"Don't be a damned fool," Jeffrey snapped. "The undercover at the Javits Center was never a problem. It was a sideshow for them, that's all it ever was. You took care of a problem that didn't exist."

The words *Javits Center* sent a shock wave through the room. The color drained from Fiore's face and Falcone looked like he wanted to find a place to sit down if he could do so without compromising himself.

"How the hell do you know so much about our business?" Fiore exploded, taking a menacing step forward.

"I make it my business to know things," Jeffrey said.

"You seem to know a lot about what's going on inside the U.S. Attorney's Office, too. Is that your business?"

Jeffrey turned to the old man, as though Fiore's insinuation didn't deserve an answer. "My training is in banking," he said. "There's no room for carelessness in that business. It's not about balls and charm. We have to know what we're doing."

Fiore wasn't about to let himself be passed over like that. His powerful hands flashed toward Jeffrey and grabbed two fistfuls of his shirt, which he ripped open with one quick, wrenching movement. And then he stopped, frozen for a moment.

This was the moment Jeffrey had been waiting for. The trap had been carefully baited. Now, with Fiore inside, all that remained was to spring the door.

He knocked his adversary's hands away, and then, with insolent calm, said, "If you want me to take off the rest of my clothes, just ask. You won't find a wire."

Fiore said nothing, because Jeffrey had left him nothing to say. He walked to the patio doors, content to let this play itself out while he studied the sea beyond the narrow strip of land. He could hear the hissing of the surf.

"I wouldn't have gone into this without a safety net, Mr. Falcone. You can understand that," Jeffrey said, pulling his shirt closed, buttoning the buttons that remained. "I knew even before I made the first transaction that federal agents followed Mr. Fiore the first night he made contact with me. It was bad weather, there was very little traffic. It should have been easy for him to determine whether or not he was being followed but he didn't do it. He could have contacted me privately but he chose my daughter's birthday party instead."

He turned to Fiore, half a room away. "A person like you showing up as a guest of a person like me is going to pique their interest."

Fiore glanced over his shoulder. "That went nowhere and you know it," he growled.

Now Jeffrey turned on him, walked toward him, his voice sharp, an accusing finger leveled at him. "Don't be ridiculous," he said. "They've been monitoring everything we do. Which one of

452 · **Philip Rosenberg**

us do you think they were following when you took advantage of my daughter and then sent for me to come and get her?"

Now Falcone was moving across the room as well. "Is this true, Charles?" he asked angrily.

Ten minutes ago he would have written Jessica off as a tramp Blaine couldn't control. Now she gave him all the pretext he needed for his indignation.

"His precious daughter spilled her guts about our whole banking arrangement to a reporter for *Newsday*," Fiore said. "Ask him how the hell she knew so much."

Now Falcone turned his anger toward Jeffrey. "You told a child about our arrangement?"

Jeffrey was ready for this. "She guessed," he said. "Mr. Fiore jumped into our lives with both feet. It wasn't hard for her to figure out what he wanted. I assume the U.S. Attorney's Office has figured out the same thing. I'd like to shut down the entire operation until you tell me it's safe, sir."

Falcone nodded his assent.

"Fine," Jeffrey said. "Is there anything else we have to discuss? It's a long drive back to the city."

Falcone studied him a moment before responding. There was an insolence about the way this banker conducted himself that he didn't like. It wasn't Blaine's place to leave until he was sent away. But Falcone was finished with him for the time being, so he turned away and waved Jeffrey out of the room with an impatient gesture.

When Jeffrey was gone, Falcone turned to his protégé. "Come, there's food," he said, gesturing toward the fruit and cheese. "Get us a bottle of wine."

Fiore went to the wine closet and selected a bottle. They touched glasses before they drank.

"That man came to me months ago with complaints about you," Falcone said. "I knew then he was looking to supplant you. I warned you at the time to be careful."

Fiore smiled. "Honest men," he recalled. "You warned me that honest men were dangerous."

When they had drunk some wine and eaten a bit, the old man

walked his guest to his car, where he exchanged a few pleasant words with Jimmy Angelisi, who had been waiting all this while. The elder Sal came up and stood by his boss's side as the old man watched the Mercedes until it disappeared around the bend in the drive. Falcone turned to him.

"You know what to do," he said. "Take your son with you."

Fiore settled in and leaned his seat back as far as it would go.

Jimmy glanced over. "Tired?" he asked.

"Nah. Not tired. Something else," Fiore said.

That had been a close call, he thought, stretching his legs out as far as they would go. Blaine was smart, but the old man was smarter. He knew a play for power when he saw one.

The salt air smell was fading as they moved away from the shore and into the village, where the Mercedes turned onto the highway. It wasn't much of a highway this far out. "Are you going home or are we going into the city?" Jimmy asked.

They still had an hour before Jimmy had to turn off the LIE for the Bronx and City Island but Jimmy always had to know everything ahead of time. He had been like that even when they were kids.

"There's nothing going on," Fiore said. "Drop me at the house."

He turned his head and watched the landscape unroll beside him. In the turned earth of a freshly plowed field he saw Eddie Vincenzo's skin the way it looked that day in the hospital. *Fuck Blaine*, he thought, jerking his attention back to the road ahead. It wasn't like his little bitch of a daughter was kidnapped. Eddie called and she came running. How was that Eddie's fault?

Maybe, Fiore thought, *we don't need Blaine anymore*. He should have made that point to the old man when he had the chance. They knew how Blaine's system worked. Any banker could do it. Maybe they didn't even need a banker. Maybe the guy who played the games with the computer for Blaine could do it just as well without Blaine. It shouldn't be hard to find out who that guy was.

It felt good to be thinking through problems again, to be going straight for the solution. The old man would like this one. Blaine was too headstrong. He was a threat to all of them.

What the hell was that thing he said about the Javits Center? A sideshow. Blaine had the nerve to call it a sideshow. Because he never saw the bubbles in the water, never saw Gus's white ass floating to the surface when it was all over. *Sideshow.* Fuck him again.

Jesus, Fiore almost said out loud, *what the hell is the matter with me?* He looked over to Jimmy, because he wasn't sure whether he actually said it out loud or not. But Jimmy had that concentrated look on his face he always had when he was driving. For a minute Fiore almost wished he could have told Jimmy to pull over so he could talk to him. But what was the use? Jimmy wouldn't have understood a single word he said. Fiore loved Jimmy like a brother, but not the kind of brother you could talk to.

Ginny was surprised when he got home so early, and even more surprised when he grabbed her from behind in the kitchen and reached past her to turn off the stove. He was never playful like that, and she didn't know what to make of it.

Upstairs, while they were changing their clothes, he sat down on the bed and said, "Have you noticed anything different about me?"

She stepped around to look at him from the side, with the light from the window behind her, and cocked her head to see him better. Then she realized that he didn't mean different that way, so she sat down next to him. He was holding the socks he had just taken off in his hand, and she took them from his hand and dropped them on the floor. "You tell me," she said.

"I'm asking you," he said.

"Because you've noticed something. Tell me what you've noticed."

He was quiet for a long time, and she said, "Just tell me the parts you can tell me. I don't need to know about things you don't want me to know."

In all the years they had been together, the things he didn't talk about simply didn't exist inside these walls. She never asked about them and never thought about them. This was the first time she permitted herself, with a word or a look or a gesture, to let him know she knew there was something missing.

"I don't know," he said, as though she were the one who had posed the question. "I went into a man's house a while ago. There was a balcony all around the living room." A sweep of his hands drew the picture on the walls around her. She could see it exactly, just in the way his hands moved. "There was a wall of books. It was morning and his wife came out in her nightgown after this man and I had been talking. I'm trying to think why I keep coming back to that . . ." He stumbled for the word, and in the end chose *scene.*

He stood up quickly and motioned for her to say nothing. When he was on the other side of the room, he turned back to her. "It's just envy, isn't it?" he said, a sneer in his voice, as though he were disgusted with himself. "Because I don't have a house like that."

"Because you don't?" she said. "No, it's not that. Because you can't."

He knew in an instant that she was right, the way one recognizes a face, all at once, without thinking about it. "Because I can't," he repeated. Obviously, his lifelong compulsion to secrecy was absolutely obligatory in his line of work. That could never change. He thought with contempt about the coke-headed oil cowboy in Oklahoma who kept receipts for everything he did, leaving an easily followed trail, like a cow that shits as it walks. And yet there was something to be said for Clint Bolling's way of life. Fiore lived the way he imagined queers lived in the days when queers married women to hide what they were. Chet Fiore couldn't own anything worth owning because it would be evidence of wealth he couldn't account for.

"You know what I'm thinking, Ginny?" he said. "Even a dog marks his territory. I can't do that. I can't leave my mark. If I'm going to piss, I've got to piss water."

"And that's sad," she said. She was still sitting on the bed where he left her.

"Here's the part I don't get," he said. "I found a way to change that. I don't have to live like that anymore. So why am I thinking about all this stuff now?"

"Because if you change that," she said, "you have to change everything."

He took a minute to think this through. *Yeah*, he decided, *she's right*. He laughed, a warm, deep laugh, the first time he had laughed in a long time. He walked toward her and held out his hands. She took them and stood. "You know what we're saying, don't you?" he said. "All of a sudden Chet Fiore wants to be respectable."

She kissed him lightly on the lips. "Good," she said. "You're respectable."

He kissed her and he thought, *Yes, of course. It makes sense.* He started out trying to change Jeffrey Blaine and ended up changing himself in the process.

They went out for clams and scallops and lobster at Angelo's, a little restaurant on a pier at the end of their street. Everything was good at Angelo's. Fiore and Ginny ate there whenever he wasn't in the city. Angelo's son was married to Ginny's brother.

The last thing in the world he expected was for Jimmy to walk into the restaurant before they were finished with dinner. He practically ran up to the table. "Mr. Falcone called. He's got to see you," Jimmy said.

"Now?"

"He said right away."

"Why did he call you?" Fiore asked.

"He must've called you, you weren't home."

That was too bad, because if he had been home to take Falcone's call, he would know what this was about. His mind was racing. Maybe the old man had taken ill. He hadn't looked good.

"How did he sound?" Fiore asked.

"He sounded okay."

"We'll drop Ginny at home," Fiore said, but Ginny said she'd walk because she wanted to talk to Angelo and hadn't finished her coffee.

"You don't have to talk to him tonight," Fiore said, but Jimmy took her side.

"If she wants to talk to him, why can't she talk to him?" he said, making more out of this than it was worth. So Ginny said she'd go, and Jimmy said, "See? You talked her out of it. Now she can't do what she wants."

"She's doing what she wants. That's what she said. She wants me to drop her at home."

Jimmy said, "That's because you said—" and Ginny said, "It's all right, Jimmy. It is."

They had had a whole bottle of a nice wine with their dinner. Fiore left a hundred on the table. They told Angelo that everything was wonderful and said good night to him.

The restaurant was actually out on the pier, with the tides lapping under it. The channel was deep and a good-sized cabin cruiser was tied up just outside the front door of the restaurant, its deep-throated engine growling a steady growl. *That's a beautiful boat,* Fiore was just about to say to his wife when he noticed the two men on the foredeck. As they turned toward him, Jimmy dove onto Ginny, knocking her to the plank floor. Fiore heard the sound of the two shotguns like bombs going off and he heard Ginny's scream, and he felt his chest ripping apart as he started to fall. Two more shells blew through him on the way down and his blood spilled through the planks to stain the water.

He just had time to think, *Oh Jesus, why did they have to use Jimmy?*

Epilogue

A few weeks into the new year Jeffrey Blaine bought the Astor mansion. There was a prodigious amount of work to be done, bringing a nineteenth-century house into the twenty-first century without compromising its intriguing idiosyncrasies. Elaine Lester came there with him often, for meetings with the contractor and the architect. For both Jeffrey and Elaine, a large part of the appeal of the place was the haunting and tragic story of uncompromising love that went with it. Born to riches, the young heiress for whom the house was built threw everything away to follow her heart. Four years later, at the age of twenty-eight, she was found dead and penniless in an unheated flat in the Cockney district of London.

One night, after the contractors had finished their work on the upper floors, Jeffrey met Elaine there for a tour of inspection. He brought wine and sandwiches. They sat on barrels and drank from plastic glasses while they ate. When they were satisfied with everything they saw, Jeffrey asked Elaine to marry him once his divorce was final.

She said yes.

Phyllis learned that her husband was buying the Astor mansion when she ran into Emily Rudin at Buccellati's. *I can't believe you're really buying it,* Emily gushed, and when Phyllis answered with a look of blank incomprehension, she said, *Oh, I hope it's not a surprise. I've ruined it, haven't I?*

"Jeffrey and I aren't together anymore," Phyllis said, and walked out of the store.

When she got home, she called Jeffrey at the office, the first time she had called him there, or anywhere else, since he moved out. Jennifer said he wasn't in, which may or may not have been true. "That's all right," Phyllis said in a pleasant tone of voice. "Can you just give him a message for me? Tell him he is the most despicable cocksucker on the face of the earth."

She had been through a lot and this felt like the last blow. Months earlier, when the newspaper headlines blared Charles's death at her, she was inconsolable but had to hide her grief from her daughter. Even before Fiore was gunned down in front of his wife—and the damn newspapers were full of pictures of the wife— Phyllis had begun to grow tired of the relationship, with its constant and tedious insistence on maintaining an implausible level of passion. Still, ending an affair and having it ended for you with such garish and brutal finality were two entirely different things, and for weeks she found it almost impossible to think of anything else. She even went back to the hotel room where they used to meet. She took off all her clothes and lay down on the bed, but after a few minutes her awareness of where she was and why she was there jolted her back to her senses. She got dressed, went home, and made arrangements to go to Europe for a month, taking Jessica with her. She couldn't very well leave the girl alone and she wasn't about to pack her off to Jeffrey.

What haunted Phyllis above all was her awareness that there was some sort of connection she couldn't even begin to fathom between Jeffrey and Charles. She was absolutely certain that Charles was somehow involved with whatever happened on that hideous day when Jeffrey brought Jessica home wrapped in a checkered tablecloth. Jessica wouldn't tell her a thing, and Jeffrey never talked to her again. She asked Charles about it one night, but he got out of bed without answering. He was dead before she ever got around to asking again.

• • •

Schliester and Gogarty were the first federal officers to respond to City Island when word came over the radio that Chet Fiore was dead. The NYPD tried to keep them out, claiming that the entire area had to be quarantined for forensic purposes. It was a big case and they wanted it for themselves.

Schliester had to put in a call to Elaine Lester, who called Greg Billings, who called his opposite number on the city side before the two agents were permitted onto the island. Where they found every newspaper and television journalist in the city already hard at work. The first colorful phrase the reporters came up with was SHOTGUN SHOWDOWN, because the use of shotguns in organized crime bloodlettings was an interesting touch the public didn't get to see all that often. Then someone started calling the hit men COMMANDO KILLERS after the police leaked the word that they had come and gone in a boat.

In a conventional homicide, family, friends, and witnesses all line up to tell you who did it even if they don't know. In a mob hit, everybody knows everything and no one says a word. It was obvious to anyone who knew anything about the workings of the New York mob that no one other than Gaetano Falcone could have authorized a hit on Chet Fiore. But that's not the same thing as having a case against Falcone. Fiore's widow obviously didn't see a thing. She was knocked flat the second the shooting started. Fiore's driver, who had had the foresight to dive for cover even before the shooting started, didn't see a thing because he was lying facedown on the pier.

The police and the feds set up a joint command post inside the restaurant. It was Schliester who noticed that the table, which hadn't been cleared, was only set for two, which meant that Jimmy Angelisi hadn't been a member of the dinner party. The owner of the restaurant confirmed this. But when a New York City detective named Lou Galamante asked Jimmy what he was doing on City Island, Jimmy said that he had been having dinner with "Mr. and Mrs. Fiore."

Angelo Monte, the owner of the restaurant, called the next day to correct a misunderstanding. He hadn't meant to give the impression that the Fiores had dinner alone. Their friend Mr. Angelisi was with them. There was no receipt to confirm this because the Fiores were relatives. Relatives don't pay.

At about the same time the witnesses who saw the killers fleeing in a boat weren't quite as sure as they had been that the boat was involved at all. Or even that there was a boat.

Schliester and Gogarty stayed with the case for almost a month, working with the NYPD's Organized Crime unit. Their initial suspicion that Gaetano Falcone was behind the murder was confirmed when week after week passed with no other bodies turning up. If anyone other than Falcone had ordered the death of Falcone's right-hand man, retribution would have followed quickly.

Other than this bit of deduction, the investigation turned up nothing. The liaison between city and federal investigators was terminated and the city put the case on a back burner, reassigning its top detectives to more promising investigations. Schliester and Gogarty returned to their office on the East River.

"We're at square fucking one," Schliester said sullenly.

"I think we're at square fucking zero," Gogarty corrected.

Jeffrey's divorce had been final for months, but Elaine never quite managed to set a date for their wedding. There'd be time enough for that, she told him, when the house was ready. She had long since moved out of her position in the U.S. attorney's Organized Crime unit, transferring back to an antiterrorist unit, which is where she had enjoyed her greatest triumphs in the office. She left while Schliester and Gogarty were still working out of an NYPD facility, so there were no good-byes.

When the house was finally ready, Elaine knew she couldn't put off a decision any longer. She promised to meet Jeffrey there for dinner on a Friday night and avoided him for the three days until then. She needed the time to think.

A team of waiters and a sommelier from Jean-Georges served them dinner in the dining room as though they were in a private room at the restaurant. When dinner was finished and the staff was gone, Jeffrey and Elaine went out onto the rear balcony, from which, in slivers here and there, they could see the river. It was on a balcony overlooking the river on the other side of the island, Elaine remembered, that she had walked away from another marriage.

"This isn't easy, Jeffrey," she said. "I'm leaving government service. One of my law-school classmates has a small defense firm in Chicago. I'm going to join her."

"I can't picture you as a defense lawyer," Jeffrey said, trying for gallantry, trying to avoid recriminations, to make it easier for her than it would have been if he let her know how much her decision hurt.

His answer felt cold to her, and she said, "Oh really? Can you picture me as a prosecutor? I've forfeited the right to be that, don't you think?"

He put his arms around her, but she said she wanted to go. She asked him not to walk her downstairs.

She looked up when she got out to the street, and she could see him silhouetted in an upstairs window. Then she turned and walked to the corner, where it would be easier to catch a cab. She didn't look back again. She thought of the Astor girl, who never got to live in the house that had been made for her.

When the term of Schliester's transfer to the federal task force expired, Gogarty figured his partner would take the vacation time he had coming and then go back to St. Louis.

"No," Schliester said, "there's something about failure. It gets under your skin. You just can't get enough of it."

Gogarty sighed and ordered another beer. *"Boychik,"* he said, "the thing about banging your head into the wall is that it's supposed to feel good when you stop. If it starts feeling good while you're doing it, you've got a big fucking problem."

They both laughed.

The next day Schliester submitted his formal resignation to the St. Louis Police Department and accepted a permanent position as an investigator in the U.S. Attorney's Office.

With Fiore dead, there was no case against Blaine at all. Not even the beginnings. Schliester and Gogarty moved on to other things. But Schliester wasn't ready to give up yet. On a brilliant but chilly spring afternoon he drove out to City Island, where he had no trouble finding Chet Fiore's house. He knew before he got there that it wouldn't be much of a house but it turned out to be even less than he expected. It needed paint in a few places. The wind came straight off the water, cold and salty. There was a wreath on the front door. It seemed to Schliester a long time to be still in mourning.

He rang the bell and waited. In a moment Virginia Fiore opened the door. She had a friendly, open smile, which made him feel funny about flashing an ID. He slipped it back into his pocket and introduced himself like one person introducing himself to another. He said he was from the U.S. Attorney's Office and asked if they could talk.

She invited him in. As they walked to the comfortable, old-fashioned living room—at home they would have called it a parlor—she said, "It's lucky you caught me in. My mother-in-law just passed away. Charles's mother. It seems like I've been doing nothing but closing up her house for a week."

So that explained the wreath. Schliester couldn't help wondering how little or how much her life had been changed by her husband's death.

He told her he was still interested in bringing the men who killed her husband to justice. He wanted her help.

"Every day after he died," she said, "before the funeral, after the funeral, even on the day of his funeral, the police told me I knew who killed him. They wanted me to tell them. But I don't know. And I don't understand why you're asking me again now."

"I'm not sure I understand it myself," Schliester said. "Sometimes we can't put these things behind us either."

"Either?" she said, very softly. "I'm not sure that I haven't."

When he left City Island, Schliester drove to Jimmy Angelisi's apartment in the Bronx. It was the middle of the afternoon. Jimmy had been working on a model sailboat and his hands were crusty with glue. "Let's go outside where we can talk," Schliester said. "Do you have to put that stuff away?"

"It'll be fine," Jimmy said, capping the glue and adjusting the order of some of the pieces on the table. He got his coat and shouted to someone in the bedroom that he was going out for a few minutes.

There was a bare hedge that ran along the side of the apartment building, separated from the sidewalk by an ankle-high iron railing. Almost all of the winter's snow was gone, but a few dirty patches from a two-week-old storm still littered the roots of the hedge. The two of them stood there huddled against the cold.

"No one's bothered you for a long time about Fiore, right?" Schliester asked.

"Is that what this is about?" Jimmy asked.

"We haven't bothered you. The city side hasn't been bothering you, have they?" Schliester said.

He sounded weird, like someone who looks at things a little cock-eyed and can't get to the point. So Jimmy figured he'd better keep it as simple as possible. "No," he said, "no one's bothered me."

"What about you?"

"Me?"

"Are you sleeping all right?" Schliester asked.

Jimmy felt like spitting at him. "Get the fuck away from me," he said, and started to walk away.

Schliester caught his arm, spun him around, and stepped right up to him.

"You set him up, Jimmy," he said. "You knew him since you were kids and you set him up. I'm not going away. I don't want you to talk to me now because you wouldn't tell me enough. Someday you're going to get tired of being reminded how you set him up and you're going to tell me everything."

He left Jimmy at the railing and walked back to his car.

That night, in a bar on Sullivan Street, Schliester tried to talk

Gogarty into staying with him on the Blaine case. He reminded his partner that the whole thing started when a random surveillance of Chet Fiore led them to a midtown restaurant. Maybe if they kept an eye on Jeffrey Blaine, they'd get lucky again.

"You call that lucky?" Gogarty said. "That's like a doctor discovering a new fucking disease by catching it."

Jeffrey got used to seeing Wally Schliester out his window or in his rearview mirror. Maybe once a week, maybe twice. No pattern to it. Day, night, skip a day, skip a week, and then he would be there again. If it was supposed to make Jeffrey worry, it didn't; if it was supposed to be an annoyance, it wasn't.

Schliester was there the night Jeffrey got a call from a police lieutenant in New Haven. "We found your daughter wandering the streets, Mr. Blaine," the lieutenant said. "She wasn't very coherent."

Jessica had been clean for almost a year when she went back to Yale. This relapse caught Jeffrey completely unprepared.

He called the garage and asked them to bring up his car. It was waiting for him when he got there. He wanted to tell that goddamn cop or agent or whatever he called himself to get the hell out of his life, that he had no business making himself obnoxious at a time like this. But he wasn't about to give the man the satisfaction.

The bastard's headlights were in Jeffrey's mirror all the way to New Haven.

The lieutenant told Jeffrey that Jessica had been sent on to the hospital. Her breathing was irregular and they didn't want to take chances.

"I appreciate that," Jeffrey said.

The hospital was just down the street from the police station. The lieutenant personally came out to the sidewalk and pointed the way.

As Jeffrey drove off, he saw Schliester get out of his car to talk to the lieutenant. The man was a hyena, Jeffrey thought. Feeding on carrion.

Jessica was asleep when Jeffrey found her. The nurse said her vital signs were stable. He pulled up a chair and sat by his daughter's bed to wait. When she finally opened her eyes, a wan smile passed across her lips as fleeting as the smile of an infant. "Daddy," she said, in a very small voice.

"It's all right, baby, it's all right," Jeffrey said. "I'll take you home. You can come home with me."

"Daddy," she said again.

Jeffrey Blaine literally did not know how much money he made working for Gaetano Falcone. He kept it warehoused in so many different accounts in so many different countries that it would have been a vast undertaking just to keep count of it. And he certainly didn't want records lying about. He bought a racehorse in England, and a villa and a boat in Italy. He bought the farmhouse in Normandy where he and Phyllis spent a few weeks just before Jessica was born, paying the farmer's widow a monthly stipend as part of the purchase price. It made him feel good to know she would keep the place ready for his arrival if he ever got around to going there.

He personally underwrote, on an anonymous basis, the Didier Fund, which was in danger of falling apart from a lack of subscribers. They did leukemia research. It was worth a shot.

He took Jessica to Normandy for a month and a half. It was good for her, and when they got back he found it possible to be hopeful about her future again.

Schliester still came around now and then, still watching and waiting.

Sooner or later, Schliester knew, Jeffrey Blaine would make a mistake. Sooner or later, Jimmy Angelisi would crack open like a seed pod.

Wally Schliester wasn't going anywhere. He had all the time in the world.

Acknowledgments

I must begin with an expression of my gratitude to and for my wife Charlotte and my son Matt. There were so many times since I started this book when I needed them so much. Whenever I turned to them, whenever I reached out to them, they were reaching out to me. I am a very lucky man.

And to my brother Stuart, deepest thanks for all his encouraging words and helpful suggestions.

I owe a considerable debt to Dan Conaway, my editor at HarperCollins, for his patience, for the soundness and the sensitivity of his suggestions, and for the dogged vigor with which they were made. In short, for making this book so much better than it would otherwise have been.

My deepest gratitude to my friend and agent Nick Ellison, who was there from the very start (and before, in fact); who knows how true it is, for once, that without him this book wouldn't exist.

I don't even know how to begin to thank my son Mark. Yes, of course for his sensitive reading of the manuscript and his invaluable suggestions. At my age—and at his—he gave me writing lessons. Which shouldn't have come as a surprise. And didn't. But more than that, a father's thanks for his being there at the top of the stairs and showing me the way down. I don't have words to tell him how much that meant and means. I hope he knows.